THE BLACK PRINCE

ARIANA NASH

CHAPTER 1

kiem

THEY DID things differently in this land, Akiem considered as the dragonkin, Lord Clarion, swung his axe down with devastating accuracy. The blade severed the elf's head from her neck and slammed three inches deep into the woodblock beneath her.

Over the years, Akiem had learned not to flinch. To flinch was to broadcast emotion. Emotions were a weakness. Weakness killed dragons.

The elf's head rolled a few feet and came to rest on her right cheek, her eyes already clouded.

Death didn't take long. Once in its grip, one rarely escaped.

Akiem had felt death's touch before. The first time when Mother had discovered a secret of his. The second more recently. At least this elf's sentence had been final. His torture persisted.

"Justice is served," the elven elder, Killian, declared. He was a tall, thin example of his race. From his narrow boots to his tapered ears, he lacked the physical presence of elves that Akiem was more accustomed to, like a swift breeze or harsh word might topple him, but he spoke with an authority his weak body belied. This elf was used to being heard. His voice carried far, filling the large receiving room, one of several vast spaces the dragon king used for gruesome spectacles.

The two elves behind their elder with their longbows and daggers certainly had greater presence than the elder, but the three of them together would be no match against any of dragonkin gathered here, including Akiem.

He couldn't recall what crime the elf female had committed. It took little convincing for King Luceran to end an elven life. She'd likely done something as simple as steal a horse, or perhaps she'd strayed into a part of the city prohibited to her kind.

He stared at her clouded blue eyes.

An elven death had never bothered Akiem before.

It didn't bother him now, he reassured himself, picking a piece of white fluff from his dark sleeve. Such things were necessary. He came from a land across the ocean, on the other side of the world, where elves roamed freely, ultimately causing chaos. No such chaos reigned here. As far as he could tell, from his short time in Luceran's territory, everything ran perfectly smoothly, all thanks to the king.

"Justice indeed." King Luceran rose from the only chair in the hall. Shaped from scrap metal roughly hammered together with planks of wood, the chair was an ugly creation, making the king seem all the more glorious in his lace-embroidered gray leathers. He stepped down a level to join the elves and the gathered dragonkin.

Luceran appeared young in human form—younger than Akiem's late twenties, if a dragon's age could be measured in human years. Slimmer and leaner, but also quicker for it, Luceran wasn't physically imposing. Akiem had known physically stronger dragons, like the metals, made of muscle and rage. If physicality were all that mattered among dragons, he would be at the bottom of the food chain. But Luceran's physical weakness disguised the whip-like mind behind it.

Luceran was diamond to his core, and just as sharp and unyielding.

The three elves who had come to witness justice regarded the king coolly, as only elves could. Stubborn, all of them. The more Akiem came to know elves, the more their stubbornness appeared to be a racial trait. They'd stare death in the face, baring tiny fangs as if they truly believed they stood a chance against powers far greater than they. Fools. Barely more worthy of admiration than the cattle Akiem ate.

Luceran was bigger than the elder's two guards and broader in the shoulders. Most all dragons were larger than elves, but Luceran had finer features too, such as his sculpted jawline and long, pale lashes, which would have earned him a quick death in Akiem's amethyst brood. A tail of long white hair licked down his back. Akiem might even call the king *pretty*—no, that wasn't right. No dragon was pretty. Such a word wasn't fit for dragons. The king's design was *striking*.

"Need I remind you of the little effort it would take for me and mine to topple your houses?" Of course, Luceran's words did remind them. His voice filled the room, filled the ears of all here too. This region's vocal accents had taken some time to adjust to. Akiem's accent had been termed as *English*, and those here called themselves *American*. Such words meant little to Akiem. The language was the same as his, just the sound of it was twisted.

The skinny elder elf bowed his head, and the guards behind him did the same. "We are forever your faithful servants."

Akiem's attention wandered to the right-most guard. Clad in leather and strips of white cotton, he seemed the resourceful type. The other guard, the one with blue-black skin, wore more daggers. Something about the stillness of the first made Akiem look deeper. The elf's russet-red hair appeared blood red under the light leaking in through the windows. He wore a small metal hoop earring at the top of his ear, drawing attention to how it tapered.

All three elves still bowed their heads, waiting to be dismissed, but as Luceran turned away, the red-haired guard looked up, straight into Akiem's gaze. The sudden eye contact stripped Akiem raw. By the Great Ones, it was as if this elf held no fear. Akiem opened his mouth to alert the king, but the elf's eyes glittered the most startling shade of green he'd seen outside of dragonkin, and the alarm he'd intended to raise fell away, inexplicably unvoiced.

The elf's bow-shaped lips ticked into the corner of his mouth, as though he knew his gaze had stalled Akiem's thoughts, and then this brazen elf did the most foolish thing: he winked.

Akiem flinched.

The king hadn't seen, and all the dragonkin watched the king. None among the crowd had witnessed the elf's ridiculous behavior. Did this one wish to die? Because Akiem could see it done. A single word to draw Luceran's attention back, would be enough. Lord Clarion, the king's broodbrother, had a well-known bloodlust for elves and would delight in wetting his axe with more elven blood.

"You are dismissed," the king said. "Leave the grounds before my hungry kin pick you off."

Akiem glanced at the red-haired elf, but any hint of a smile now hid behind a stoic mask. Had he imagined the eye contact, the wink? Surely not. Yet, of late, his mind had been showing him things, dreaming things that tried to twist his thoughts in knots.

"Akiem." Luceran clicked his fingers, and Akiem glided into motion to stand beside the king.

"Yes, my liege?"

"What are your thoughts regarding the elf's death?" Luceran asked.

It was a perilous place, to be seen beside Luceran. Akiem had learned that early on. This court was full of teeth, and like any trap, it was armed and ready to spring shut. Dragons looked at him—the newcomer—with envy. Behind his back, they schemed and snickered. Akiem knew their games and how to play them. He'd been playing them all his life. They were all dangerous, but the most dangerous of them all was beside Akiem, and as long as the king remained such, Akiem would stay by his side.

Akiem regarded the cooling pool of elven blood and the axe lodged in the block. "A quick death. Few could ask for such a merciful end."

Luceran considered the words, then a smile touched his lips. "Indeed."

Lord Clarion—as white-haired as his brother but physically stronger—slung the elf's headless carcass across his shoulders, caring little for the stream of blood that soaked the back of his shirt. He snatched the severed head by the hair and carried it alongside him, letting it bump against his leg. The head would prove something of a whimsy for dragon kits to tear into.

The hall's closing doors drew Akiem's eye. He glimpsed the darker-skinned elf, but the cocky red-haired fool had gone on ahead. With an attitude like his, a dragon would soon deal with him. Perhaps his head would be thrown to the kits next. At least his end would be final.

CHAPTER 2

ane

"Who do you think the king's new pet was?" Jevan bit into the roasted chicken leg and tore off a chunk of meat. He soon followed that with a tankard of whatever swill this inn served and gulped half its contents without stopping for breath. A quick wipe with his sleeve and the whole display started again.

Zane stared at his friend, openly disgusted by the male's ability to eat like a fat horse, yet secretly impressed. His own stomach turned over at the thought of food so soon after what they'd witnessed at court. He hadn't known the victim of the king's wrath, but he'd heard she'd been foolish enough to steal food. There was nothing wrong with that—everyone had to eat—her mistake had been in getting caught.

"What new pet?" Zane asked, feigning ignorance. He kicked his boots up on the table and leaned back in the chair, fingers laced together behind his head as he claimed the entire tabletop as his. The lower angle also offered the best view of the server's ass. A little young for his taste, maybe eighteen, but if the earlier smile and brush of the shoulder were any indications, he'd be game for a frolic. Zane wasn't much older, but he preferred males who knew their way around themselves and others. Besides, the young were too quick to fall in love. Still, he hadn't tapped *that* ass yet, and it really was the kind he couldn't resist.

Jevan dropped the gnawed-on bone into its bowl and wiped his hands on a cloth. "The dragon you spent the whole time eye-fucking."

Zane mock-scowled. Of course Jev had noticed his wandering glances. "I have no idea what you're referring to. An elf of my esteemed character would not be interested in an uptight, egocentric dragon."

Jev barked a laugh. "You're so full of shit. I saw his face while you were eyeballing him. He about shifted on the spot. You're lucky he didn't squeal to the king."

"Just some extra piece of ass that washed ashore. The king's obviously fucking him," Zane said, answering the earlier question.

"Must everything be about sex with you?"

Zane grinned. "Said like a male who isn't getting any."

Jev showed him his middle finger in a gesture they'd picked up along the north-east coast.

Although, to be fair to Jevan, Zane had been eye-fucking the dragon dressed in black. The beast had looked wrapped up so tightly in all those buckles and belts that he could pop at any moment, and Zane wanted to be there when that happened. Strictly speaking, elves and dragons didn't mix, unless a dragon happened upon the docks near the full moon to see if they might find an elf to satisfy their *other* hungers. He'd heard rumors. Didn't plan on ever going there, though. Zane didn't need to solicit such attention when, more often than not, it was thrown at his feet.

Still, Luceran's shadow was interesting—so dark beside the king's diamond-whiteness. He had an emptiness about him, as though someone had hollowed him out and left him standing. If given the opportunity, Zane would gladly spend the night filling him right back up again.

He shifted in the chair. He rarely had such thoughts about dragons. The fascination with the dark one bothered him more than he let on to Jevan. Dragons were abusive assholes at the best of times, and at their worst they were fucking monsters. Better to forget the dark one and move on to someone more likely to reciprocate his advances.

The server was looking over. With his hair cropped short and his ears pricked high, adorned with small hoop earrings and studs, he clearly liked to advertise his prettiness. Zane flicked a hand up and jerked his chin, summoning him. The male added a sway to his narrow hips that wasn't there when dealing with other customers. Good, because Zane really needed the company.

"What can I serve you, sir?" He wore a bracelet made of plaited leather and beads. What other trinkets did he have about his person that Zane might discover?

Zane gave him a smile that had melted hearts up and down the east coast. "Besides some time alone with you when your shift is over, I'd like some wine. Make it strong."

The server cocked an unimpressed eyebrow and flounced to the bar.

Zane pursed his lips, unaccustomed to anyone refusing him. "Did I misread him?"

Jev twisted in his chair to get a long look at the server. He faced Zane again, mouth chewing up a laugh. "Maybe he's heard of the red-haired devil fucking his way through every town on the east coast."

"You think?" They'd been in these parts for weeks now, working as hired muscle for what little coin there was rattling around. Zane *had* sampled some of the goods in the local bars. Where else was an elf supposed to get some ass?

Jev snorted and rolled his eyes. "By Alumn's light, you're so freakin' gullible when it comes to your number one love."

Zane frowned. "My what now?" Love? Shit, there was no need to bring love into this.

Jev laughed harder. "*You*, numbnuts. If you weren't my friend, I'd punch some of that pretty right off your face."

Humor plucked at Zane's mood, brightening it. Gesturing at his face, he replied, "This pretty is untouchable." He puckered his lips for Jev, instantly silencing his friend's laugh.

"Don't." Jevan pointed a thick finger. "Take all that and your ego"—he waved his hand at Zane—"to one of your fuck boys."

The server chose that moment to dump a tankard in front of Zane and scoop up the coin waiting on the tabletop. He left with a huff, making it clear he'd heard every word.

Zane watched the missed opportunity stalk away, all the lean and muscled inches of him. With a sigh, he picked up the drink and found Jev scowling at him from across the table. "What?"

"I'm wondering what I did to piss off Alumn for me to get stuck with you as a friend."

"Oh, come now, what have I done that's so bad?"

"At the execution, didn't you care?"

His mood abruptly soured. He'd come here to *forget* about the execution. "She knew the fucking rules." He took a drink, needing it more now. The hot, spicy liquid went all the way down and tried to burn a hole through his soul. Damn, that was good stuff. "Don't fuck with dragons and we all get to live."

"You're all heart, huh?" Jev grumbled.

What was Jev's problem? Zane planted his boots on the floor, leaned in, and looked his friend in the eye. He could remind him how they'd crawled out of the westland mud while dragons screeched above, but the shadow in Jevan's eyes suggested he knew. Here, on the east coast, King Luceran did things differently, and that was a *good* thing. Sometimes, an elf paid with her head so the rest of their race could roam mostly free. Her death had hit Jev harder than Zane. His dark skin had turned wheaty. "Go get some light or get laid."

"Yeah, maybe I will." Jev stood, grabbed his tankard, and stumbled to the bar. He'd probably stay there for the rest of the night, and maybe tomorrow he'd soak up some of Alumn's generous warmth. Sunlight could fix just about any grim mood.

Zane huffed through his nose. The combined chatter from the elves rose and fell in waves, washing away his rattling nerves. Being around his people and hearing normal talk helped, but what he really needed was a few more of these tankards and someone willing to get personal with him for a few hours. The guilt for his own survival would return tomorrow. Until then, he'd do his damnedest to drink and fuck the memories into submission.

~

ZANE REACHED for the wall of a nearby building to prop himself up. If the street and houses would just stop spinning for a few seconds, he could get his bearings. Rubbing at his face helped scrub off some of the drunkenness. The cool evening air cleared the rest.

Spectacularly wasted and deliciously numbed, all he needed was someone to warm his bed. He smiled at the fat moon hanging low over the city's jagged skyline and felt laughter bubbling.

Huh, the moon was full, and here he was, a stroll from the old docks. Well, that seemed fateful, didn't it? As he happened to be in the area, he'd take a quick look to see if the rumors were true. The goddess Alumn had guided his boots here, and no elf would risk incurring her wrath by ignoring her.

He crossed an old road flanked with half-battered high-rises. Rumors claimed the buildings had been glass and steel once, and they'd lined the streets like enormous palisades. Elves had since remade them into towers, patched them up with wooden scaffolding, and turned each level into homes, creating a new shantytown.

He fell into step with other elves headed toward the waterside. These folks were wandering toward the docks for a reason, but they couldn't all be after the company of dragons, could they?

Following the winding streets, he eventually came to rows of market stalls overflowing old sidewalks. Hanging lanterns lit the stall corners, lighting up the market. As the street narrowed and the stalls increased in number, the bustle enveloped him, sweeping him along. This was the intrigue? A night market held on the full moon?

He browsed the wares and spied a few thieves working coin from the pockets of those in the crowd. In the past, he'd done the same, but unlike the unfortunate elf who had lost her head, Zane had never gotten caught.

He'd met Jevan on a street like this. His friend had been wearing scruffy clothing, with his hat in hand, begging for coin. Zane had stolen his hat and coin, and the asshole had tracked him down. They'd scrapped in the gutter as if their lives depended on it. Jev had won, but instead of beating the shit out of Zane, he'd offered his hand. Right after, Zane had proposed they work together. Eight years of surviving side by side, taking coin, working the grind, and traveling from town to city to town. It wasn't a bad life. At least it *was* a life, which was more than any of the extinct humans could say.

He plucked his coin pouch from his belt and tucked it deeper into his pocket, just in case any little-fingered elfling took a shine to it.

The stalls sold old-world trinkets: hooks and boxes, bells and pots, twisted things that made no sense. A little windmill, perched atop a stall roof, powered a music box, which played human music, of all things. Interesting, but there was nothing on offer he needed. There was no use in carrying anything other than weapons and a spare pair of boots. He didn't have roots, or a home, and didn't need strange human fancies weighing him down on the road. But some folks lived in homes, and they traded what little coin they had for the curiosities of the long-gone human world. He'd seen elven homes brimming with bits of the old world, their owners like magpies collecting shiny shit to line their nests. There were villages outside the city that practically overflowed with all this junk; they even had electricity to make their lights glow. Zane didn't see the point when Alumn's light was enough to feed the soul.

A citrusy tingle on his lips alerted him. Dragonkin. Scanning the crowd, he spotted her—a tall, imposing female—then saw others mingling among the elves. Really, they didn't mingle so much as carve their way from point A to point B, brushing aside anyone in their path. Some talked with elves, and some browsed the stalls. The deeper into the docks Zane wandered, the dirtier the lamps became, and the distance between elf and dragon decreased.

Zane knew sex. He reveled in it—life was too short not to partake in pleasure wherever available—but the one thing he'd never realistically entertained was sex with a dragon. Yet here it was, out in the open. The beginnings of it anyway. He saw their touches and how the dragon's body language crowded the elves. He saw their coy smiles and illicit touches. Dragons and elves getting more than personal was forbidden by Luceran, but there were plenty here who hadn't gotten the message, and the rest appeared to look the other way.

Coin changed hands. Everyone got what they wanted.

Then it occurred to his alcohol-addled mind that none of this was consensual. Dragons held the power. If an elf said no, that elf would lose his or her head, coin or not. No elf was strong enough to stop a dragon from doing whatever the fuck it wanted.

He recalled the sound of the axe coming down and how the elf's sobbing had suddenly ceased. Such a simple thing, but witnessing her end had been something else entirely.

He'd seen death.

What elf hadn't?

But he didn't seek it out. He was paid to guard higher-society elves, mostly, and to look the part, but he wasn't a killer—not by choice, and only on the frontline, when Jev had pulled him from the mud.

Memories jostled for purchase. Mud in his mouth. Its gritty taste mingled with blood. Jevan's hands around his waist, pulling him free, dragons screeching, elves dying.

His gut flipped in warning.

He hadn't eaten, and now the wine was coming back to haunt him too.

Someone thumped into his shoulder, almost whirling him around. His drunkenness tried to dump him on his ass in the middle of the street, but hands grabbed his arms, steadying him.

Kind eyes smiled, setting Zane right again. "Hey, sorry there! Didn't see you." The male elf patted him on the shoulder, then stomped on, head down.

"Sure, fine..." Zane wavered on the spot. He'd been going somewhere, hadn't he? He distinctly recalled coming downhill to the docks, so he needed to go uphill to get back to the lodge. He'd seen enough of the docks to know he didn't need to linger or return.

"Oy!" a young'un shouted behind him.

Zane turned. A tall figure cloaked in black lifted an elfling off his feet and held him dangling like a worm on a hook.

"Hey!" Zane barked before noticing the cloaked figure had the same square set and substantial presence of all dragons.

The dragon's shoulders tensed.

Nearby chatter fell away.

Shit. He couldn't win a one-on-one fight with a dragon.

But, by Alumn, he wasn't standing by while a dragon beat on a little elf either.

"Hey you..." He stepped forward, found that his bravado held, and kept right on walking until he was almost chest to chest with the hooded beast.

The dragon dropped the elf. The little scout rebounded fast and darted off, leaving Zane facing a hooded figure that, in dragon form, would fill this street and crush every elf inside it.

A shaft of light cut across the male's whiskered chin, but the rest of his face remained well hidden beneath the hood, as though he'd deliberately cloaked himself from head to toe.

Zane's instincts pulled on him to apologize and back off, saving his neck from Lord Clarion's blade. The only problem was, his feet wouldn't budge and any apology had lodged in his throat. The dragon wasn't moving either. According to protocol, Zane should dip his head and turn away, but as the dragon hadn't called him out on it, his mischievous streak demanded he see how far he could push his luck. Some witty remark would be perfect right about now, but Zane's thoughts had all stalled. He managed a cocky smile, tucked a thumb into his pocket, and pretended he wasn't facing down an apex predator.

"Your coins." The dragon produced a money pouch, just like the one Zane had.

What? Zane tapped his pocket. Empty. That damn little elf, the one he'd saved, had stolen from him.

"That little rat." Zane plucked the offered pouch from the dragon's fingers. "I er... Thanks."

"You're welcome."

He didn't speak like anyone Zane had ever heard. His accent was all angles and edges. Zane wanted to hear him speak some more. He tried to think of something to say, something to keep the dragon from leaving, but the seconds passed, and the silence grew sharp and uncomfortable. Damn, he was usually better than this.

The dragon dipped his head, moving only the hood and shadow, and stepped around Zane.

The exchange was over, yet Zane wasn't done. He sensed the dragon had wanted to say more, or perhaps that was Zane's imagination making more of the male's strange silence. But there was an opportunity here, wasn't there? A hint of *something*. The dragon had helped him. It seemed only fair that Zane return the favor.

Zane turned. Beneath the heavy cloak and hood, the male could be anyone. He could be vicious or cruel. Zane had no reason to think he was any different from all dragons. But why hide his face? The other dragons here announced their presence. They walked through the crowd like they owned every elf on the street. This one was quiet. Too quiet. If he hadn't stopped the thief, he likely would have continued to move among the crowd unseen. So why help at all?

"Were you looking for someone?" Zane asked before common sense could stop him.

The dragon pulled up short.

Zane could taste his damn heart beating in his throat. It wasn't wise to provoke them, yet he'd done just that. This was one of those moments Jev had repeatedly warned him about, the moments when Zane went too far, pushed a little too hard, asked one question too many, and kept right on doing that *thing* until it got them locked up, or fired, or both, like that time in Oldport.

The dragon turned his head, all cloak and hood.

Nothing of his face or expression showed. Was he angry, intrigued, insulted?

Alumn, this was a terrible idea. Damn the goddess for guiding him here. He'd be having words with her the next time he prayed. He'd heard a rumor that the elven goddess was part dragon, so maybe she was behind his actions tonight. Little else made any sense.

"You know..." He laughed and waved off his own foolishness. "Forget I asked."

He'd head back to the lodge, crash on the bed, and write this off as a drunken misadventure. But the way back was past the dragon, and despite the street being some forty feet across, the male somehow filled it. That left him with one way to go: deeper into the docks, where fewer lanterns flickered.

Fuck it. His pride dictated that was the only way out. How bad could a night get anyway?

Zane turned and walked deeper into the dark.

CHAPTER 3

kiem

Akiem hadn't come here for *that*, though he knew other dragonkin did. He'd just needed to get out of Luceran's compound, to hide under a hood and walk and walk. Taking to the wing was too painful. Old and new scars pulled every muscle taut. These days, flight was always the last option. After he'd walked the streets for an hour, nothing hurt save for his feet, and nobody cared to look twice at him. Even the elves paid him no mind. He was nothing here. Invisible.

Nobody cared to even *see* him, unlike at Luceran's court, where eyes crawled over him every moment of every day.

He could have walked all night if not for the red-haired elf with his constantly moving smile, like it had a mind of its own, and glitteringly mischievous eyes.

The same elf from the execution. The same elf who had *winked* at him.

Akiem had seen him ambling through the crowd. The thief's partner had bumped into him while a young elf had used the distraction to free the coin pouch from his pocket. They'd played the red-haired elf for a fool, and something about that had triggered Akiem to interfere.

He'd come to the docks for the air, for the people, for the pleasure of being a shadow, not to get involved.

Were you looking for someone?

The question had been simple, really, yet Akiem had lost his voice. He hadn't thought he'd been looking for anything in particular, but upon hearing the elf's question, he'd stumbled.

He knew what happened in these parts: propositions and coins changing hands. Courtly dragons spoke of it in whispers. More than goods were traded at the docks. More, like pleasure.

Dragons came to dally with curious elves. It was all beneath Akiem. Elves were animals, cattle, food. Yet standing there, with the elf's words ringing in his ears, he'd understood the appeal of having company. Part of him ached so badly to no longer be alone, but a larger part recoiled deeper inside himself at the thought of intimacy of any kind.

Then the elf had said to forget it, leaving Akiem with an alarming sense of loss. He had turned to stop him, to ask what he'd meant, but the elf had already vanished into the dark. Did he know where he was going? What if another dragon found him? Someone likely to hurt a lost elf? He'd appeared a little unsteady, nothing like his rigid, poised self at court.

He should leave him to his fate.

An elf such as him didn't need him interfering.

Akiem tapped his fingers against his thigh. This elf attracted trouble. He was also intoxicated, and few dragons could resist such easy prey. If he continued on his current path, he'd be hunted down by any number of the dragonkin here.

Akiem sighed and followed the distant figure deeper into the waterside section of Bayston city, where empty structures hugged the water's edge and old metal cranes hung like enormous gallows across the sky.

Trouble soon appeared in the form of a pair of dragonkin in human form. They peeled away from shadowed doorways and closed in behind the elf. Only moonlight licked the old streets here. Either the elf was a fool, or he was deliberately leading the dragons along. Akiem had known elves who would trap curious dragons this way, but those on this side of the ocean didn't appear to possess the same murderous or suicidal streak. Maybe this example of elvenkind was about to prove Akiem's assumptions wrong?

One dragon lunged at the elf. The elf produced a small dagger and got a slash in, but such a small weapon was no deterrent for a dragon. The big male grabbed for the elf, causing him to tip over a curb. He fell onto his side.

Akiem's pace quickened.

The dragons towered over the fallen elf. Bad times flickered across Akiem's vision. How many memories featured Akiem falling the same way? With someone bigger, stronger, heavier crowding close? He'd experienced the great weight of an unwanted dragon pressed over him, inside him, tearing him apart. Akiem had deserved it, but he would not witness such a thing again, not even on an elf.

He tore off the cloak and whistled through his teeth.

The shrill sound darted like an arrow across the empty street. The dragons jerked their heads up.

One had his hand on his crotch, indicating where he intended the assault to end.

Rage warped Akiem's better judgment. Distantly, it occurred to him that Luceran might not appreciate him brawling in the streets, but the need to see this end before it properly began crushed that thought.

Heated power rushed in, filling him up and pooling fury into the emptiness. He couldn't have stopped the shift if he'd wanted to. He breathed in, collecting the rush of raw power through his entire being, then breathed out, freeing the truth. Matte black scales exploded outward—too many missing, scarred, or broken. His soul stretched far, swallowing all the pain and hurt, until it became part of who he was and what he'd become.

Dragon.

Armored scales as black as night.

Teeth sharp and bright.

He stoked the amethyst fire low in his throat, lifted his head, and bared his teeth, giving the dragonkin a moment to understand he was not posturing.

He clamped his jaws around the first dragon before he could retaliate. Magic tingled on his tongue, a warning that his prey was about to shift. Keeping his teeth caged around the dragon's body, he freed his amethyst fire. Dragons were resistant to his fire, but not in human form. The one he'd bitten screamed for all of two seconds before the superheated purple fire consumed him.

Akiem tossed his roasted carcass aside and focused on the second dragon. This one had been about to rape the elf.

Akiem lowered his head, pinning the foul male under his gaze.

He hadn't shifted and seemed reluctant to. Whatever he was in dragon form, it was weak enough for him to drop to his knees and blubber like a runt. "Don't tell Luceran! By the Great Ones, please!"

At the mention of the king's name, Akiem's fire simmered hotter, burning his throat, seeking freedom. He'd killed worthless dragons like this one the moment they'd hatched from their eggs, giving them the mercy of a quick death. Dragons were different here. Luceran tolerated sniveling weakness. Akiem did not.

"Please," the runt snuffled. "He'll—"

Akiem might have had mercy in him once. Not anymore. He snapped his teeth through the dragonkin's middle, cutting him clean in half, and tossed his torso aside too.

The fallen elf watched on. Akiem expected him to reek of fear. If the elf ran, Akiem would struggle not to give chase, considering how hot his blood pumped. Impossibly, however, the elf didn't smell of fear. He didn't tremble. He looked up, the tiny dagger clutched in his hand as though it might protect him from a dragon the size of a dockside building.

Were you looking for someone? The fool had asked a monster to his bed.

Akiem huffed, blasting the elf with air and dust. He spluttered and coughed, then rubbed at his eyes to clear them, but still he looked on, unfazed.

Impossible creature.

Akiem was done here. He opened his wings but found the dockside too narrow to expand them fully for flight. Pain danced down his back. Old scars lit up like fireworks beneath his scales. The one on the back of his neck, too close to his crown, burned the most. It was old, older than Luceran's new scars. He grunted off the pain and climbed the outside of a derelict building, needing the elevation to take to the sky properly.

At the top, he turned in a circle, taking in the glittering elven town, which had been reclaimed from a much older human one. Oil lamps throbbed warmly. It seemed almost peaceful from above, more peaceful than any life Akiem had known. He resisted the urge to open his jaws and scream at the elves to frighten them into their homes. The old Akiem would have, but he was a shadow here. Shadows did not scream into the night.

He spread his wings, gave them a few experimental flaps to measure the airflow, then dove off the side, skimming the dockside where the elf lay before soundlessly gliding out across the water.

The elf watched him the whole way.

"You were at the docks last night?"

He should have known Luceran would find out, but he hadn't expected the news to travel so fast.

"Yes." There was no point in denying it, and besides, Luceran hadn't ordered him to stay on the grounds.

The king walked the grounds of the old compound, like he did every morning, rain or shine. An hour earlier, to Akiem's shame, the king had found him tucked in a corner of his chamber, shivering and muttering like a crazed lower. Luceran had brought him around with a simple touch on the shoulder. Akiem distinctly recalled growling at him—*as a man*. It had taken him too long to come around from being dragon. He'd liked it there, buried beneath scale and fire. The physical pain still plagued him as dragon, but the mental torture didn't persist. Only as a man was he haunted by the past. Maybe he was losing his mind to the darkness inside him. Maybe he *should* stop fighting and let his mind go.

"You don't have elves among you, in your land across the sea?" Luceran asked.

"Not free like they are here."

"It must have seemed strange to walk among them at the docks?"

It had been strange at first, but as he'd drifted unseen through their crowds, he'd found a strange comfort among them. Elves were *safe*.

"I found it"—*liberating*—"interesting."

Elves, humans, dragons—they'd been at war in Akiem's land, a place known to these people as Europe. Humans had been almost wiped out, but elves persisted. Akiem had spent a lifetime hunting and killing them. Seeing elves living alongside dragons was taking some getting used to.

"You killed two dragonkin while at the docks," Luceran went on, tone level.

The king had spies everywhere. He had to, to keep the elves and dragons under control. Akiem knew that, but he'd hoped his excursion and its outcome would go unnoticed. It would have, if not for the foolish elf and his invitation. Akiem should have left him there.

"The dragons and I had a disagreement." Akiem paced alongside the king, reading him out of the corner of his eye.

Luceran often invited him on these walks, speaking

little, as though the king sensed how silence alone could be a gift. As far as Akiem knew, no other dragon had ever been given this courtesy. He wasn't sure what to make of it, but Luceran had his desires, like any dragon.

Luceran arched a pale eyebrow. "Must have been some disagreement."

The king hadn't asked for an explanation, so Akiem didn't offer one. Akiem seldom lied, or never used to, but he would about this. Luceran had seen him weak, seen him broken and near death. If the king knew why Akiem had killed the dragons—to protect an elf, of all creatures—he'd have a weapon to use against him.

"Any disagreements must be dealt with properly, lest the rule of my law break down. You're new to us. Mistakes are to be expected. Do I need to discipline you?" He said this as though he were asking if Akiem enjoyed the sunshine on this fine morning. The tone was light, but it held a razor's edge.

Old wounds throbbed. "If I overstepped, I apologize."

They walked some more, passing through an old human tunnel with arches and doorways before exiting onto a barren street. All part of Luceran's sprawling territory.

Luceran walked with his hands clasped behind his back and his face tilted toward the morning light. His snow-white hair fell down his back, unbound and silken. A breeze teased the locks. He looked like a fantasy Akiem's half-broken mind had conjured, like he'd turn to mist if Akiem dared to touch him. Warm, pink, bitable lips held a contented smile. In the sunlight, he was ... *stunning*.

Akiem forced his gaze away. Such thoughts were not for him. In another time, another place, these desires, if discovered, would have seen him severely punished or killed. As the incident at the docks had proved, he was still finding his way among the laws here, and while he hadn't seen anything to suggest that males desiring males was considered wrong, he also hadn't seen any evidence to prove it was acceptable. Besides, it *wasn't* acceptable. It was a rot at Akiem's center, like so many others he harbored. A rot he denied.

"When I found you broken on the beach, I considered killing you," the king continued whimsically.

You almost did, Akiem thought. He'd accepted death that morning on the beach. The diamond dragon had come upon him, and he'd recognized the look in his violet eyes: death. Luceran had sought it for Akiem, and Akiem might have begged him to deliver it had he had a voice left to beg. The journey had stripped him raw.

"You survived," Luceran went on. "I've welcomed you, housed you, brought you under my wing in a position of trust that few others enjoy..."

He trailed off, and when his pace slowed, Akiem slowed beside him until they both came to a stop. The sun baked this section of cracked road. Butterflies flitted over waving grasses as tall as men.

"Yet it's been weeks." Luceran held Akiem's gaze. His eyes, so pale, held an open honesty so rare in dragons. "And I don't know you any more now than I did then."

This was a dangerous conversation. Akiem did not know why Luceran had spared him on the beach, but he suspected it was the mystery about his origins and what lay across the sea that kept the king so enthralled. Gossip at court told of how the king had had other... *fancies*, mostly males. They'd been found dead once Luceran had tired of them.

Facing the king, he squinted into the sunlight framing him. "There is nothing to know."

"In all the years I've patrolled this coast, nothing has washed up alive on my beaches. Nothing. Yet on a morning just like this one, there you were, scales stripped raw from your journey, too exhausted to lift your head, and half mauled by something far bigger than you."

An ache spread across Akiem's forehead and down around the back of his neck. He rubbed it, trying to ease the memories. He did not want to remember the time *before*. Remembering was what caused him to curl into corners at night. It was easier to believe he'd died crossing the ocean and been reborn in this new land with Luceran as his king.

"What terrible thing were you fleeing from?" the king asked, blinking astute eyes.

"Everything," he replied, revealing too much and nothing at all.

Luceran studied his face, reading between every thin line. He'd seen Akiem's scars, as man and dragon, and read those like a map charting every bite and gouge. What Akiem could not say his body said for him. Luceran understood that.

Gods, Luceran was beautiful.

He almost reminded Akiem of himself. His old self. Proud. Strong. Untouchable. But he wasn't alone like Akiem had been. Luceran had a brood, a court, a vast network of dragons who knelt at his word, and a township of elves who did the same. Had Akiem been king in his own land for longer than a few weeks, he would have created something like Luceran's vision. Akiem admired him and his creation.

He noticed how the light played in Luceran's pale hair

and lashes and kissed his cheek, adding a touch of pink to match his lips. His mind wandered along the fine edge of the male's jaw, and he yearned to run his fingertips there.

Luceran lifted his hand. Akiem flinched, expecting the worst and revealing his fear of it, but the king's fingers settled warmly on his cheek.

"Whatever happened to you," he said, "whoever hurt you, it's over. The ocean delivered you to me, and now you are mine." The words were kind, even soft, but the king's eyes darkened. "But you must follow my law. Do not think to play games with me, Akiem. It will not end well for you."

Fear snagged the breath in his throat. Play games? "I wasn't—"

Luceran's fingernails scratched furrows down Akiem's cheek. "You do not kill my dragons, and you do not walk the docks, fraternizing with elves—"

"That's not—"

The backhanded slap brought Akiem to his knees, facing the dirt. Blood pooled in his mouth. He spat into the grass and tongued the split on the inside of his cheek. He felt nothing. He was nothing. This was the way of things now. He was grateful for Luceran, for everything he'd done to return Akiem to some measure of sanity. *Loved* him, even, if that was the strange feeling darting inside him. He owed Luceran obedience.

"You're confined to your chambers for a week." The king's command fell hard.

Akiem swallowed blood. He rocked back on his heels and lifted his head, losing his gaze in the mocking blue sky. Throbbing heat burned his cheek and jaw, joining the rest of the hurt from invisible wounds. "Of course."

Luceran nodded and returned the way they'd come.

Akiem stayed alone in the empty street, among the ruins of an old world, breathing slowly while the sun tried to thaw the ice in his veins. He didn't think he'd ever feel warm again. He lived with the cold, because it was all he deserved.

CHAPTER 4

ane

HE COULDN'T DECIDE if it was thunder or drums outside the door of his lodgings, and he didn't care either way, as long as both ceased so he could sleep off the mother of all hangovers.

"I swear on Alumn's tits, Zane, I will kick this door in and drag your ass through the street if I have to."

Not thunder. Jevan. And if he was mentioning Alumn's tits, he was pissed.

The hammering started up again, rattling the door on its hinges.

He wouldn't go away. Jev didn't quit.

Zane lifted his head from under the pillow and squinted into the gloom. Sunlight blasted through a slit in the drapes and sliced through his skull. It must have been an excellent night, because he had no memory of making it back to his bed. He grasped at memories from the past few hours and came up with the sight of the terrifying black dragon swooping over him. Fuck, he hadn't drunk enough to forget *that*.

Someone groaned beside him. A naked leg hooked over Zane's.

He blinked at the handsome male sleeping beside him and struggled to recall *anything*. After the goddess-awful incident at the docks, he'd returned to the bar. Ah, the bar. Right. The server lad. Shit. He'd told Zane his name sometime between feverish kisses and thick-fingered groping. Now here they were.

Zane scrabbled around his mind for the name. Adam? Abraham? His waist curved inward slightly, and his sun-touched skin brought Zane's thought back around to running his fingers down his side, kisses following. He'd tasted like life-giving sunlight. The male had hidden tattoos in various nooks, like his ankles, behind his knee, between his thumb and fingers. Zane had kissed them all. And the lad, whatever his name was, had found Zane's tattoos, the delicate one running around his little finger and the smaller one at his hip. He'd traced each swirl and dip with his tongue.

A wrecking ball hit the wooden door, flinging it open so hard it hit the wall and rebounded. Jevan stormed inside, stomping straight for the bed. He grabbed the sheet and yanked, exposing Zane and his bed companion to the cold air.

"You." Jev pointed a finger at the server lad, who'd startled awake. "Get your shit and get out."

Zane watched the male peel himself from the bed, and at the delicious sight of his sunlit nakedness, he realized he remembered a good deal about last night after all, and much of it centered around that delightfully pert body. If there was any wasted skin on the male, Zane hadn't found it. Every part of him had a purpose, and Zane had made sure to explore each one.

"And you…" Jev turned his scolding glare on Zane. Zane stretched, naked from head to toe, reveling in the cool morning air. Jev's rage-tensed cheek twitched, but he wouldn't look away. He knew Zane's games too well. "Get the fuck dressed."

The server lad pulled on his pants, and with the rest of his clothes bundled in his arms, he made for the door, tossing a long, appreciative look over his shoulder, like someone already grieving the loss of a wonderful thing.

A balled-up sheet thwacked Zane in the head.

"We're due at the elder's house in fifteen minutes, and you're still drunk." Just like that, Jev ruined a perfectly good afterglow.

Zane swung his feet over the side of the bed and waited for the walls to stop wobbling. His clothes were scattered about the room in spectacular fashion. The server lad had been a firecracker once he'd gotten him back inside these walls.

"Focus," Jev barked, propping himself against a chest of drawers and folding his arms. There was no arguing with him when he was like this.

"All right, all right." Zane found his shirt, threw it on, and tracked down his pants, passing by Jev's disapproving glare. "Didn't dip your wick in anything last night then, eh?"

"Unlike you, I have standards."

Zane snorted. "I have standards. They're just real low." He flashed his friend a grin.

Jev's eye twitched. He was thawing.

Once dressed, Zane tightened the shirt laces, tugged

on the snug-fitting overcoat, and raked his fingers through his hair, brushing out a few knots. A bath would have been ideal, but there was no time for that. "I thought the execution would be the end of it. What does that weed of an elder want with us now?"

"More guard duty. A note was shoved under my door early this morning."

Early this morning? By Alumn, it was still early, wasn't it? Zane crossed the room, parted the drapes, and peered into another late summer day. The sun had already made most of its arc across the sky, stretching the shadows long again. The city of Bayston—it's old human name forgotten—had all manner of buildings clustered close. Some tall and skinny, some squat, some made of timber, some stone built. Elves moved along the old street routes, busying themselves with trading and fixing. Some lay sprawled like cats on rooftops, soaking up Alumn's life-giving rays. The empty buildings outside Bayston's center, with their glassless, vacant windows, looked inward like silent sentinels. They were ever-present reminders of what happened to those who fought dragons.

"We're to accompany him to the west gate," Jev explained.

"And stand behind him, looking like we care?" Zane turned away from the window, plucked his daggers, and slotted them home in their hip sheaths. "If he wasn't such an emotionless plank, he wouldn't have to buy friends."

Jev's lips twisted. Definitely thawing.

"You know I'm right." Zane headed for the door.

"It's easy coin," his friend grumbled, clomping behind. "When was the last time we could say that?"

True enough. They'd fought a war not so long ago. He

had no wish to fight another. There weren't enough coins in the world to buy away those memories.

"Zane…" Jevan's strange tone had Zane pulling up short by the door. His friend looked pained. "You all right?"

Zane shrugged. "Why wouldn't I be?"

"It wasn't you at the docks last night? You didn't see the black dragon kill two of its kin over an elf?"

Zane tossed him a throwaway smile, opened the door, and strode out onto the lodge house landing. "I was here all night."

"Talk is the elf almost got killed. If anything happened to—"

"Must be one lucky bastard to survive a dragon."

He wasn't sure why he'd lied or why it mattered, just that he'd seen a little of what went on at the docks and a lot more of a dragon up close than he ever wished to again. He'd seen dragons before, of course. At three years old, he'd watched a small one rip into his father. But he'd never seen one as close and none as devastating as *that* golden-eyed beast. The damn thing had flown silently off the dockside building. If Zane had blinked, it would have melted unseen into the darkness. Dragons weren't supposed to be that quiet. They were all bluster and noise.

He'd heard the king's "consort" was an obsidian jeweled with golden eyes, and those were rare, which likely meant the dragon who had saved him at the docks was the king's new pet, and that was not a thought he wanted to linger on. Luceran had a reputation for viciously guarding his shiny toys, and Zane had already poked that sleeping dragon more than once.

After the next job for the town elder, it would be time to move on. He preferred to keep his head on his neck, not at Luceran's feet.

∼

THE EVENING ARRIVED EARLY in the shadows of the ruined buildings. Zane didn't know why humans had built them so high. Perhaps they'd wanted to reach the sky like dragons. The crippled towers acted like a ring around the elven sectors. Bayston's elves believed the ring protected them. Few dragons were brave enough to fly through the standing monoliths, and so that's where the elves made their homes, under Luceran's watchful eye.

Elder Killian waved them over. Behind him, a line of rusted junk cut the street in half, dividing the habitable city from the barrens beyond.

"You will stand behind me," Killian said, not bothering with pleasantries. "Don't say or do anything unless I am threatened." The elder had his hair braided in a dozen painfully tight tails that pulled on his already narrow face. He'd clasped his hands together in front of him and locked them there.

"Are you likely to be?" Zane asked.

The elder held his gaze. "If I wasn't, I wouldn't need you, would I?"

Zane dipped his chin, opting for silence instead of the reply that would see him sacked and unpaid.

Jevan had taken up his position on Killian's right. He adjusted the longbow at his back and observed the barrier. Zane had left his bow back at the lodge. In the city streets, long-range weapons had little use, but Jevan wore his to complete the threatening picture. Jev arched an eyebrow behind Killian, echoing Zane's unease. The location was too isolated, too overlooked. It plucked on Zane's survival instincts.

Killian scanned the street beyond the barriers. The

elder stood motionless, like a rabbit caught out in the open. He wasn't even dressed as he should be. Instead of the elder's simple attire, he'd wrapped himself in light leathers, presenting himself more like an elven scout than an official elder.

One more job and Zane was done with this city. He and Jev would head south for the winter and work the cold months with the sun-loving southern elves. They were always game for a laugh.

The wind whipped up dust and leaves as it tore through the street. A citrusy smell tingled his nose and throat. Dragons. Three emerged from farther down the street. All male.

Zane exhaled and shook out his hands, keeping his sheathed daggers within easy reach. The males were big, naturally. Dragonsight made their eyes slightly luminous in the building's shadow. They didn't wear weapons, believing they didn't need any. They had ample space between the towers to shift, although they'd have a hard time taking flight. That thought was too close to the memory of seeing the black dragon shift in front of him. That thing had been enormous. And now, facing three of the beasts, knowing exactly what they were inside their human skins, he considered that should they want the elder and his guards dead, it would happen. Zane's little daggers and Jev's longbow wouldn't stop them.

Jev sent a worried glance toward Zane, brow pinched.

They'd be all right. It was just a meeting. They'd been through worse.

Shit, but this felt different. Maybe it was because of what he'd seen at the docks.

He balanced his stance, acutely aware of the many exits, should they need them.

The black dragon had fucked up his instincts, that was all. These dragons wanted no more trouble than Killian did.

"Killian," the lead dragon greeted with a smile full of teeth. His long white hair flowed about his shoulders, only restrained from the wind by a single band tied low. The wind rippled his loose clothes. Zane narrowed his eyes. This one had swung the axe at the execution: the king's brother.

"Lord Clarion." Killian bowed his head.

Zane's heart jolted. He skimmed the pair standing on either side of Clarion, recognizing them now that he had context. Why, by Alumn's light, were Clarion and his courtly dragons meeting with Killian? This wasn't official business, not on an unlit backstreet. This was something else, something both sides wanted kept quiet.

Clarion's gaze fell to Jevan before skipping to Zane. His thin lips lifted in a toothy dragon smile. Zane's blood chilled. Whatever the reason for this meeting, the dragons were eagerly anticipating something.

"Why the muscle?" Clarion asked. The male's deep voice made the words rumble. "Don't you trust me, Killian?"

Killian shifted on his feet, moving for what felt like the first time since the dragons' arrival. "These parts are unruly," he quickly said. Too quickly. He reeked of anxiety, and not only because of the dragons' presence.

Clarion's eyes flashed. "Oh, then it isn't us you guard against?" His companions' smiles inched wider. "Are we not worthy?"

He was fucking with Killian, like a cat with a mouse.

Zane grimaced. Killian was supposed to represent the

elves, but right now, he just represented a wet-behind-the-ears fool.

"No. I-I..." Killian's hands fell open pleadingly. "It is merely... My reputation, of late, has been... somewhat lacking—"

"Trouble among the elves?" Clarion chuckled, talking over him. His dragons echoed his laughter, filling the street with their bass rumbling. He stepped closer to the elder, crowding him. The dragon was bigger in every way —taller, heavier, broader.

"The last batch was underfed." The lord's tone rumbled a warning.

"My apologies." Killian dropped his gaze and turned his head to the side so he didn't have to stare the male in the chest. "The harvest yield has been poor this year."

Clarion's mouth twisted, bored and impatient. He stepped back and waved a hand. "Bring out the fodder."

Killian lifted his arm and clicked trembling fingers. The wind tore the sound away, washing it down the street behind them. Zane dutifully stared ahead, avoiding the smirks from the courtly guards. Next time, he and Jev would need more information. A note shoved under Jevan's door wasn't enough. If this went wrong, he wasn't prepared.

The wind blessedly eased, and in the new calm, the sound of shuffling drew his attention behind him. He looked and would forever wish he hadn't.

An elf led a line of elflings, each with a burlap bag over their head, from behind a building. But that wasn't the worst of it. The elves were small and reedy. From their size, Zane guessed that their ages ranged from the likes of the little one who'd stolen Zane's coin last night, to those on the cusp of maturity. They shuffled along in scuffed, worn shoes and tattered rags, hands roped to each other.

What was this?

Clarion brushed by, shoving Zane back a step. Killian said something, but Zane's thumping heart drowned it out. He knew what this was, but there had to be another explanation. This could not be happening.

The elf who had brought the line of elflings out disappeared back down the street. Zane should have watched him go, but Clarion had reached them. The dragon lord pinched an elf on the arm. The small male whimpered, but he didn't cry out.

Clarion screwed up his nose, unhappy. "They'll do."

The lord clicked his fingers, and his dragons moved in. One took the front of the line, lifting the rope to lead them on, while the other followed behind. Both had the blown pupils and glazed look of hungry dragons.

They were taking the elves.

That's what this meeting in the middle of nowhere was for: a trade. Elflings... for what? Was Killian selling them into slavery or worse? Clarion had called them *fodder*.

"What is this, Killian?" The wind dropped, making the question louder than he'd intended.

Killian stiffened and flung Zane a scathing glare. "You do not speak. Those were our terms," he hissed. "And you will address me as *Elder*."

The elder was more concerned with protocol than the lives of twelve elves he was supposed to *protect*. A restless sense of injustice burned Zane's patience away. "Where are they taking them?"

Killian's eyed widened, showing their whites. He was so blatantly afraid that he trembled. He reached for Zane, but Zane grabbed his wrist, twisted, and shoved him back.

The elder stumbled over his feet. "You fucking coward. *Where are the dragons taking them!*"

Jevan lunged in, clutched Zane's arm, and pulled him back. "Leave it. Leave it, all right? This is not our fight." His friend shoved Zane in the chest, inserting himself between his friend and Killian.

Leave it?

Those dragons were taking the elves for fuck knew what, and Killian was letting it happen!

Zane yanked his fist free and shoved Jev off him. He was right—this wasn't their fight. Zane knew it. The sensible thing to do was back down, be the mute guard, get paid, and move on to the next town, where he'd drink and fuck the memories away, just like all the other horrors he'd seen. But how could he? How could Jev let those twelve be led to their deaths and say nothing?

"They're young'uns, Jev." Zane frowned. "You know what will happen to them. *You know!*"

Jevan's jaw worked, making his cheek twitch. Jevan was not heartless. He knew this was wrong. He'd seen the same shit Zane had and maybe lived worse. "It's. Not. Our. Fight," he repeated, holding Zane's glare.

"Shut him up," Killian snarled, "before they hear."

Too late. Clarion lifted his hand, halting the line. The lord turned on his heel and stared back at them.

Killian dropped to his knees and spread his arms out on the ground, like a willing servant. Zane watched the elder prostrate himself. Bile burned the back of his throat. Was that excuse for an elf what they'd all become? Weak, bullied, compliant? By Alumn, this display was disgusting. Zane knew the law—elves submitted to dragons—but he had some pride left. Everything happening here was bullshit. Nobody would fight for those twelve elves because Clarion sanctioned the trade. Zane couldn't live with that.

"You have a problem, Red?" the lord demanded, jerking his chin.

"No." Jevan whirled and thrust out a steadying hand to stop Clarion. "No, my lord. He doesn't have a problem. We're leaving—"

"Yes, I fucking have a problem." The words were forever out, and with that knowledge came a stab of fear. But what was a little fear against the lives of twelve children? Zane jerked his chin, flicked open his dagger sheaths, and slid the weapons free.

"Zane!" Jevan snapped. "Stop!"

Clarion's nostrils flared. Instead of addressing Zane, he snarled at Jevan, "Is your companion simple?"

Jevan might agree, just to defuse the situation, and maybe it'd work. Maybe they'd go back to the lodge, shrug it off, and move on. That's what should happen. Zane knew it.

But Jev's posture changed. His shoulders tightened. He lowered his hands onto his weapons. They'd fought alongside each other, knee-deep in mud and blood and shit, and they'd lost, but Alumn be damned, there were fucking limits to how much the dragon bastards could be ignored, and taking elven children was a line that should never be crossed.

Clarion saw the change in Jev, and briefly, the male seemed confused, like two elves defying him was utterly unthinkable. He laughed, long and loud. His kin joined in, until the street rumbled with their laughter all over again, only this time the sound hid more of the dragons' growls.

Still chuckling, Clarion shook his head in disbelief. "Some advice." He gestured at Jev. "Take your friend and go. Leave it at that. What you saw here is just one trade among hundreds. You can't save them all. This is not a fight you can win, little elves."

Hundreds? Zane tasted fury on his tongue. It burned inside his chest and tried to split him open. "When word gets out about this, my kind won't stand for it."

Clarion's smile vanished. The dragon straightened. The change in him wasn't as subtle as in an elf. Violence shimmered in his eyes, in his snarl, and in the way he curled his hands into fists. He was made for rage.

He swung for Jev, but the elf had been watching for it and whirled aside. Then, lunging in, Jev slashed both daggers across the dragon lord's belly, opening up a thin bloody line.

It should have been enough.

But Clarion didn't slow. Didn't hesitate. He grabbed Jevan by the neck and reeled him in close, locking Jev's back against his chest. Jevan kicked and bucked, but the dragon had him.

Zane flung a dagger. The big bastard twisted, avoiding the blade.

He plucked his own dagger out of thin air—one of Jev's —and lodged it under Jevan's chin. The tip summoned blood and shortened Jev's breaths.

Shit, this hadn't been meant to happen.

Jev stopped fighting and shook his head as much as the dagger would allow: a warning to stop.

Don't, his eyes pleaded. *Don't make this worse. Get away. Survive.*

Zane had one dagger left. Just one dagger against three dragons.

There was no winning this. Clarion deserved to die, but Jev was right. They wouldn't be the ones to kill him.

Zane lowered his blade.

"Thank you." The lord grinned. The only evidence of the brief fight was a few loose strands of hair whipping across his cruel face and the red stain on his shirt. "This one is now mine. He is my guarantee that you'll keep your mouth shut about what happened here and what will continue to happen after every full moon, you little elf prick. If I see any sign of dissent in the elven districts, your friend loses his head."

Zane didn't feel the punch to his lower back until he was face down on the ground, trying to breathe around the pain. The other dragons had moved in. One snatched his dagger from his hands. A kick to the gut came next. It landed hard, stealing his air. He curled around the thumping agony, his lungs struggling to work. Another kick landed against his back, this one ripping a cry from his lips. He might have heard Jevan shout something, or perhaps he had cried out again. The pain became too much to think around. He let it happen, let them land their fists and boots, knowing it would end. And when it did, he'd hurt every single one of them for what they'd done.

ane

TWO DAYS PASSED before he could face crawling from his bed to wash off the crusted blood from his body. Another day before he could walk without needing to cling to the wall, and another before he left his room to check Jevan's lodgings.

The bed hadn't been slept in, and Jevan's small collection of personal items still lay on the dresser. The air smelled stale. He hadn't returned. Zane hadn't expected him to, but he'd hoped that maybe it had all been a horrible dream.

Clarion had Jevan, all because of him.

Zane picked up Jevan's silver locket from the dresser and popped it open. A curl of dark hair was nestled inside. Jev never wore it, but he always had it with him. The hair likely belonged to a lover or child—someone lost to him—

but he'd never said who. He'd seen Jevan weep over it, seen him clutch it close when they'd both needed comfort.

He dropped it into his pocket, cleared out the rest of the items, informed the landlord of the vacant room, and headed to the bar.

Too many days had passed since the trade.

The elflings were lost. Without having seen their faces, Zane had no hope of saving them. But the dragonkin would take more children, and that made him want to take up a blade and kill any damn dragon that dare come near him. Then there was the matter of Jev. He could handle himself, to a point, but no elf could stand against a dragon. Short-lived battles from the past proved that devastating fact.

Clarion had said he wouldn't kill him. Yet.

Zane ordered a drink at the bar and winced as he picked up the cup. By Alumn's grace, the dragons hadn't touched his face, save for a split lip. They'd known to keep the wounds below the neck. The swelling had subsided enough for Zane to at least function again.

He plucked Jevan's locket from his pocket and rested it on his palm.

Everything hurt.

What he'd seen at the west gate hurt the most.

Killian was handing the dragons elven young. For servitude, fucking, or eating, it didn't matter. The outcome was always the same. They'd suffer and die.

Jev had been right: it wasn't his fight. Zane should have kept his mouth shut, should have watched it all happen and come back here, to the bar, to drink the horror away, just like after the execution. Had he done that, Jev would be beside him now, bitching but free. He could imagine him telling him he was an ass. Instead, Zane was alone because he'd opened his mouth like a fucking fool, and Jev was paying for it.

He'd get Jev back. Somehow. He just had to get into Luceran's court and find Clarion. This time, he'd be prepared for the meeting.

"Hello, lover." The server lad set a tray of drinks down on the bar and unashamedly dragged his heated gaze over Zane. "I figured you'd have breezed out of town by now."

"I'm not going anywhere." He recalled his name now: Arlo. Funny how these things came back when one didn't try to remember. He'd been sure he'd forgotten it. With everything that had happened, he'd almost forgotten about Arlo too.

Arlo rested a hand on Zane's arm, right over where an angry bruise throbbed. He winced. Arlo saw and withdrew his hand, the lust in his eyes snuffing out. He'd read the wince as rejection. Collecting his tray, he managed a small smile. "Let me know if you need anything."

Zane nodded and let him think the worst as he left. He could have called him back, could have forgotten himself in him for a few hours, or at least distracted himself with a quick tumble, but it would have raised questions about Zane's many bruises. Arlo seemed like the type who got attached too easily, and Zane had a rule not to fuck them more than once. Plus, he had other, more important things to consider.

He couldn't attack dragons head-on. That never ended well for elves. To get to Clarion, he needed to find another way. He could fight his way through, if he had the element of surprise, or use stealth. But getting into Luceran's compound wouldn't be easy, and if the dragons scented elf within their territory, it wouldn't end well.

There was another way.

One he'd already tested the waters of. It would require some... finesse.

Zane downed the drink and waited for the bruise to stop throbbing.

He'd find Clarion, and this time, he'd make sure the cuts went deep enough to ensure the dragon never traded in elves again.

CHAPTER 6

kiem

A WEEK CONFINED to his chambers—locked in isolation. The madness began on the third day. He knew the signs: tightness in his chest, rapid breathing, racing heart—all the symptoms of fear with no outward source, because the reason for the fear didn't exist, not on this side of the ocean. But his mind didn't care for facts, and his body followed along with the madness. He considered taking flight from the window, but Luceran's punishment would be worse than the mental torture he endured. So he paced and breathed and kept on living, because there was no other way. Every step was time passing, moments combining into a day and then a night. On and on and on.

The whole time, Luceran was in the adjacent room.

He heard the king, at times, moving about his chambers. Heard the doors open and close and voices in the hallway outside. *Company.* So close but out of reach. On the last day of his punishment, he picked up the pieces of his broken mind and slotted them back into place. They seemed to fit from the outside, but on the inside, they felt as fragile and sharp as ever.

He waited at the window looking out over the empty city. It looked like freedom, but Freedom was not a place. It wasn't something that could be given or taken. It was a state of mind. Or so he assumed. He'd never had freedom to know it. His mind was a prison he couldn't escape.

The connecting door between his and Luceran's chambers snicked, and the king breezed in, wearing layers of cream cotton, brown leather, and gold lace.

Akiem observed the male from the corner of his eye while continuing to stare out the window. If he moved from the window, he might do something foolish, like drop to his knees and beg the king never to shut him away again. Luceran couldn't know how Mother had repeatedly punished him this way. She'd tell her court she'd sent him on a faraway mission, and nobody would suspect he was deep inside the tower, locked in the dark for days on end, denied food, water, light, life. Denied *company*.

Luceran didn't know, but just as Akiem had heard the king moving about his chambers, the king must have heard Akiem's feverish mutterings. Akiem would never admit it to him, or anyone, but Mother's torture had made him stronger. The fact he was no longer strong wasn't her fault; it was his.

Luceran approached the window. "The Feast of the Rising is this evening. Do you celebrate such things where you're from?"

That was how his punishment ended, with no flare or ceremony. It was just another day to Luceran, while Akiem clung to the shredded pieces of his mind.

"No, we do not."

Feast of the Rising sounded like an homage to when the first great metals had broken from the ice and claimed the human world as their own. The jeweled had come later, when humans had flung their nuclear weapons into the fray, thinking the world-sundering explosions could kill dragons. It hadn't worked; the dragons had mutated instead, becoming the faster, more vicious jeweled dragonkin.

The king leaned a shoulder against the window frame opposite Akiem's. "Would you attend at my side?"

He asked as though Akiem had a choice.

Akiem turned his head, intending to tell him exactly that, but in the seven days spent lost in his head, he'd forgotten how deep Luceran's influence had hooked into him. The male reclined against the frame, his body tied up and buckled inside slate-gray trousers and a fitted boned waistcoat that tapered at the waist. Over one shoulder, he wore a half-length sheer cloak, transparent but for a slight flitter, like dragonfly wings.

A sudden, terrifying rush of heat flooded his veins, like his body had been triggered to attack. He saw himself crossing the few strides between them, shoving the king against the wall, and tasting his mouth, just to see if he tasted as sweet as he looked. The fantasy was pin clear. So clear, in fact, that its impact physically hurt. Disgust at his own filthy desires kicked him into motion. Akiem pushed away from the window and headed for the chamber door. His punishment was over, and he could leave. He had to leave before his body betrayed his arousal.

"Stop."

He stopped, marooned in the middle of the room, halfway between the door and the king. Breathing through his nose, he waited. If the king came to him, he wasn't sure what he'd do. He'd spent too long locked up alone. He couldn't do *alone*, but he didn't want to be seen either. Gods, he didn't know how to be *Akiem* here, with Luceran, with these dragons in this court on the wrong side of the ocean. He wanted to be different, to change things, to change himself, but he didn't know how.

Luceran's hand landed gently on his shoulder. It felt like a lightning strike. The king slowly—so slowly—stood in front of Akiem. He was perfect. Eyes a deep violet. His hair done up with pins and curls, ready for the feast. His damn clothes all clipped and neatly edged. In winter, back in his homeland, he'd liked to roll in the snow as dragon, just to upset its soft perfection. Luceran was like that snow. Akiem wanted to destroy the picture standing in front of him, to rip it to shreds and fuck it until the male screamed his name, either in lust or fear.

The thoughts shocked him. Luceran said something. Akiem watched his lips form the words, saw the perfect teeth and the tip of the king's quick tongue, but he didn't hear his voice over the sound of his thunderous heart. *Wrong, wrong, wrong,* his heart said. He heard a chamber door slam inside his memory and felt the darkness bury him in isolation until Mother believed he'd suffered enough for his foul thoughts.

This was the king's fault.

Luceran should never have locked him up. He was too dragon to be shut away. *This* fucking insanity burning up his veins was the result.

"Get out of my way," Akiem growled. *Or you won't like what I become,* he finished inside his mind.

Luceran's hand stroked Akiem's chest.

Akiem snatched the male's wrist, held him still, and

squeezed. The king's eyes blew wide open. Good. Let him feel the strength of the beast he toyed with. On the beach, Akiem had been near death. Luceran had taken advantage of that weakness. Akiem was not weak today.

The king's infamous smile tilted his lips, and instead of backing off, he stepped in. With his free hand, he cupped Akiem's painful erection. Akiem hadn't even registered he'd become so aroused. The contact jolted another dangerous blast of lust through his veins. The king's hand was hard, his grip firm, and Akiem's body rebelled against the horror of having a male hold him there by driving his erection against Luceran's touch, seeking glorious friction.

It was wrong. He'd be shut away again. But Mother wasn't here... Nobody was here to stop this from happening. "I don't do males."

Luceran's lips cut a wicked smile, and his hand squeezed.

Akiem grabbed roughly at Luceran's pretty hair. Knotting his fingers in the locks, he yanked him forward. His mouth was on Luceran's, his thoughts racing to catch up. He didn't want to think. Luceran tasted of ice, of a cool autumnal morning before the heat of the day. He tasted like a different kind of sweetness from the one Akiem had imagined, but by the gods, he wanted more.

Luceran's tongue darted, and the male opened, pushing as much as giving, rocking with Akiem's assault. Akiem looped his free arm around his back and pulled him close, clamping his wrist between them. Luceran's hand, the one placed firmly on his cock, ground over his erection, driving a dangerous wildness through Akiem. He didn't do males —he didn't—but this...

And then the wretched memories slammed in.

Another's tongue thrust into his mouth. Hands held

him down. Teeth at his throat. A dragon who smelled of metal. Images flashed, each one as real and cutting as lashes from a whip. The dragon wasn't Luceran, and he wasn't here, but Akiem's mind had conjured him up. Luceran's hand on his cock groped and grasped, taking without permission. Akiem tore free and shoved Luceran back.

Breathe.

He needed to breathe.

He couldn't. It hurt. Everywhere hurt.

Claws groping, invading.

He reeled away, hit the bedpost, and almost fell.

Luceran was there, looming over him, but it wasn't Luceran. The male was huge, his muscles slick with sweat, smelling of metal and blood. Akiem remembered praying for death, praying to any god who would listen, even Alumn, the elven goddess, to make it end, and the metal dragon had laughed sickeningly.

"Akiem..."

Luceran.

Didn't matter.

He sank down the bedpost and buried his head in his hands.

Smaller.

He wanted to be smaller, to curl into a ball and hide.

A touch sparked at his shoulder.

Akiem sprang forward, lunging at Luceran's middle. Cornered, he had no choice but to attack. This wasn't reason; it was instinct. Only, Luceran somehow caught him and yanked Akiem off balance. Akiem met the floor face first. Cool, strong hands caught his arms and held them behind his back. A knee sank into his back.

"Stop."

Heated power crawled beneath his skin. The shift. It would tear him open and make him dragon and he welcomed it. Needed it.

"Breathe," Luceran said, calmly.

Breathe. Akiem let out the breath he'd been clutching, blowing puffs of dust off the floor. His cheek hurt where splinters dug into his skin. His back hurt too from Luceran's weight pinning him down. Luceran. Nobody else. There was no one else here. From the floor, he could see the dresser, the window, the end of the bed. He'd been alone. Luceran had come. Nobody had tried to hurt him. It was all in his head, in his past.

The urge to shift faded, sinking him back inside his human-like skin.

Acting on the urges in his head, he'd attacked Luceran in more ways than one. This was the madness in him, the dragon, the truth hidden at his core like a rot. The part of him he'd never fully realized. The ugliness he saw every time he looked in a mirror.

"Forgive me," he whispered.

The weight lifted off him, and Luceran's hold on his wrists vanished. The king offered his hand. "We'll work on that, my black prince."

Black Prince.

He'd been called that before, half a world away.

Akiem winced, pushed onto his knees, and looked at Luceran's offered hand, then up at the king. His hair was all mussed up and his dragonfly cloak all shifted out of place. The color on his lips had smudged, yet still he smiled.

"Not everyone is out to hurt you, Akiem."

The words choked him and had his vision swimming. He wanted to believe that, but Luceran was fickle, his desires more so. And Akiem had pushed him, teased him, and attacked him. Any dragon worth their scales would have retaliated, but not with this strange kindness.

"I don't deserve you." He clambered to his feet without taking the king's hand and cast his gaze toward the window, avoiding Luceran's messed-up appearance. He'd have done worse to the king. Ravaged him, if they'd continued. In many ways, it was good his fucked up past had ended his lust. He wasn't supposed to be this way.

"You have no idea who I am. How can you know whether you deserve me?" The king's words pulled Akiem back into the room. Despite Luceran's upset appearance, or perhaps because of it, there was an honesty about him. "Come to the feast. Sit with me or don't, but come." He headed for the adjoining doors.

"If I don't, will you sentence me to solitude again?"

The door clicked closed behind him with the question unanswered.

Akiem drew in a breath and let it out slowly. It appeared, he was going to a feast.

ane

ZANE DISCOVERED two things about dragons after luring a lower courtly type away from the docks: they're easily manipulated at the promise of sex. The second chance discovery was that they were susceptible to valerian root. His mother had taught him the benefits of the plant. It was one of the few things he remembered of her, and it served him well.

After the dragon had smuggled him into the compound and a "room" apparently meant for similar encounters, if the ready and waiting bed were any indication, Zane dropped a small vial's worth of valerian root into the dragon's cup. The beast's groping began again right after he'd taken the drink. Zane delayed, opting to pleasure the male slowly rather than have his hands provoke his bruises. He took his time unlacing the male's pants, putting some art into it, more than concerned that he might have to go through with the act, but shortly after lying back, the dragon lost interest in the positioning of Zane's hands and mouth and fell asleep.

He picked up his jacket and shirt, throwing both back on and hastily tying them in place, then headed for the window. Outside, torches lit the compound pathways across open areas. Lamplight illuminated the windows of other buildings. Beyond, a larger blocky building signaled the center of Luceran's court. The important dragons would be in there.

The second he climbed from the window, he'd be risking his head.

Moving about anywhere near the torches was suicide.

After quietly opening the window latch, he swung the pane open and leaned out, looking up. Cool evening wind wrapped its chill around him. He could just make out a downpipe, which led to the roof, and as the houses were all connected, he could, in theory, make it all the way to the central compound without anyone spotting him—unless there were dragons in the sky. He hadn't seen any, but after watching the black one sail right over his head silently as a moth, the idea of running along the rooftops at night didn't seem as foolproof as before. Still, it was up or risk the gardens, and as good as Zane was, movement among the lights was more likely to catch the eye of any dragon looking outside.

"You'd better thank me for this, Jev." He climbed onto the sill, used the open section of window to lean out, and grabbed the downpipe. The iron creaked and groaned but held. Once he was on the roof, the wind bit at his face. Flicking his collar up, he hunkered down and kept low to hide his silhouette. The rooftops were uneven, adding a challenge, but he made it to the end of the row of houses.

Now all he had to do was cross to the central compound and find an open window. Once inside, finding Jevan would be difficult, but he'd worry about that if he got that far.

The dragonkin he had seen were all headed deeper into the compound, and they were dressed in fine colors. So, this was a night of celebration. All the better for Zane. He could use the distraction.

The grounds appeared clear, but that didn't mean there weren't any dragons watching. Torches didn't light all corners.

"Alumn, you owe me." He pulled his hood up, started down the pipe, and hit the ground running.

"Hey!"

He'd made it almost two-thirds of the way when the shout went up. Zane ran harder, darting around a corner and in through an open window. Clothes. Sheets folded and piled high. A laundry. Good. Breathless, he gently latched the window behind him and blew each wall lamp out. In the dark and quiet, he waited, hand on a dagger. Moments went by, and then footfalls thumped closer outside.

"Right around here," a female said. "I saw her come this way."

Her? The dragons weren't expecting an elf. They thought they'd seen one of their own, but a slimmer female.

"You smell elf?" a male asked.

Zane squeezed his eyes closed. Damn.

The painful seconds dragged on.

"Must be tonight's entertainment." The female laughed, her voice moving away.

He waited until their voices had faded altogether before approaching the laundry door, cracking it open, and looking out into the hallway. All the hallways looked the same. He'd only walked down a handful, and that was when he'd accompanied Killian to the execution. But dragons weren't complicated. Social creatures, they mostly stayed together in the hub of the brood—the nest. The lowers spread out, forming their own smaller nests close to, but away from, those at the top of the food chain. Zane's unsuspecting date sleeping off the valerian root had been a lower and an idiot. After a few questions, he'd even mentioned roughly where Clarion's chambers were, too hungry for elf ass to care why an elf was asking about the lord.

Keeping his ears pricked, he dashed light-footed down the hall, slipping into the shadows of doorways to listen for any company. Whatever event was happening, it had them enthralled, and it gave Zane the break he needed to locate Jevan.

CHAPTER 8

kiem

A FEAST at the amethyst court—the court he'd grown in but was now nothing but ashes—had consisted of mountains of food, noise, dragons, blood, and sex. It had been a time to display how virile a dragon you were. Luceran's feast was... different. The hall was just as large as the one used to behead an elf over a week ago, although the ceiling here was higher and crossed with exposed timber beams. Inside the vast space, tables lay scattered about, each topped with spreads of meats and vegetables. There had to be over two hundred dragonkin present. Clarion headed a table right of the king's. Luceran sat at the center, surrounded by his dragons. Akiem had assumed he'd be seated off to one side, where he could observe them and have none at his back. He seemed unconcerned. If anything, he glowed among those at his table. High officials. His trusted council. Dragons Akiem avoided as much as they avoided him.

He'd arrived late. A lower had found him appropriate clothes, and he'd asked her to fix his hair in the correct fashion. The amethyst court hadn't cared much for beautifying things. The practical was more important in times of war. Again, things were different here. Dragons wore their hair in elaborate twirls and tufts and wore uniquely cut and colored clothing. The result had him curiously self-conscious as he entered the hall. The lower had chosen for him a flattering mix of a dark purple vest—to bring out the night colors in his hair, she'd said—and high-waisted black pants with a line of silver buttons up the outside. She'd tied much of his hair back but left enough to braid and pin alongside the loose tail. The vest left his arms exposed, revealing more skin than he would have ever dared show at such a gathering.

More than a few glances lingered too long. Most were heavy with the usual scorn, but a few had lightened appreciatively, even becoming hungry in their assessment.

He hadn't deliberately sought Luceran's attention, but as he drifted among the tables, he found he already had it. The king had eyes only for him in a room of hundreds. He'd had someone fix his hair and appearance and looked exactly as he had before Akiem had tried to rip into him. Only now a new heat lingered in the king's stare—an obvious one none could mistake for anything but attraction. Akiem's withered heart stuttered in its cage. A larger part of him wanted to shun the affection, but the shame had faded some. Luceran hadn't rejected his advances, rough as they'd been. So then males lusting after other males seemed... acceptable here, at least to Luceran. And really, his opinion was the only one that mattered.

There was no place for him at Luceran's table, he noticed. The king had asked him to sit beside him, but perhaps he hadn't meant it literally, and now Akiem found himself without a seat or a destination in a room full of dragons who would soon notice how foolish he had been to think he—an outsider—could sit among them.

He felt their gazes crawling over him again.

Clarion brushed by. The lord laughed, planted a cup in Akiem's hand, and nodded for Akiem to follow him across the room to his table, where a spare chair waited.

Akiem fought the urge to glance back at Luceran, and then wished he hadn't at the open disapproval on the king's face. A mistake, then, to go with Clarion, but he'd had little choice.

"Don't mind him." Clarion pulled the chair out for Akiem. "He thinks I'm luring you here to talk politics and maybe persuade you to my bed."

"Are you?"

All six of Clarion's close circle of dragons at the table laughed.

"No." Clarion pointed at Akiem. "Not least because I rarely do males, though I don't begrudge those who do. Besides, Luceran has a special fondness for you, his *black prince*." The crowd snickered. "I wouldn't want to disrupt that."

"I..." He'd been about to deny it. He'd always denied it since Mother had threatened to bite off his wings if he didn't stop his wandering gazes before they became a real problem. He bowed his head in submission and agreement. Not a verbal answer, but an answer all the same.

Those at the table already assumed he and Luceran were... whatever a male pair was called. They hadn't had a word for it in the Amethyst brood, at least no words besides *wrong* and *forbidden*.

"You're a mysterious one, eh," Clarion went on. "Dropped out the sky and suddenly you have Luceran in knots." He began to fill his plate with food, as the others were also doing. "Some here don't trust you."

"There is no mystery," Akiem said, his mind wandering to the food. There had been talk among the lowers of famine among the elves, but there was no sign of a food shortage here. He tentatively loaded his plate too, finding curious meats that smelled sweet and delicious. In Akiem's own lands, amethysts ate mostly beef. Little else was left large enough to satisfy their appetite. Akiem had taken the occasional deer. Elf, too, when he could catch them.

"We don't see many obsidian scales here. There's one, that I know of, and he keeps to the outskirts. Just diamonds, some topaz, and a couple of amethysts."

"Any emerald?" Akiem enquired. He picked up a slice of white meat, sniffed, and bit down. Delicious. Smooth but with enough texture to grip with his teeth—and familiar, though he couldn't place it.

"Emerald? None."

"Metal?" Akiem asked.

Clarion recoiled as though the question surprised him. "Metals! They died out centuries ago."

Akiem was in no mood to correct him. Better that the metals stay far away and never bother this land or Akiem. "Plenty of elves, though." He quickly diverted the subject from the metals before he lost his appetite.

"Elves," Clarion snorted. "Like rats. They're everywhere. Get into everything. I'd kill them all."

Those around the table jeered their agreement.

Akiem had heard similar sentiments before, but this

was coming from the king's brother. No wonder Luceran hadn't looked pleased when Clarion had drawn Akiem over. Like all brothers, tensions existed between them. Clarion and Luceran had the same diamond-white coloring, but they seemed to share little else. Did Clarion covet the king's crown? It wouldn't be the first time a brother had sought to unseat the ruling king. Wars had been fought over less. Had this been an amethyst brood, one brother would have killed the other long before now.

He ate some more of the exotic meat, surprised to find himself ravenous.

"Good?" another dragon asked. She was diamond too. It showed in her eyes, multifaceted and shimmering. But her coloring was darker than the brothers' pale skin and light hair, her skin and hair a warmer shade of chestnut.

"Hm, what is it?"

"Elf." She grinned. "The kitchens salt and smoke the carcasses, hang them for a few days, and then slow bake it. Brings out the richness in the meat."

"Abbey here is our resident hunter-gatherer," Clarion explained. "She likes to hunt them herself. Not the ones in the city, mind. They're useful. Just the ones outside."

Akiem swallowed hard. He somehow managed to keep the broken pieces of his smile from collapsing. So the meat was elf. Didn't matter. That's how they did things here. Amethyst wasn't so different. Any elves found were killed. Some eaten, as dragon. Akiem had eaten elf, but always as dragon. Not like this. *Prepared.*

"Surprisingly nice, right?" Abbey beamed. She scooped up a few slices with her fingers. "We eat the little ones too, bones an' all. Fucking delicious."

"What was your trade in your homeland?" Clarion asked between mouthfuls of meat and wine.

Akiem reached for his wine. "I was... a flight leader." *And a prince. Briefly a king.* He kept those last thoughts to himself.

The male's eyes narrowed. He openly appraised Akiem's figure, noting his arms and their ladder-like scars. "A fighter?"

"On the wing." Akiem let him look. He'd lost weight and muscle since arriving here, and if Clarion ever saw him as dragon, he'd doubt Akiem's words then too. Luceran's reception had nearly killed him. He hadn't fared much better since, and he healed slowly. He'd always healed slowly. He knew he appeared too slim, too *weak*. That's how things were now.

"Who'd you fight?"

The others were intrigued, all leaning forward as the gathering continued behind them. Akiem tried to sight Luceran in the crowd but couldn't find him among so many. "We fought wild dragons to the north of our territory, mostly."

"And the others?" Clarion pushed, sensing Akiem was holding back.

He rubbed his neck, trying to massage the ache away, like always.

"Bronze," he said, tasting blood, a memory.

"Metal?" Clarion's eyes widened. "You fought fucking metals?"

His insides grew cold. "It didn't start out that way. We were allies, but the bronze were difficult."

"Shit," Abbey said. "Now I know why you're scarred like you are." Her gaze made the marks on his arms sizzle.

The ache grew. They had no fucking idea why he was scarred.

"What are they like?" she asked.

More wine went down to fill the growing hole inside, but instead, it only made him feel more empty. "What do you think?"

"Big," another dragon said.

"We heard they'd all died?" Abbey asked.

"No, or maybe they have now. I don't know. Don't care. I left and..." He felt teeth pierce his skull, the memory so damn real he almost gasped. Claws scraped his back, his wings. Teeth tore muscle and scale from his body. Mud tried to choke him, blind him, and deafen him all at once. It clung to his wings, and through it all, the bronze held him down. Always held him down.

Akiem's hand shook. He pressed it against the tabletop.

"Is that why you came here? To get away from them?"

Akiem stood so quickly his chair toppled backward and hit the floor, startling nearby dragons. He scooped up his drink. "Excuse me."

"Hey—" A hand grabbed him.

Akiem didn't think. There wasn't time to. He swung for Clarion, using his left fist, so it was never going to land well. It clipped the male's jaw and startled him enough to have him fall backward, and in doing so, he caught Akiem's arm and yanked, pulling Akiem down, eye to eye.

The diamond's eyes sizzled with restrained rage. "You're mine."

Akiem bared his teeth and yanked his arm free. "I'm not your bitch—or your king's. Threaten me again and I'll rip your wings off while you sleep. I've mauled far worse than you, *bitch*."

The lord blinked, frowned, and barked a torrent of laughter. He picked up his cup and drank deeply while the others laughed at the hilarious thought of Akiem beating Clarion.

Akiem left the table before he could get drawn into another brawl—with the king's brother, no less. He searched for Luceran, but his attention snagged on the elf making her way into the room. Her flowing pale gown rippled like water over her bare feet. Warm honeyed skin glowed. She didn't look real. Akiem blinked, expecting her to ghost away. But she stayed, walking along the outside of the room, drawing attention her way. She smelled of the forest at dawn, of wood and wildness. There wasn't a dragon here who didn't see her.

Then she stopped, faced the room, opened her mouth, and sang. The sound she produced was smooth, melodic, haunting, and spellbinding, and all at once, Akiem had to leave. She didn't know the dragons feasted on strips of her kin. Nor did she know she wouldn't make it out alive, or if she did know, then all the more reason for Akiem not to stay, because if she knew she'd die here, that made her far braver than him and worthier of life.

The hallways all looked the same.

Akiem took a few random turns, stumbled down steps, passed from one building to another where they'd been knocked into one long compound. He was sure most dragons knew the twists and turns like they did their own tails, but Akiem was lost. He didn't care. Walking was getting away. Like at the docks, he just had to keep moving to escape the memories. Just keep moving.

A hooded figure blocked his path.

He lifted his head.

Red hair.

Green eyes.

Elf.

Akiem frowned. Had his thoughts conjured the elf from the docks here? "What—"

The elf's green eyes widened. He bolted left, down another hallway.

Akiem lunged after him out of instinct, mostly. Few dragons could resist a chase.

The elf's red hair might as well have been a flag in the torchlit corridors. As he ran, his hood fell back, making his long hair fan out behind him. His footfalls were almost silent. And damn, he was fast. Akiem tossed his cup and ran harder. Just like at the docks, if this one came across a less friendly dragon, he'd surely be killed. Akiem wouldn't allow that to happen. For the elf back in the compound, for the elves who had died to feed gluttonous dragons. This red-headed fool wasn't dying as well.

"Stop…" he called, but not too loud. Most of the dragons were at the feast, but it would take just one to spot them and raise the alarm.

The elf was outrunning him, bouncing off corners like water flowing down a drain. Shit, he was too damn fast. He darted around corners faster than Akiem could keep up, until the flag of red hair fluttered out like a torch and was gone. The hallway came to a dead end. No elf. Four closed doors, two on either side.

Akiem let a smile lift his lips. He sniffed the air, scenting elf, but that didn't tell him what door the intruder had taken. "I don't want to hurt you." Of course, all dragons would say the same, and little would convince this elf that Akiem spoke the truth. "You shouldn't be here."

Why was he here? This was the last place an elf would willingly come. Unless he'd escaped from inside the compound? Perhaps he'd been meant to be part of the entertainment too—and die for it.

Akiem's patience frayed. Games were one thing, but he was trying to help this fool escape dragons.

He opened the first door to the left and found an empty room inside. No furniture. A closed window. Nothing. The first door to his right in the hallway opened to a storage room, its air musty. The elf hadn't gone inside. That left the two at the end. He tried the left. Locked. The right door then.

Akiem closed his hand around the handle. He cracked the door an inch and smelled the fresh, woodsy scent of the traditional elven homes. Akiem swung the door open. One step, another. Darkness greeted him. Sheets covered the outlines of a chair and couch. The rest of the furniture was difficult to make out.

Akiem entered, hands up. "I'm not armed."

"You don't need to be," the voice said from the far corner. Akiem couldn't make out where the elf was among the layered shadows.

"True enough." He lowered his hands.

Voices sounded from far down the hallway. Akiem swallowed. "I'm going to shut this door. If I leave it open, another dragon will likely discover you."

The elf didn't reply.

Akiem toed the door closed and then backed against it, plunging himself into the darkness. He found himself in a dangerous position. As man, he was vulnerable to the elf's sharp daggers. The elf had better night vision too. He knew exactly where Akiem stood, whereas Akiem had yet to pinpoint him among the piles of junk.

"I don't want to hurt you," he said again, finding the words truer the more he said them.

"Why chase me?"

Akiem zeroed in on the crouched shape behind the

couch. "Because there are five hundred dragons in this compound who do."

The elf straightened, armed with a dagger in each hand. Cloaked in shades of gray, he was no less intriguing than he had been at the dock. It seemed impossible that they should meet again, just as impossible as an elf roaming a dragon compound.

"Why are you here?" Akiem asked. "Are you looking for someone?"

As Akiem's eyes adjusted to the dark, he saw the elf smile.

As he emerged from behind the couch, Akiem took in the make of him. He wore softer leathers than those he'd worn at the execution. They clung to him and kept his profile lean, all the better for infiltrating dragon strongholds. The daggers would no doubt be sharp when he stabbed Akiem—which was surely about to happen.

Akiem lifted his chin.

Still, the elf strode forward, unafraid, and the closer he got, the more his features sharpened in the dark. He had smooth freckle-marked skin, pale in a way that made him glow instead of making him appear sickly. The hair was a mess of ruffled lengths. Some locks licked his jaw, some fell to his shoulders, like he'd hacked at it himself.

The blade was at Akiem's throat and the wall at his back before he could draw his next breath. He didn't fight and kept his hands out, submitting.

"You're not afraid?" the elf whispered, eyes narrowing. His breath was cool where it touched Akiem's chin.

"Of death? No."

The elf's eyebrow arched. "You could have chosen *not* to chase me, to let me go, but here we are."

He hadn't had much choice. Run and he'd give chase. The instinct was ingrained into all dragons.

The elf's eyes flashed a warning. "What do you want?"

The dagger dug in; whether intentionally or not, the blade still bit and stung, drawing blood. Akiem did have a choice, and he decided now. He brought his arm up, fast enough to knock the elf's hand back, and locked his fingers around the elf's wrist. Snagging the other dangerously armed hand, Akiem pulled and turned, slamming the elf into the wall, his wrists captured high. The elf cried out. One dagger slipped free, and then, as Akiem pushed in, drilling his glare into the elf's, the elf relinquished. It clattered to the floor, leaving the elf disarmed, but his kind always had more blades on them.

Akiem had planned to pull back, to show him he truly had no intention of hurting him, that he'd just wanted the blade away from his neck, but a curious sensation had overcome him. The elf's breathless panting from the run brushed his chest against Akiem's. Their breaths mingled. His tasted fresh, clean.

"It appears I am at your mercy." The elf's voice had turned sly, and a crooked smile rested on his lips, asking for things it shouldn't.

Akiem slowed his own breathing, aware that his heart hadn't slowed at all. If anything, it raced faster than before. He licked his lips, saw the elf's gaze pin to his mouth, and froze beneath the scrutiny.

"You smell of wine and revelry, dragon. Perhaps you should start thinking more with your head." The elf blinked slowly, pinched his bottom lip between his teeth, and let it spring back. "And less with your cock."

If Akiem hadn't been aroused before, he was now, in this dark storage room with an elf pinned to the wall.

Nobody need know. Even he didn't fully believe it. Was this wild elf also aroused? Akiem didn't smell fear. He knew fear. The red-haired temptation with his wrists pinned overhead was a long way from being afraid. That alone teased Akiem's instincts to provoke a reaction. Who was this elf that he wasn't afraid of dragons and males in dark rooms?

"As much as seeing you struggle with your desires is a fascinating journey into dragon psyche, I do have somewhere I need to be, so if you don't mind..." He pulled at Akiem's hold, a token gesture. He could have pulled harder.

He should let him go. If he didn't, he'd be no different from his kin. But there was something between them. He knew there was. It had sparked to life when the damn elf had winked at him, and it had burned a little more at the docks. Fate kept putting this one right in his path.

"Dragon, kiss me or let me go. I'm sure we both have lives that need us in them—"

His lips were soft, and with Akiem brushing his against them, they were also blessedly silent. The elf parted his mouth enough to grant permission. Akiem didn't move. He wasn't sure he could. If he took what the elf offered, what did that make him?

The elf leaned in, sealed their mouths, and forced his tongue in. Suddenly breathless and robbed of thought, Akiem fell into the kiss. By the great gods, he needed this. The gentleness made him ache. It wasn't like any other time, with any dragon. It wasn't like anything else he'd known. The elf came alive against him, his mouth and body hungry. He tried to pull forward, to tempt Akiem in, but this... just this kiss... was enough. It was just... right.

The kiss ended like all things must, but it ended slow,

full of promise and want, as though it were a beginning and not an end. Lust shone in the elf's eyes. In this dark room, the elf was a forbidden delight, a secret, a wonder.

"Did you enjoy my gift, dragon?" the elf purred.

Even the words he used, and how he spoke them, drove Akiem to distraction. He wet his lips, careful to keep his voice level. "More than you know."

"Good. Here's another."

The elf slammed his knee up, exploding agony through Akiem's balls and up his back. He might have sworn, but he certainly cried out and stumbled backward, reaching for the couch so he didn't drop to his knees and throw up the horrid meat he'd unwittingly eaten at the feast.

The elf was out the door and running.

Akiem staggered out the doorway. He clung to its frame, the pain sapping him of his strength. He wouldn't go after that elf until he could at least see through the throbbing stars crowding his vision. And by then, he'd hopefully be gone, destined for freedom and not Clarion's chopping block.

He still didn't know his name.

His Red. The one whose kiss had been a fucking delight and not a horror. He touched his lips, tasting elf in a way that went against everything he knew and every-thing he'd been taught. The kiss. Gods, the wild kiss. He waited for the shame to smother him, but it didn't come. He waited for the past to crowd close and make him weep. He felt nothing but heated desire to have *more*. Akiem had never relished the feel of a knee in the balls, but this one he'd never forget.

ane

PLAN A HADN'T WORKED, but with some modification, it might. He'd first snared a lower. That had gotten him inside the compound, but the place was too big. However, as he'd searched for Jevan, he'd also somehow, inexplicably, snared the king's new toy. That had seemed like too good an opportunity to pass up. That was the only reason he couldn't get the kiss out of his head. The same reason he couldn't stop thinking about how the dragon had tasted. Delicious, with a hint of spicy warmth that had Zane's unruly cock twitching. But he didn't do dragon. His enjoyment of the kiss had been a ruse to get away, nothing more. If he hadn't kneed him in the nuts, he'd have ended up dragon food. He'd done the right thing.

So, to Plan B:

Use the king's new toy to get to Clarion and/or find Jevan. As terrifying as the dragon was, he seemed reasonable as man, and if Zane had to fuck him to get what he wanted, it wouldn't exactly be a chore. He hadn't had much of a chance to get his hands on him, but what he had seen in the dark had been pleasing enough. The male's biceps had held a defined curve while stringing Zane up high. The dragon's smile had briefly appeared, softening his entire face. Without the smile, he had a severe intensity to him, like his glare could melt metal. He probably could melt metal, as dragon. As long as Zane didn't forget the monster he was, everything would be fine.

He paced his room.

It would all be fine.

He just had to find him again. Seduce him. Get Jevan's whereabouts from him. The rest he'd deal with when it happened.

There was one place they had crossed paths before. A place seduction was expected.

He'd have to win his trust.

Make him believe he was genuinely into him.

"Easy enough," Zane told his lodgings.

The dragon was definitely interested in Zane, but if he gave him what he wanted too soon, he might miss his chance to get answers. No, this had to be a seduction. A work of art. Not a dirty fuck against the wall, as much as the idea had Zane's already alert cock hardening further. Alumn be damned, this wasn't personal. This couldn't be personal. Not with a dragon. Get Jevan. Get the hell out of this wretched city. He owed Jevan that. And fucking a dragon would be the price.

A knock sounded at his door. He'd almost missed it, along with the sound of boots hitting the boards.

"Yes?" he called.

"Zane, it's Arlo..."

Gods, yes.

Zane opened the door. Arlo was dressed in his bar attire—plain black pants and a white shirt.

"Is everything all right?" Zane asked, already picturing him out of his work attire.

"Yes, fine. I wanted to ask—"

Zane caught him by the shirt, pulled him in, and kissed him up against the wall, using a boot to kick the door closed beside them. Thank Alumn's light, the male's hands were on him instantly, roughing up his shirt, trying to yank it free from his pants.

Zane chased his mouth and delighted in Arlo chasing him back, going so far as to groan as tiny sharp teeth nipped at his neck. Zane pulled his shirt open, sending a few buttons scattering. He spread his hands over Arlo's chest and ran his tongue down and around a nipple, sucking it before riding down the ridge of his abs. He was too slim and lithe to be dragon, not that Zane was comparing. He wasn't. Just an observation. He unlaced Arlo's pants and had his cock in hand, then between his lips and over his tongue.

"Fuck," Arlo spat, thumping his head back against the wall. His fingers sank into Zane's hair. "Oh gods, Alumn... don't."

"Don't?" Zane mumbled around the mouthful.

"Do!"

Zane rolled his tongue, applying pressure, and used his hand on the hot, hard shaft while his mouth did the rest.

"Fuck, Zane."

Please do. Zane straightened, kissed Arlo hard, and claimed him, working the slickened cock against his palm and through his fingers. Arlo rocked, hips thrusting. He threw an arm around Zane's shoulders and fucked his hand, grunting in a way Zane never would have expected from him. When he kissed him again, he fucking devoured him. His cock in his hand, his tongue tangled with Zane's, his body trapped. Arlo pulled free, flung his head back, and came so fucking hard Zane couldn't help but grind his own throbbing cock against his thigh.

"Zane, please…" Arlo shoved his pants down, turned to face the wall, presenting the curve of his back, and thrust out a tight, round ass, which Zane remembered well.

"Wait." Zane rummaged in the dresser drawer, found the oil, and spread it over himself and Arlo's crevice. He sank two fingers in to help ease the tight ring of muscles.

"Goddess, *just do it.*"

Zane took his arousal in hand and held Arlo's thigh as he guided himself into the tightness he needed so desperately he couldn't think straight. Arlo arched his back and rocked his hips, opening himself, and Zane closed his eyes, easing in deeper. Pleasure was a cruel tease, and he chased it down, falling into a rhythm that had him clutching Arlo to him, his chest to Arlo's back. He fucked him until he lost all sense of himself, the room, the world—all but the damn dragon he'd kissed in the dark. He imagined that kiss again, reliving it in exquisite detail. The taste of fear on the male's lips, a fear the dragon had overcome. He was a monster, a beast of flame and claw, and still he'd kissed as though he were broken and didn't know how to fix himself.

By Alumn, Zane wanted to show him how, to make him whole again, and he didn't damn well care that he wasn't supposed to think that way about anyone, especially a dragon. He wanted that monster in his arms, beneath him, over him, in every way. He wanted him to spill his seed and whisper Zane's name in a kiss, just like the one they'd shared in that dark room.

He came suddenly and hard, pleasure uncoiling and snapping, spooling free, leaving him panting over Arlo's golden back. He kissed and nipped at Arlo's shoulder.

Braced against the wall by a single hand, he closed his eyes and saw the dragon beneath him, his back rippling with strength. Alumn, it couldn't happen soon enough.

THE DRAGON WASN'T at the docks the next night or the night after. Plenty of dragons came and went, many from Luceran's court. None were the dragon he wanted to see, and none sparked the same breathless fluttering in his chest. Their numbers tapered off, and by mid-month, the market trade and the dragons had all but dried up. It ebbed and flowed like this, a trader told him. On the next full moon, the dragons would return.

There was no other way to reach him. He knew a way inside the compound, but the place was much bigger than he'd anticipated, and he'd only gotten out without anyone seeing him by luck. Chancing it again felt like one chance too many.

Zane walked the dockside, deliberately close to the water's edge. There were traders here. The area was lit well enough. He was safe, and perhaps that was the problem. The dragon had so far shown up twice, and each time when Zane had been running headlong into trouble. Perhaps he should play the damsel in distress again to see if the dragon emerged from the shadows.

Of course, this was all part of the plan.

None of these *urges* were personal.

He stopped by an old ship's anchor tie, the concrete projection shaped like a large mushroom rising from the dockside. There weren't any ships at the docks. Ships hadn't sailed for centuries. Some lay rotting in the channel. None of those huge human machines, whether it be cars, planes, or ocean liners, moved in the air or on the ocean anymore. Zane had only seen those human things in water-stained antique books belonging to the elves who paid him to work.

Work he sorely needed.

He had enough coin for another week's lodgings, and then, if he didn't find work, he'd have to resort to stealing like the little elf the dragon had caught.

His memory chose that moment to supply the image of the twelve young'un's being led to their fates with bags over their heads.

By the next full moon, that bastard Killian might have caught a new batch. How the sick asshole slept at night was beyond Zane. At least Zane was *trying*. When he got Jevan back, they'd damn well tell the world what was happening here. Let Killian pay his way out of that scandal.

Zane picked up a stone from the walkway and tossed it into the black water some fifteen feet below. It plopped in and disappeared beneath the surface. The tide was in, slopping about the dock wall, stirring up salty odours. Looking up, he followed the water's rippling surface out into the bay. Farther on, half a world away, were there other elves and dragons? The king's new toy had come from *out there*. He'd flown in from that impenetrable darkness. Had he come for a reason, or had he been running from something? It was said no dragon could fly across the ocean. One had. Something or someone must have driven or pulled him here.

"A lovely view." His unmistakable voice, the accent sharp, set Zane's blood pumping.

Zane could see farther out to sea than the dragon, and he found the view bleak. "There are better views." He didn't dare turn. If he turned, the dragon might be there, or he might discover he'd imagined him, and he wasn't sure which he wanted more. "I see only darkness out there."

The dragon stepped up to the dock's edge beside him. He was taller, something Zane had forgotten in the dark room during that kiss. It was dark here too, but a different darkness, licked by the occasional torch. The dragon's hair fanned around his shoulders. Torchlight set some of its strands ablaze, while the rest fell in inky lines. His profile held all the stern edges of typical dragons. Jawbone and cheekbone equally sharp. Zane knew he could be vicious. He'd seen him kill two dragons. At a glance, he looked like a ruthless killer, but there was more in his golden eyes, more he *chose* to hide.

"What's your name?" Zane asked.

The dragon cocked his head and smiled but didn't turn to look. He didn't answer either. Fine. Two could play that game. Zane had no intention of giving up his name either. Names were personal. They didn't have to go there. This was the plan: seduce, get information on Jev, and get him out before Clarion or Luceran got wind of this.

If Luceran discovered him here... Shit, what the hell was Zane doing? Luceran would kill him, maybe the dragon too. If Jevan knew he was here with a dragon, *Jevan* would kill him.

He sank his hand into his pocket and caught the locket in his palm. Jevan wasn't here. This had to be done. He needed this dragon to open up and fall for him. He looked up at the clouds passing over a waxing moon. Time was not on his side.

"I keep asking myself why you were inside the compound," the dragon mused, his gaze locked on the faraway ocean.

"So you thought you'd visit the docks again to get your answer and maybe tap some elf ass while you're here?"

His shoulders stiffened. Ah, this wasn't the dark room, and such things said out in the open made him uncomfortable.

Zane glanced behind them. Others were here, although nobody cared about the elf and dragon standing beside the water. But the dragon cared. Maybe he was shy, or maybe it was more than that. Luceran had well-paid spies among the elves. Perhaps the dragon had already been punished for coming here? Yet he'd come back.

Zane watched the dragon's tension hold him. They couldn't do this out in the open. "We can go somewhere else, if you'd prefer?"

His shoulders dropped. "I'd prefer that, yes," he said, then quickly added, "To talk. Nothing else."

Nothing else. Sure. He'd come down to the docks, hunting for an elf to talk to. Did he even know he was lying? "Take the north street. At the top, where the road splits, go left at the fork. There's a bar along there. You can't miss it."

"A bar?" Now he deigned to look Zane in the eyes.

Zane blinked. Alumn, he was a pretty dragon beneath all the scowling. "A bar. Where you buy drinks and spend time with friends. You know, *a bar.*"

"Fine, yes, a bar."

He had no idea what a bar was. What kind of backward wasteland did he come from where kin couldn't get together to drink and relax?

"Will there be others?" he asked, dark lashes shuttering his gold-rimmed eyes.

"Others?"

"Elves?"

"Yes. It's a bar. You'll be fine." Zane smiled, more to ease the dragon's anxiety than anything else. "Wear the hood."

He left the dragon at the dockside. Maybe he wouldn't come. Zane ignored the sharp bite of nerves working to undermine his confidence. Of course the dragon would come. Zane's lovers *always* came.

ZANE SAT at the table tucked against the side of the room, the one beneath the unlit lamp. Usually, he'd plant himself in the middle of the room to annoy Jevan by attracting too much attention, but tonight wasn't about open flirting. Tonight he had a target.

Fifteen minutes later, a cloaked dragon walked in. Even though he wasn't as large as others of his kind, he had that undeniable build that could never pass for elf. The air changed, as though an ocean storm had poured in through the door. A storm that could destroy every-thing and everyone here. There was no hiding what he was.

The crowd quieted, but these were street elves; they'd seen it all, and a dragon in their bar barely raised an eyebrow.

Zane watched him scan the crowd before he finally headed over, pulled out a chair, and sat. His every move was precise, as though he calculated exactly how he presented himself to others.

Zane waved, caught the bartender's eye, and held up two fingers. Arlo wasn't on shift. A blessing. Things might have gotten awkward if he had been.

"Do they know you well here?" the dragon asked, his accent clipping each word.

"No, I'm just passing through." Nobody knew him well. Nobody but Jevan.

The dragon lowered his hood and leaned back in the chair, making it creak. He'd drawn more than a few eyes, and not just because he was dragon. Zane had seen him at court, dressed in black. He'd thought the color suited him. His dark presence beside Luceran's light had left an impression, but that was before he'd seen him in purple beneath the torch-light while Zane had fled through the compound, the dragon giving chase. The same purple color he sported now, in a dark purple button-down shirt over dark pants. He looked like an angry storm trapped in a human-shaped bottle.

The dragon's gaze flicked over elves at other tables. It wasn't fear, but there was definite anxiety in seeing them.

"They won't rat you out. They're elves. We have some honor left." *Unlike dragons.*

The dragon's slightly raised eyebrow suggested he'd heard the unspoken words.

"Why were you at the compound?" He asked, sliding his gaze back to Zane and pinning it to his face.

The scrutiny set Zane's nerves twitching. The dragon barely blinked his golden eyes, and when he did, it seemed deliberate, not involuntary. He was accustomed to wearing a mask, the one that had slipped during the kiss they'd shared.

A stocky elf delivered the drink and eyed the dragon like she was trying to figure out how to tell him he wasn't welcome here without losing her head.

"Why are you so concerned about my presence at the compound?" Zane dug around for his coin pouch, but the dragon got there first. He slipped four coins into the server's hand, paying double, ensuring her smile and her silence.

"Old habits," the dragon explained before sipping his drink. After tasting it—probably for poison—he drank deep. His throat bobbed, drawing Zane's eye.

His mind wandered back to the dark room, when the dragon had pinned his wrists to the wall. He suspected the dragon had wanted the kiss to travel down his neck and other places. Zane shifted in the chair and took a drink, veering his thoughts off their path before they showed on his face.

"What were you, before you came here? Your trade, I mean, if you had one..." Zane asked.

The dragon set the drink down. "Flight leader... Guardian. Executioner." A shadow darkened his eyes. He had more to say but no further explanation came. Guardian and executioner to whom? Then he'd killed elves? It was hardly a surprise. But after the chase, he'd said he was trying to help Zane escape. Why would a hunter help its prey?

"And what is *your* trade?" the dragon asked.

"Mercenary. Bodyguard. Among other things."

"You're paid to fight for a cause not your own?"

"Something like that." Paid to do many things, although never sex. The dragon didn't need to know that. This was beginning to feel like an interrogation, on both sides. He needed to steer the conversation back to more pleasurable things.

"Do you... lodge nearby?"

"I do." Zane's lips twitched. He leaned on the table, shortening the distance between them. In the shadows, the dragon's eyes held a shimmer, often referred to as *dragonsight*. Some saw in different tones and shades than others. Did this one see Zane differently? "Do you have something in mind, dragon?"

From the heated sizzle in those eyes, he had a lot on his mind, and much of it indecent. Would he really be this easy?

He didn't seem to know how to answer, and Zane stole the moment to drink deeply, finishing the tankard in one. With nothing left to say, he stood and headed for the door, with the dragon in tow. His lodgings were a few doors down, and he was aware of every single step the dragon took behind him, but the closer they came to his temporary home, the more Zane's heart fluttered. Taking a dragon to his private space was a terrible idea, but where else could one fuck a dragon around here?

He continued on, passing his lodgings, and headed up the street where the oil lamps flickered, fighting back more shadows.

"Where are we going?" The dragon's steps drew closer.

"You'll see."

That nip of anxiety returned. He ignored it, like he had before, and reminded himself this was necessary and nothing more. An empty building lay ahead, one of many abandoned high-rises along this street. Once, it had climbed high into the sky, but the top floors had long ago tumbled into the street. Now the upper floors gaped at the stars.

Zane vaulted over a broken barrier and headed inside. "Elf?"

He turned. The dragon's eyes churned molten in the low light as he waited outside the barrier.

Zane opened his arms in invitation and backed up a few steps. For a few seconds, the dragon didn't move, which was wise. Following anyone into a dark, abandoned building ranked up there with sheer stupidity, but he was dragon, and Zane an elf. *He* had the power here. The dragon must have realized the same, because he climbed over the barrier and started up the steps.

The stairs climbed higher and higher, dog-legging back in a large open spiral, forming the spine of the building. Grass and vines had tried to claim the walls, rooting in cracks and holes. Broken windows afforded ever-higher views of the half-abandoned city. The entire building was hazardous, but whenever Jev inevitably had them returning to Bayston every year, Zane always came to this tower. It had stood for hundreds of years and outlived the humans. It wasn't going anywhere tonight.

Finally, the stairwell opened to an exposed floor and star-glittered sky. Old concrete struts acted like columns, holding up a ceiling no longer there. Rusted steel rods, bent from huge forces, made for excellent grab handles as Zane picked his way across the open floor. The air smelled sweeter up here, away from the oil lamps and ocean. Zane breathed in, filling his lungs, and approached the concrete pillar near the far corner and the edge.

The dragon drew up alongside him and stopped at the half wall. One more step and he'd plummet the eight stories to the street below.

"Now that's a view," Zane said.

Bayston's streets sparkled far below. The city had been

altered over the years—added to, patched up, built around, repurposed. Some blocks, the unsafe ones, lay dormant, like the one they stood in now, but most shone. The city had once bustled with humans and their wheeled traveling machines. It didn't seem possible looking at it now.

The dragon stared out over the lamplit cityscape. The wind teased his long hair away from his stern face. Reading him was nearly impossible. His mask was too good. But the view didn't seem to impress him, and Zane's fluttering nervousness returned.

"Every time I pass through Bayston, I come up here," Zane said, then regretted it. This wasn't supposed to be personal, yet here he was, bringing the dragon to one of his favorite secret places. He should have taken him to his lodgings and fucked him.

The dragon looked down, teetering on the edge.

Zane folded his arms to keep from reaching out like a fool. "Could you shift before hitting the ground?" he asked carefully.

The dragon's cheek twitched. He met Zane's gaze. A hungry intensity burned in his eyes again. Zane's heart stuttered. Was this what all his prey felt like before he devoured them?

Zane's breathing sharpened, adrenaline kicking in. The dragon likely sensed it all. Maybe bringing him up here really had been the wrong thing to do. Nobody but Jevan would miss Zane if he met with an *accident*, and Jev was hardly in a position to fight for another dead elf.

The dragon stepped forward.

Zane instinctively backed up.

Another step. The dragon's eyes blazed.

Zane's back bumped against the concrete pillar. He should run, like he had in the compound, but the dragon was blocking the only exit. This feeling, though, wasn't fear. He didn't want to run. The sensations pouring through him had everything to do with *anticipation*. The kiss in the dark room had lit Zane's match, and now he was yearning to feel that heat between them again.

The dragon crowded close, his scent tantalizing, his presence too big to think around. His fingers touched Zane's. Cold metal landed in Zane's palm. He looked down. Three coins rested in his hand.

"Service me, elf."

His words threw more fuel on the fire, drenching Zane in lust. He'd never been ordered in such a manner, and never by a dragon. The coins in his hand warmed. Payment for sex. With a dragon. Fuck, Zane would do him for free just to hear him growl those orders again.

He pocketed the coins and rested a hand on the dragon's chest. He couldn't feel his heart, not through the layers of leather, but his radiating warmth wrapped around Zane like his solid arms might. Zane ventured his hand lower, feeling his way over the flat, hard plain of his stomach, then around and over his hip. Beneath the cloak and clothes, the dragon was made for strength, for fighting his way to the top, but all that muscle and masculinity was frustratingly hidden from Zane's touch. He wanted to tear into the buckles and straps, rip his layers off, and suck him dry.

Zane lifted his gaze, bringing his mouth close to the dragon's, now set in a firm, stubborn line, and whispered, "What will you have me do, dragon?"

kiem

WHAT AKIEM WANTED WAS to turn him around, take the mischievous red-haired elf up on the signals he broadcasted, and fuck him against the concrete pillar, raw and fast like Akiem had been denied his whole life. But it wasn't that simple. Nothing was ever that simple.

He hadn't been able to get Red out of his head since that terrible kiss, like the damn elf had somehow infected him with yet more madness. It couldn't be Akiem. He didn't have these thoughts, not for elves. He couldn't. Could he? But this one... This one was different. Red had been at the docks again, soliciting certain pleasures.

Pleasures Akiem didn't need or want.

But he'd gone to the docks, hoping to find Red waiting there. His wretched heart had leaped at the sight of him near the water's edge, the wind in his hair, his gaze cast out toward the endless sea and Akiem's home.

This was forbidden.

This wasn't for Akiem.

It couldn't be for many, many reasons.

What will you have me do, dragon?

And now they were here, on the roof of the world, this elf's secret place.

The lust wasn't fading. He couldn't bury it like he had before. He'd hidden his desires all his life. He'd had little choice. It was survival. Now... this red-haired devil had undone it all with a single kiss, and he kept pulling on Akiem's strings, unraveling him.

Akiem closed his eyes and shuddered out a sigh.

What will you have me do, dragon?

The elf—Red—waited, his mouth tantalizingly close, his body pressed closer. Every word Red said was designed to undo him. Akiem closed his hands into fists, fighting every instinct—some to stay, some to go, some to shove the elf onto his knees and have his mouth on his most intimate parts. He didn't move. There was Luceran to consider. If the king discovered this... But it was nothing— a transaction. Coins had changed hands. This was a service.

Red's hand found Akiem's clenched right fist. His fingers peeled his fist open, then slipped inside, locking their hands together. Akiem looked down at their entwined fingers. Red's little finger was tattooed. A little swirl of black ink, like a ribbon around his finger. The city noises found them, tossed their way on a breeze that shifted locks of the elf's red hair over his eyes. Still, this didn't feel real.

This was different. So very different. That elven hand in his had ripped him open.

The elf's eyes were full of want, need, and terrible

understanding.

Nobody understood Akiem. He didn't even understand himself and never had. He knew that now. He'd been someone else for others, for a queen and mother who had never loved him. For a broodbrother who barely saw him. For his amethyst brood who took from him and never gave. For the life of a prince in a faraway court in which he had never truly belonged.

"Is this what you want?" Red brought Akiem's hand to his own arousal straining inside his tight pants. The touch —feeling a solid rod of maleness in his palm—scorched parts of him he hadn't known existed.

The elf arched a russet eyebrow. He stood on his toes, hooked his free arm around Akiem's neck, and met his mouth. Gently, at first, like it had been in the compound. A careful test. Warm, soft lips created a raging fire inside him, where before there had always been a hollowness. Gods, he was so fucking afraid of this.

Red's mouth taunted, urging him to open, to submit. If he gave back, the raging want running wild through him would make this unstoppable. His need was a breathless, maddening thing, and it wanted out.

The elf's tongue teased. Akiem opened, feeling himself falling, as if the world were tipping him over the edge. Red had tipped everything upside down. He kissed him back, slowly at first, so damn carefully, afraid of it all, afraid of what it meant.

But this didn't mean anything.

He'd paid.

Emotion—feelings—didn't come into it.

Red's hand rose to Akiem's hair, fingers cradling the nape of Akiem's neck, and then his other hand stroked down the curve of his back, settling over his ass, where Red gripped, claiming him.

It wasn't like before, with dragons, with Luceran, or with the worst of them all—the monster of a male who had torn Akiem open.

His breath caught, the kiss coming apart. Fear and madness and memories pushed in, but the elf's mouth found his jawline, and his tongue swirled and his little teeth nipped. Akiem turned his head away, inviting more of the touch that chased away the dark he'd thought was a permanent part of him. He wanted to touch him but didn't know where to start. He knew what he liked, but was Red the same? Were elves the same? How did one pleasure an elf?

Red caught his hand and placed it on his own ass.

"Right there is good," he mumbled against Akiem's neck, just below his ear, as though sensing Akiem's thoughts. Then he mouthed that spot below Akiem's ear, sucking just enough to shoot a dart of lust straight to Akiem's cock. He gasped, giving himself away. Too late to hide now. This elf impossibly already knew more about him than anyone else alive.

Akiem cradled the male's erection against his palm. So strange, to feel another male's desire for him. So good to feel its straining hardness, so very like his own.

The elf eased back, throwing both arms over Akiem's shoulders, and looked him in the eye. It didn't need to be said that Akiem hadn't done this before, not willingly, but Red wasn't mocking him. The look in his eyes fucking understood and made this all kinds of right—and so wrong.

He lowered his gaze, auburn lashes fluttering, then slid

down Akiem's body to rest on his knees, putting his head at waist height.

Akiem swallowed. His arousal, evident in the bulge upsetting the line of his pants, seemed so shameful. There was wetness too. His mouth tightened. Shame tried to crawl beneath his skin, but the elf planted both hands on his hips, holding him steady, and looked up, licking his lips in anticipation.

Red's elf-quick fingers plucked the laces of Akiem's pants free. He pushed the waistband down, but only an inch, making the pants rest low on Akiem's hips.

Akiem ran his fingers through Red's messy hair. The male responded by mouthing over Akiem's hipbone. Akiem's fingers tightened. The elf's tongue flicked and probed, teasing a path downward.

He was temptation in male form. A prize, a dream, and everything about him made Akiem forget how to breathe. Yet breathe he did, too fast, too obvious, his emotions spread bare for the elf to see, and he didn't care. Couldn't think to care. His want was visceral. His cock throbbed. His heart pounded. And he didn't care to hide it. His secret was safe with a nothing elf who sold sex to dragons.

Back home, he would have been punished for admiring another male and killed for touching an elf this way. That made all of this impossible. He didn't want to make sense of any of it. The old Akiem did not do this. *Couldn't* do this. But he was new, different, and so was this.

Red slid his hands up Akiem's thighs, his constant crooked smile a wicked delight. He paused there, his hands on Akiem's hips, his eyes full of lust. He waited, because he knew—somehow *he knew* Akiem needed control. Akiem nodded once and audibly swallowed.

Red's tongue poked into the corner of his mouth as he

worked free the remaining laces of his pants. Akiem's smile parted, growing.

"Laughing at me, dragon?"

"Admiring." It was all he could say. If he said too much, the elf would know how much this meant—a weakness he couldn't afford to reveal.

This should have been an easy transaction, but nothing about the elf on his knees and about to service Akiem's cock was easy.

Red freed Akiem's cock and wrapped his strong, warm fingers around the straining length. The contact shocked Akiem's thoughts into silence, making him forget about everything but the tight feel of his hand. The elf purred at the back of his throat, a sound Akiem had never heard from an elf before. Akiem's heart hammered louder, if such a thing were possible. The elf knew what he was doing, and Akiem's arousal was obvious, although having it exposed to this elf was another layer of vulnerability entirely.

He'd never had another male touch him willingly. Not like this. But he'd wanted it. Gods, he'd ached for it since he was a kit. It was the first secret he'd told Mother, and the first time she'd almost killed him.

The elf straightened suddenly, rising, and angled his hand around Akiem's cock. The motion brought his mouth kissably close, and this time, Akiem took it, opened it, pushed his tongue in, needing more elf inside him than he cared to admit.

Nobody was here in this secret place above the city to deem it wrong. Nobody *cared* how two males sought pleasure in each other.

Red kissed him back, arching forward as his warm,

expert hand worked Akiem's cock. Akiem gasped inside the kiss, but the elf didn't back off. An urgency sizzled through his moving body, and Akiem matched it. He clamped his hand against the elf's back, holding him close while the male's hand worked him toward the edge of insanity. To have a male's hand on him, a hand that wasn't his own, emptied Akiem's mind of everything but the good. The elf squeezed, and stroked, and teased. Then he tore free from the kiss, and his hand was gone, replaced by his hot, wet mouth and probing tongue.

Akiem plunged his hands into the elf's hair, holding him. He lifted his head and rolled his hips, angling deep into Red's accommodating mouth. He wrought pleasure from every inch. Gods, he was falling, falling so far into something that didn't make any sense, but it felt so damn right, felt freeing.

Pleasure crackled and sharpened to a fine point. He looked down himself at the elf with his cock in his mouth. Red's beautiful eyes locked on his. The contact struck a match, lit the touch paper, and blew every doubt out of Akiem's mind.

Ecstasy tore a tumble of growls from his lips, making the elf's tight mouth smile. It was more than he could take. Ecstacy snapped, and he came hard, teeth gritted as he rode the blinding wave and panted out his excess as the elf lifted off him. Red used a thumb to wipe his smiling mouth clean and then crawled up Akiem's body. He touched Akiem's face to make him look, then kissed him. He tasted of elf and seed, a new combination Akiem had never considered might arouse him. He wanted more.

The kiss filled with growls. Akiem shoved Red back against the pillar and plundered his mouth. Great gods, it wasn't enough. He dropped his hand, tore at the elf's pants, and plunged a hand inside, taking all of him in hand. Red threw his head back, panting hard.

Akiem admired his rapturous face, slightly turned away. The straight nose and almost feminine jaw, and the tapered ear with its twinkling hoop earring.

Red caught him studying him and smiled coyly. "Who knew you liked elf in your diet?"

The comment struck too close. Akiem flinched, but Red grinned, like he knew exactly how it sounded but he'd said it anyway. He seemed the sort to say *anything*. The wink at the execution.... He was clearly a wild one. The center of attention. Impossible to chain. No wonder he charged for his time. He was worth every coin.

Red clutched the back of Akiem's neck. His smile fell away, and his eyes turned fierce. "Will you bend for me, dragon?"

Something inside tore free. Terror, maybe.

He couldn't.

Memories flashed.

Rough hands holding him down. Hot panting against the back of his neck where the elf's hand burned now. The feel of *male* forced inside. The growls, the pressure, the heat, and the hurt of it all.

Akiem recoiled, stumbling. Sudden, vicious sickness rolled through him.

"Wait..." The elf stepped forward. Horror paled his face, because he knew. Akiem had revealed too much. He'd revealed the worst of his wounds.

No, no... this had been a mistake. His knee hit the low wall—the only barrier between him and the long fall onto the street below. He could fall and end it now. There was peace in death, wasn't there? He'd thought so. He'd tried to find it once, but death had tossed him back.

"Dragon... it's all right..." Red approached, hunched, making himself smaller, less threatening, and offered a hand. "I won't hurt you."

Akiem tasted metal. It wasn't real. The male who haunted his dreams wasn't here. But it felt real. He could hear his thick, boiling laughter. *Submit for me, prince.* And Akiem had, because he'd had no other choice.

The elf looked at him, eyes full of pity.

"This was a mistake." What was he doing here, with an elf? He turned, facing the vast open space, and let the wind push and shove him.

"What's your name?" the elf asked behind him. "Tell me your name and step back from the edge. We can go to my place—"

He couldn't tell him. Names didn't matter in transactions. "The Black Prince."

He stepped off the edge. The shift took him long before the street could rush up and death could claim him. He flung open his wings and soared low over the rooftops, away from the elf and the terrible things Akiem had done.

Akiem had a lower draw him a bath and take his clothes to the laundry. He smelled of elf and sex, evidence of his indiscretion.

He flung open his chamber window, allowing the wind to blast in, and then soaked in the bath by the open fire. Steam rolled in the chilled air, but the bath was warm. With his arms braced on the sides, he ran his gaze over his scars. They'd faded some. A few were only visible when the light caught them, but they'd never fully vanish. He remembered the weight behind every cut. Remembered the smell of hot metal and how it had laced his throat, filling him up. He'd kept his shirt half on during the encounter with Red. Red hadn't seen his scars, but he'd witnessed Akiem's horror at the thought of being... mounted.

Resting his head back, his eyes closed, and he drifted somewhere between wakefulness and sleep. The night-mares usually found him here, but they didn't rush him. What he did find waiting for him in this warm, soft place was the elf's wicked mouth and how he'd been able to summon hidden parts of Akiem to the surface. He began to harden, and his mind wandered. He recalled the elf's soft mouth taking him in deep. Recalled spilling his seed into the elf's mouth in mindless pleasure. Red was a whore. Sex was his profession. Akiem could see why. He was damn good at it.

"Where were you?"

Akiem opened his eyes. Decades of restraint hid his panic before the king could notice. "I walked the northern boundary," he lied smoothly.

"Did you?" The king glittered in whites and golds. He approached the bath, rolling up his white bell sleeves. He loomed on Akiem's left, glanced down into the water, and roamed his gaze over Akiem's body. His gaze snagged on Akiem's erection. His lips parted and fresh tension simmered a warning around him.

Akiem waited, keeping his face blank. If Luceran wanted more from him, he wasn't sure he could give it, not after what he'd experienced with Red. Whatever he had with Luceran, it wasn't anything like what he'd felt with the elf. The lust Luceran roused in him was dark, born of the king's control these past few months. Luceran spoke to that mindless part of Akiem, the part he tried to bury.

Luceran perched on the edge of the bath and crossed his wrists over his thigh. "Do you think me a fool?"

He knew exactly where Akiem had been.

Akiem locked his jaw. "No."

"I'm tired of lies. It's bad enough I hear them from my brother, but from you? Where did I fail you for you to betray me so?"

He moved to heave himself out the water. "I haven't—"

Luceran's hand found his throat and pushed Akiem down. Water rushed up his nose and down his throat. He gasped, swallowing more water. His lungs burned. His body bucked, trying to writhe free. He clawed at the hand holding him under, twisted and thrashed. The shift tried to tear through him.

Luceran let go.

Akiem thrust upward and spluttered up water. *Breathe.* It wasn't mud; it was just water. He clutched the edge of the bath, vision a blur, his past trying to drown him too. The bronze had held him down, forced him into the estuary mud, and the mud had pulled and sucked, wrapping him in coldness. He'd died then. Death was cold. So cold.

Shivers robbed him of his control, and he hissed through his teeth.

Luceran walked away. "Go to the elf again and I'll make you watch as Clarion takes his head."

The connecting door slammed behind him.

Akiem panted into the cold, empty room. There was no choice. He couldn't return to Red, even if he wanted to.

Ever. The mercenary elf would leave the city, and Akiem would never see him again.

It was for the best.

A sob rolled up his throat. He swallowed it, and the others that followed, keeping any betrayal of emotion hidden inside.

ane

SOMEONE HAD HURT the Black Prince. The hurt had gone bone deep. When Zane had suggested he might want to be fucked and the dragon's eyes had widened before he could hide the response, Zane knew. Whatever he'd endured, it had scarred him inside. Zane's heart fucking ached for a dragon.

Alumn, he was doomed. Now the dockside killings made sense. Those beasts had been about to rape Zane, and the prince knew exactly how that felt.

Shit.

Had he known, he would have approached things differently.

Maybe Zane could save him too?

A crazy thought. A fool's thought. It had been a job, like any other.

"Service me, elf." The way he'd demanded it... his tone,

the strength behind it, the typical dragon assumption that all elves lived to serve. But, Alumn help him, Zane had *enjoyed* obeying.

It was just the game. He didn't truly care for him. He had a plan: seduce the dragon and get answers. He just had to get him talking.

Jevan would think him insane.

The next day passed too damn slowly. He spent the morning asking around for jobs, and when dusk came, Zane headed to the docks.

The dragon didn't come, but he would. He was starved for what Zane could give him. That much had been more than obvious. He'd come again. They always did.

He didn't come the next night either—or the next.

A week passed. Nothing.

Maybe they hadn't shared a connection, but he was sure he'd felt something between them, something intangible. Zane fucked around. It made life on the road tolerable; he'd dare say even fun. The kiss, and then having the dragon in his hand and mouth, watching him thaw and come undone. That had been real. The *Black Prince* had revealed his true self on that rooftop—his mask had fallen away—and by Alumn, he was so fucking beautiful. Zane wanted him to visit again, and unless Zane's instincts were way off, the dragon wanted it too.

So, why hadn't he come back? It couldn't just be the mistake he'd made in asking him to bend, could it?

What if something had happened to him?

What if Luceran knew?

Shit. All that was out of Zane's control.

Zane needed another plan to get to Jevan. The prince wasn't his concern. Couldn't be. He was dragon, for fuck's sake. Elves were his *prey*.

He collected his knives, threw on his hooded jacket, and went out into the night. Forget the dragon, the kiss, the rooftop blow that had left Zane so fucking wired he'd taken his own cock in hand the second the dragon had jumped off the roof and dealt with his pleasure, coming so damn hard he'd needed a pillar to hold himself up. Forget all that. There was another way around this.

Elder Killian's home wasn't guarded. It didn't need to be. He was the city elder, leader of the elected council. He stood for control and peace and maintained good relations with the dragons. Now Zane knew how he accomplished that peace, but it wouldn't be enough to tell others. He needed proof.

He chose a rear window, out of sight from the main thoroughfare, and after smashing a pane with his elbow, he reached in, flicked the lock, and let himself inside. The house was quiet. Killian would be asleep at this hour. He'd have household assistants, but if Zane played this right, they wouldn't wake. After a few false starts in bedrooms where others slept soundly, Zane found the elder's room. He plucked his daggers free and approached the bed. The elder slept alone—of course he did—snoring lightly. The fact he killed elflings every month didn't appear to keep him awake at night.

Zane loomed over him. He could slit his throat and leave. He rarely desired to kill someone. Killian was the exception. But then nobody would know why the elder had been murdered in his bed, and the why was important.

Bracing an arm against the headboard, he leaned in close and pressed the edge of his blade against the male's throat. Killian's lashes fluttered. He opened his eyes.

"Remember me?"

Killian sucked in air through his nose.

"Make a noise and you'll be dead before help comes."

The male panted, eyes wide. He should be afraid. He deserved to feel fear, the same way those elflings felt when they smelled dragon and knew their fate.

"What possessed you to hand them over?" He had to know. No explanation could excuse it, but maybe there was a reason he couldn't see.

"They'll kill us all if I don't," the elder whispered.

Zane bared his teeth in a snarl. "They told you this?"

"That lord—the king's brother—he told me."

"It's bullshit. They won't kill us. They need us to keep the city working. Clarion's bluffing."

Killian swallowed. His throat moved against the knife's edge. "I can't take that risk."

Zane pushed in. "Yes, you fucking could. They're kids, you son of a dragon's cunt. You're supposed to protect them—and us."

"I am. By doing this! I have to."

Alumn, give him the strength to spare the sniveling coward. "When is the next trade?"

"Six days."

Six days until the next full moon. Six days before Killian handed another line of elves over to the dragons. He'd see an end to it and Clarion, and then he and Jevan would leave, hit the old roads down the coast. The dragons wouldn't find them if they kept to the hills, and this whole nightmare would be over.

Zane straightened. "You have coin?"

The elder nodded and reached for the bedside table. Zane got there first and found a money pouch with enough coin to see him until the end of the month.

"That's mine…" Killian protested, sitting up in bed.

"Be grateful I'm not leaving you in a pool of your own blood."

"You're just a thief—a coward like the rest of us. What will you do, huh? Drink the coin away in that tavern and pretend you can make a difference? Look around you. We don't fight them. We can't. Some elves die so the rest of us can live. That's how it is."

Zane backed away from the bed before he stuck his dagger in Killian's belly. He tucked the money pouch over his belt and stared back at the elder. "I'm nothing like you."

"They'll kill you."

"Maybe."

"You'll die like all the humans who stood up to them. Upset Luceran's rule and it will be on your head, sellsword."

"Do they kill them, the elves you deliver? Fuck them too?"

The elder flinched.

"You make me sick." He didn't even try to keep his voice low. "We had pride once. We were better than this, better than you. Maybe we can be again, but not if we let them take our young!"

"Those who think like you will die fighting them."

"At least they won't live to see you sell their children for some mockery of peace."

Zane was done here. He left the room and met a household assistant in the hallway. She saw him, saw his knives, and screamed for help. He jogged down the stairs, passing others, and bolted out the door to the sound of an alarm whistle.

He couldn't go back to the lodge, not while they might be hot on his tail, so he walked the city limits, keeping to the piles of rubble that sprouted weeds bigger than him and hid his passing from prying eyes. He knew he'd walked too far when a screech overhead sent him ducking into the tall grass. The dragon circling above blotted out much of the starlit sky whenever it swooped low. Alumn, the thing was huge. Its scales shimmered, each one touched by shimmering moonlight, making the beast's whiteness *shine*.

Clarion or Luceran. Zane didn't know either well enough to distinguish them, but the dragon was definitely diamond. He watched the beast settle atop a flat-topped building. It spread its wings, giving them a settling few flaps before tucking them against its back. The crown—a ridge of bone that spread outward behind the skull, which all dragons had—fanned backward, each tip as sharp as a blade. Luceran was said to be beyond vicious and Clarion brutal, but the king's crown of blades was well known. This was Luceran. He shifted, warping the air around him, pulling it in, flipping it over, and with a blinding flash, all of that dragon was contained in the body of a man. He opened the roof access door and disappeared inside.

Zane scanned the torchlit adjacent buildings. This was the compound. He crouched outside its wire- and metal-stakes boundary, but he'd seen enough to know where the king resided, and likely where the Black Prince did too.

He knew how to get inside and how to get to him.

He wet his lips. Six days until the full moon. He couldn't do this alone. Years ago, he should have died in a battle defending a dream that had been doomed anyway. Elves weren't strong enough to fight dragons—alone. What if they had a dragon among their number?

He wrapped his fingers around the locket in his pocket. Hundreds of thousands had died, Jevan's love among them, whoever they had been. An entire species wiped out because they'd fought back. Humans had been brave. They'd had honor. They hadn't given up, even when it was over. They'd fought, never surrendering, while elves had fled.

Jevan had saved him from the mud that day during the battle, and Zane had tried to understand why he'd lived, while thousands upon thousands hadn't. He'd demanded answers of the ever-silent Alumn, but with none in sight, he'd fallen into wandering, fallen into anything and anyone so he might feel again.

What if this was the reason he'd lived? What if that reason had brought him here in time to find an obsidian-scaled prince?

He had to get inside that compound.

Tonight.

kiem

LUCERAN WATCHED him at all times. During breakfast, Akiem sat beside the king. Dinner too, when the king was in residence and not patrolling his borders. Luceran hadn't spoken more than a few words, and those were to order Akiem where to sit, what to eat, and when to retire. The king's fury was all the more deadly when silent. He'd snap, and soon. Akiem knew of only one way to subdue wrath, and that was to give the king what he wanted and reveal the mystery of himself, along with other truths. Whether he mentally and physically could was another matter. If he didn't, he'd feel the edge of the king's axe.

He mulled this over while walking the warren-like compound hallways, passing dragons he recognized from court. Few spoke to him. Scorn burned in their gazes. Leaving Luceran wasn't an option. His wings were too weak, too scarred for distant flight. A dragon as weakened as he was wouldn't survive long outside the king's guardianship.

It hadn't always been that way.

"Akiem," Clarion purred, catching up with him in a corridor. His boots clipped the stone floors, striking like a hammer punching in nails. "The Black Prince." He gave a sweeping, mocking bow and grinned on rising. "After he fucks you, you'll be a dead prince. How does that make you feel?"

Clarion wasn't wrong, and Akiem might have continued on without acknowledging him had he not been curious as to why the lord had tracked him through the compound.

"You already know that, though," Clarion acknowledged, striding close. Where Luceran's violet eyes sparkled, Clarion's were deeper in color, as though they sought to pull their observers in and smother them instead of merely bespelling them. "You've held out longer than the others. How long do you think you can keep the king dangling on the end of your tail before he bites it off?"

"What do you want, Clarion?" Omitting his title had the lord's lips twitching.

"You have me curious," the lord mused. "The king sent me to find you, but it seems to me you might appreciate a longer route back to his bed, no?"

Akiem didn't relish the thought of sitting silently beside the king while he sizzled in his anger. He had no wish to return to that painful scrutiny. He bowed his head in agreement.

"Come," Clarion urged, quickening his pace. "It's time you and I got to know each other."

Akiem fell into step beside the lord. They passed through maze-like sections and traveled down flights of stairs, descending below street level. The air cooled and dampened. Even the flickering torches struggled to burn off the moisture.

"The king and I... It's not what you think." Akiem wasn't sure why he'd said it, perhaps to cover his own hide. "We're not... together like that."

Clarion laughed. "I'm sure his last toy thought the same."

Lowers dipped their heads as they approached and averted their eyes. How long until word got back to Luceran that Akiem was walking the halls with his brother? He wondered if Luceran had indeed sent his brother here. Luceran had mentioned his brother's lies, right before plunging Akiem under water.

Clarion stopped outside a thick, windowless door at the end of a windowless corridor. "How would you like"—he opened the door, unveiling the sight inside—"a distraction?"

The smell of wet metal hit Akiem first, then elven blood. His nostrils flared and guts churned, memories clawing at him. Clarion swept ahead into the room, straight to the female elf pooled on the floor. Thick ropes, looped around her wrists, tied her to metal loops in the floor.

The singer from the feast.

Others were here too. A pair of elflings, twins, huddled together in the corner. These were Clarion's *pets*.

Sickness burned at the back of Akiem's throat. None of this should have surprised him, and he wasn't supposed to care. For the longest time, he hadn't cared. Hadn't he also chained elves to dungeon walls, beating answers out of them for his now-dead queen and mother? Gods, that life and those memories didn't seem like they belonged to him, not anymore.

"This one…" Clarion caught the singer's chin and yanked her head up. Tears stained her cheeks and crusted her swollen eyes. "…sang like a bird every year at the feast. But this year…" He sighed. "This year she decided she had grown bored of my company. So I cut out her tongue." He discarded her and turned to the twins. The pair shied away, clutching each other. Clarion grabbed their leashes and pulled, toppling them forward onto their hands and knees. Two females. It had been difficult to tell before, but now Akiem saw the curves of their hips and slimmer shoulders. "These two are delightfully feisty, but they still take dragon cock. Most of it." The lord threw a grin back at Akiem, expecting his approval.

Akiem looked on, outwardly bored. Behind his back, his fingers curled into fists.

"Ah, but wait, there's one more." He threw the twins down, flung open another door, and beckoned Akiem inside the dark, damp room. The windowless room opened like a cave mouth and smelled of decay and shit, just like the room Mother had locked Akiem inside.

His heart lurched like a rabbit in a snare. Briefly, his blood pumped too loudly, drowning out the sound of whimpering elves. If he didn't get a grip, Clarion would see the weakness on his face. Clarion looked at the dark-skinned elf chained to the wall. He didn't see the pieces of Akiem's mask crumbling away.

"This fucking one." The lord stopped in front of the elf and looked down.

Akiem had been in a position like this before, with a stubborn elf chained to the wall. This one was just as fierce looking. On his knees, he pulled on his chains, arms straining. He hadn't been here long. Soon, the lack of light would eat away at his strength. For now, he was full of hate and disgust. Recognition tugged on his memories, but before he could place the male, Clarion flung a look over his shoulder.

"He's not to be touched, so he watches through the door. I think he likes it."

The elf spat at Clarion's feet, missing by miles. The lord laughed it off and turned. "So, which will it be?"

Akiem blinked. "Which what?"

The twins' sobbing chipped at his broken mind.

"Fuck them, cut them, do as you like. They're elves. They're ours. You look like you could do with a release. Call it a gift and when you're done, perhaps you and I can talk some more?"

This was the one time Akiem's preference might save him. "I prefer males."

Clarion sighed and looked again at the black elf staring through him. "Well, then, maybe it's time this one joined in instead of observed? What do you think?"

"Fuck. You," the elf snarled, baring tiny canine teeth. "Come near me and I'll bite your fucking cocks off, you yellow-bellied overgrown lizards."

Clarion's smile grew. "He'll be a delight to break."

Akiem wet his lips, his mouth dry. He'd known this happened. Dragons picking up elves at the docks was just the start. Most ended up in rooms like this one. He hadn't *seen* it or needed to think on it, but now here it was, thrust in his face like the meat he'd mistakenly eaten at the feast. He ground his teeth.

"Me..." Clarion returned through the door to the twins. "I prefer them fresh and young." He said it loud and clear, without shame. "Some before they've had their first monthly bleed. Have you ever fucked your prey and then eaten it, Akiem?"

Akiem swallowed bile. "I don't believe I have."

The elven girls buried their heads against each other and sobbed.

Clarion eyed them, teeth bared, body bulked out as he towered over their prone forms. The sight was exactly how they did things this side of the ocean. Elves were bullied, abused, and treated like nothing, and after all that, they were killed for sport. Amethyst—his brood—as brutal as they were, hadn't tortured elves for fun—besides Mother, who'd tortured everyone and everything for pleasure. It had been war. This was... abhorrent.

His mouth twitched. A growl rumbled from his depths. He swallowed it down. "If Luceran smells elf on me, he'll have my head." His voice came out rough, broken into pieces and ground down to dust. It sounded like lust, not the rage it was.

Clarion turned, eyes sparkling. "Shame. Perhaps the king won't be around much longer to pull your leash, *Prince*?" He waved a hand. "Though, of course, I would know little of such things."

Shock at the brazen treasonous words had Akiem too stunned to think of a response. He dipped his chin. "If you'll excuse me, I must return to my chamber and await the king."

"Another time, perhaps?" Clarion nodded toward the black elf seething in the dark.

"Another time." Akiem strode from the room and closed the door on the sound of the girls' whimpering becoming more urgent.

~

THE MADNESS CRAWLED under his skin again. He walked, not seeing the path ahead. Walked and walked and walked because he couldn't fly and he couldn't run. Walking was all he had.

They were just elves.

Just fucking elves.

None of this should matter to him.

He was Akiem, dragon prince to a dead court and the Black Prince with a heart of darkness. Untouchable. Immovable. He'd commanded flights. He'd ruled, briefly, until the metals had torn him down. He had been the pinnacle of dragonkin. He did not *care* for elves.

Fucking elves. Why was it always the fucking elves who ruined everything!

He tore into his chamber, slammed the door, fell back against it, and thrust his hands into his hair to squeeze out the thoughts. No, he didn't care. No, it didn't mean anything to him. The prick had cut out the singer's tongue. So? He'd done worse for years. She was just one of many. It went on everywhere here. It was life here. The elves lived with it, so why couldn't Akiem?

Someone cleared their throat.

Akiem snapped his eyes open.

An elf stood at his window, backlit by the waxing moon. An elf was in his chamber, inside the king's compound. Not just any elf. His Red.

Akiem blinked. Still there.

"Hello, lover."

No. Impossible. Insane.

He shoved from the door and made it to the end of the bed in three strides. The elf lifted his chin, defiant and prepared. He had his knives but hadn't reached for them.

"You..." Akiem's voice cracked. "You can't be here."

Red approached, hands out placatingly. "Look, okay... this is an intrusion, I understand that. And what happened on the rooftop... I didn't mean—"

"Stop."

Red stopped. His green eyes shone, open, expectant, waiting.

He couldn't damn well be here. Akiem's heart thumped too hard, thundering over his racing thoughts. He pointed at the closed connecting door and whispered, "That door leads into the king's chamber."

Red looked at the door, frowned, and then looked back at Akiem. "Someone has separation issues," he whispered back.

No. No! Akiem growled a warning. "You must leave. Now."

Luceran could be next door. He might be listening to every word. He'd kill Red or let Clarion have him for his menagerie of elves, which would be far, far worse.

Akiem broke his locked stance and closed the distance between them. He grabbed Red's jacket and yanked him toward the window. "Get out."

Red resisted, tugging back and digging his heels in, but his strength could never match Akiem's.

Akiem shoved him at the open window. "Get out!"

Red fell against the glass and clutched the sill, but he still wouldn't leave.

Akiem would shove him out if it came to it. He towered over him and sneered, adding more dragon to his next words. *"Get the fuck out. You're not welcome here."*

Red flinched. It stabbed Akiem in the heart, but by the gods, he wasn't backing down. Of everything he'd found in this new land, Red was the only damn thing that had given him a moment's respite from the madness, that had made him *feel* again. If Red didn't leave, he'd die like the rest of his kin, and Akiem couldn't—wouldn't let that happen.

"I need your help," Red said, eyes pleading.

"I don't care." He grabbed the elf by the throat. Red's racing pulse fluttered against the pad of Akiem's thumb, so fucking fragile. "I'm not what you think," he whispered.

"I know. That's why I'm here." The words, the way his mouth shaped them, and the tiny tremors running through his body, threatened to undo Akiem.

"No. Gods, no." His grip eased, and with it came the realization that he had the elf pinned awkwardly against the window frame. He snatched his hand back. Redness blushed across the elf's neck. Akiem had hurt him. He knew what it felt like to have hands around his throat. "I can't help you." He wet his lips. His fingers roamed up the elf's jaw and skimmed his cheek, his ear, like his body had its own wants and wasn't listening to the horror his mind screamed. "I can't..."

Who was he telling? Himself or the elf?

Red caught his wrist and gently lowered it between them. "I know somewhere we can go. Will you just listen?"

"There is nowhere."

"There is. Come with me." He slipped his hand into Akiem's.

"I can't." Akiem braced his free hand on the window frame, holding himself back. Gods, he wanted to flee with this elf, to run away from these halls, from these dragons, from their ways and his past.

Stupid thoughts from a stupid mind, his mother had said time and time again.

"Luceran won't know. Trust me."

Trust him? Akiem trusted no one, least of all himself and certainly not a whore of an elf.

Red ducked out the window and was gone in a blink. Akiem should have closed the window and left it at that. Their forbidden tryst wasn't worth the risk. It couldn't last. It shouldn't last. It was folly, misadventure, nonsense. He just wanted more coin.

Akiem leaned from the window and saw the elf three stories below, looking up. His mouth lifted in a smirk that hooked into Akiem's heart. By the great gods, how had this elf ensnared him so?

He swore, clambered through the window, and dropped, landing in a crouch beside the elf. Straightening, he sighed hard, resigned to whatever happened next. The elf nodded and waved him into a sprint through the shadows, keeping close to the buildings to avoid the pools of light beneath the scattered torches.

Akiem followed him into an outer section of buildings, mostly unlit and unattended, through narrow, half-crumbled halls, and then into a dark bedchamber. Red pulled the thick drapes across the window and lit a single oil lamp, using matches from a drawer. He appeared to know his way around the room remarkably well.

Akiem turned the lock over on the door, drawing Red's gaze. He nodded, carried the lamp to the fireplace mantle, and placed it in front of a mirror to illuminate the room.

Akiem sniffed the air. A mingling of scents lingered, mostly elf and dragon. They were still inside the compound, yet the scent of elf was strong here. "How do you know this place?"

"Don't ask."

Red stood by the cold fireplace, his eyes serious as he watched Akiem wander the room, assessing the made bed and empty cabinets. Someone used the space, but they hadn't been here recently. He pulled open a bedside drawer and eyed the thin bottle of massage oil, then the bed, and then Red, his eyebrow arched. So, that was what this room was for: sexual encounters. Red knew of it because he came here regularly. Akiem should have expected it, but jealousy squirmed inside his gut at the thought that *his* Red had been here with others. "It is a wonder you have lived as long as you have."

"Skill," Red said like he believed it.

"Luck, more likely."

"Alumn watches over me."

"You should not have come." With the room assessed as safe, Akiem rounded on Red, stopping beyond his reach but close enough to make his point clear. "You should have left the city. What possessed you to break into the compound again? Are you a fool? Do you wish to die? Because that is how this ends for you. Luceran knows about you. He will kill you."

Red's eyes widened. "I am no fool, *dragon*, and I have good reason to come to you."

"Sex? Is that why you brought me here, into a room you know? Am I another conquest? Some dragon fancy to warm your bed? I'll not pay another coin, so if you came for that, you can leave." He didn't want to believe that others regularly used Red, didn't want to let his trade get beneath his skin, but as Red turned his face away, the truth was obvious. The elf was more than familiar with dragons. He'd asked him in the bar what his profession was, and he'd told him mercenary, among other things. He took coin from dragons for sex. That's why he'd been at the docks and why he was here now. It was his *only* reason for being here. The rooftop encounter had been... eye-opening. Though it meant more to Akiem than he'd ever let this whore know, he couldn't do the same again. It already hurt, and it would only hurt more if he fell for this clever elf's sexual wiles.

"You need to leave here and never return. Leave the city, find another place to sell your *talents*, elf, before Luceran catches up with you." *Before I tell him what you are.*

Gods, why did it hurt so?

"I can't."

"You need my help?" Akiem laughed dryly. "Fine. What do you need me for?"

"Clarion has kidnapped a friend of mine. I have to free him."

Akiem backed up, needing distance from Red, from this room. He knew the elf he spoke of. The elf had stood beside Red at the execution. He saw the connection now. It was all falling into place. Coincidence hadn't brought them together. Red sought to use him. "I can't help you."

"I just need to know where he is. That's all."

Akiem leaned against the bedpost, needing the support. It wasn't just about the room, the bed, and the coin. "You meant to seduce me to discover this information?"

Red swallowed. "Initially, yes, but—"

Akiem made for the door. What a damn fool he was. He'd wanted company so badly he'd followed an elf and paid him to *do things*.

Why was he so surprised? He'd been used his whole life, and now here too, by a worthless elf. Always some-one's bitch. Always someone's toy. As a son, a prince, a pet. A fucking tool.

"Wait—"

Akiem whirled, batted Red's reaching hand away, and snarled, "Don't touch me, elf!"

Red lunged and pushed his arm under Akiem's neck.

His back hit the wall. Pressure crushed his throat. The fear came hot and fast, drenching body and mind. He gasped, tasted metal, and stopped. Everything stopped. *Lie still. Let it happen.* It would be over faster that way.

Red sprang back, shock blanching his face. "Shit, I'm sorry. I just... I didn't mean to hurt you. I'm... It's just, I need your help. You're the only chance..." He stood still, breathing hard, watching Akiem's face, reading all the signs. *Seeing fear. Knowing.*

Akiem closed his eyes, squeezing out cold, useless tears. He waited for the panic to subside, for his body to thaw and become his own again. Lying still, turning cold, had been his safe place for so long that he couldn't stop it from happening. It made him *prey*. The same assault on his senses that always happened shuddered through him, his body rebelling against his mind or vice versa. Minutes passed, and eventually, the panic subsided enough to explain.

"He was dragon," Akiem said, eyes still closed. The past brushed up against him, making his skin burn and itch. "Metal. One of the first great metals who broke from the ice and changed the world forever. He was a monster." He grimaced, tasting the bronze chief inside him all over again. "The bronze dragonkin will mount anything that moves. Dokul was... the worst of them." His mouth pulled into a mockery of a smile. He opened his eyes and found Red sitting on the edge of the bed, face stricken. "He kept me. He..." Akiem's throat clogged. He cleared it with a low growl. "He fucked me, as man and dragon. Repeatedly. For weeks. Forever." It was the first time he'd said the words out loud. It didn't hurt as much as he'd expected. In fact, telling his truth this elf eased some of the aching guilt he'd carried for so long.

"Why?" Red rasped.

"*Why* is the easiest question to answer: because he was dragon, because he was bronze, because he could." He tapped his head where the agony still lived. "I deserved it, but... things came to a head. We fought. He killed me. At least, I think he did. I was never going to beat him. He drowned me in the estuary mud. I can still taste it some-times, in my dreams..."

Pain and pity crossed the elf's face, like he understood more than he should. Akiem could never voice these truths to anyone else, but he didn't fear this elf would use the truth against him.

"But I survived. I don't know how or why. I crawled from the mud as dragon and fled. Flew to the ends of the Earth. I didn't think. I just needed to chase the horizon until the world ended or I did. That's how Luceran found me."

Sadness replaced the pity on Red's face. "Nobody deserves that."

Akiem laughed. "You do not know me, elf."

"I'm so sorry, for all of it. I never meant to hurt you." He almost seemed sincere, this elf who kept throwing himself at dragons for coin.

"I cannot help you. You're elf and I'm dragon, and that's how things are." Akiem couldn't stomach the pity in his eyes and the compassion he didn't deserve. "Now leave. Our business is done."

"He's taking our young." Red stood, breathed deeply, and approached slowly, as though he were approaching a skittish wild animal. "Every full moon, Clarion accepts a trade from our elder in exchange for peace. It's bullshit. I have to stop it."

The sight of the young elves huddled close in Clarion's

chambers attempted to undermine Akiem's determination to forget any of this had happened. He'd tasted elf flesh during the feast and listened to an elf's final song before Clarion cut out her tongue. Whatever he thought of Red, those elves didn't deserve such a fate.

"I discovered the trade and threatened Clarion," Red went on, gaining confidence now that Akiem hadn't shut him down. "He took Jevan to guarantee my silence and had me beaten. Help me find Jev. Help me stop the trades."

"This friend of yours, his skin is black, like my scales?"

Red stepped closer again, but Akiem tensed and the elf backed off, raising his hands. He frowned, his mouth pinched tight. "Yes. You've seen him?"

"I know where he is." Red's breathing stuttered in relief, but that relief was short-lived as Akiem continued. "He's unharmed for now, but if you try to get to him, you'll die. He's deep within the compound in a room Clarion has guarded night and day."

"Shit." Red started pacing. "There must be a way. Windows?"

"None."

"Clarion can't always be there?"

"You won't get inside." Akiem watched him walk and listened to his boots strike the boards. This elf had repeatedly risked his life to save his friend. They had a special relationship. "Your friend... is he your lover?"

Red laughed dismissively. "No. It's not like that, though I did try it on with him once. He threatened to cut my balls off." The elf's smile returned, albeit briefly. "He saved my life. I owe him the same."

Akiem wiped the drying tears from his face. He'd failed most of his life, beneath one ruler or another, but in this one thing—saving one elf—perhaps he could do some good? He'd pay for it, either with his body, or mind, or with his life. But what else was there? He was under no illusions. He'd die here eventually, likely beneath Clarion's axe. His death should stand for something, and if that something was the life of an elf, it seemed fitting. Mother would have raged at him, despised him more, shut him away for weeks, alone in the dark. That thought decided it for him. He'd save an elf to spite her. To spite them all.

"I can get to him."

Red's pacing ceased. He looked up. "You'll help me?"

"Not for you. For him. I know what it is to be chained by dragons." Akiem unlocked the door, stepped outside, and paused. He didn't want to look back. Looking back would imply he cared, and the elf did not care for him in return. "Be here tomorrow night."

"Wait—"

He hesitated.

"My name is Zane."

"I do not care to know your name, *elf*." He closed the door and retraced their steps, opting for the door to his chamber instead of the window. A breeze had swept through his room, wiping away any scent of elf. He closed the window and locked the latch. If Red tried to reach him again, he'd find his way barred. That was the only way. His brief encounter with the elf was just that. Now he had to turn his mind to the king, to Clarion, and what he could do for a single elf who didn't deserve to die beneath dragons.

kiem

THE DIAMOND DRAGON flew in hot, claws out, wings clutched close. At the last second, he flung them out and parachuted perfectly into the abandoned tower's gaping mouth. Akiem waited at the back of the huge room, as man, not dragon. Clarion hadn't yet seen him as dragon. Only Luceran had seen his scars. He intended to keep it that way.

The diamond—Clarion—shook his head and narrowed his dark violet eyes on him. The effect was meant to make Akiem feel small, insignificant, and easily crushed, and it would have worked on a lesser dragon, but Akiem merely waited for the lord to finish preening and said, "I've reconsidered." He had to raise his voice to be heard over the dragon's bellows-like breathing.

Clarion snarled, lips rippling over rows of sharp teeth. Unlike Luceran, his skull didn't carry a crown of lance-like bone protrusions. His spikes were fewer and blunt. There was no denying he was a magnificent beast, with pearly white scales, claws of black obsidian, and an envious wingspan.

Clarion shifted with a magical scattering of light, and ear-popping pressure forced Akiem to look away. The king's brother approached, shrugging his plain cotton shirt and tan leather pants into alignment. He tilted his head, popping muscles in his neck, and then flashed Akiem a grin. "The black elf?"

"I want him."

The male's eyebrows lifted. "Figured you might." He waved a hand. "Walk with me."

Akiem obliged. This part of the compound belonged to Clarion. The lord slept with his own brood in his own area, within Luceran's territory. He and the king rarely crossed paths. It seemed they avoided each other deliberately, perhaps for the sake of Luceran's stable rule.

"You know my brother will kill you when he's done with you, of that there's no doubt," Clarion said.

It was no secret. While Clarion sated his urges with elves, Luceran did the same with lower dragons—the same lowers who delighted in telling Akiem how he'd soon experience the king's wrath.

"It's why I've yet to submit." Among other reasons.

They walked some more, Clarion's grin growing with each step. "If you think to outmaneuver him, don't. He's already two steps ahead." Interesting words, as though this were all an elaborate dance. "What if there was another way?"

It needed no explanation. Clarion had his eye on the throne. He was recruiting dragons to his cause. How much of a force did he already have? Enough to overthrow

Luceran? There was a time, not so long ago, when Akiem might have warned the king. With Red's—*Zane's* betrayal, he'd considered the same again. But his feelings for Zane, even though they weren't reciprocated, had shown him the truth of his twisted attraction to Luceran. He'd find no sanctuary in the king's arms.

"I could use a warrior like you," Clarion went on. "You have it in you. No other fucker could cross that ocean and live. You fought metals and survived. You have that look about you, Akiem. You're a killer. Luceran ignores your potential because you fascinate him. He's been at the top so long he's forgotten the fight to get there. I'm sure you've noticed how I'm different…"

Different, indeed. He liked to torture elves. Akiem knew who and what Clarion was: a typical jeweled dragon. No mystery. No pretense. He took, and he owned, because he could.

"Have the elf," Clarion said. "I'll cover for you. I'll get more for you. They're easy to obtain. Young, old, black, pink—whatever you fancy. But you will do one thing for me."

"Name it."

Clarion stopped, forcing Akiem to stop as well. They were alone in a tunnel-like hallway, heading down toward Clarion's chambers. "Luceran's peace will not hold forever. When I need you, you'll stand beside me, and you won't even have to fuck me to do it."

His eyes were cold, colder than Luceran's. Akiem was no safer beside one brother than the other. At least with Luceran, he saw the killing blow coming. Clarion schemed too, and this was surely part of it, but it didn't matter. Akiem didn't fear death. In many ways, he welcomed it.

"Very well."

"Good." Clarion gripped Akiem's shoulder. His fingers dug in, and when he leaned closer, his violet eyes darkened to amethyst. "Now let's get you some elf."

~

JEVAN, Zane had called him. He looked up when Akiem and Clarion entered the torture chamber and stared straight into Akiem's gaze. If looks could kill, that one would be surrounded by dragon carcasses. A good thing elves weren't as strong as dragons, a fact made perfectly clear when Clarion detached the elf's ropes from the floor loops and pulled him to his feet. He had plenty of fight left in him, but he was wise enough to preserve his strength for when he'd need it most.

"Do you have somewhere you can take him?" Clarion asked.

"I do."

The lord reeled Jevan in. The elf hissed, setting off Clarion's laughter again. "Are you sure you can handle him? It'll be my ass Luceran comes for if his new toy hurts himself."

"I wouldn't be dragon if I couldn't." He took the loop of rope.

The elf spat. Wetness dashed Akiem's cheek and cooled as it dribbled down his chin. Clarion raised his hand in what would have been a devastating blow, but Akiem flung the length of rope around Jevan's neck and yanked, lynching him tight. His eyes watered and bulged, but still the stubborn elf stared back. This one had fight and spirit, and he'd see Akiem dead at his first opportunity.

Akiem held the loop tight until the elf's struggles

slowed, then quickly loosened it to a torrent of splutters and gasps. "Do as I say and that need not happen again."

The elf hung his head, too focused on breathing to fight back.

Akiem led him stumbling along through the chamber that held Clarion's other pets. They turned their heads away, trying to look small.

"Just... don't kill him, Akiem. I need that one alive," Clarion said, his focus falling on the twins.

"Why?"

"Only until the full moon. After that, he's all yours." The lord waved, shooing him on.

"What happens at the full moon?"

"The red-headed devil friend of his dies." Clarion's attention drifted onward, to the silent singer glaring his way. "Nothing you need concern yourself with."

Jevan yanked on the rope, lunging for Clarion. Akiem almost didn't catch him. He hauled the elf back under his control and looped an arm around his neck. The fool bucked, his head striking Akiem's chin.

"*Stop*," Akiem hissed in his ear, too low for Clarion to hear. "*Stop fighting me and you and Zane will survive this.*"

The elf froze at the sound of Zane's name.

Clarion's hideous laughter bubbled. "Keep him tied, Akiem. Lose him and it'll be your head rolling. Understood?"

"Perfectly."

They made it out of the torture chamber without further incident. Akiem's words had calmed the elf, but it wouldn't last. He hurried him along, veering into the emptier parts of the compound. It didn't matter if anyone saw him. All of this would be over within a few hours, and then Akiem would deal with the consequences of having lost an elf under Clarion's care.

The bedchamber was as he'd left it, although Zane had yet to arrive.

"I'm not fucking you. I don't fuck dragons. And if I did, I wouldn't touch the king's leftovers."

"You'd do well to keep your mouth shut." Akiem tied the end of the rope to the bedpost. Jevan could work it loose given enough time, but the binds only needed to last until Zane arrived. "Zane is coming for you."

"What?"

"You heard." Akiem collected the oil lamp, found the matches, and lit the wick, just as Zane had done the night before. He could still smell the fresh-cut-wood smell of elf, as if Zane had left moments ago, not hours. The bed drew his eye again, his mind seeing Zane servicing other dragons between the sheets. He'd never thought of himself as the jealous type. He'd coveted his broodbrother's freedom and the attention Mother paid him, but nothing else. Strange that he should feel it now, over a promiscuous elf.

"Then you aren't... you're not going to..." Jevan gestured at the bed, as much as his tied hands would allow.

"I have no interest in you."

An ache pounded behind his eyes. He rested his elbow on the fireplace mantle and rubbed his temples. Everything would be so much simpler if he didn't care. But how to go back to that? Now that he genuinely cared, he couldn't get the damn elf out of his head.

"Is this... Are you screwing with me?" Jevan queried. "Is Zane really coming, or is this some sick dragon trick?"

"If I wanted to screw with you, I'd set you free and

chase you down. Now sit there, shut up, and be grateful you have a friend who cares."

The elf blessedly fell silent, but it didn't last.

"How do you even know Zane?" he asked. He was sitting on the edge of the bed now, arms still tied to the post. Some of his fight had fled. "How did you and he... How does that happen?"

Akiem opted for silence. *I paid him for sex* wasn't something he wanted to reveal to anyone.

"What about the others?"

Akiem tipped his head back and closed his eyes. Maybe he could just leave the elf tied to the bed and return to Luceran, but then he'd miss Zane. He'd miss the damn elf who took coin and didn't give a shit about Akiem's *feelings*, confused as they were. Gods, what was he doing?

"The girls, Helana and Teone? And..." The elf swallowed hard. "You can't leave them there with that monster. They'll die."

Akiem leveled his glare on the elf. "That's the part I meant when I said to be grateful you have a friend who cares. You get to live. They do not."

The elf's face pinched in disgust. "Why are you doing this?"

"It doesn't matter." The ache thudded heavily, beating in time with his heart. He pushed from the fireplace and found a chair to sink into. This room smelled like elf and sex, and it reminded him of a time on a rooftop with Zane on his knees. To his shame, he'd pay Zane again to relive that moment.

Ropes scraped, and the bed creaked. Akiem looked up to find the elf trying to loosen the knots. "You can't run."

"I'm not leaving without them." He tugged at his ropes.

Zane's friend was testing Akiem's patience. "Without who?"

"Helana. Teone. I'm going back to get them."

Elves. They'd become the bane of his life. "No, you're not."

Jevan stared at Akiem. "That sick monster holds them down and fucks them both. He finishes in one while the other watches and makes her pleasure him until he's hard again. Then he takes them wherever he can—mouth, ass, doesn't matter. They're just pieces of meat to him, and I won't fucking leave them there!"

Akiem fell forward and dug his elbows into his knees. He laced his hands behind his head, needing to squeeze out the memories the elf's words had summoned. The pressure of such invasions had been worse than the pain. The feel of *another* violating him... Sickness flushed his skin hot and cold. For the first time since crossing the ocean, the marks on his arms tingled, his fingers itching to find a blade and add to their number.

"They're too afraid to open their mouths to scream. You have no idea what they endure. You don't even care! I don't know why you're doing this, but if you leave them there, you're worse than he is, because you could do something, but you won't!"

He had the chair in his hands, saw the wall, saw the chair shatter against the wall, and still he didn't register he'd moved until his heart slowed.

He tossed the bits of chair at the fireplace, not caring that most missed. It wasn't enough. He wanted to crush the memories out of himself. Needed to crush something before his veins exploded and the shift rolled through him.

The dresser toppled beneath his hands, smashing apart, and still it wasn't enough. He was breaking apart. It was more than he could take. Oh, he knew what it felt like to be afraid to scream. He knew what it felt like to be forced to open for a dragon and weep silent tears in the dark.

He had the elf in his hands, his throat so delicate. The whites of his eyes showed. Fear, he reeked of it.

A twitch and he'd be dead. Maybe that would work to Akiem's advantage. He'd toss the carcass at Clarion's feet and tell the lord he followed no orders save his own. He'd tell Luceran how his own broodbrother plotted against him, and maybe Akiem would wield the axe *for* the king, as another executioner, another guardian, but for a king this time, not a queen. He was fucking Prince Akiem of the amethyst brood, and the world needed to remember he'd been bred to rule.

"I've killed hundreds of your kind." He forced the words through gritted teeth and smelled the rich spiciness of fear on the elf. The dragon in him rolled in the scent. "Shredded them, placed their heads on pikes, eaten them alive. Don't think I won't do the same to you."

"You're just like them." Hatred dripped from every word.

Akiem blinked.

No, this was what he didn't want. This was what he was trying *not* to be. He flung himself away, found a corner, and wedged himself in, eyeing the door and waiting for Zane to come and take his friend away.

Gods. He looked at his hands. Killer's hands. There was a rot at his core he could never escape from.

At least the elf had stopped trying to free himself. He'd stopped talking too.

Zane pushed open the door some time later and toed

through the broken bits of furniture to reach Jevan. He glanced over, checking on Akiem, and neatly cut Jevan's ropes with a dagger. They embraced.

Akiem looked away. What must it be like to care for someone so deeply you'd go against the worst of monsters to free them?

"Thank you," Zane said, drawing Akiem's gaze back to the pair. Zane seemed sad and wary, and that was a crime. He had a face made for laughter and delight, not sadness.

"Clarion will be waiting for you at the next trade," Akiem growled. More dragon sounded in his voice than he'd expected, the words rough-edged and uneven. "Leave the city. You can do no more here."

Zane's brow pinched. "Some things you can't run from."

Oh, Akiem knew all about running in circles. Even now he didn't know if he wanted to help these elves or kill them. He didn't know if what he felt for Zane was more than lust, because his mind wasn't capable of more. If he genuinely cared, he'd do more, wouldn't he? Just like Jevan had said. Half of him wanted to rage at the world, but the other half just wanted to be held. He heard Mother's voice: *stupid thoughts from a stupid mind.*

Jevan rubbed his neck, where fresh bruises bloomed. The movement snagged Akiem's wandering mind. *Prey.* The elf winced and swallowed, then became aware of Akiem watching him. "Clarion said you'd die if you lost me."

Zane swung a questioning glare at his friend, almost as though he cared, but then he turned away, casting his gaze at the ceiling. Now that the trade was done he couldn't meet Akiem's eyes. Their business was over.

"I've died before, elf." Dragon rippled beneath his skin, rising to the surface. He was losing control. "Leave."

Zane took in the mess and opened his mouth to speak. This time Akiem did growl, cutting him off. "Go!" The shift stretched his mental chains, stretching, yawning.

They left, and just in time. The shift had him, turning him over, remaking him. He breathed out, spilling dragon into the small room and filling it up until the walls groaned and cracked, then finally burst apart. Akiem flung his wings out, shaking off dust and rubble. He lifted his head, climbed from the ruined house, and opened his jaws, stoking the fire low in his throat. He tasted elf in the air, and that would not do. Throwing his head high, he freed the fire, lighting the sky with purple flame.

Another cry sliced through the night.

Luceran. He'd known... somehow... and now he was here.

The king banked in the dark sky, presenting arched wings like a crescent moon.

Akiem lowered his head, laying his crown against the back of his neck to protect the scars around his skull.

So be it. Death had stalked him for months, ever since he'd fled across an ocean and landed on the beach of this strange new world.

Luceran pulled his wings in, sharpening his body into an arrow, and plunged in fast. Fire burned in Akiem's throat. He boiled it, readying, breathing hard. It seemed cruel that in what might be his final moments he felt almost as alive as he had with an elf.

CHAPTER 14

ane

"By Alumn, *that's* the king…"

They had almost made it outside the compound when Zane heard the dragon's roar and felt the warmth of purple fire. He'd turned to see the diamond banking over their heads, fixing the Black Prince in his sights.

"Luceran knew?" He must have known. How else could he have gotten here so fast?

"He'll die, just like he wants to. C'mon—" Jevan tugged his arm, but Zane pulled back. What did Jevan mean? Who wanted to die? Not the prince? "Wait. He saved you—"

"And?"

Dragons screamed, chilling Zane's blood.

Jev blocked his path back. "You want to get in the middle of that?"

An inferno warmed the sky. The sound of claws and

teeth on scale set his teeth on edge. Alumn, their screaming was unearthly.

"The king will kill Akiem for letting me go. Let them kill each other."

"Akiem?" Who was Akiem? The Black Prince? "Jev, shit…" He couldn't abandon Akiem after the prince had saved Jev's life. Maybe he could create a distraction or something?

Jevan grabbed Zane's shoulder. His fingers dug in, but his glare dug deeper. "If we don't leave now, we'll get caught in that firestorm."

Akiem wasn't strong enough to fight the king. Even Zane knew that. Akiem knew it too. Oh, Alumn, he'd sacrificed himself, knowing this would be the outcome. His life for Jevan's—for an elf's.

Zane shoved Jev's grip off. "I can't leave."

Pain flashed across his face. He tasted dirt and grass, realized somewhere in the blur that Jev had struck him, and then nothing.

FIRE THROBBED through Zane's jaw. Groaning didn't ease the pain, but it seemed fitting that Jev should hear. He cracked an eye open and found his friend in a chair beside his lodgings bed, frowning. Nothing new there. "You hit like an elfling."

Jev's lips turned down in regret. "I told you I'd knock your pretty off."

Zane grunted and swung his legs off the bed. He still had his clothes on, so it hadn't been one of *those* drunken nights. Then he recalled the purple fire and the screams of dragons and why Jev had hit him: Akiem. That was the dragon's name. It was a good name, for a dragon. "Is Akiem dead?"

Jevan let out a long sigh. "I went back because I knew you'd damn well ask. There's blood—not enough for a kill—and some ruined buildings. He's alive, or he was when he left." He didn't seem pleased about that.

Zane prodded his jaw, finding it swollen. He *would* have gone back for Akiem, and it would have been the wrong thing to do, but only because Zane was elf. There was nothing he could have done to stop the battle between Akiem and Luceran. Had Jev saved his life? Again? "You're a bastard."

Jev finally grinned, any awkwardness fading. "What happened between you and him? You didn't fuck him...?"

"No. Maybe."

Jev fell back in the chair, rolling his eyes.

"I mean, it wasn't like that. It was, but... Okay, fine, yes, I took his coin and used him to get you out." Hearing it out loud made it sound like a shitty thing to do, but it had worked. Jev was here, alive. That had to make it all worth it?

Jev offered his hand. "You're insane." He smiled, and that smile offered Zane some relief from the guilt.

Zane gripped his hand, yanked him close, and wrapped an arm around him. "You mispronounced, '*Thank you, Zane, for saving my life.*'"

Chuckling, Jev extracted himself from the embrace. His laughter faded. "I know you. In every town we pass through, you act like you don't care about anyone or anything, but I haven't forgotten Oldport." Jev let the name-drop simmer in a small silence. "You'd have gone back for the dragon, even knowing what he is."

The mention of Oldport had Zane burying his face in

his hands. Shit, Oldport had been a clusterfuck of mistakes and imprisonment, and escape right after. He'd done some things, said some things, maybe gotten his heart broken too. But this was different.

Zane had been about to deny this was anything like Oldport, but Jev continued. "Whatever went on between you two, he's not right in the head. You must see that?"

That was why Zane couldn't stop thinking about him. "Akiem is different."

"Yeah, the mad kinda different. He nearly killed me." Jev rubbed this neck.

It wasn't as though Zane thought Akiem was good. He knew what the Black Prince was capable of, but Zane had only seen him show aggression toward other dragons, not elves. But Jev *was* bruised.

"He hurt you?" Zane asked, dreading the answer.

Jevan rose from the chair and headed to the window. "I told him the truth."

"The truth about what?"

"About what he is. About him being a coward. He knows what Clarion does to elves, and he doesn't give a shit. That makes him as bad as the rest." He leaned against the wall beside the window and crossed his arms.

Zane could imagine how that conversation had gone, and perhaps why half the furniture had been smashed before his arrival. If Clarion raped them, Akiem definitely gave a shit.

"Clarion has others?" he asked. Of course the lord did. Every month, he got a fresh delivery of elves to fill his belly and satisfy his needs. "You saw them?"

Jev nodded, looking outside. "We won't let this stand."

He'd been lucky to get away. Had Clarion touched him too?

Jev caught Zane's rapidly falling expression and added, "He didn't hurt me, not like the others, but he would have, eventually. I guess I owe your dragon thanks for that, if nothing else."

Shit. This whole damn city was cursed, but Zane couldn't leave, and from that determined look on Jev's face, he wasn't going anywhere either, not until they stopped the elf trade, one way or another. "The full moon is in five days—"

"Four. You slept through a day."

"Clarion will be waiting for us."

Jev sucked in air through his teeth. He stared out the window like he could see the future and their place in it. "He knows we're coming."

Jev put on a brave face, seeming like a pillar of strength. He always had. He was Zane's rock, but he had cracks too. "Are you up for this?"

His throat bobbed. "I've never wanted to see a dead dragon more than that diamond-lizard."

Zane dug in his pocket and, approaching Jev, held out the locket. "Didn't want it to get stolen while you were gone."

Jevan's face fell. He took the locket, pooled its chain on his palm, closed his fingers around its tarnished shimmer, and swallowed. "It's time we fought back," he said with conviction.

"Yeah, it is."

CHAPTER 15

kiem

HE TUCKED his nose under his tail and squeezed his eyes closed. The pain had never left him. He still felt the king's claws and teeth beneath his scales. Shifting would fix that, as long as the wounds were clean. He'd licked them as best he could. But shifting meant thinking as man, talking as man, and living with the hurt and confusion as man, and he wasn't ready. Dragon was easy. Dragon was better. He had scales to hide behind. Teeth to display in warning. Claws to scratch. Nobody but Luceran dared approach him.

The ungrateful elf, Jevan, had gotten away. Zane too.

That was good.

Only, he had the gut-sinking feeling they'd be back. Zane alone might have left, but not his angry companion, and they were a team—a small pride of elves.

Elves didn't know when to quit.

Then there was the problem of the elves in Clarion's *care*. Zane had said the lord collected them at the full moon.

Akiem had a problem with that. He'd saved one elf, but it wasn't enough. Denying he cared just delayed the inevitable. He'd denied himself many things his whole life. His attraction for males, the ability to think and fight for himself, the fact elves were as worthy of life as any dragon. That last one would get him killed quicker than the rest. Gods, Mother would laugh to see him now. It had begun with her. He hadn't seen it, couldn't see it. He'd always been on the inside looking inward. Now, from the outside, looking at himself, the view was very different.

He'd always tried to be something for someone else. He'd never tried to be himself.

To be anything, though, he needed to survive.

He had to play this smarter.

Play it harder.

All here thought him weak, thought him beaten and pathetic, thought him Luceran's pet who came when called and was beaten when he misbehaved. So he'd play the pet. He'd damn well revel in it, because if he knew anything about jeweled dragons and their courts, it was that when one fell, another stole its place. Clarion eyed the throne. Luceran either didn't know or didn't care. Beneath it all, elves looked on, beaten just like Akiem and abused... waiting to bite the dragon-hand that fed them.

Eventually, Clarion would destroy Luceran or vice versa. Akiem just had to nudge them along to speed things up. *That* he could do. If he were more confident, like Zane, he could play the king's desires, but there were other ways to manipulate. The Amethyst Queen had taught him, and he was fucking amethyst. Defiance was in his blood.

He huffed at the empty chamber, untucked himself, and invited the shift, spilling all his dragon-self into the tight restraints of wingless flesh and human muscle, then went in search of his chamber, fresh clothes, and a king to topple.

~

AKIEM WAS NOT PERMITTED inside Luceran's inner council. No one had told him as much, they didn't need to. As an outsider, he had no seat at the command table and never would, but there were few better places to make a statement than in front of the most powerful dragons this side of the ocean.

Nobody expected him to walk into the meeting, and so nobody stopped him when he rounded the table, knelt beside the king's chair, and took his slim hand, placing a delicate kiss across the back of his fingers. Akiem rubbed his cheek across the same spot, letting some dragon bleed through. "Forgive me."

Luceran pulled his hand free and threaded his fingers into Akiem's hair, stroking it back from his face and summoning a purr from him.

"Please excuse us," Luceran dismissed the others. Akiem caught Clarion's narrow-eyed glimpse before he strode from the room behind his lordly peers.

"I did not expect to see you so soon." The king's lips lifted in a small smile. With Akiem on his knees, Luceran peered down at him.

"I could not waste time recuperating, knowing what I do. I fear for your safety. There are plots—"

"Ah, Clarion."

Akiem dared to place a hand on the king's thigh. His

warmth reminded him of another's, one with a smile made for late nights by firelight. He wasn't afraid, not now. He could fear this later, after it was done.

Luceran stroked Akiem's cheek and hooked a finger under his chin, urging him to rise. He did, but only enough to press himself against the king's knees. Seduction was not in his nature—seducing males was unbroken ground—but he'd felt Zane's readiness in his hand and kept that thought at the forefront of his mind. The elf had given him a gift. Akiem had tasted male pleasure and wanted more. He could use that gift for his own means, perhaps in the same way the elf had, but Luceran paid Akiem with trust, not coin.

Luceran parted his knees and bowed forward. His braid of white hair fell from his shoulder. Akiem pulled the band free and teased the interwoven locks apart. Luceran's eyes observed, reading his face. The king moved in, his mouth so close to Akiem's that anticipation sizzled on his lips.

"Why now?" he whispered.

"Change is coming," Akiem said, matching the king's breathless tone, teasing his mouth away. "Clarion sought to recruit me, bribing me with gifts."

"The elf who escaped you. He was a gift?"

Akiem swallowed. "Clarion poisons your brood from the inside. He undermines you, even now."

The king's hand slid into Akiem's hair again. His fingers twisted, applying enough pressure to turn his head away and expose his neck. The king's soft, warm cheek brushed Akiem's in a dragon-like gesture.

"You think I do not know my own brother?" A dangerous note tightened Luceran's voice.

"I do not presume to know what you think. I owe you

my life. I am yours. He believes he can manipulate me and turn me against you. He is wrong."

Luceran's lips skimmed Akiem's jaw, the touch featherlight. "Then you are the first," he whispered. "He excels at finding my pets' desires, bribing them, and turning them against me. Why do you think all my previous lovers have perished?" His whispers brushed the corner of Akiem's mouth, a tease and promise. Akiem's breath raced. "But not you, my black prince. You are different." His fingers tightened in Akiem's hair. "And dangerous because of it."

The king's mouth crashed against Akiem's, ferocious with urgency. The strength behind it rocked Akiem on his knees. He dug his fingers into the king's thighs, wrenching a gasp from the male and notching up his own need. But it wasn't Luceran Akiem kissed, not in his mind. The damn elf had rooted himself in place of the king, his mouth the perfect and wicked tease, his body strung tight like a bow. Luceran tasted like dragon, citrusy and sharp. Akiem's mind wiped that fact clear and replaced the taste with the sweetness of pine and forests at dawn. The king tore the kiss apart, wrapped an arm around Akiem's back, and dragged him forward.

"I fear for you," Akiem said against his neck, placing the words close to his ear. How easily the lies came now that he'd given them permission. Was this how Zane did things? Had he thought of another while they'd been together? Had any of it been real?

"Don't fear for me, my prince. There's no need."

"Kill him," Akiem hissed, so very dragon. "See it over with."

"And there is the truth of you, my black prince." His teeth grazed Akiem's throat, the warning clear, the pleasure exquisite, until he recalled another dragon's teeth at his throat.

Fear tried to sink its claws in. Akiem pushed back, holding Luceran down with one hand while he pressed the other against his cock. The position saw him higher than the king, but Luceran either didn't notice the lapse in protocol or didn't care. He clutched Akiem's hand, grinding it where he needed it.

Akiem climbed into the chair, straddling Luceran's thighs, trapping him, and kissed him hard and fast, like these were his last breaths. If he failed in his seduction, they might well be. If he succeeded, they might be too. The balance was important. Not too much. He needed the king keen, needed him fucking lost in want and distracted by the chase—a chase Akiem had no intention of finishing.

Akiem pulled away and rose. He flicked his hair back and threw Luceran a look he'd learned from an elf, not entirely sure it would work. He bit his lip and ran his gaze down the male's heaving chest, envisaging elf beneath him. Acknowledging his wrongs, and owning them, made this so much easier.

Luceran's hands rode up Akiem's chest, bunching the shirt and skimming over bruises the king's claws had delivered.

Akiem flinched.

"Not yet..." The king measured his breathing and glanced around him, recalling where they were. The passion in his eyes snuffed out in a blink. "Rest. Heal."

The unexpected withdrawal and oddly sympathetic words tripped Akiem's thoughts. Luceran wasn't supposed to think like that. He was all want and take, like all drag-ons. This was... baffling.

He fell in for another kiss, hoping to reignite Luceran's lust, but the king turned his head. "Rest," he growled. "Heal. When this happens"—he grasped Akiem's hair and ran it through his hand—"and it will happen—it will be glorious." He pushed Akiem away, got to his feet, and straightened his clothes.

Akiem leaned heavily against the table, lips tingling. He hadn't expected this... kindness. It wasn't how things were meant to be. Luceran was cruel and vicious. He was jeweled. All they cared about was owning and taking and controlling.

"Retire to your chambers," the king said, delivering weight behind the order by holding Akiem's gaze.

"Are you punishing me?"

"No," he replied curtly. "Akiem, both parties must be willing." The king bowed his head, took a moment to collect his thoughts, and said, "You are not ready."

How did Luceran know? Akiem filled his lungs and sighed. He wasn't supposed to look at him this way or think this way.

"I am no beast," Luceran said. "I will not do to you what was done in the past."

Akiem's heart seized. The diamond king *cared?*

Luceran nodded, his point made. He left without looking back, and Akiem wondered if he truly knew the dragon he was about to betray.

"I TOLD you not to lose the elf!" Clarion marched down the corridors toward his tower.

Akiem followed, keeping up with his breathless pace. "I'll deal with it."

"Forget it." The lord laughed his typically hollow laughter. "The problem will resolve itself once his companion dies."

Zane. That's where Clarion was headed. Akiem had steered clear of the lord during the last few days but kept within range to watch for his departure on the full moon. That moment was now.

Clarion threw open the door into the chamber with its one open wall. Outside, a fat full moon hung low in the night sky.

"Allow me to make amends."

"I warned you he was fiesty. Did you at least get what you wanted from him?" Clarion saw his expression and snorted. "Akiem, if you cannot handle one little elf, how can you handle what is to come?"

"Luceran knows you're plotting against him."

"Of course he does. We're of the same damn brood." Clarion approached the edge of the building. The wind whipped inside, stirring up dust devils. That same wind took hold of the lord's hair and lashed it across his face, as it did with Akiem's, forcing him to sweep a hand up to hold it back.

"I hatched moments before him," Clarion said. "His rule should be mine. All our lives he's known I'd come for him. Every day he wonders, *Is this the day?* It's my own game." Clarion backed toward the edge. Throwing his arms out, he presented a compelling image of a dragon on top of the world, his white shirt billowing and his snake-like hair scattered by the wind. "Everything is about to change, Akiem. This ridiculous peace with elves... it is not the dragon way. You know this. I see it in your war-weary golden eyes. Are you ready for a revolution?"

"Let me fly with you."

The lord grinned. "Very well, but keep up."

He stepped backward off the edge and dropped from sight.

Akiem's stomach flipped empathically moments before the diamond dragon soared high. Clarion opened his jaws and roared at the moon, appearing to swallow it. He looked silver in the moonlight, but he wasn't metal, just jeweled.

Akiem's heart stuttered its irregular beat. Hot, hungry blood warmed his veins, itching for the shift. He broke into a run. The edge came closer, the darkness yawning beyond it. His boot hit the lip, and he launched away from the safety of the building, and fell. The wind took him, toyed with him, tore and snatched at his clothes, hair, and skin. Gods, falling was freedom. The shift exploded through him, ripping him open. He flung out sore, battered wings a moment before the ground could embrace him.

He swooped low and pulled up, gravity yanking on his insides. But by the Great Ones, there was no other feeling like it.

The city streets and buildings peeled open below, lanterns glistening in nooks and corners like dew on long grass. Human towers clawed at the sky. Akiem skirted around them, cutting in close enough to dislodge rubble in his wake. His tail flicked, lashing wide, streamlining his balance.

Clarion shone ahead, threading through towers. Moonlight made him knifelike and lit him up for Akiem to follow.

Akiem beat his wings and gained altitude, but slowly. Still, the higher he climbed, the more of the city he saw. Colder air nipped at his wingtips and tail. In the dark, he was hidden from any onlookers, while Clarion was a beacon.

The lord slowed, needing to climb now that the buildings were too dense to fly through safely. Akiem circled above and watched two jeweled dragons glide in. The three alighted atop a smaller building and shifted. Akiem opted to circle and observe, knowing stealth kept him hidden. Hidden above it all was how he preferred it. Even in the moonlight, he'd be difficult to pick out from the ground.

It was then he saw a slice of light to the west, sliding in from outside the city. Another dragon. Another diamond dragon with a jagged crown. Luceran.

Below, Clarion didn't know his brother approached.

Akiem stayed high, stayed hidden, and watched.

ane

CROUCHED IN THE RUBBLE, downwind from the west gate, he watched the meeting in the street unfold. He had his longbow angled sideways to keep its arch hidden. Clarion made the perfect target, as did the sniveling Killian, but Zane's arrow was not meant for the elder. Not today, anyway.

He couldn't see Jevan, but he'd be where they'd planned, his bow similarly lined up on the target. If Zane missed, Jev wouldn't.

"Good to see you again, Killian." Clarion slapped the elder on the back and embraced him in an overly familiar hug that rattled Killian to the core. He paled and wiped his brow.

Zane cast his gaze farther into the darkness behind the dragon. Clarion wouldn't have come alone, so where was his entourage?

"What do you have for me tonight, elf, eh?" Clarion hooked his arm around Killian's shoulders. "I wonder, do you ever make a list and pick the elves that pissed you off this month? The ugly ones? Eh, tell me. I won't tell another soul. Your secrets are safe with me."

His behavior was off, almost drunk, as though he were deliberately overexaggerating. Zane nocked an arrow but didn't pull the string back. He needed to see the elves Killian intended to trade first.

"Come now, don't be shy." Clarion grinned, showing perfectly white, blunt teeth.

"Hello, brother."

Zane blinked. The gray-clad king approached along the same path Clarion had used. Clarion stilled. He hadn't expected his arrival. The lord's arm slipped from around the elder. He turned to face Luceran and lifted his chin.

"I put an end to this barbaric practice last year, did I not?" Luceran tilted his head and glanced up, as though seeking something above, but the look happened almost too quick to register.

Clarion snorted. "It's just elves."

Luceran's gaze thinned. That had been the wrong thing to say. Luceran didn't care about elves, but he cared about dragons following his laws. Apparently, his brother wasn't exempt. "Killian, I apologize on behalf of my brother. He should not be trading with you. All agreements are rendered null and void. You may leave."

A growl rumbled from Clarion while Killian scurried off.

"You apologize to them?" Disgust dragged Clarion's tone down and curled his hands into fists. "Have you gone mad?"

Luceran squared up to his brother. Their differences

were stark. Luceran was the cut diamond, while Clarion was uncut and rough. "Peace is an art, one I don't expect you to understand."

"Peace?" he snorted. "Fuck peace. Treat them as equals and they'll rise up against you."

"Equal, no, but we have an understanding, and because of that understanding, our city grows, as do our dragon broods. This equilibrium serves both races."

Clarion recoiled. "It's like we weren't hatched from the same nest."

"Sometimes, I wish it were so."

"Then what is this?" Clarion shrugged. "Will you punish me like your little pet?"

"No. This ends now."

The breeze washed the taste of magic from the dragons and over to Zane's hiding place. They were close to shifting, and if that happened, they'd be impenetrable to arrows. He couldn't wait for one of them to come out the victor of any impending fight. He wouldn't have another chance like this, with Clarion out in the open and distracted.

"Brother..." Clarion spread his arms. "Take your best shot."

The shot would be Zane's, and he had to take it now. He drew the string back, the wood creaking, aimed at Clarion's back—

Jevan's arrow flashed toward the dragons—toward Clarion—but the wind changed, whipping dust around the street and dislodging the arrow's trajectory, sending it straight into Clarion's sights. Impossibly, the dragon saw. He twisted and caught the arrow in mid-flight. Carrying it forward, he punched it home, straight into his brother's chest.

It happened so fast. Zane blinked, struggling to register the truth. Luceran shifted in a blast of white scales, filling the street with dragon. His roar was a terrible thing never meant to be heard. He clawed at his chest, tearing scales off, and lurched sideways. The arrow was still embedded in his chest. The shift had migrated the arrow, lodging it somewhere inside him—a death sentence.

Darkness flew in over Zane's head. Zane ducked.

Akiem skidded into a landing, tearing up asphalt under his claws. Clarion hadn't shifted, and when Akiem's wings lifted, the lord wasn't anywhere on the street. Zane searched the ground, the rubble, but there was no sign of the lord. He must have fled.

Luceran staggered, wings thrust out, awkwardly trying to catch the wind as though he could escape the arrow killing him with every breath.

Zane knew a dead dragon when he saw one.

With Clarion gone, it was time to leave. He backed away through the rubble, careful to stay low while keeping watch on the dragons. Akiem tore at the king's chest with his teeth, ripping open a fresh wound, but the king was down, panting his last breaths, his struggle dwindling.

Zane turned away. He didn't need to see the king die.

A terrible keening sound smothered all other noise—a lonesome, empty whine that followed the dying into their final moments. The sound came from Akiem, and it did something to Zane's heart. His breath hitched.

Zane stayed quiet, and slunk away.

The king was dead.

Clarion was king.

That changed everything.

Tomorrow would be a darker place for elves.

"WE NEED TO MOVE." Zane shoved everything he owned into his traveling bag and cinched the string tight, then slung it over his shoulder.

"We can't leave the city." Jevan stood guard at the window, his fingers peeling back the drapes an inch, enough to watch for oncoming dragons. "We started this, we finish it."

Finish it? Finish it how? Panic clawed at Zane's thoughts. The arrow had been meant for Clarion. That would have finished things. Now they'd started something far worse. Clarion's death would have changed things for the good of elves. Luceran's death changed *everything*. The king had kept the peace. The wrong diamond was dead. How had that even happened, and why the fuck wasn't Jev racing to get the hell out of here?

"Not leave the city, just... leave this lodging, this area. We need to go to ground before dawn, before we're found—"

Bells chimed nearby, rattling the windowpanes. Zane hadn't known this city still had bells. He looked at the window, at the red light of dawn creeping around Jevan like a warning.

Gods, Clarion would spin the king's death to his advantage. Elves had assassinated the king, and they'd all be punished.

"What did we do?" he whispered.

Jevan turned and pointed a finger at Zane. "We didn't do this, yah hear? That wasn't... It wasn't supposed to happen like that. It was me. I did this. I... the wind... and Clarion—he was fast. I've never seen a dragon move so fast."

And Akiem's whine, Zane silently added. Had the Black Prince cared for the king after all? Akiem might have seen the arrow from above, might even know who'd fired it. He might come for them.

Zane adjusted his bag over his shoulder. "There're lodgings at the southside, by the old Alumn chapel. It's farther from the compound. We'll hole up there and figure this out."

"I meant to hit Clarion," Jevan said, as though repeating it would change the outcome. He ran a hand through his tightly braided hair and bundled it against the back of his neck, wincing hard, holding himself in check. There wasn't time to patch Jev up. That would have to come later.

"It's done. We have to leave."

They'd made it outside the lodging when a familiar figure approached. Although cloaked, Arlo's slim frame, light-footed walk, and chinking bangles gave him away.

"Go on," Zane told Jevan. "I'll be right behind you."

"You're leaving?" Arlo lowered his hood and glanced back at Jevan, already marching away. Arlo had paled, or perhaps it was the ominous red dawn light that made ghosts of them all. So much had happened that Zane hadn't given Arlo much thought.

Zane drew him into the shadow of the lodge's doorway. "You should leave too. Things are about to get difficult around here."

"The bells? Did you hear them? You know what happened, don't you?" He gently rested his hand on Zane's arm. Zane covered it with his own and carefully removed it, giving his fingers a squeeze.

"The king is dead. Clarion will rule. It's no longer safe for us near the compound."

Arlo rocked back and fell against the wall. "The king is dead? Alumn help us," he breathed. "Where are you going?"

"Southside. Do you have anyone, any kin you can stay with?"

He bit his lip and shook his head. "I came up the coast alone. Bayston was supposed to be a sanctuary. I don't have anyone or anywhere to go."

The story was the same for most elves, because there was nowhere else to go. Alumn, Zane's heart ached for his kin, and for what was surely about to happen. "Go to the southside. I'll meet you there and help you find somewhere until... until this blows over."

He offered what he hoped was a confident smile.

Some of the lines around Arlo's eyes softened. He nodded, pulled his hood up, and stepped away, his hand reluctantly falling from Zane's.

Zane watched him turn and hurry back toward the bar. Other residents stirred awake, disturbed by the now-silent bells. He couldn't warn everyone. It was better he didn't and slipped away unseen. There was still a chance Clarion wouldn't act, that nothing would change and the dust would settle.

Pulling up his own hood, Zane ducked his head and walked south, along roads the morning sun had soaked red.

kiem

HE LANDED SOFTLY and lowered the king's body on the rooftop, freeing it from his jaws. The arrow must have struck his heart and stayed there when he'd shifted. The shot had been fatal the second it landed. Akiem aligned his wings, pulling them in close. These feelings were... unfamiliar, as though he had been tipped off balance, or like he was watching everything through someone else's eyes. It seemed impossible that the king lay dead. Luceran was still warm, and if it weren't for Akiem's own thudding heart, he was sure he would hear the king's heart beating still.

Lifting his head, he spotted three dragonkin by an old elevator stack, all waiting in their human forms. One he recognized from Clarion's table during the feast. The other two were new faces.

Akiem shifted and approached. "I witnessed it all. The

king's death was an accident." True enough. He had seen it all from above: the hidden elves with their bows drawn, and Clarion's men coming in behind them, intent on ambushing them. Luceran had abruptly stopped the meeting; he'd known about the elves too. The arrow should not have landed where it did, for more reason than just the change in the wind's direction. Reasons Akiem planned to investigate after he'd seen Clarion.

"An accident?" one of the dragons asked. "How convenient for you."

Akiem slowed, and the dragons fanned out, preparing to flank him. "I had no hand in Luceran's death."

"Killed him before he could kill you? It always ends the same way for his toys, but I didn't think you had it in you... outsider." The dragon produced a length of reinforced chain from behind his back and pulled it tight between his fists. "Come along easy now."

"It wasn't like that..."

The second and third dragons circled behind.

Akiem stood his ground, anticipation of violence drying his throat and sending adrenaline pumping through his veins. "I didn't kill him."

"You'll face the axe before the entire city." The one with the chain grinned. "The elves working with you have already been dealt with."

Zane and Jevan were dead? The unbalanced feeling he experienced almost tipped the world on its edge. Akiem staggered back a step. They saw a conspiracy to bring down the king, one Akiem had been a part of. He'd let the elf assassin escape, he'd conspired with them to kill the king. Arguing his innocence wouldn't save him from Clarion's axe. The lord had likely planned this all along. Akiem was Clarion's scapegoat. Gods, he should have seen it.

He breathed in. There was only one way out of this, with blood and violence and the rabid part of him desiring such things stirred awake. The leftmost dragon lunged in. Akiem had seen him tense for the strike and twisted away. He carried through with the movement and landed a punch to the dragon's throat, dropping him. All the restrained rage and bitter injustice broke from Akiem's control wide open. He lunged at the second, sidestepped a haymaker punch, and kicked the dragon's weight-bearing leg out from under him. The clumsy fool reeled and fell.

The chain looped Akiem's throat. Metal bit into his neck, shutting off his air. He clawed at the links, tasting metal on his tongue. Or maybe it was blood. The fallen dragon clambered to his feet. Akiem yanked himself and his captor forward, spat in the face of the one on the floor, and thrust an elbow back, knocking the air out of the dragon holding the chain. Its links loosened. Akiem tore the chain free, whirled, and whipped the chinking links across the dragon's face. Blood and bone sprayed. Akiem wasn't done. He swung the chain down on the one he'd blinded with his saliva. It didn't end there. The dragon fell to his knees. The chain landed across his back, ripping a cry from him. Blood splashed Akiem's smile. Again, Akiem brought it down, the thudding in his head too loud for reason to break through. Again and again. His veins *burned* with the violence now set free. Blinded by vicious rage, he wanted *more*.

When it was over, the three of them lay torn apart, steeped in pools of cooling blood. He tasted their blood on his lips, so very much like metal, and tossed the chain among their ruined bodies. He should care more, care for *something*, but he felt only the lust for violence sizzling through his veins.

He was done with dragons.

Running to the edge of the roof, he shifted and climbed high into the red-soaked morning sky. Bells rang out in alarm behind him, either to announce the king's death or Akiem's escape. Either way, there would be no returning to the compound. He had another destination in mind, and eyeing the waking city below him, he prayed to whatever god would listen that he wasn't too late to save two elves.

CHAPTER 18

ane

HE PAID TOO much of Killian's stolen coin for a week's rental of an old brownstone terrace, propped up by its rundown neighboring buildings. Alumn's abandoned chapel, with its broken windows and torn flags, gaped from across the street. Zane hoped it wasn't a sign of the desolation to come.

He slotted the key into the front door and pushed inside the cold dwelling. Jevan followed. Morning light spilled in through the windows, revealing modest rooms with minimal mismatched furniture. It would do. Zane dumped his bag in the hallway and climbed the stairs. There were more rooms than they needed. Perhaps Arlo might be grateful for a place to stay? Although inviting him under the same roof as him seemed like a bad idea. The lad might get the wrong idea. Others would need help

"

too, though Zane could only stretch his coin so far. He couldn't save them all. *It still may not come to that.*

He opened the door to the attic room. The strong scent of blood and dragon wafted over him. The door swung inward. Zane reached for his dagger. Jev did too, judging by the rustling behind him.

The Black Prince sat upright and regal in a chair by a huge open window. Dark stains marked his dark clothes. Blood splatters had dashed his face and dried there. He didn't smile. Just the slightest pinch of his brow acknowledged Zane before his gaze slid to Jevan. The frown darkened with suspicion.

"There are two dragons approaching this residence from the front," he said. "They're here to kill you."

Jevan made a low-throated growl. "We're supposed to believe you're here to save us?"

He turned to tell Jevan to back down, but a thump from downstairs signaled the three of them were no longer alone. Jevan darted silently out of the room. Zane freed his second dagger but caught Akiem's gaze. The dragon arched an eyebrow.

"You aren't with them... the dragons downstairs?"

Akiem's mouth ticked. "I'm not with the dragons, no."

That was good enough for now. Although, by the way he'd spoken, he had more to say on the subject.

Zane crept onto the landing and, peering down between the staircase, saw the two dragons making their way up. They wouldn't shift. They weren't here to make a scene by destroying a block of houses. Clarion had sent them to tidy up the loose ends so the new king could create his own version of events.

Zane ducked into a side room and let the door swing mostly closed. Jev would have done the same.

Akiem's help would be real useful right about now, he thought the second boots hammered on the boards outside the door. Someone yelped. The sounds of a scuffle filled the next few seconds and ended with a sudden thump.

Zane eased the door open.

Akiem knelt beside a body on the landing, his dark coat pooled around him. He had hold of the dragon's oddly misshapen and clearly deceased face, but let go and straightened when Zane emerged from the room. "Clarion will send more when these ones don't return."

Zane sheathed his unused blades. Rescued again. This was becoming something of a regular pattern between them.

Akiem skipped his gaze toward another room. "Jevan is fine, although I don't believe he appreciates my interfering."

"Are you all right?" Zane asked. The question sounded stupid now that he'd voiced it. Covered in the blood of his kin, he wasn't likely *all right*.

"Surprisingly, yes." A strange little smile hooked into the corner of his lips. A genuine one, Zane realized. He really was all right.

Zane regarded the cooling body. Yet again, Akiem had protected elves from dragons. Did he even know it was becoming a habit of his? "How did you find us?"

"Your friend Arlo at the bar."

"Did you hurt him?"

Akiem returned a dry look.

"Okay..." Zane sighed and rubbed his hands on his thighs. They'd need to deal with the dead dragon. He'd have to dispose of it in a city already on high alert. Maybe Akiem could eat it? He looked up and found the Black

Prince observing him in that unblinking, golden-eyed way of his.

"Jevan?" he called.

"Here."

Zane followed the voice back to the attic room.

"There's a body down the hall," Jevan said. His hands shook as he reached up to wipe his face. "Alumn, I need a drink."

He looked over as the Black Prince entered the room. Zane felt the weight of dragon at his back, and his skin prickled. Jevan eyed him coolly. There was no chance of the two of them getting along anytime soon, but he had bigger concerns.

"Clarion has declared that the three of us worked together to assassinate the king," Akiem said. He'd placed himself against the far wall. "I am a traitor to the crown. All dragons will be urged—*compelled* to kill us on sight."

Jevan fell into the chair Akiem had occupied earlier. "We can't leave."

"Leaving would be for the best."

"We need to think this through," Zane suggested. Leaving was beginning to sound like the only option, at least until they could form a plan. Akiem was here... and considering the dead bodies, he wanted Zane and Jev alive. That had to be a good thing.

"Thinking it through won't bring the king back." Akiem held Zane's gaze, saying something important in the silence.

The dragon blinked and turned his heavy glare on Jevan. "Why did you kill Luceran?"

"I didn't... I didn't mean to. Shit. I was aiming for Clarion. The wind caught it."

Akiem narrowed his eyes but said nothing more. His

attention drifted back, and now that the adrenaline was easing, Zane questioned his faith in this dragon. Zane had technically used him. Akiem had enabled Jevan's escape and likely paid a high price for it, but he still lived. The dragon had as many lives as an elf.

"I was told you were both dead. I'm glad to see that's not the case," Akiem said.

Zane considered telling him he'd been thinking the same, but Jevan's glare was drilling too deep into them.

"The king… did you care for him?" Jevan asked, probably wondering if Akiem was here for revenge.

The dragon dropped his gaze. "You believe I'm capable of caring?"

In their short time together, Zane had seen something in the prince, something more than the black-heated ruthlessness of all dragons. On the rooftop, there had been a vulnerability to him, a fragility, but he was doing a grand job of hiding it now. Yet Zane had heard his pain upon the king's death. Akiem *had* cared, and he did hurt, and that made his presence here equally fascinating and dangerous. Did he want revenge or something else from them?

Akiem shoved from the wall and strode by Zane out the door, trailing the pungent smell of dragon blood in his wake.

"Where are you going?" Zane asked.

"To wash."

Jevan looked up, his eyes pleading with Zane for something he couldn't fathom, and called, "You're staying?"

"I have nowhere else to go." The dragon's voice sailed back to them, joined by the sound of his boots marching across the landing.

Jevan frowned. "He's staying?"

What, by Alumn, was Jevan expecting Zane to do?

"He's covered in dragon blood. He crushed a dragon's skull in front of me. You want to be the one to tell him he can't stay, be my guest."

"He's dragon," Jevan whisper-hissed.

"We are all aware."

"He's a killer."

"Apparently, so are we, and he's as wanted as we are. That puts him on our side."

"I don't think that's how it works."

Jevan wasn't wrong, but neither were Zane's instincts, and they told a whole other story about the Black Prince, like maybe he was here because he wanted to be. He could have flown a thousand miles by nightfall, but instead, he'd come to warn them, even killed to protect them, and now he was staying. That spoke volumes, even when the dragon himself did not.

Sighing, Jevan stood and approached the door. "Don't go there, Zane."

"I don't—"

"He'll rip out your heart and eat it. I'm telling you this as your friend and someone who's seen you fall before. *Don't. Go. There.*"

Zane held his glare, insulted that Jevan would even think that such a thing as Zane falling for a dragon was possible. "I don't plan to."

Jevan left, and Zane went to the window, checking that the fixings were all sealed and locked. The front door had been locked on their arrival. Akiem must have gotten in through the window or the skylight overhead. In daylight. To have known where they lodged, he must have tracked them... from above. That was a slightly unsettling thought.

He braced his hands on the sill and peered across Bayston's rooftops. Distantly, in the part of the city he'd fled that morning, dragons speckled the sky. After the battles, he'd planned never to incite their ire again, knowing it was an unwinnable fight. He hadn't planned on staying longer in this city than necessary either. And now? Zane was no fool. His easy life was over. If he stayed, he'd die. If he left, he could never live with himself. He hadn't planned any of this, and hadn't planned on meeting the Black Prince either. The fact Akiem was here had to be by Alumn's guiding hand. Akiem had already proven himself. It looked as though they needed him. He'd saved Zane at the docks and saved Jevan from Clarion—even if the fool wasn't grateful. His rescue had been more Akiem's doing than Zane's. Now the dragon was here, with them, and showing no signs of leaving. That last thought made his insides flutter with anticipation.

No, Zane didn't plan on *going there,* but he was having a hard time ignoring how the prince's presence tied his thoughts into knots, muddling them with hope and a sense of opportunity. Bizarrely, in all the years and all the places he'd passed through, Zane had never felt safer than with Akiem in the next room.

kiem

THE HOUSE HAD a thing elves called a shower: a wonderful closet full of stove-heated warm rain. Such a thing didn't exist back home. He reveled in it, spreading warm hands against cold tiles, relishing the feel of water running down his back and over scars. Even after it ran cold, he lingered, letting the chill mottle his skin. Pleasure was a strange pursuit he'd never allowed himself, and certainly not in this human skin. Maybe he was coming apart. He saw no other explanation for how he had changed these last few weeks —becoming a creature of *want* where no desire had dwelled before. It couldn't all be the elf's doing, could it?

Stepping out, he found an old, rough towel and a pile of fresh clothes waiting for him. They weren't Zane's; he knew the elf's scent. This was a gift from Jevan.

He dried off, tied his damp hair in a loose bun, and pulled on the pants and shirt, both slightly too small. The shirt he let hang open but rolled up the sleeves. The pants would have to do, tight as they were. Better that than dressing in the clothing soaked in his dragonkin's blood.

Jevan waited for him in the bedchamber. The elf's eyebrows rose as Akiem emerged from the wet room.

"It's all we've got," he said, noting the tight fit.

"Yours?" Akiem tugged on the shirt's hem.

The elf nodded.

"I appreciate it."

"Look, about... the arrow." Jevan lowered his voice and glanced at the closed chamber door.

"And why you're lying?" Akiem asked.

Jevan strode closer. Akiem stiffened, making him halt. He wasn't armed, but his anxious manner frayed Akiem's already short nerves.

"The wind. It was the wind," he said again, gesturing like the comment were hardly worth voicing. He continued to look around, avoiding Akiem's steady glare.

"I'm dragon. I know what the wind was doing. I was riding it when you loosed that arrow."

Jevan clicked his tongue against his teeth, dismissing Akiem's words. "It's not what you think."

"You aimed for Luceran, not Clarion. Clarion helped it along." Zane couldn't have seen the truth from his angle, but from above, Akiem had seen it all. He'd seen the elf line up the shot on Luceran, and he'd tried to dive in to stop it. Instinct more than emotion had driven him to protect the king. "Both you and Clarion wanted the king dead."

Jevan swallowed, his throat undulating. "It was a mistake."

Was it shame that kept the elf's head turned away?

"You're familiar with a bow. You read the wind's direction and speed. Your aim was true."

Jevan stiffened and looked Akiem in the eye. "Have you never loved, dragon? Do you even know how to?" Jevan grimaced and laughed dryly. "Of course you don't. There are things your lizard mind can't understand."

"There always are." Akiem had loved once, long ago. He'd loved for his broodsister, the only true light in his otherwise dark life. Mother had butchered her. He'd found it easier not to love at all after that.

"Don't tell Zane," Jevan said.

"Your secrets are of no concern of mine, elf. Dragons will soon come for us. Whether their motivations are built on a lie doesn't matter. This was inevitable."

"Give me your word."

"My word?"

"As a prince, or whatever you are..." The intensity on Jevan's face crumbled, revealing his vulnerability. "Just say you won't tell him the truth."

There was much more to Jevan and his actions than the elf let on. His emotions were all over his face, but there were too many for Akiem to read accurately. "Why did you do it?"

"I—" he clipped his sentence, sealing his lips shut.

"You knew this would be the outcome. You know your actions will kill thousands."

His shoulders fell. "I know."

"Then why?"

Pain, that expression was real. "Just don't tell Zane. If you do, I'll tell him you raped me in that room while you had your hands around my neck."

Akiem smiled, revealing a hint of teeth. The elf's threat reeked of desperation. "Don't threaten me, whelp.

It's not been so long since I've tasted elf and might gladly do so again." He lunged forward a step, and the elf jerked back, his hand dropping to his empty sheath. "You're alive because you're Zane's friend. He cares about you. I don't. Put him at risk and I won't hesitate to remove you as a threat."

Jevan's top lip curled back. "Whatever you believe is happening between you, it's bullshit. If you're here because you think you have a chance with him, look elsewhere, *dragon*. He used you. It's what Zane does. Move on."

Akiem's smile thinned. He no longer found this elf amusing. "I'm here to help stop a war before it begins. I could just as easily leave you and your kind to your fate."

"Maybe you should. Elves don't need dragons to save them."

Akiem turned away and busied himself by picking up his discarded clothes. By the time he straightened, the door had clicked closed and the elf was gone. Zane trusted him, but trust was blind by its very nature. Akiem trusted no one, least of all the angry elf who had killed the king.

DUSK FELL EARLY, hastened by dragons darkening the sky. From Akiem's rooftop position, he watched with human eyes as they glided over the distant compound. Dying light stroked over jeweled scales, making his kin shine.

He'd spent his life trying to fit among his kind, trying to do what he thought was right, what a dragon *should* do. It had been a fucking waste.

"Thought you'd left us..." The red-haired elf leaned out of the skylight, facing up the slope of the roof.

Akiem narrowed his eyes.

When Zane didn't get a reply, he hitched himself out of the window and into a crouch. "Are you going to make me climb up there?"

"It's your choice." He'd be a fool to. If he slipped, he wouldn't survive the four-story drop to the street below.

Zane started to climb.

Akiem clenched his jaw. Was the elf fearless, or did he not see the danger? Of course, it was no concern of Akiem's should the elf wish to kill himself. Zane displayed an impressive command of balance, but still Akiem's fingers twitched to reach out for him. Finally, he perched on the ridge beside Akiem and brushed the dust from his hands and pants.

"I figured you'd catch me if I fell," he said, looking out at the dragons. Bayston's ambient light sparkled in his eyes.

Akiem might have, although it wouldn't have been pretty. If the elf had gone over the edge, he'd have needed to shift, and shifting took precious seconds. Akiem would have destroyed half the building trying to save him, and they both would have landed hard in a street too narrow for a dragon. "I'd appreciate it if you didn't test that theory."

Zane snorted, but his mood soon soured when he looked again at the dragons. "They're gathering."

"There's blood in the air." Akiem didn't mean it literally, though it would be true soon enough. His kin sensed an impending slaughter. Clarion would have called them back to the brood. Nightfall was almost upon the city. The lord might wait until dawn, or he'd attack at night, when the elves slept.

"You could have left us," Zane said. "Could have flown away." He swooped a hand through the air.

"Yes, I could have." Saying the truth aloud eased some of his mental wrangling. He'd saved Zane and Jevan, and now he'd save more, and those were the simplest, most perfect thoughts he'd had in years. "No matter how far you fly, there is one thing you can never escape."

Zane blinked. "Yourself."

A smile tugged at Akiem's lips. "Indeed."

This elf *saw* him. Not the Black Prince. Not the outsider dragon. He saw *him*, the truth trapped beneath layers of pretending, and all for the price of a few coins. If a few more coin should change hands, what other secrets might Zane reveal?

"Do you know where the bells are?" Akiem asked. He looked up at the jagged skyline and away from the elf, fearing his face gave away too much of these strange, shifting emotions he'd yet to understand fully. He'd been scanning the horizon, looking for the source of the earlier ringing before Zane's arrival.

"There." Zane pointed into the distance, where a spire cut into the skyline.

Akiem leaned closer to Zane, seeking a clearer view. Higher towers, all abandoned but bulky enough to impede flight, surrounded the human structure. Reaching the bells would take precise flying. One wrong flick of the wing and he'd hit those towering monuments.

"Why are you asking about the bells?" Zane asked, facing him.

Akiem adjusted his focus to the elf seated too close beside him. He should move back again, but now that he was looking, he noticed how the elf's hair held gentle waves. He'd wanted to run those locks through his fingers before, and he wanted to again now. One wayward curl had fallen over the elf's forehead. Akiem fought the urge to tuck it behind the elf's pointed ear. He hadn't cared about such little things with dragons. He'd fucked females, he'd had to else risk Mother's wrath, but it hadn't been gentle—no light touches or breathless kisses like that damn kiss in the dark room.

Zane's green eyes fixed bravely on his—challenging or questioning, Akiem wasn't sure which, perhaps both, but he had no answer.

Zane had asked something, hadn't he? But lost in Zane's exquisite beauty, he couldn't recall the question, and now the silence had stretched too thin. He wanted to kiss him. He waited for the terrible weight of guilt and shame to bury him, but none came. The need to feel Zane's mouth opening against his lips, to hear his breathing hasten, to watch desire pool in his stunning eyes, it consumed Akiem's body and mind.

Akiem blinked and turned his head away, breaking the spell. He pulled a knee up to rest his wrist on and observed the distant jeweled dragons swoop and spiral. "They'll come at night, perhaps tonight. The darkest hour will see them move through the streets as dragon. They'll take your kind from their homes and kill them. Your only advantage is that they can't fly inside your narrow city streets, but it will still be a slaughter."

Horror blanched Zane's face. He flung a glare at the circling dragons. "How do you know?"

"It's what I would have done, once."

"We need to warn them..." He looked toward the spire. "That's why you asked about the bells."

"I'll ring the bells to alert the city to the danger. It will force the dragons to launch their attack early, robbing them of the element of surprise. Elves will die, but more will escape into the lands beyond the city. They'll be safer there, among the trees."

Zane assessed Akiem as though trying to see through something. He clearly wanted to ask why Akiem was helping, and Akiem had no idea how to answer him. Perhaps it was for the many elves he'd slain over the years, but in truth, it was more for himself. He *could* change. He could do good. Saving Jevan had been the start, and now that he'd had a taste, he wanted more. So easy these thoughts came to him, without the others to smother them.

Instead of asking why, Zane asked, "Won't they burn us out?"

"Eventually."

Zane breathed in and sighed. "Fuck. You really think it'll go down that way?"

He knew dragons. "It will."

"I keep seeing the arrow and Clarion grabbing it... It shouldn't have been possible."

Akiem drew in a breath. "Do you trust Jevan?"

"With my life." Zane stiffened. "Why?"

Jevan's disgust toward Clarion had been evident after Akiem had saved him, but it could have been a lie. Perhaps something else had happened between the angry elf and the dragon lord during his time in the torture chambers. If Akiem told Zane, Zane would deny it. The elves were too close, and Akiem was dragon. It would look... forced, like he was jealous of the pair, or he hoped to drive a wedge between them. Zane trusted Jevan, and maybe that was enough. What was done was done. Knowing why Jevan had aided in killing the king would change nothing.

"He's a hard-ass," Zane explained. "He's had to be. We all have. This world is not kind to elves."

It wasn't kind to certain dragons either.

"Are there elves where you come from, across the sea?" Zane asked. "Boats used to ferry messages to us, but they stopped coming before I was born. I grew up assuming the elves had all died out."

"There are elves there." Akiem had known several, in the end. They had fought with a relentless persistence that had led to most of their deaths.

"What are they like?"

Those memories were sometimes the hardest to recall. "Prideful, stubborn, ruthless. They brought down my brood in a roundabout way." Gods, if Mother could hear him now, she'd bite off his wings. It was freeing to speak so honestly. To *believe* the words, to believe in *anything* and not be punished for the truth.

The words didn't brighten Zane, as Akiem had assumed they would. If anything, he seemed further burdened. Had Akiem said the wrong thing?

"You sound as if you admire them," he said sadly.

Akiem admired them now, but he hadn't in the past. "There's a fierceness in your kind." A passion he admired too, though he kept that admission to himself.

"We are..." Zane picked at the moss between the roof tiles, tearing tufts off. "We've forgotten what we once stood for. We were protectors. My ancestors were supposed to protect humans, and now we live among their ruins like rats. We failed in every way. We're cowards." His sharp teeth showed behind the harshly spoken words.

"A coward did not break into a dragon stronghold to save his friend."

"No." Zane smiled. "That was you." He stretched an arm behind him and twisted at his waist to face Akiem. "And I haven't thanked you enough."

A roof slate slipped beneath Zane, jolting him downward. Akiem grabbed him and held him firmly as the dislodged slate sailed on, flicked off the roof, and smashed out of sight on the street.

A moment of absolute silence followed.

Zane looked up and grinned. Gods, did he take nothing seriously?

"Theory tested," he said.

Akiem became very aware that he had Zane pulled against him, the male's hip digging into his thigh and their legs locked together. The position would have been intimate had they not been perched precariously on a rooftop. Any lower and the view of Zane looking up at him from between his legs would be similar to the one he regularly summoned and also tried to forget.

"You should go inside. Jevan will be wondering where you are." He didn't want to let him go but holding on to him didn't seem right either.

Reluctantly, he loosened his grip, and Zane shifted off him.

"Jevan left to find Arlo—my friend you stalked and terrified."

"Unintentionally terrified."

Akiem's heart lurched at Zane's quick smile, and then the elf dropped back inside the attic.

Akiem drew the air across his lips and tongue. Night tasted like dampness and cold. It also tasted of dragons. They would come soon, and the killing would begin. The night would be long. He feared for Zane and his people. Zane had been right—the elves here were different. They were not assassins or killers, fighters or protectors. They had carved a different path for themselves, straight into the belly of their enemy.

Akiem sank a hand into his pants pocket and found some coin, transferred from his old clothes by Jevan.

His gaze traveled to the open attic skylight and then back to the sky. They had some time...

He climbed back inside the dwelling and found Zane in a bedchamber, emptying his traveling bag onto a bed and sorting through what little he owned, oblivious to Akiem's presence in the doorway. His clothes wrapped him in snug layers, highlighting tight thighs and the curve of his ass. What would he look like out of those layers? His skin of ivory beneath Akiem's hands, eyes of green shining with desire, hair of fire knotted in Akiem's fingers.

Zane stiffened.

He turned his head and caught Akiem standing frozen in the doorway. His smile froze, waiting.

It was just coin. A transaction. Zane did this nightly.

Akiem stepped inside the room and closed the door behind him with a small *snick* that sounded too loud in the silence. His hand lingered on the handle; he knew when he looked up, Zane would know what he wanted and there would be no going back.

There was no shame here. Akiem needed to feel, and the elf needed coin. Simple.

He looked up to find the elf had turned toward him. He had his arms folded and an eyebrow cocked in question.

ane

THE DRAGON WAS HUNGRY. Zane had seen it in his eyes on the roof, right after he'd manufactured the fall to see if Akiem was here for the right reasons and not to see Zane dead for helping to kill the king he'd cared for. The Black Prince had caught him, proving he didn't mean them harm. The opposite, in fact. Oh, this dragon was good at hiding his desires, but Zane was better at revealing them, layer by layer by layer.

Akiem stood in front of the closed door, warring with himself. If left too long to dwell on this, he'd talk himself out of what he wanted. Maybe it would be for the best— Jevan would think so—but considering this might be their last night together, Zane was more than happy to oblige the dragon's desires, once he took that first step forward. It had to be the dragon's choice.

A mystery, this one, and pained, troubled, and tied up

tight in invisible restraints. He clung to those chains as though they defined him. His eyes burned, but not with dragonsight. *Lust*. Zane had unleashed a wildness in this black prince, and he'd be a liar if he denied that he wanted to see where that wildness led.

The dragon took one step and another. Then he was crossing the floor, coming in hot, all gold-tarnished dark eyes and black hair. Gold and black, like a summer storm breaking a too-long drought. Zane felt that heat burning him up.

Akiem halted with one final step to go, as if someone had pulled on his leash. Zane reached for his face to draw him in for a kiss, but the dragon caught his hand, twisted it, and planted two coins in Zane's palm.

Zane looked at the coins. Just two? He'd paid three before. A good thing the coin didn't matter or he might have been offended. "I'm not..."

He'd been about to say he wasn't a whore, that he'd do this without payment, but the fierceness in the dragon's eyes stalled the words on his lips. He needed this to be a service. That was how he justified fucking an elf. Without the coin, it would become personal, and Akiem didn't do personal.

Zane lifted his chin and dropped the coins into his pocket. The second his hand came away empty, Akiem struck. His warm, rough hand brushed Zane's cheek, and the other he thrust into his hair, claiming him. He pulled, and Zane answered, clashing into a kiss carried on the dragon's growl. Fuck, he hadn't been like this before. His mouth burned. His tongue invaded. Zane arched into him, opening up, surrendering to something larger and more powerful than him. Akiem closed an arm around his back and trapped him close enough to feel every inch of hardness beneath his clothes.

The sweet and tart taste of dragon tingled on Zane's tongue. The taste should have meant danger, should have scared him off like it had the elves from history. They'd have been afraid, but Zane wanted to taste more, so much more. He wanted to crawl over this damn dragon and devour every inch of him, to make him moan and undo all his restraints. Fuck Jevan's advice and that voice in his head that said this was doomed. Zane needed this. Akiem needed this. The why didn't matter. The coin didn't matter. Zane's heart ached for this tortured dragon nobody had loved. Akiem didn't need to say it; it was in his terrified touches, his fearful kisses, and the reverent way he stroked Zane's cheek.

Akiem's fingers dug into Zane's ass and hauled him so close the hard ridge in his pants nudged Zane's hip, a clear signal of his overwhelming desire. Zane rocked his hips, answering with evidence of his own raging arousal, and ran his hands up Akiem's back. The dragon trembled, but not from fear. He was holding back.

Zane tore free from the kiss and brushed his jaw against Akiem's cheek, whispering into his ear, "Tell me what you like, dragon."

His growl rumbled through Zane's chest, spilling need into Zane's eager cock. Akiem's hot, wet mouth brushed against Zane's neck, and the dragon shuddered out his obvious desire. He wanted to bite, like dragons did.

"Do it," Zane said.

His teeth clamped down, pinching the skin and sparking a barrage of pain. Zane gasped. Akiem could do more, could do worse, and the thought of walking that line between pleasure and pain had Zane's heart pounding and his thoughts emptying of everything but the feel of Akiem.

Zane cupped Akiem's cock and ground the pad of his thumb downward. The dragon gasped, freeing his teeth from Zane's neck. He sighed, breaths hot and heavy against Zane's ear. Moments ago, he'd sat on the rooftop, distant, restrained, locked behind his mask. Now he was free and in Zane's arms, his body alive and in motion.

Zane yanked at Akiem's trouser ties, loosened them, and plunged his hand inside, finding the dragon's erect cock and fitting it neatly in his grasp.

The dragon's growl bubbled again. He walked Zane backward, his mouth on Zane's, their tongues and lips giving and taking. The backs of Zane's legs nudged the bed frame, trapping him between the dragon and the bed. Akiem's pre-seed wetness soaked Zane's palm, smoothing his strokes. Zane wanted him in his mouth, inside the rest of him too. The heat of need pulsed through Zane's cock. All of him ached to be filled. Zane dropped onto the bed. Akiem shoved his knees open. A pause stilled them both in the eye of the storm. Akiem stood over Zane, lips parted, breathing hard, eyes devouring him. Zane stared back, fucking alight beneath the dragon's intense glare. In all his time on the road, of all the towns and cities he'd fucked around in, no one had looked at him in such a way.

Akiem's glare owned, and Zane's body sang with need, making him so fucking hard he couldn't think. For the first time in a long time, he wanted to feel a male inside him, to feel the power of this dragon touch him in places he hid from others.

Zane pushed up into a seated position and worked on the few buttons holding Akiem's shirt closed. After exposing his chest, Zane took a moment to admire the rack of abdominal muscles and the tight V that guided his gaze downward. He spread his hands over Akiem's chest, soaking himself in the dragon's warmth. He was so fucking hard and so damn vulnerable. Akiem's breathing raced, as did his heart. Zane fancied he could hear it thudding.

Zane traced the tip of his tongue down to Akiem's navel. The dragon's hand clamped against the back of his head, holding him, guiding him, *controlling* him. Zane licked and nipped, clutching the dragon's hips and roaming lower, until his chin brushed the tip of Akiem's erect cock, still partially restrained inside his trousers. Zane flicked his tongue over the head. Akiem twitched. His body said what he could not. His desire was alive, and Zane was happy to answer its needs. He hooked his fingers into Akiem's trousers and pulled them down, off his hips, exposing the dragon's erection.

Alumn, dragons had it where it counted, and Akiem had more than enough to keep Zane satisfied. He took him in deep between the lips, stroking the silken tip against the roof of his mouth. The dragon's shudders grew more prominent. He tasted of salt and citrus. Zane wanted more. He wanted it deeper in a way that couldn't be met like this. Zane flicked his gaze up and found Akiem watching him with a new superheated shimmer to his eyes. The idea that Akiem might take him from behind sent pleasurable twinges down his back.

Akiem's fingers speared into Zane's hair, driving him on. Zane clutched Akiem's thigh, holding himself steady, and swallowed him down, then almost freed him, using his tongue to massage the erect shaft. The dragon's open groans signaled his pleasure. Alumn, Zane wanted to pull him onto the bed and have him braced over him.

Maybe he would be open to more, if Zane were gentle.

He pulled free, smiled coyly at the dragon peering down, and unbuckled his jacket. After tearing it off, Akiem reached in and flicked open Zane's shirt buttons, his fingers precise and fast. Zane leaned back, bracing both arms against the bed while Akiem ran his hands over his upper chest and shoulders, levering the shirt over his shoulders and down his back, where it snagged, his arms still trapped in the sleeves.

Akiem lunged in, cradling Zane's head with one hand while the other danced down Zane's naked chest. The dragon's mouth and tongue did wonderful things to Zane's neck before trailing lower, over his collarbone. Zane let his head fall back and then the rest of him. Akiem was right where he wanted him, towering above Zane, a knee braced on the bed beside Zane's hip, his shirt open, his cock exposed, his hair and eyes wild.

Akiem's hand went to the bulge in Zane's pants, the movement so sudden Zane flinched. Fear widened Akiem's eyes. He was going to bolt. Before he could lose himself in those thoughts, Zane covered his hand with his own and pushed down while bringing his hips up to meet the friction, showing Akiem how much he desired his hand there. How all of him wanted to be there, sprawled beneath a dragon, laid out for him to explore.

The fear flickered and snuffed out, and then Akiem scooped an arm under Zane's lower back and lifted him higher on the bed. His mouth was a hot, wet tease on Zane's hip, his tongue swirling. Zane looked down himself to find the dragon engrossed by the small tattoo he'd found there. Akiem flicked his golden eyes up, lashes fluttering. Zane smiled and lifted a hand, showing him the tattoo's partner on his little finger.

The dragon prowled up Zane's body, his silken black hair tickling Zane's navel, and then Akiem gently took Zane's hand and slipped the tattooed little finger between his lips. Warm, tight wetness rode over the knuckle, and Akiem's golden eyes burned, watching for a reaction.

"Fuck..." Zane panted. The tight, wet pressure promised pleasure for other parts of his body currently throbbing uncomfortably. Akiem let the finger and hand fall free. He reached down between them, cupped Zane's raging erection, and brought his mouth down to tease Zane's nipple.

Zane tipped his head back. Every touch and every tease had him wired to blow. And now Akiem was plastered against him, his chest against Zane's, his hip pushed in, and his cock trapped between them, in the dip of Zane's waist. It was all too much and too little. He wanted more, wanted Akiem arched over him, his cock deep inside. He clenched his ass just thinking of the fullness.

Zane cupped Akiem's face, making him look. "Will you fuck me?"

The dragon's stunning eyes darted, his body going rigid. "I..."

Zane pressed a finger to his lips. "It's all right. You don't have to."

"No, I..." He swallowed. "I want to. I just..."

Did he not know how, or was some other thing stopping him? Something more to do with how he trembled, restraining himself.

Akiem jerked his head up. His glare shot to the window, his eyes narrowed. Then he was moving off the bed and realigning his clothes, tucking himself away behind buttons, belts, and ties.

Zane feared he'd lost him again, but the look he threw over his shoulder at the window had nothing to do with sex and everything to do with war.

"It's begun."

Zane hastily dressed himself, pushing the ache of loss away. When he stood, Akiem was in front of him, too close. Longing and regret sizzled between them. For a creature who hid his feelings, he had a great deal of them crossing his face.

"Go," Zane said, hating the word.

Akiem opened the door and was gone in a flurry of black hair. His leaving struck a fragile, untested part of Zane. Akiem was confronting danger *for elves*. Nobody would thank him—nobody even knew him—yet still he fought for Zane's people. He fought more than the elves did. A dragon was fighting for elves. It was... impossible—a miracle, even.

Zane dashed out the door and leaned against the landing rail, looking up toward the attic room, where the sound of Akiem's boots struck the floorboards. "Akiem?"

Moments passed in silence.

Akiem peered over the banister above, his loose hair spilling around his face. "Yes, elf?"

Shit, now he had to speak and admit too much. "Will you return?"

"If there is anything left to return to."

"Come back. For me."

The dragon's eyes widened. Too much, he'd said too much, revealed too much, like maybe he wanted Akiem for more reasons than coin.

"You paid, and our session isn't over." He tacked on a cheap smile, a wriggling sense of guilt eating him up inside, because it was a damn lie. Akiem made Zane want to be better, to do good, *for him,* for the dragon who cared. Akiem gave him hope. He made him see the good in the world and made him want to do good. He had to come back. They were only just beginning.

The dragon nodded curtly and disappeared.

Zane winced at his foolishness. What if the coin meant Akiem was using him for sex and nothing more?

The audible snick of the attic window closing reached Zane's ears.

He returned to his room, where the ruffled bed mocked him. A shudder tracked through him. Jevan was right. Zane was falling for Akiem and falling hard. A few coins in his pocket had never felt heavier. He didn't do love. Not since Oldport. Not since he'd had his affections thrown back in his face and almost gotten himself and Jevan killed over so-called love. He'd been used then, like Akiem was using him now. The dragon paid for sex. He wasn't buying Zane's fucking love.

Zane wandered to the window. Things would be easier if he could stop his foolish heart from loving those who didn't love him in return.

Maybe Akiem wouldn't return, solving all of Zane's problems.

A roar shattered the night, so loud it shook the window glass.

Akiem.

The sky was black. Akiem had vanished into the darkness blanketing the city, hoping to save it. That was why Zane's wretched heart had fallen for him. Even after everything he'd been through, when nobody else cared, Akiem fought on. Akiem made cowards of them all.

~

THE BELLS RANG OUT SHORTLY after. It wasn't like the sound that had woken them that morning. The bells clanged out of tune and order; they sounded as though the city had come to life and screamed its alarm.

It started slow, like nothing had changed, and Zane hoped Akiem was wrong. Then the sky above parts of Bayston began to glow, and soon, embers fizzed in the dark, like darting stars. The screams started right after. Word was spreading quicker than the fire. Dragons had attacked. More and more elves spilled from the north, filling the streets, carrying bags and the young. Some stumbled, painted in ash. Others ran blindly.

Zane stumbled out onto the street and into a steady stream of elves. They carried with them a malaise of smoke and ash and death.

It didn't seem real.

He'd started this.

Elves would die, the city would burn, and it was his fault.

Jevan and Arlo fought through the flowing crowd. Zane handed Jevan's bag over. "Tell anyone who will listen to head for the trees. They'll be safe there. I'll meet you by the old cable bridge at dawn."

The bridge was on the outside of inhabited Bayston but within the old city limits.

Arlo's gaze darted. "Can't I stay with you?"

"No. I'm going north to help others." *Toward the fires.*

A dragon sailed above the buildings, screaming its presence. Its scales shone. The firepit low in its throat glowed. The beast banked, coming back around. Akiem had said they wouldn't fly into the city, but they didn't need to. They had fire to clear the streets for them.

Zane shoved Arlo. "Go! Go now!"

The beast's firepit glowed hotter. A building blocked Zane's view, but he heard the screams. The crowd broke into a run, buffeting him.

"C'mon." Jevan grabbed Arlo. "Stick close!"

A wave of heat and light poured into the street from above. The noise *consumed*. Zane flung himself away, burying his face under his arm and against the road. Furnace-like heat washed over his back, so hot it burned his throat.

He'd die here, in the street, like thousands of others. Alumn hadn't spared him in the past for some grand gesture. It had all been for nothing.

He wished he'd told Akiem the truth, fuck whatever that meant. The coin was bullshit. They'd both needed to hear it, and now he'd never know.

The flame ended as abruptly as it had come, leaving Zane's head full of pounding and screaming.

He took a breath. Ashes and embers stung his tongue. He coughed, stirring up clouds of ash. His vision blurred, smudging the fires orange against a background of gray. Screams. Someone running. Flames tore at a figure, eating him from the outside in. Zane launched off his back foot, ripped off his jacket, and slammed into the burning male, knocking him down. He got the jacket around him and patted it down, over and over. Fire tried to leap up Zane's arms and lick at his hair, but eventually, it snuffed out.

He tasted burned flesh.

The male beneath him wasn't moving.

A glance at his face, at his shriveled lips, missing cheek, and sunken eyes said enough.

Zane scrabbled off him, retching at the stench of burned skin and hair. There were others burned and fallen, dead in the street, their clothes still ablaze. He choked on ash and stumbled. So many dead in seconds. It could have been him. So many…

"Zane!"

Zane snapped his head up at Jevan's shout.

Arlo wasn't with him.

Zane searched the faces of the dead around him.

"He ran!" Jevan called.

Arlo had run. That was good. Zane looked up. The sky glowed with embers.

"Go," he called back to Jev. "The bridge. Dawn."

A dragon call filled the streets. It swooped in low, pulled up, and landed on a nearby rooftop. The downdraft from its wings whipped up a storm of ash and fire.

Zane brought his arm up to guard against the burning dust. His people scattered in every direction.

"South!" he yelled. "The forests, go south!" He snagged an elfling running at full tilt and turned him around, shoving him away from the flames. "South, to the woods! Go!"

He bolted, and in moments, clouds of ash ate him up.

Zane stumbled into a run, heading north to where flames clawed at the sky and steering those he came across in the right direction.

More dragons filled the sky, their calls endless. More dead lay on the street, their remains smoldering. The smell coated his throat and clung to his lungs.

He'd done this. He and Jevan. If they hadn't gone, if Jev's arrow had hit Clarion instead…

He had to save them all.

A blue-scaled dragon prowled the narrow street ahead.

Blood dripped from its jaws, leaving a river of red in the gutters. Zane ducked into the smoldering remains of a house and found a dozen pairs of elven eyes watching him —and the rheumy eyes of an elf he knew well.

Killian either didn't recognize Zane or didn't care. He huddled near the front of the group, hands in his lap, rocking back and forth, muttering prayers to Alumn. His world had been turned on its head, and it was partly his fault.

Zane pressed a finger to his lips, signaling for them to be quiet, and shrank down in the debris.

Claws clicked against the road.

Growls bubbled so close they trembled through Zane's bones.

Alumn, make it move on.

The beast huffed close by, upsetting the air with more dust and ash. Zane met the frightened gazes of those looking on. Twelve lives, like the twelve he'd failed to save from Clarion. These weren't all children, but it didn't matter. A life was a life.

He could make a difference here, make things right.

That knowledge burned beneath his skin and through his veins, just like the fire burning the city down around them.

If Zane had fired his arrow sooner, Clarion would be dead.

There would be no bodies burning in the street.

No elven flesh sizzling.

No young'uns screaming for their mammas.

Killian bolted from safety and ran past Zane, fleeing into the street, his white and gray robes flailing.

There was a breathless moment when it seemed he might make it, and then the dragon plucked the elder off the street in his jaws, threw its head back, and swallowed. A growl burbled up its throat. It swung its head around and stared straight into the sanctuary.

Zane burst from the building and dashed under the dragon's nose. The beast reared and loosed a startled squawk. Zane glanced back. Fuck, it was huge, with a jagged crown of uneven bone.

Zane bolted over fallen blocks and slowed once the street had opened some. The beast looked on. Its glare narrowed on Zane, but it was still too close to the house. He needed to draw it farther away from the others.

Zane waved his arms above his head. "C'mon then, dragon…"

He backed up, stumbling over fallen blocks but staying upright.

The dragon saw its chance, lifted its head, rippled its lips, and started forward.

The twelve in the house would live. Maybe Zane would not. He was oddly okay with that.

"You want me!" He threw his arms wide. "Come get me."

Between one blink and the next, a wall of black plowed into the blue, thrusting claws into its side and tearing the blue clean off the street. Vast black wings blasted open, yanking the dragon's arrow-like trajectory up short. Using the sudden deceleration, the black released the blue and tossed it into the base of a tower.

Debris rained down. The tower groaned and buckled but stayed upright. As the dust settled, the blue stumbled from within the hole its impact had created.

The black lunged and crushed the blue's skull between his jaws, as if its death were no more troublesome than cracking an egg.

The black turned its head. Golden eyes locked on Zane. It prowled forward.

Akiem.

Zane staggered out of the debris.

Something, maybe a plank of wood, bounced off Akiem's neck. He pulled up and growled at the tiny figure. Just an elfling. He'd been hiding in the building with the others.

"Don't!" Zane stumbled forward. "Don't... it's all right." To the boy, he said, "He won't hurt you. He's..." What was Akiem? "He's with us." Zane looked up at Akiem, not needing to say a word. This close, with Zane standing almost beneath him, Akiem appeared as tall as a high-rise and as wide as a street, but he ducked his head and backed off.

The others emerged from their hiding place, warily watching the black dragon.

"Trust me. Trust him..." Zane waved them out. "You need to get out of the city."

Ash-stained faces blinked at him.

"Then what?" a female asked. Beneath all the ash and dirt, she wore the clothes of those with more coin than Zane.

"Worry about the rest tomorrow, eh?" he suggested, trying to smile.

Another dragon, circling above, roared.

Akiem looked up and bared his teeth. He spread his wings, stretching the dark canopy over Zane and the others, but the other dragon had already seen. It landed atop a building and crawled down the façade, dislodging bricks under its claws.

Akiem galloped forward and slammed his crown into the beast's side before it could balance itself on the street.

The dragons struck the building, taking out half its foundation supports. The heavy top floors swayed.

"Get back!" Zane shoved and pulled them away from the chaos.

Thunderous tremors and hot air blasted against his back. Dust scratched his throat. He turned, coughing like the others, and saw wings thrashing and teeth flashing in the dust cloud. Akiem unleashed his fire, painting his prey in liquid purple fire. Before the other dragon could recover, Akiem buried his teeth in its throat and ripped out a mouthful of muscle, scale, and blood.

When he whirled and stalked back toward Zane, the elves huddled behind him whimpered at the sight. Zane couldn't blame them. Blood and flesh dripped from Akiem's jaws. His eyes blazed their fury. There were bigger dragons, brighter dragons, louder dragons, but Zane could believe there were few as vicious.

Akiem lowered his head, pressing his belly to the ground. He made a gentle noise, part snort, part purr, and waited for something. Zane blinked. Was he suggesting they... climb on?

"You er... you want us to..." He frowned, struggling with the idea. "Get on?"

The dragon huffed.

Climb a dragon. *Ride* a dragon? Ride *that* dragon?

The young'un who'd thrown the makeshift spear rushed past Zane. Akiem lowered a wing, pressing as much of his body as he could against the ground. The elf scrambled up the wing's leading edge and clambered to where Akiem's long neck met his shoulders.

"You all wanna live?" he called. "Get on!"

Wasn't that supposed to be Zane's line?

The rest scrambled up the wing and nestled in place,

Zane the last to climb on. The wing alone felt all kinds of wrong beneath Zane's hands—tough and rough, like the scales latticed up his back. Up close, he saw the scars. Missing scales too. So many dislodged and torn.

Akiem lifted his head. Zane's stomach dropped. He fell forward and hugged a scale the same size as him. This was fine. It was all fine. The world tipped and swayed. Heat soaked into Zane's body. Akiem climbed over the rubble and circled back. Akiem looked up. The orange-tinted night sky was clear of dragons. If they met one in the air, what would happen then? Zane dug his fingers between the scales and clung on.

Akiem beat his wings and thundered forward. The wind tore at Zane, trying to pull him off. He hugged the dragon, pressing himself so close nothing could get between them, and prayed to Alumn he survived what came next.

Akiem landed somewhere along the coast, outside the city limit where the forest met the sea. Other elves had already gathered on the beach. They scattered when Akiem landed but watched from among the trees as he delivered his cargo of elves.

Zane spilled off and fell to his knees. It wasn't the flight, although that might have been enough to drop him to his knees. It was what he'd seen when Akiem had carried them into the air. All of Bayston was ablaze.

Hundreds dead. Maybe thousands.

Zane fell onto a hand. His lungs wouldn't work, and his throat burned. His body was shutting down. He smelled smoke and blood and burned flesh. There were elves close by, watching him, watching Akiem, and none of them knew Zane was partly responsible for this, all because he and Jev had tried to do the right thing.

He didn't deserve to live.

A warm hand settled between his shoulders.

Zane sensed the great weight of dragon, even in his human form. He'd saved them. He'd killed for them. He'd done more for elves than Zane ever had.

Alumn, Zane was a coward. A selfish, shallow coward.

Akiem's hand burned against his back.

Zane's lungs burned too. He clutched his chest.

"Breathe," Akiem said, as if it were that simple.

"I killed them." The words came out torn. His throat burned. He could still taste the dead. His gut heaved, retching up nothing.

"Clarion killed them."

Tears blurred his vision. He lifted his head and saw the elves along the shoreline, some wounded, most crying, and others sitting on rocks, staring out to sea.

"Alumn, why? Why did this happen?" he asked. He'd always been good, done good, tried to do good, tried to fight for good. Why this?

"So many, Akiem..."

Akiem's hand slid from his back to his shoulder. It felt solid and strong, like nothing could bend or break him. Zane knew that wasn't true, because someone had broken him, but he'd survived. He'd turned it all around, making himself good despite everything that said he shouldn't be. Akiem was different. Akiem was better than them. Akiem was a fucking miracle.

Zane straightened and turned toward the touch. Akiem stood there, his clothes disheveled, his hair knotted, his face a mask of nothing, until the smallest smile tucked into his cheek. It was too much. Zane threw his arms around Akiem and reeled him in. Akiem instantly stiffened, but Zane buried his head against his shoulder, *needing* his strength, his warmth. Whatever the cost for this, he'd pay it. He just needed to *feel*.

CHAPTER 21

kiem

The elf was embracing him.

Akiem's heart skipped. His breathing stuttered. He wanted to embrace him back but didn't know what it would mean if he did. It was different here, on this beach with the ocean at his back and the city ablaze. It had become *personal*.

He bowed his head, breathing in the smell of elf and filtering out the stench of war. He'd seen him on that street, goading a dragon to chase him. At first, Akiem had raged over Zane doing yet another stupid thing, and then he'd spotted the elves hiding in the ruined building and the rage had turned from an inferno to icy cold. The topaz dragon would have killed his elf.

Zane fisted Akiem's shirt. Zane wasn't thinking. He was emotional from what he'd witnessed. That was all.

Akiem wrapped his arms around him, feeling him sigh

and melt against him. Strange, how he fit so seamlessly in Akiem's arms. For a moment, Akiem forgot they were on a beach, with dozens of curious elves watching them. He listened to the waves lapping against the rocks, listened to elves murmuring and the *thud-thud* of Zane's heart as it slowed. The elf just needed someone, anyone, to hold. Akiem was happy to provide comfort, even if it didn't last.

Zane pulled free, and without looking at Akiem, he clambered over the rocks, back up the beach. Akiem watched him go, feeling oddly cold as he stood alone.

"Thank you."

"What?" He hadn't even seen the older female elf approach or the boy huddled beside her, the same boy who had thrown a stick at him as dragon.

"You're the Black Prince," she said, her eyes soft and wet with tears.

He blinked at her and the elfling.

"Thank you for saving us," she said again, as though he might not have heard her the first time.

After bowing her head in respect, she and the boy made their awkward walk back over the rocks to the tree line, where her kin waited, each one looking at Akiem with the same awe in their eyes.

An uncomfortable twisting inside made Akiem uneasy.

Following her path, he approached them. "I don't deserve thanks, not from any of you."

They blinked bright elven eyes at him, disbelieving his words. Damn elves.

With a frustrated growl, he moved on, seeking a quiet place where he could unpack everything that had happened and bury it somewhere in his mind all over again. He was surprised to find Zane tending the wounded instead. His senses had led him back to the elf, the dragon in him seeking him out.

Akiem watched from a distance as Zane helped those he could, but Zane's hands shook, and more than once he needed to reach for a tree to keep himself upright. When he took off, away from the makeshift encampment, Akiem followed.

"No fires." Akiem grumbled, passing by a pair of elves attempting to start one. "Not yet."

Dragons would be watching for smoke. It was bad enough they were all huddled together along the shoreline.

He found Zane tucked against a tree, his elbow propped on a bent knee, his face buried in his hand.

The elf's shoulders shook. He was... crying. Zane stared into the darkness between the trees. Diamond-like tears glistened on the male's filthy face. Akiem silenced all thoughts that demanded he leave Zane there. He ached to go to him, to sit beside him. Nothing more, nothing less. Just company.

The elven woman had thanked him, but she did not know who Akiem really was.

He could not care for this elf.

His place was not among them.

He turned away, about to disappear into the night.

"Stay," Zane croaked.

Akiem sighed. He turned back and settled against the tree, tucked among the roots like Zane beside him. After a short time, the elf laid his head against Akiem's shoulder. His breathing slowed shortly after as sleep finally relieved him of the horrors he'd seen.

Akiem stared into the trees, watching for dragons, for threats, for anything that might threaten to steal away his elf. He was insane to feel such things, but denying it didn't make the feelings stop. The dragon in him knew the truth.

Were you looking for someone?

Come back. For me.

Akiem squeezed his eyes closed.

He cared for Zane in a way he hadn't allowed himself to care for anything else in his entire wretched life, and that truth terrified him. Caring made him vulnerable, made him prey. Caring was not the dragon way.

He looped an arm around Zane's shoulder as he slept and tucked him under his chin. Akiem was done with the dragon way. Whatever happened, with the elf or not, he'd find his own way going forward. The right way.

~

"Hey."

Akiem blinked awake and fell straight into Zane's smiling eyes. Shafts of sunlight streamed through the tree canopy. It was morning. He hadn't dreamed, but he almost believed this to be unreal. Except, the more reality sharpened everything around him, the more he noticed Zane's hair was matted and bloody, and he still smelled like ash.

Zane offered his hand. Akiem took it and let the elf pull him to his feet. Zane's grip lingered on his hand a moment too long before letting go, or perhaps that was wishful thinking.

"You snore," Zane said.

"I—what?"

"Just a little." Zane showed him the smallest gap between his finger and thumb. His cheeks still wore the tracks of his tears from the previous night, although he'd smudged much of them away. His smile was bright, like the morning Akiem had found himself in.

Akiem blinked at him, words suddenly difficult. He should tell him how he admired that smile, but in the morning light, speaking such things seemed whimsical and foolish.

"We have to go back." Zane started to make his way through the brush. "I told Jevan I'd meet him at the cable bridge. He'll be there. He might have Arlo with him."

Akiem knew of the cable bridge. It was miles within the city. "It's not safe."

"I can't leave them there."

Akiem didn't see why not. Jevan was resourceful. He'd make his way out and bring Arlo with him.

"Can you er... can you, yah know, fly me in there?"

Akiem stopped.

Zane marched on a few strides before realizing Akiem wasn't following. He sighed and turned. "Honestly, I don't relish the idea either. I spent much of my first flight with my eyes closed, praying to Alumn, but I gave Jev my word. I have to go back, so I either spend the day walking back, or"—he gestured at Akiem—"you can get your dragon on and we'll be there and back in an hour."

"'Get my dragon on'?"

He waved the same hand he'd gestured with and frowned at the ground. "Yah know, shift." He dragged a hand down his chin, hiding a wince.

Honestly, Akiem would have already said yes, but he was rather enjoying watching someone usually so confident stumble over his words.

"It's not easy, carrying an elf." He stepped closer. "You're not particularly streamlined. I must constantly adjust to keep from tipping you off. My speed is also hampered. Too fast and you won't be able to breathe. My range of movement is limited—"

Zane rolled his eyes and dug into his pocket. "I'll pay."

At the sight of the coin, Akiem lost his smile. He brushed by the elf and continued toward a clearing with enough room to shift. "Keep your money, elf. I don't shift for coin."

"What's that supposed to mean?"

He hadn't intended to rile him up, but his tone had carried an edge to it. "Nothing."

"*Nothing?*" he said, mocking Akiem's voice. "Wait a second."

They reached the clearing. Akiem stepped into the sun, already imagining warm rays on his black scales. The elf appeared in the corner of his eye.

"I'm not a whore." Zane threw a collection of coins at Akiem's feet. They shone in the bed of pre-autumnal leaves. All the coins Akiem had paid him. "I don't take coin for sexual favors." Zane moved around to face him. His cheek twitched. "I should have told you, but you needed the coin to make it happen, so I let it go."

He'd lied and taken coin anyway? How was that any better?

"The distance," Zane explained.

Akiem frowned.

"You needed the distance to make it impersonal, because I'm elf and you're dragon and that's the way things are. If I hadn't accepted the coin, you wouldn't have gone through with it."

No, he wouldn't have. "You don't take coin from dragons for sex?"

Yet twice he'd taken coins from Akiem. What was he supposed to make of that?

"No. And I don't fuck dragons as a rule. You were—"

"You only got to your knees to pleasure a dragon for your friend. I understand." Akiem stepped around him and headed into the open area. Better to be dragon where all this emotional baggage meant nothing. He flexed the mental muscles, freeing the shift. "Stay back, elf."

"I'm sorry, okay?" Zane called.

"No," he replied too softly for Zane to hear. It was not okay, because if the coin meant nothing, what did? Was any of it real? Did Zane want those things, or had he been fucking with Akiem all along? The first time, yes, to save his friend. But earlier, before the city fell, what had that been for, if not to save his friend? Just for fun? Out of pity because he knew Akiem's past?

"Akiem? You're pissed. I see that. Maybe flying isn't... such a good idea. I can walk. It's... it's fine. I'll just walk..." He mumbled the last words.

"Scared I might drop you?" Akiem called back.

The shift tore through him. When he next turned to look at the tiny elf, he towered over him as dragon. Bringing his head in low, he pinned Zane beneath his glare and sighed through his nose, upsetting his flame-red hair and the leaves around him. His tiny elf looked angry—or perhaps frustrated. It was difficult to tell through dragon eyes.

Zane sighed back. He pursed his lips and rested a hand on a hip. "You've gotten the wrong idea, and I can't say it's not entirely my fault." Looking up, his green eyes widened some, drinking in the sight of dragon. "You're real big as dragon, by the way, but curiously easier to talk to."

Akiem huffed again and lifted his head so as not to crowd him.

"All right, fine," Zane growled.

A chuckle tried to rumble up Akiem's throat. So little, so angry, so elf.

"I don't usually do this," Zane continued. "Get *involved*. It's not how I play things. I can't, else I'd leave a piece of me in every place I visited until there was nothing left." He stalled, restless on his feet again. "I'm shit at this. You're shit at feelings too. Half the time, I think you want to eat me, and not in a good way, and the rest you look at me like... like we're equal. I'm getting mixed signals all over the place. Maybe you still need the damn coin, I don't know, but if you do, I'm not taking any more, so we're done. You can buy your elf-kink elsewhere."

Akiem bared his teeth. A hint of a growl began low in his throat, but it was enough.

"Shit. Fine. I wasn't straight with you, but it wasn't all an act. Most of it wasn't, actually." His confession slowed. "I don't pretend to know what's happening here, between us—if there is anything between us, and that's a big *if*. You're a dragon, for fuck's sake." He swept a hand at Akiem. "I've never done dragons. I don't do dragons. You're all selfish, self-righteous, vicious assholes." He puffed out a breath. "All but you."

Akiem chuffed a laugh. What an unexpected pleasure it was to see Zane flustered. He hadn't been sure anything could unsettle him, but evidently real *feelings* did. Perhaps they had that in common, if nothing else. Every word Zane had spoken was true, and Akiem delighted in hearing it, because it meant Zane was having as hard a time with this whole relationship as Akiem was.

Zane winced. "I didn't want to hurt you, okay? I didn't set out to do that. It was meant to be a simple seduction and I'd be gone. But I hurt you, and for that, I am truly sorry. You didn't deserve it, no matter what you seem to think. You have more than proven yourself as good. I'm the prick here."

Akiem growled again, but this time, when he brought his head in low, he brushed his chin against the ground, as close to Zane as he could get without knocking him over. The position was subservient, but Zane couldn't know that, making it safe. He blinked at the elf, almost crossing his eyes to see him standing at the end of his nose. He seemed sad again, and that wasn't right. Zane wasn't made for sadness.

"So, after we've met up with Jevan, can we maybe deal with some of this shit between us? No coins. Just you and me and the truth?" He placed a tiny hand on Akiem's nose. The touch was warm and painfully gentle. "I owe you that."

The truth? He wasn't sure he knew what the truth was, but he was beginning to understand some of it. The only things that had felt right, felt true, were saving the elves and being with Zane.

Akiem nuzzled closer, prompting Zane to bring his other hand around and place it by the first. He spread his fingers, and Akiem briefly closed his eyes. Yes, things were more simple as dragon. He liked this elf's touches. More than liked them. More than liked him too.

Zane rubbed his scales, and a purr strummed at the back of Akiem's throat.

"You like that, huh? *The big-ass angry dragon likes nose scratches...*" He scratched some more, working his hands around and between scales.

Akiem nudged, almost knocking him off his feet. He laughed. Gods, that laughter was free and rich and delicious—a fine thing to hear.

Zane stepped back and gave Akiem a strange, sidelong

glare, his smile climbing. "We should have tried talking like this before, as dragon, I mean."

The elf hadn't been ready before. Rising a little, Akiem brought his wing ridge down and waited as Zane climbed on.

With the elf safely tucked in, he took to the air, skimming the trees with his belly, keeping low to avoid breaking the horizon line.

Were you looking for someone?

He had been. Now he both feared and hoped he'd been looking for Zane, and perhaps he was ready to discover what that meant.

CHAPTER 22

ane

OVER THE YEARS, most of the cable bridge had collapsed. Its towers leaned in, and the old cables had frayed in places and drooped. It couldn't be crossed but made for the perfect landmark.

Akiem landed gently, obviously for the benefit of his passenger.

Zane clambered off, grateful to be on solid ground, and patted the ridge of Akiem's wing, signaling he was clear. The dragon gracefully rose to his full height and scanned the nearby broken buildings, long overgrown with trees and brush. The place was more wild than Zane recalled, meaning locating Jevan might take some time. Hopefully, he'd seen them fly in.

"I'll go look for him."

Akiem barely spared him a glance. His attention stayed dutifully locked on the sky.

Zane climbed over mounds of crumbled concrete and through the brush, heading for the river. He'd said a few things back in the forest clearing—maybe said too much—but after everything Akiem had done, it was only right. After waking that morning, alarmingly content in the dragon's lap a few personal words didn't seem like such a big deal.

He'd needed Akiem last night, and the dragon had been there.

If Zane hadn't cared before, he more than cared now. He cared that Akiem should see himself for the good person he was, not a monster. He cared that Akiem deserved someone, because he was so damn alone, and Zane knew what being alone felt like. He cared that nobody should touch Akiem in a way he didn't want ever again. If Zane were dragon, he'd make that happen, but he was elf. An elf wasn't enough in a world ruled by dragons, but he'd try to make it mean something, if Akiem would have him.

He'd talk with Akiem later, male to male, without trying to seduce him. Zane chuckled at the thought. It should be easy, *just talking*, but Akiem had no idea how tempting he was. All that restrained power and the way he softened beneath Zane's touch, while other parts of him hardened... the dragon had no idea how he turned Zane's thoughts upside down. If he knew how easily Zane had fallen for him, he'd be dangerous.

They'd just talk.

Once Jevan and Arlo were safe. Once this was over.

"Zane..."

His name pulled him up short. Jevan crouched among the brush, blending in perfectly with the greens and browns. He appeared unharmed, although ash-covered and wide-eyed.

Zane crouched beside him. "Is Arlo with you?"

"No, I haven't seen him. Where's Akiem?"

"Near. He'll take us—"

"We have to leave. Now." Jevan grabbed Zane's arm and pulled him along behind him, toward the broken bridge and away from Akiem.

"Jevan, stop." Zane yanked his arm free. "Akiem will carry us out of here. If we just—"

Jevan rounded on him. "Clarion is here."

"*What?*" Zane stepped closer to the brush, hoping to camouflage his outline from above. Clarion had to be above. Alumn, if Clarion was here, he had to warn Akiem. "Where?"

"I don't know. He was here and then when he saw the Black Prince, he left."

Something in Jevan's tone, and in his gaze too, set Zane's heart thumping. He stared too hard at Zane. Was this because of Akiem?

"Jevan..." he whispered. "We have to get back to Akiem. He'll carry us out of here. We can't fight Clarion."

Jevan closed his eyes. He raised a hand and rubbed his forehead. The locket dangled from his hand. "Alumn, I just wanted this to end."

This didn't make any sense. How had Clarion known they'd be meeting here? "Why is Clarion here? Did you... speak with him?"

Jevan dropped his hand, revealing his pained expression. "This is all my fault."

The things he'd seen last night had hit him hard. Zane squeezed his shoulder. "We just need to get out of here, all right? Follow me."

"I can't. We can't. Clarion... He knows Akiem is here. He wanted you, but... when he saw the dragon fly in, I guess he changed his mind."

Zane dropped his hand. Jevan had been speaking with Clarion, and he'd told the new king about this meeting? Why? When? "You're not making any sense. How is Clarion here?"

"It's better this way. He said it was inevitable. Your dragon... I mean... he said it would always end like this."

"Jevan, you're in shock. Trust me, Akiem won't hurt us. Just follow me and we'll be out of here—"

"He's not going anywhere." Lord Clarion's voice carried far in the quiet. "Isn't that right, Jevan?"

Zane turned slowly, dropping his hands to his daggers. The dragon stood beside a dead tree, as human, his white shirt and hair spotless and too perfect against the ragged elf he clutched against his chest, blade at his throat.

Arlo.

Blood had dried on his chin from his split lip. His right eye was swollen.

"How lucky I was to find this one in the rubble, squealing about knowing the two elves who have eluded me."

Zane held out a hand, trying to calm him and the situation. "Don't hurt him. He hasn't done anything."

"And his innocence matters because...?"

"What do you want? You want me? Is that it? Let him go." Zane plucked his daggers free and tossed them in the dirt.

Arlo's eyes widened.

"Take me." Akiem would be nearby. He'd hear this. He'd come. He always saved them. Zane just had to buy time.

"It's funny"—the lord grinned—"how you believe you have any power here."

He pulled the blade across Arlo's throat, opening a bloody curve, and then kicked Arlo forward. Zane caught him and fell with him to his knees. Arlo clawed at his throat, mouth opening and closing, fighting to breathe. He convulsed, almost bucking out of Zane's grip.

"I've got you..." Zane hissed, holding him tight. "I've got you, okay?" Panic shattered Zane's thoughts. He forgot Clarion, and Jevan, and Akiem. "Arlo, it's going to be okay..."

But Arlo's writhing slowed until he fell still in Zane's arms, his eyes open.

It happened so fast. It wasn't right.

"You son of a—" Zane sprang off the ground, lunging for Clarion.

The dragon swung a fist. Pain exploded across Zane's jaw, slamming him facedown into the ground.

Too strong. Didn't matter. Zane got his hands under him and pushed up. Steely fingers grabbed him, rolled him, and then Clarion's fist was on his chest, pinning him down.

"I asked Jevan, once, why he didn't tell you his secret—"

Jevan... what? Zane shoved, but the dragon's arm was an immovable steel rod. He grabbed Clarion instead, trying to force him off. He didn't move. For all his human appearance, he was dragon and a hundred times bigger than the man pinning him down. Zane couldn't fight him, but he'd damn well die trying.

"I see now," Clarion said. "You think you're good-hearted." The dragon leaned in. "Your friend thought the same about himself too, but even the good ones can be turned. It just takes the right motivation."

Zane rolled his tongue and spat.

Saliva dashed Clarion's cheek. The lord used a cuff to wipe it clean. "He was Luceran's spy before he was mine. Didn't tell you that, did he?"

No, that wasn't true. Clarion was full of shit. Zane had known Jevan for years. He couldn't be a dragon's spy. He was Jevan. Jevan *despised* dragons.

"A little persuasion applied to the right pressure points, and his arrow found its mark."

Zane didn't want to look for Jevan, didn't want to find him standing behind Clarion, not moving to help, not denying anything Clarion said. But he did look, and there Jevan was, his face haunted. Alumn, Clarion was right. Jevan had killed the king and started a war, and he'd done it for Clarion.

"Why?" Zane asked.

Jevan's hand tightened around the locket.

Clarion must have tortured him to make him do this. He wouldn't have betrayed his kin willingly. He'd never endanger so many elven lives. Jevan was better than this. There was no way Zane would let a dragon come between them.

Clarion sighed. "You're all startlingly easy to manipulate."

Zane bared his teeth. "One day, an elf will cut your throat from ear to ear and end your wretched life, dragon."

"It won't be you." He pulled him forward, face to face.

Zane gritted his teeth and tore at the arm, but he could no more shove the dragon off than he could move a boulder.

Clarion slammed Zane down. Sparks exploded through Zane's skull and burst in front of his eyes. It didn't hurt so much as rip the world away, making space for a sudden darkness to rush in. Zane clutched his head. The dragon's weight on his chest had vanished. He tried to roll, to stand, but he couldn't see, could barely breathe. The sounds of scuffling tried to pull him back from the edge of unconsciousness, but Alumn, the heat in his head thumped too heavily, bleeding its way out of his skull and down the back of his neck.

Zane rolled onto his front and dug his fingers into the cool dirt. "Akiem...?" he whispered.

The world was falling away and taking him with it.

A new growl rumbled through the air, followed by four glorious words, "These elves are mine."

Akiem.

That final thought chased Zane into the dark.

HE SMELLED the sea and dragon and ash, and then rain. Its patter gently lured him back to consciousness. Pain throbbed down his neck and tried to empty his guts, but as he hadn't eaten in what felt like forever, he was spared that indignity.

Alumn, why was it so cold?

"Hello, elf."

Akiem crouched beside him, an arm draped over his knee. Dark brows pinched together, giving Zane the impression that someone was in trouble. Oh right, that someone was him. He'd needed saving. Again. He'd have been fucking embarrassed if everything hadn't hurt so much.

"Jevan...?" Speaking split his head open. "Gah." He fingered down the back of his skull and found dried blood knotting his hair.

Akiem's lips turned down. "I don't know." As he rose, he winced and tried to hide it by clamping an arm against his waist. The fresh metallic scent in the air wasn't from wet blades—Zane had lost his. Akiem was bleeding.

"You're hurt."

"It's nothing."

Of course he'd say that. Akiem drifted toward a nearby tree trunk and gingerly lowered himself between its roots. The wound was bad enough to impede his movement.

"Did you kill Clarion?" Zane asked.

"Regrettably, no." He clenched his teeth and dropped his head back. "I am not the warrior I once was, nor the dragon..."

Zane saw the blood then, wet and heavy, dragging Akiem's borrowed shirt down and gluing it to his chest. That was no minor cut.

Akiem closed his eyes. Rain patted against his pale face, dampening his dark lashes. He could be about to sleep or die. Zane heaved his wrecked body forward. His jaw ached from Clarion's punch, but the worst of the pain throbbed down the back of his neck. It wouldn't kill him, though. Akiem had stopped Clarion and taken the brunt of the lord's fury.

He knelt by Akiem's leg and touched his hand, the one clutched to his waist. Akiem's lashes fluttered, his eyes opening slowly.

"It will heal..." he slurred.

"Will you allow me a look?" Zane wouldn't touch him without permission.

Akiem dipped his head in an almost indiscernible nod.

Zane opened the lower buttons and peeled the shirt back. The cut was clean but damn deep. Did dragons bleed like elves? If so, the blood was dark. Not a good sign.

Wounds like that could kill if left untreated, and they were likely to get infected. Akiem needed stitches. Zane rested back on his heels and scanned the area for anything useful. The rain continued its relentless beat against the canopy. With no dry wood, a fire was out of the question. He had no supplies and no coin.

"Where are we?"

"I have no idea. I picked you up and... this was as far as I could get."

Then he'd been dragon and shifted with this wound. Such things were risky. Their magic sometimes moved wounds around, turning a minor wound fatal.

"Do dragons heal quicker than elves?" Zane asked, hopeful.

"Some do." Akiem closed his eyes again. "I'll just... rest awhile," he sighed.

Zane sat in the wet leaves beside him and then shuffled closer, so his arm brushed Akiem's. His thigh brushed Akiem's too. The dragon was *warm*. He remembered that from waking sprawled across the dragon that morning.

He checked to see if Akiem was even aware he'd moved closer and caught a small smile. "This is just... It's real cold."

"It's perfectly fine," he said, voice gruffer than it had been moments before. The same foreign-accented voice Zane had fallen for on the dockside.

Life had sure kicked him in the nuts these past few days. He'd started out with little more than a traveling bag and a friend, and now he had neither. "Clarion has something on Jevan. I know him. He wouldn't have done this willingly."

"I agree," Akiem replied, keeping his eyes closed.

"You never trusted him, did you?" Zane asked.

"I saw him aim at the king," he said, eyes still closed. "It was no accident. I don't like him, but he cares for you, and that I... That is true."

So Jev had killed the king for Clarion. If he was still alive, he'd be in the heart of the compound by now and well out of Zane's reach.

It didn't seem right. Elves had done nothing to deserve this. They'd lived by dragon laws, kept peace with them, served them, but none of it had mattered. Arlo had died for nothing. Thousands had died for nothing. Clarion had taken away ten years of peace in one night.

"The humans fought them, and they all died. We fought them, and we surrendered." Zane picked up a twig and snapped it in two. "And still they kill us."

"Destruction is the dragonkin way," Akiem mumbled.

But destruction was not Akiem's way. If they hadn't been both exhausted, beaten, and bloody, he'd have asked why Akiem was so different, but that was a conversation for another time.

"What do you intend to do about it?" Akiem asked, wincing around pain. Opening his eyes, he blinked too quickly, and gently shook his head, trying to focus.

"What can I do?"

"Nothing." Akiem faced Zane, his attention suddenly pin-sharp. The dragon had a new kind of heat in his eyes, one that stoked the waning fires in Zane's heart. "Alone."

Did he mean what Zane thought he meant? "You'd fight for us again?"

Akiem didn't answer and turned his gaze to the clearing. When he next closed his eyes, his shoulders softened, exhaustion taking him. He seemed younger without the permanent scowl, more vulnerable too. A hard life had aged him, made him rough and cold on the outside. But beneath all that, he had heart.

"Don't move."

A scout emerged from the bushes, her bowstring stretched and arrow aimed at Zane's chest. She wore her long hair bundled back, pinned with dagger-like needles. Her two-tone hair faded from dark at her roots to silver at its tips, sharpening her appearance. She didn't appear to be wearing daggers, but the bow was dangerous enough. Small and lightweight, it was meant for close-quarter combat. In her hands, she'd kill with it.

She jerked her chin at Akiem. "The dragon dead?"

"No, actually." Akiem opened his eyes. "Though I'm in no condition to stop you, should you wish me to be."

Talking shit like that riled Zane's protective instincts. "I'll stop you." He staggered to his feet and offered up empty hands. "We're not here to hurt anyone. We're both wounded, hungry, and cold."

"You come from Bayston?" She narrowed her eyes. "We heard the city is burning."

"Yes and yes."

She eyed Akiem a few moments more, weighing the risks, and then lowered her bow. "You hurt bad, dragon? Can you walk?"

"If I must."

She nodded. "Get up and follow me." She turned and plunged back into the brush. "Come. There are wolves nearby, and you both smell like easy meals."

Zane helped Akiem to his feet, more concerned than he let on when Akiem leaned heavily into him.

"This elf is more like those from my home..." Akiem said.

"More honorable?" Zane asked.

"More likely to kill me."

Zane mustered a smile. "Maybe it's time I protected you for once, eh?"

~

ZANE HAD HEARD of the settlement, not by name but by their eccentric practices. Electric lights were strung from poles along a winding central village street. Old human ruins had been patched up using debris from the old world. Windows glowed with electric light. He'd ask how they harvested electricity once he'd rested up, but for now, he admired the light as the scout led them into a house. She flicked a switch on the wall and a central light lit up the entire room.

"Dragon, get on the bed."

Akiem had barely settled on the bed before she approached with gauze, bandages, and a needle and thread. He eyed her as though she were approaching with a blade. "If I shift, any efforts to stitch me will dissolve."

"Don't shift then." Setting the implements down on the bedside table, she assessed her patient. "Do you want to remove your shirt, or shall I?"

Akiem grunted, peeled off his shirt, and tossed it aside. The pair glared at each other, and Zane, from his position propped against the wall, caught a touch of heat in the scout's cheeks. She was checking him out. Unexpected jealousy stoked the possessiveness Zane hadn't known he harbored.

"He's bleeding again," he said flatly, breaking their shared glare.

"Lie back," she ordered.

Akiem arched a brow at her tone and deferred to Zane.

Zane nodded. If she was going to hurt either of them, she'd have done it by now.

She worked quickly, her hands light and fast as she cleaned the wound and stitched it up. It must have hurt, but Akiem didn't protest or flinch. He stared at the ceiling, going wherever he went in that complicated head of his.

If she got to check him out, then so did Zane. He still hadn't seen enough of him naked, and it was the scars that drew Zane's eye. Dozens of them. Most on his arms. Some small nicks and others deeper. They were too uniform to be the result of an accident. Someone had methodically cut him—or he'd cut himself.

Fuck. The surface scars were a fraction of the wounds he'd been dealt. The dragon way was harsh. They routinely fought, but this was different. He'd been systematically tortured *for years*—maybe his entire life.

"Let me check that head wound of yours," the scout said to Zane.

He'd been so lost in thought, staring at Akiem's now-sleeping form, that he hadn't noticed her approach. "I'm fine," he grumbled.

She sighed like she'd heard the same a thousand times. "If the big bad dragon can let me stitch his side, you can let me take a look at your head. Sit."

He sat and leaned forward. Her fingers gently probed through his hair, around the bruise.

"I know you," she said. "You came by my old village a few years ago. Left some controversy behind, if I remember correctly?"

"What was the place called?"

"Oldport."

He swallowed. "Never heard of it."

"No? A guy by your description shacked up with one of the gang leaders for a while. Didn't last, though. You—or he—left, taking a shit ton of coin with him. That wasn't you?"

"Must have been someone else."

"You'll live," she declared, backing up and wiping her hands clean on a cloth. She scrutinized him some more, her attention roaming over his face and landing on his hand.

Zane looked down at the tattoo on his finger. He curled his fingers, hiding it.

"The stove's alight, there's hot water, and I'll get you both some fresh clothes. When you're ready, you can join us for breakfast."

Zane lifted his head. She tidied away the bloody pads, moving about the place as though she knew it well.

"What's your name?" he asked.

"Suzanne, but most everyone calls me Annie. You're Zane, from Oldport. The tattoo..." she said, reading his shock at hearing his name. "Your friend's called...?" She nodded at the sleeping dragon.

"His name's Akiem." Her hunter eyes sparkled at that, like she'd seen prey. "Why are you helping us?"

"Because of the haunted look about you, friend." Finally, she smiled, and her prickly persona softened. "You've seen enough darkness. A little light goes a long way. And because he's obviously the Black Prince everyone is talking about."

She turned and left before Zane could ask how she knew the Black Prince. His gaze fell to Akiem again, like it always did now. He'd fallen asleep on his back, on top of the covers, shirtless. One arm hung carelessly off the bed while the other lay behind his head. Zane readily imagined being poised over him, about to enlighten the male on the pleasures denied him. He wanted to show him some goodness, some light, just like Annie had said. A life spent in darkness was no life at all.

Akiem's countless scars were bright in the artificial light, thawing Zane's rising lust and turning it into anger.

kiem

THE LAST FEW days were broken into so many pieces that Akiem struggled to fit them together in his mind. Zane featured in them all. There was blood, and Clarion, and pain, and an elf with black and silver hair who'd spoken to him as though she were dragon. Her hands had been on his skin. Gentle hands. Light hands. And now he was in a strange house with its harsh, relentless electric light and old-world furniture, smelling of elf.

He woke feeling *light*. He'd dreamed of bad things, but it hadn't hurt. He hadn't woken trying to claw the marks off his arms. He hadn't found himself tucked into a corner, barely able to string three words together.

He knew war. The things he'd seen in the city didn't alarm him, only the things in his head wounded him, but even those appeared to have fled.

He tried to sit up. The wound screamed, making him

gasp. Clarion had slashed his belly. He was lucky the lord hadn't disemboweled him. Lucky he'd gotten away. He'd fled with Zane in his claws, not knowing whether the elf was alive or dead. Impossibly, Clarion hadn't given chase.

He'd been afraid when he'd landed, exhausted and with his belly bleeding, but not for himself. He'd lain the elf down on the leaves as carefully as possible, freeing him from his claws, and waited, watching for any signs of life. Those moments... not knowing... they'd torn Akiem open. What if the elf was dead and gone from this world? What was left for Akiem then?

Zane entered the house, a tray of food balanced on one hand and a cup in the other. He kicked the door closed behind him and set the food down on the end of the bed. His hair was damp, darkening it to a chestnut color. The clothes were fresh. He smelled of another elf.

An uncomfortable spike jabbed Akiem in the chest. He rubbed it. Could he be jealous of the other elf he smelled on Zane?

"You're famous." Zane grinned, perching himself on the foot of the bed. "Apparently, there's a black dragon saving elves from the fires. Word spreads fast in these parts."

He thought of the elf on the beach and her elfing. He'd saved them, but that hardly seemed like enough to warrant the awe.

"I see where your thoughts are going," Zane said, circling a finger at Akiem. "That look that says you disagree. You can't deny it. Your actions speak for you. You saved elves."

Akiem tried to rake a hand through his hair, but it got snagged. He still smelled of fire and his own blood. "They would not idolize me if they knew my nature."

Zane rolled his eyes and stood. "Eat. Clean yourself up. Nobody here wants to kill you. They're all desperate to get a look at you, their dragon hero."

Akiem's frown dug deeper. "How far are we from the city?"

Zane's smile faded. "A few days' heavy trek. On the wing... maybe a day."

"Then Clarion will come."

"Just..." Zane puffed out a sigh. "Just rest, Akiem. You've earned it."

Akiem tracked his path out the door and waited in the quiet, listening to his racing heart. He hadn't earned this kindness. He did not deserve the food, although his stomach rumbled, overruling his head. He reached for the tray and froze. In the harsh electric light, his scars almost glowed. So many. Zane had seen. The female elf who'd fixed him up had seen too. They knew.

He looked at the door, then at the window where sunlight baked the closed drapes. He could leave. Just get up and go. He'd fled once, crossing an entire ocean to get away. What was west of here? More vicious dragons? Death? He'd ached for death before, but not so much now.

Leaving meant abandoning the elves. They'd all die if he did. Zane was right. The elves here had forgotten how to fight. They'd forgotten who they were, just like Akiem had. They needed to rediscover themselves, same as he. Maybe they could do so together.

After eating, he washed in the hot closet, dressed in more elven clothes—this time, they fit—and stared at the dragon looking back at him in the mirror. Tarnished eyes, straight hair, hard jaw and mouth, but it was the eyes that haunted him.

He sighed, looking away.

He'd seen the elves pin their hair back and, after finding pins in the dresser drawer, attempted to do the same. The clothes and hair didn't change him from being dragon, but it went a long way in remaking him into someone else, someone he was still trying to find.

"You look good."

The words stilled him. He hadn't heard Zane enter. Quickly resettling his thoughts, he straightened and leaned back against the dresser. Zane's gaze wandered over him. He found the scrutiny welcome, especially when Zane's ever-moving mouth pulled into that familiar little twitching smile.

"I've been thinking about what you said," Zane began, "about not being able to do anything alone..."

Akiem waited, watching Zane wrestle with his thoughts. He thought a lot, this one. More went on behind the shallow smiles and laughter.

"It will take more than me to inspire my kind to fight, more than impending war, even. Some people from Bayston came through here before us. They talked about the Black Prince."

Akiem dropped his gaze. His sense of unworthiness tried to sneak beneath his skin and undermine him.

Zane stepped forward. "I know you aren't who you were, but I think that's a good thing. Don't you?"

"You have no idea what you ask of me."

"I think I do." Another step. Zane held his gaze. His cheek fluttered. "You're stronger than you know."

Akiem let a smile lift the corner of his mouth. "That's not the problem."

"Then what is? Tell me," Zane pressed. "Help me understand, because I think you're wrong about yourself.

At every turn, you've done the right thing, more so than the rest of us."

"I hurt your friend."

"Jevan's an ass. I've lost count of the times I've wanted to kill him."

"I... I've tortured your kind."

"In the past. Considering what I've heard of the English elves, I'm sure they'd have done the same to you."

"That is... true." He had to admit that. It had been survival. War.

Zane was closer now and looking at him as though waiting for Akiem to speak the real truth. Of course, there really only was one truth about Akiem. "I'm dragon."

Zane shrugged. "And?"

Akiem pushed off the dresser and closed the final few strides between them, holding Zane's defiant glare. Zane was determined to find good in him, but it didn't work like that. Not everything had good in it, not everything should be saved. "I'm not the hero your people are looking for."

"Your actions say differently," he replied, so full of himself, like he knew everything, every last surprise Akiem could throw at him. The elf's eyes were full of hope, and that was part of what made Zane so impossible. What did he hope to get from Akiem exactly? "I'm broken inside. I've been broken inside my whole life. You cannot fix me. What I am, it's blood deep."

"Have you heard nothing I've said? I don't hate you." Zane frowned and flung a hand at the closed drapes. "They don't hate you."

Zane reached up, but Akiem caught his wrist, holding him back, making the grip tight enough for Zane to frown. "I am not some savior you can all pin your hopes on."

He shoved past him and headed for the door. Let the

people outside see him if that was what they truly wanted. See the dragon that would inevitably fail them, like he'd failed at everything else.

"Why do you hate yourself so much?"

The question yanked Akiem to a halt. He lifted his head and turned to find Zane waiting, arms crossed, hip cocked, the picture of cocky defiance. He was so damn sure he knew it all. Fine, then he could really know the ugly truth. Maybe then Zane would leave, and this ridiculous relationship would turn to ash, like it should.

"What color are my eyes?" Akiem asked.

He frowned. "Gold."

"Look again."

He ventured closer, bringing them almost toe to toe, and peered into Akiem's eyes. Akiem blinked, the elf's proximity crackling over his skin. Lust, desire, want, and, gods, so much more.

"What am I looking for? I see gold and flecks of darkness, the same color as your scales."

"It's not gold you see. Gold shines."

Confusion pulled his smile out of line. "What difference does the color of your eyes make?"

"I'm amethyst, like my mother, the queen of the land I come from. I'm amethyst—my fire proves it." A tremor undermined his voice, but it was too late; he'd started to reveal his fears, and now he had to spill them all. "It's what I told my mother, over and over. She'd lock me away, and I'd say the words over and over against the closed door, knowing she heard, but she never believed me because of what she saw in my eyes. No other obsidian has eyes like mine. They betray the truth to all who care to see."

"I don't understand."

"One of the three first great metals, the beast who

fucked me for weeks on end until I bled…" Gods, it hurt to say and tripped his voice. "Dokul is my father." Now that the truth was out, more tried to rush free. "It's not gold you see in my eyes. It's bronze. I'm a monster inside. It's always been there. Every time I look in the mirror, the truth stares back at me. I can't be your hero. I can't save your people because of his poison. I'm not good, Zane. No matter how many lives I save, I'll never be good. Inside, there's a need—a desperate desire to destroy everything I touch. Metals are the worst of us, and it's inside of me. *He's* inside of me every day. I can't cut him out." He thrust out his arms and pulled up the sleeves, exposing the cuts. "I've tried, Gods, I've tried. I can't escape it. That's *why* I hate myself."

He'd said it, the terrible truth. His mother was dead, and despite his efforts to make her care for him, she never had, because of Akiem's father, because of the bronze in his eyes and veins. Whether Dokul and Mother's union had been an agreeable one or forced, didn't matter. When the clutch of eggs came, she'd destroyed all but one. She'd kept that single egg for years, until raising another clutch —all amethyst this time. All but Akiem, the secret, the rot, the bad apple. *Stupid dragon.* She'd told him once she'd wanted strength, not sniveling weakness. He'd tried to find that strength she sought, but had failed every single time. Nobody else had known. Dokul had never spoken of it, never once mentioned the bronze in his eyes, although he must have suspected. The bronze chief hadn't wanted jeweled weakness in his brood, the same as Mother didn't want the bronze brutality in hers. And now Zane knew. Now he'd hate him too, because there was nothing to love about the bronze, and there was nothing to love about Akiem.

Zane searched his eyes, standing so close that Akiem had to stop himself from grabbing the elf and shaking sense into him.

"I don't care that you're dragon," Zane said. "I don't care what color your eyes are. None of that makes you you."

He didn't understand, no elf could. "You should care. You haven't seen the metals. You don't know. You think Luceran is the worst of us? Compared to Dokul, he's nothing more than a kit playing in ashes. Dokul would pin him down and bite his scales off, one by one, and that would just be the beginning."

Zane's scowl darkened. "You're afraid you're like him?"

A knot in Akiem's throat blocked the reply. The rage, the lust, the madness threatening to consume him. *I am like him.*

"How can I make you see you're not?"

"You can't," he croaked.

Zane pushed in, chest to chest, and looked up. "You think you'll turn on us. You're afraid you'll hurt me?"

Gods, this feeling that racked him every time he was around Zane ate him up inside, made him want things, made him lust so hard he feared he *would* hurt him. "Dokul destroyed me in every way. I do not trust who I am."

"I know..." Zane whispered, his mouth so close the words brushed across Akiem's lips.

"I'm afraid I'll do the same to you." He spoke so softly he might not have spoken at all.

"You won't."

Zane didn't know. He couldn't. Akiem had hurt others, tortured those of his brood, even his so-called brother—because he was bronze. The metal ran through his veins, made him vicious, made him lustful and rough, made him all the things he despised.

The door opened. Akiem stepped back and whirled away, reaching the cup of water on the dresser, for anything to create space between him and Zane and the disgusting truth.

"Oh, I... Akiem, would you like to join us for lunch?" Annie asked.

"No." He sighed and flicked his gaze up, catching Annie's glowering reflection. She wouldn't ask if she truly knew him. None here would.

"We're working out some... personal issues," Zane explained. "Thank you."

"I see. I'll let you work on your... personal issues some more then." She backed out the door and closed it neatly behind her.

Zane sighed. "Akiem, you're..." Maybe he finally understood, because his argument died on his lips. "About us—"

"There is no us." Akiem snapped. He pressed his fingers into the dresser top and kept his head down. When would he listen? "What we did was a transaction, nothing more." It was *everything more*, but for both their sakes, he couldn't allow himself to feel that way. "I paid you to fuck me. It's done."

"All right," Zane conceded. "If that's truly what you want."

"It is." Akiem drew in a sharp breath, one Zane didn't see or hear.

"Then you won't help us?"

He shouldn't even be asking. "I'm not a leader, and I'm not your savior."

"That's not what I asked."

"I will help you, where I can, but I'm no leader, not... anymore."

The sound of the door closing signaled Zane's departure and Akiem's relief.

Akiem's reflection mocked him. He looked into the eyes of the male he despised, saw the old scars on his arms, reminders of the days he'd rocked in the dank cell, trying to claw the metal from his veins so Mother would see him, and he wondered when the torment would end.

IF HE'D STAYED ANY LONGER in the elven house, he'd have shifted out of his skin. Wandering about the village wasn't as bad as he'd feared. Villagers threw a few glances his way, but the elves carried on around him, as though a dragon among their number was no more noteworthy than a traveler passing through. Like at the city docks, he enjoyed their company, because they ignored him.

He drifted through the shadows cast by the low evening light and watched their ingenious electricity flicker on. Zane was among them, and he'd drawn quite the crowd. Akiem pulled back and watched, out of sight, as Zane made his audience laugh. He talked with animated movements, always smiling, his eyes bright with mirth, and those who joined in seemed equally relaxed in his presence. He naturally drew people to him, like a flame others gathered around.

Akiem had done the right thing. Seeing him here, now, thriving among his kind, proved his decision to shut down their relationship had been right. Zane deserved an elf like him, someone who could make him smile like that every day. Still, tucked into the shadows, Akiem admired his

Red. Zane laughed at something one of his companions said, and the need inside his chest spiked again, hurting. He wanted him in every way, in dangerous ways, but it could never be. One mistake, that's all it would take, and he'd ruin his Red.

A dragon call pierced the revelry.

Distant.

Akiem looked up.

The call came again. Zane stilled. His gaze shot straight to Akiem, seeing through the darkness in which he'd been hiding.

"Turn off the lights!" Akiem ran for the cleared area they'd walked through on their way into the village. The shift poured through him moments after he'd passed the last house, opening up the wound in his belly. He mentally shoved the pain aside, flung open his wings, and beat the air, lifting himself above the trees. He needed to turn the dragon around before it saw the village lights.

Rain kissed his scales and drenched his back, weighing down his wings and trailing water from their tips. There was no sunset and no moonlight, just clouds and wetness and the arched outline of an oncoming dragon. Not Clarion. Another obsidian, like Akiem.

Akiem snarled and stoked the fire low in his throat, making himself glow against the dark sky. He wanted the dragon to give chase and never know it had almost stumbled upon an elven village.

A warning screech reached him. The dragon had seen him.

Akiem banked left, his back and wings aching under the relentless pressure. He beat harder, climbing higher, breathing heavily, feeding blood and oxygen to his heart, driving ever forward.

Away. He just had to draw the dragon away. Whatever happened after was up to fate.

He dropped his head, searching below for the obsidian, but the beast melted into the darkness. It was here, though.

He soared, wings riding the air, and listened. His heart thumped too loudly. Rain hissed against his scales. There—above to the left and coming in fast. Akiem tucked his wings in and rolled. The obsidian overshot his downward lunge, screamed in fury, and reeled mid-flight. Akiem was above him now. He let loose the boiling purple flame, sizzling the murk and clouds away and scorching a line down the dragon's nearside wing. It shrieked and pulled up, catching the air like a kite and stalling. Then it twisted back and dove.

Akiem folded his wings in and dove too, giving chase. He used the weight of his tail to flick himself on course and overshoot the obsidian. The ground, with its rolling blanket of trees, each one like spikes, rushed up. Akiem was slimmer than this obsidian and faster. Down it flew, and down Akiem plunged after it, his veins hot, his heart ablaze. Yes, this was living. This was freedom.

The obsidian pulled up.

Too late.

Akiem flung out his wings and threw out his claws. He caught the beast along its back, hooking in and wrenching it out of its flight path. It screamed and swung its head back to unleash the flame. Akiem grinned, revealing rows of teeth, and drove the dragon into the tree line, holding it down as the timber raked the beast's belly. Momentum plowed them forward. The wind beneath his wings pulled Akiem level. Trees snapped. Timber splintered. He smelled dragon blood and felt the beast in his claws fall limp.

He wanted to scream at the world, wanted more blood, more dragons to sink his teeth into, more death.

He tossed the dead dragon into the trees, wiping out a swathe of forest. Akiem landed in the fresh clearing and crowded his kill, spreading his wings wide to claim it. He didn't care who it was. A male, he saw now. Didn't care he had once had a life. This territory was now Akiem's, now the Black Prince's. He sank his teeth into the beast's throat and tore it out, then gorged on the torn entrails.

A twig snapped.

Akiem brought his head around toward the sound and saw Zane among the trees, breathless atop a white horse.

Prey.

Akiem prowled forward, snarl burbling.

Prey.

Zane's horse shied.

Akiem shook his head, wincing around another urge, a very different one. *Protect.*

The conflict tore through him, two desires ripping him apart. The shift imploded, packing everything dragon back beneath the tight confines of human skin. *"Get rid of the damn horse!"*

Zane dismounted and whacked the beast in the hindquarters. "Yarh!" It squealed and darted back into the forest.

Akiem's vision blurred, the shift still settling, dragon still trying to pour out of him all over again. *Prey.*

Zane smelled of horse.

A horse that had just fled.

Chase. Chase. Chase.

"Akiem?"

His name.

That was good.

"Say it again, elf." There was too much dragon in his words, his body full of rage and hunger and want, his wound forgotten.

The elf wasn't afraid, the fool.

Zane spread his hands. "Akiem." He smiled and kept on walking closer.

Akiem panted through his nose.

"They saw you. They saw what you did. You saved the village."

He was done with stupid human words. Akiem had Zane's face in his hands in the next moment, and then his mouth on his, *owning, taking.* Zane tried to push back, and that made it worse. His growl claimed them both, and Zane shuddered like he wanted this. Akiem dragged his nails down Zane's shirt and clenched the fabric while driving the elf against a tree. The sudden stop pressed *elf* into Akiem. He tore from Zane's mouth and dragged his teeth over the pulsing softness of his neck. He was raging hard, a fact Zane's hand had found. Trapped somewhere between dragon and man, Akiem pulled the elf's shirt apart, popping buttons, and tasted the smooth warmth of his shoulder. He moved down over his collarbone to a pert nipple. His teeth ached with the urge to bite. He thrust his cock into Zane's hand instead to distract his wild mind.

If Zane said no, he wouldn't listen.

Akiem clutched the elf by the hair and held him back, his throat exposed, his body pinned beneath his. "I can't..."

I can't stop. I can't do this. I can't hurt you. I can't be who you want me to be.

"Do it."

He didn't know what he asked of him!

There were more growls than words now. Zane's fingers pulled on the laces of his pants, loosening them. He breathed fast, and when Akiem dropped his hand to Zane's crotch, he found the elf equally hard and wanting.

Zane clutched Akiem's face and bared his teeth. "Fuck me, dragon, like you've wanted to since we met." His eyes blazed ocean green. Need burned where humor had glittered before.

Akiem couldn't stop this.

Nothing in him was strong enough to stop it.

He clutched Zane's hips, near madness. There were too many layers of clothing between them. Akiem was considering ripping them off, when Zane made quick work of the ties of his pants, grabbed Akiem's hands, and plunged them into the back of his pants, forcing his hands to ride over his ass. Zane gasped close to Akiem's ear. He was a writhing, hot, muscular thing made of desire, and Akiem was losing his fucking mind to him.

Zane faced the tree and thrust his ass against Akiem's crotch, rubbing against the part of him that strained and beat as though filled with its own dragon fire. Akiem needed it quenched.

Zane planted a vial of liquid in his hand. Somewhere in all the raging chaos, Akiem understood what he asked and pooled the oil in his hand. Then he slid a finger down Zane's crevice and eased it inside the puckered, heated hole.

"Deeper."

The elf's groans plucked on Akiem's nerves, the ones that lined up directly with his cock. He sank a finger deeper, and Zane arched.

"Fuck me. Now. Dragon."

Akiem stroked the oil over himself, widened Zane's

hole with two fingers, then probed closer, testing. Something inside Akiem snapped. Control, maybe. He gripped Zane's shoulder, clasped himself tighter, and Zane shoved back, lifting his ass. Akiem thrust in, losing himself to the feel of elf. There was no going slow. He pushed down on Zane's lower back, seeking the right angle to penetrate and thrust. Zane gasped, swore, and groaned an elven word Akiem had no hope of understanding. Again, pleasure trilled. Again, he was falling, losing himself and finding himself all at once. He thrust harder, deeper, finding a maddening rhythm that chased the fine line between pleasure and pain, making it pull tighter and tighter. Zane flung a wicked look over his shoulder, and Akiem came undone. He spilled his seed and growled out his claim.

Zane tried to move, but Akiem reached around and found his hardness. Akiem pulled Zane up. Zane's back met Akiem's chest, and still inside him, he rolled his thumb and palm over Zane's erection. The elf bucked and twitched. Zane's breath hastened, his heart too. Akiem heard it all, strumming Zane's pleasure higher until he too broke open. His beautiful mouth spilled curses while his cock spilled his seed.

Akiem gently bit his shoulder, and when Zane turned his head, he kissed him, slow and messily. Zane turned in his arms. The kiss deepened and became real now that Akiem saw the shimmer in Zane's eyes.

"You're a bullshit liar, Black Prince." Zane nipped at Akiem's mouth, then his chin, and purred, "There absolutely is an *us*."

He could hardly deny it, though much of him wanted to. No coin had changed hands. This was all Akiem, all dragon, and by the gods, he wanted—*needed* the elf in every way, and that was fucking terrifying.

"Don't you dare shut down on me." Zane held Akiem's face and forced him to look, to see. "You didn't hurt me. There is no shame in this. Do you hear me, Akiem? You did nothing wrong. In fact..." He grinned. His grip softened, and his thumb stroked Akiem's cheek. "You did everything right." The kiss was all teasing, nearly touching lips and tongues, and a promise of more. "You save elves now."

"I guess I do," he grumbled back. One elf in particular. He slid his hands down Zane's back, marveling at the sensation of *male* and how good he felt beneath his touch and how right this all was. Zane *was* right. He didn't feel shame, not with him. He felt free.

"As much as I'd love to stay here, the dead dragon will attract wolves ..."

He reluctantly withdrew and heard Zane sigh the same regret that pained Akiem inside. The carcass drew Akiem's eye; its glistening insides spilled across upturned trees. Gods, Akiem had forgotten the carcass and the vicious killing need that had driven him to own Zane. He laced up his pants and watched Zane do the same. Something like an apology stuck in his throat. Zane had said he was fine, but Akiem had been blind with lust. He'd been rough. He must have hurt him.

Zane's hand slipped into Akiem's and squeezed. "C'mon, tall, dark, and deadly. You frightened my horse, so now we walk."

"Good. I do not ride my food."

"Are you sure about that?" The look he tossed Akiem scorched his soul and made his cock harden all over again.

Zane looped an arm through his, startling Akiem with its familiarity, but within a few steps, he found the closeness comforting. He'd never had anyone just walk with him before. Those who had gotten close in the past had always wanted something in return, had always *taken* pieces of him until there had been nothing left. Zane only gave, and Akiem's hollow heart swelled.

Elves were... fascinating, heartwarming, honest—mostly—and kind. All things dragons were not. He hadn't cared to know them before. Now it seemed he cared too much, perhaps even *loved*.

ane

His body throbbed in all the right ways, and while there were more important things going on around them, Zane had a hard time thinking around the dragon that had fallen into step beside him. They entered the village from the side and slunk into their borrowed house unnoticed. Akiem went straight for the shower, and Zane watched him go, thinking about following. Alumn, he couldn't get enough of the paradox that was the Black Prince. Vicious and deadly on one hand, protective and vulnerable on the other.

The shower hissed on. The door was closed. Akiem hadn't invited him inside, but he didn't know *how* to invite him inside.

Zane planted his hands on his hips. That fuck against the tree should've sated him. His body couldn't take another round, but his mind wasn't done with the dragon, not by a long shot.

After Akiem had dashed out of the village, shifting in full view of the startled elves, Zane had climbed to the rooftops along with the others and watched the two black beasts tear strips off each other, lit by Akiem's purple fire. He'd never seen anything so devastatingly beautiful, and when the dragons had come down, he'd taken a horse and galloped out to find him, fearing he'd vanish and never return. He needn't have worried, and now every elf here knew Akiem protected them.

It was insane and impossible, but that was Akiem. Dragons didn't care for elves. They ate them. Akiem *cared*.

Zane knocked on the shower door, staring at the pile of clothes dropped outside it. He'd have thrown the door open and stepped inside with anyone else, but Akiem was just as likely to shove him through a wall if startled.

The door opened. Akiem reached out, grabbed Zane's shirt, and pulled him inside the shower filled with steam and dragon. Bronze eyes glowed in the mist. Zane's breath caught. And then Akiem's mouth slammed into his. He was all hardness and strength, but somehow also soft and precious. Water soaked Zane's clothes through in seconds, weighing him down. He didn't care. The kiss breathlessly shattered. Akiem boxed him in, arms braced on either side of him against the wall. Water poured down his face, painting his black hair over his shoulders and down his chest. The wound low at his hip had scabbed over, but it still looked raw enough to bother most people. But Akiem wasn't most people. He knew pain better than he should.

Zane followed the half-lifted rise of his lips and the shimmer of dragonsight in his eyes. He didn't look real, or maybe he was too real and Zane's mind couldn't grasp what he'd captured.

"You're so fucking beautiful..." He touched Akiem's face, tracing the hard line of his jaw.

Akiem's lashes fluttered down. He didn't believe the words. Zane's heart ached for his wounded dragon. He'd make him see the beauty inside him if it took an elven lifetime.

"I'm sorry," Akiem whispered.

Alumn, he had nothing to be sorry for. Zane cupped his face and ducked his head, seeking Akiem's shying eyes. "You have done nothing wrong."

"I don't understand what this is... what we are..." He spoke so softly, his voice broken by tremors.

"Let me show you."

Zane kissed his jaw and ran his tongue along its edge, teasing the dragon awake all over again. He needed to taste all of him, *feel* all of him. Zane dropped his hands to Akiem's chest, mapping every ripple of muscle and relishing his strength. To know he had a dragon's heart pumping for him, his body alight beneath his hands, was a power trip Zane desperately needed more of. More than that, he wished Akiem could see himself the way Zane saw him.

Akiem's hot mouth was at Zane's throat, his tongue circling, teeth nipping. It was too much and not enough. Zane pulled him closer and hooked a leg around his, feeling every inch of Akiem grind against his hip.

Akiem's mouth traced the corner of Zane's, his tongue probing, but as Zane went to answer it, Akiem pulled back, teasing or still unsure. Fuck. And Akiem thought he couldn't do this. If he were anyone else, Zane would have grabbed him, flung him against the wall, and owned him, mouth and hands and cock, but not Akiem. He needed this gentleness and to be in control. Zane had always known it instinctively, but now knew why. If Zane ever met the bronze who broke his dragon, he'd rip his fucking heart out and pin it to a tree.

The shower ran cold, but Akiem radiated heat, and Zane lost himself in his dragon—Akiem's touches so achingly gentle and reverent, so different from before— until he no longer knew where he ended and Akiem began.

Akiem shut off the water, lifted Zane under the thighs, found the bed, and lowered him down. His eyes blazed their possessiveness, and Zane blinked half-lidded eyes back. There was nothing to be said, no words that could make this more perfect. Zane vowed to keep Akiem's dragonheart safe, whatever their futures held.

MUCH OF THE village was going about their morning tasks when Zane found Annie stringing a bow at a table outside a dwelling.

She arched a brow, which Zane translated as, she knew exactly why he and Akiem hadn't made an appearance since the dragon saved the village. He wasn't sure what the elves here thought of a dragon and elf relationship—if what he had with Akiem was a relationship. He hoped it was.

"And how is our grumpy dragon this morning?" Annie asked.

He couldn't help but smile. "He's lurking somewhere, watching the sky."

"How did you snare him?"

The personal question caught Zane off guard. "It's a long story." And not one he wanted to share with her.

"Seems like an unlikely pairing, is all."

Whatever he had with Akiem was between him and Akiem. "I wanted to speak with your elder about what we can do for you."

"Don't got one." She shrugged. "We govern ourselves in this little corner of the world. Anyone who doesn't like it can move right along." She tested the bow by pulling back on the string, making the wooden limbs groan. "What is it you think you can do for us, Zane?"

The way she said his name and glanced at the tattoo on his finger reminded him of the accusations he'd left behind in Oldport. "Okay, look... you heard some things about me in Oldport. The situation there was unusual. Much of it was personal. I left. It's over. Can we move on?"

"Sure." She beamed. "You moved right on to dragon from your 'personal issues.'"

Zane pinched his mouth closed and sighed through his nose. "Is that a problem?"

Was Akiem the problem here or Zane's past?

She waved the comment away. "Ignore me. I haven't slept. Refugees are still passing through. Dragons circling. It's a lot to take in."

It was, and they'd all seen horrors these past few days. Zane's nerves were more rattled than he was used to. "This place is close to Bayston. The dragonkin will come eventually. Akiem can deter them for a while, but you'll need to move farther out."

She tutted. "Can't do that."

"Part of the old world were rediscovered underground during the war. You'd be hidden from dragons."

She turned her bow over in her hands, admiring her

work. "Yeah, no. That doesn't work for me and probably won't for the rest of the people here."

Then they'd all die, but Annie didn't seem concerned. She hadn't seen people burned alive in the streets or tasted their ashes on her lips, but if she stayed, she would. "I saw Bayston fall, and before that, I fought against dragons in the westland. There's no use in repeating the mistakes of the past. Perhaps we can stand against dragons in the future, but not now."

"Can't we?" She set the bow on the table and focused all her attention on Zane. "Do you think Alumn brought you and the Black Prince here, Zane?"

"I don't know..." he answered honestly. He'd tried not to think too long on what any of this meant.

She nodded. "I'll show you why we're not going anywhere."

He followed her out of the village, along a well-worn trail to a metal hatch in the ground. Sweeping aside fallen leaves, Annie heaved the hatch open and descended down a long set of steps. Electric lights flicked on, illuminating her way. As Zane followed, electric lights buzzed overhead. "Where do you source your electricity?"

"We have a solar farm nearby."

Impressive.

"Before my time, the village had a few humans among them. They knew how to wire up the solar cells to a converter and taught electricity to the residents, until the dragons rounded them up and killed them."

Zane reached the final step and stared into a vast, hollow darkness. Annie flicked a switch on the wall. Light flooded into a massive windowless warehouse.

"That clearing you arrived through... this bunker is

beneath it," Annie began, moving into the space, shrinking with every step. "We keep it camouflaged, for obvious reasons."

Small boxes lining the wall blinked red lights. They were placed at intervals around the entire subterranean building. "And those are?"

"Wired explosives." Her words echoed.

Zane looked again at the blinking boxes. There had to be fifty of them, all set and ready to blow.

Annie stopped, placed a hand on her hip, and sent her gaze far down the building. "We think it was an aircraft hangar. This whole area was laid with asphalt, like maybe it was meant for their winged machines. I cleared it last summer and wired it with a stash of what the humans called C4. I think it'll work."

"What will work?"

"Your dragon can lure the new king here."

"And then what?"

"Boom." She grinned.

"What about Akiem?" Akiem wasn't bait for the enemy.

She reappraised him, the manner not entirely friendly. "You're protective of him?"

Alumn, his breath hitched. Yes, he was fucking protective of Akiem because of that predatory look in her eye. "He's been used enough."

"And you wouldn't use him to help destroy Lord Clarion? Zane, who steals from his lovers? Who leaves wreckage wherever he goes? You really wouldn't use a dragon who's fallen into your lap?"

Zane laughed dryly. All right, so this was personal. She knew a whole lot more about Oldport than rumors alone could account for. "Who close to you did I screw over in Oldport, huh?"

"The elf you stole from was my brother."

Ah.

"You broke his heart."

And he fucking broke mine. He let his smile linger, wearing it like armor. The male he'd left in her village was one of the reasons he'd sworn off having multiple sexual encounters with the same person. He'd happily warmed her brother's bed for a few weeks, gotten too close, and thought maybe it was more than a passing fancy. Zane had even told Jevan he was putting down roots. But love was blind, and so was Zane, back then. Annie's brother was an asshole; he'd just hidden it well. He ran the Oldport gangs. It had been thrilling at first, until her brother had gotten heavy-handed and abusive. "Your brother's misplaced love is hardly my fault."

"You left without a word *and* stole his coin. You've got a chance here to do something right, and all it'll cost you is a dragon."

A dragon Zane cared a great deal about. Annie thought she knew him, thought she knew what had happened in Oldport too, but she was wrong on both counts. "What are you suggesting here?"

"We lure Clarion right inside and I press the trigger. No more king."

"An ambush." Zane narrowed his eyes. "And Akiem? What happens to him?"

"He can look out for himself."

That wasn't an answer. "You don't give a shit about him, do you?"

"He's dragon... How many of us has he killed?" She approached and looked Zane deep in his eyes. "You don't think he genuinely cares for you, do you?" Her laughter was sharper than Zane's and heartless. "You do! The infamous Red Devil Zane has fallen into his own trap *with a dragon!*"

Zane might have had a come-back, but her words hurt too much to summon some wit.

"He's dragon. Do you think you'll live happily ever after like in those old human stories?" She laughed harder, knotting Zane's insides.

He hadn't thought much beyond tomorrow, but a small part of him had looked farther ahead in search of a place for them. It sounded ludicrous, but he'd hoped, and Annie was laughing all over that small glimmer of hope, snuffing it out.

She patted him on the shoulder. "Oh, lover," she sighed. "Selfish, shallow males like you don't get happy endings."

He shoved her hand off. "Your brother was no saint. I did what I did to survive. You don't know me, and you don't know Akiem. He'll help you if you ask, because he's a better man than me. He won't even care that you don't give a shit what happens to him. He'd expect nothing less. But I won't allow you to use him."

Her smile was full of pity. "It's not your choice, though, is it?"

Akiem had found a purpose. He'd save elves, even if it killed him, and that's what Jevan had meant all those nights ago when Akiem had saved him and faced Luceran right after. Akiem's purpose was to take as many dragons down *with him,* because he believed he deserved death.

Zane left Annie in the hangar, retracing their steps up the stairs and out. It might be Akiem's choice, but Zane wouldn't stand by and let him throw his life away. He deserved so much more. Akiem didn't see it, but he would. He just needed time to understand who he was—time Zane wanted to give him.

He headed toward the village perimeter, seeking his dragon before Annie found him first.

kiem

HE HAD FULLY INTENDED to walk the village outskirts, checking for signs of dragons, but he'd stumbled on an elven school and inexplicably couldn't tear himself away. The little elves listened attentively to their tutor. She talked of dragons and the war the humans hadn't survived. Akiem listened. As an outsider, this war was different from the one he'd fled half a world away. The elves here were different too. More gentle, like Zane's touch.

It didn't feel real.

The frantic need to own Zane after the kill hadn't been Akiem's finest moment, but afterward, in the rain closet, and after that between the sheets... Those times were a wonder. He hadn't known a male of any race could summon in him such wonderful sensations. Love, such a strange concept. He'd never experienced it. He'd thought he had, with his broodsister, in his devotion to Mother and beneath Luceran's controlling hand, but he'd been so very wrong. Love wasn't being owned. There was no submission. No fear. No power play. He and Zane were equal, a fact he'd have denied to his death not so long ago. Zane had shown him another way of life, and Akiem wanted so much more. For the first time in months, he wanted to live this new life, perhaps alongside Zane, if the elf would have him. Zane was too kind, too gentle, and Akiem did not deserve him, but maybe one day he would.

Luceran stepped from the shadows behind the tutor.

The sight of the diamond king was so sudden and unexpected that Akiem's heart seized. No, it wasn't possible. He blinked. Still there. The king glistened beneath sunlight like a glorious work of human art.

But he was dead. Akiem had carried him back to the compound himself.

The little elflings whimpered.

A wicked smile lifted the king's thin mouth.

This was no hallucination.

Akiem bolted down the center of the class, his only thought on blocking Luceran.

The elven tutor saw Akiem rush her, and like all good elves, she'd do anything to protect her little ones. A dagger flashed, drawn from inside her sleeve. Akiem veered, avoiding the slash, but the distraction gave Luceran an opening. The king stepped around the unsuspecting tutor. He tore the dagger from her hand and drew a bloody line across her throat.

Tiny, horrified screams erupted around Akiem.

No. No!

The tutor fell to her knees, hands clutching Akiem's legs. She hadn't seen the king and still didn't know he stood behind her, watching her die, a blank look on his face.

Other elves would come in seconds. Luceran was alive. He'd killed this female. Nothing about this made sense.

"Why?" Akiem asked.

"You do not belong to elves, my black prince."

How was the next question, but it died on Akiem's lips when Luceran stepped forward and stroked a finger down Akiem's cheek. "They'll despise you for this," the king said.

This hadn't been Akiem's doing. He would never do this, not anymore. Before... before yes... he had killed elves. So many. So much blood. Memories tore at his mind.

"Leave!" Akiem hissed at the king.

Luceran offered his hand. "You are dragon and you are mine."

This was wrong. It was a trick. Luceran was dead. But if Luceran was dead, how was the tutor dead at Akiem's feet? Was any of this real? Had Akiem killed her? The king slotted the dagger into Akiem's hand and closed his fingers around it. "You're a killer, Akiem. Look what you've done."

The dagger burned in his grip, the feel of it shockingly real.

"Akiem!"

Zane's shout whirled him around. He stood with others of his kind, holding them back. Zane saw the dagger too. This *was* real. His face fell.

He turned away from Zane, away from the pain. Luceran was not there. Akiem had a sickness inside him; the bronze in his veins made it so. Fragile thoughts cracked and then shattered. He didn't know who he was. He'd thought he was good. He'd thought he was different, but this... this was who he'd been before. This was who he really was: the amethyst prince, a killer for a queen, vicious and ruthless. Dragon.

"Akiem... wait..."

Zane. Akiem had told him this would happen. He shouldn't have gotten so close to the elf. Elves and dragons could not be together. This was the result. Always.

He had to find Luceran, to know the king was real, to know he wasn't losing his mind.

"Akiem, don't!"

He ran, darting between homes and into the brush. The king had to be here. He had to be real. If he wasn't, then Akiem had killed the tutor, making him the monster he feared the most.

ane

ZANE BOLTED after Akiem's dark outline, plunging into the brush a few strides behind him. Branches tore at his face and clothes. He had to get to him, to tell him they knew he hadn't killed the tutor before Zane lost him. He *was* losing him. He could feel it. There was something precious between them, but so very fragile, and it was about to break.

An arm shot out in front of him. Zane veered too late. Fingers snagged his hair and yanked. Zane's head snapped back, and pain tore down his neck. His back hit the ground, knocking the wind from his lungs. Clarion was on him, the dragon pinning Zane's wrists down. He growled, low and deadly.

Zane breathed hard through his teeth. He couldn't wrestle free—he'd tried that before—so he stayed still, guarding his strength for any slip in Clarion's grip or lapse in concentration. "Let me go."

Clarion leaned in, close enough to kiss, but the snarl on the lord's lips was not an invitation. "What a fabulous idea."

He pushed off Zane, climbed to his feet, and beckoned Zane to stand.

Slowly Zane rolled onto his side and stood.

Clarion's pupils were so black they filled his eyes. "Run for me, elf."

Akiem was close, chasing after the ghost of Clarion's brother.

Going back to the village was out of the question. He couldn't lead Clarion to them. He *had* to run.

"How is Luceran alive?" Zane backed up a few paces, feeling his way on the leafy ground.

"Games, elf... It's all about the *chase*." His violet eyes blazed. "Run and run and run—"

Clarion lunged.

Zane smashed through the undergrowth in the direction he hoped Akiem had taken. He *could* outrun a dragon in this brush, unless Clarion shifted and sniffed him out. The lord wanted a chase, and Zane would give him one to remember.

Following the rise and fall of the terrain, so sure Akiem would be around the next tree or over the next mound, his heart pounded and his thighs burned, then the ground fell out from under him. Falling wasn't the worst of it. His knee struck first, sinking into a bed of thick mud. Zane plunged forward and threw out a hand, but the mud took that too, embracing him up to his shoulder in cold.

He floundered. Mud splashed into his mouth. Panic made his thoughts race.

Not mud… anything but mud.

He heard dragons circling all over again, so like before. "Alumn, no…"

He had to find Akiem. He was here. He was close. He had to be. The mud sucked Zane down. With every pull, every twitch, the thick slop sucked him deeper into the cold, inch by painful inch. It was like before. He saw bodies in the mud, those drowned as they'd fled the battle-field. Reaching skeletal hands. Wide, mud-covered eyes, their faces forever locked in horror.

His lungs weren't working. His heart beat too hard, like it might burst out of his chest. Couldn't breathe. Couldn't think. Clarion was here, chasing… Couldn't think about anything outside of the mud climbing up his waist, pressing against his chest, squeezing the life right out of him.

"*Help…*" he gasped. He clawed at the mud, trying to dig a path out, knowing, somewhere in the back of his mind, that it was better to stay still, but rational thought had fled.

Mud crept over his shoulders and up his neck. He snagged a branch, only for it to snap off and drop him deeper. Mud smothered his chin, crawled higher into his mouth. He threw his head back, breathing hard through his nose. Alumn, not like this! It wasn't fair. Why save him in the past for him to die here…?

He sucked in air through his nose.

Mud poured over his eyes.

The thundering was inside, his body screaming, until the thundering of his heart swallowed him whole.

kiem

HE'D GOTTEN TURNED AROUND, and now every inch of him demanded he shift and take to the air. He couldn't see in the thick forest, and Luceran's scent surrounded him. He had to shift and take to the sky to see from above.

A streak of white hit him like a lightning bolt. Luceran's fingers found his throat. Akiem slashed low with the stained dagger and caught the king, hearing him gasp. Akiem pulled back to drive the dagger in deep to keep him from shifting, but a root or a rock caught his foot and they tumbled to the ground in a tangle of limbs.

Luceran landed a punch to Akiem's gut, reopening the wound. He cried out and thrust an elbow around, striking the king in the jaw and throwing him off balance. Akiem shoved the knife forward. Luceran caught his wrist in both hands and jerked his head forward. Pain blasted across Akiem's nose. He swallowed and spat blood, recoiling.

Teeth fixed onto his throat.

Akiem froze, instinct overruling everything.

Don't move.

It'll be over quicker that way.

He can't do anything Dokul hasn't already done.

The pain would end.

It always ended.

Luceran's growls permeated the sound of Akiem's thudding heart.

Akiem thought of Zane, his half-cocked smile and hungry, illicit glances.

Luceran's teeth slid from his neck. The king knelt on Akiem's chest and prized the dagger from his loose grip. "Return with me and your elves will live another day."

Akiem blinked at the diamond king. The hollowness Zane had filled returned, emptying out all emotion. "You'll leave them alone?"

"I will."

"And Zane?"

Luceran's top lip curled. "He'll live, but you'll never see him again."

"But he's... safe?"

The king's lashes shuttered. He leaned forward, his face filling Akiem's vision, leaving no room for thoughts of another. "You're mine," he growled. "You were mine when I dragged you off that beach and you're still mine. Nothing and nobody escapes me. Did you think you had? Did you think you were free?"

He stroked his knuckles down Akiem's face. Akiem turned his face away. The king's growl rumbled. "I opened the door and you ran, my black prince. You were a beautiful chase, but the time has come for the game to end."

His icy touch burned into Akiem's cheek. "Your death was a lie. Why?"

The king slowly blinked his violet eyes, and the real dragon peered out from behind all the dazzling prettiness. A dragon at the top of the food chain. Cunning and manipulative. Jeweled to his core. He'd played Akiem since that day on the beach, playing with his mind and hidden desires. The strange words and stranger behavior, letting Akiem think he cared. It had all been lies. Akiem swallowed.

"You made the mistake of thinking my brother and I are different. We are one and the same. He is my eyes and ears, and I am his claws. He saw rebellion in you. I saw a game like no other."

"I had no intention of hurting you."

Luceran's smile was cutting. "You think I do not know a predator when I see one? You *were* a prince. I smell it on you. Your blood beats differently from other jeweled. You look through me, seeing where best to sink your teeth. You want my throne. You want destruction. *It's in your eyes.*"

Akiem breathed in and bared his teeth in warning. "You're more right than you can possibly understand."

"You're dangerous. You're a threat. The chase has proven it." He straightened, his weight still an uncomfortable pressure on Akiem's thighs, reminding him too much of past horrors. "But for all your potential, you are weak and broken. Return to my side and no more elves need die."

Bile burned the back of Akiem's throat. "You burned a city and killed elves... for a game?"

"It was time the elves remembered who controls

them." Luceran freed Akiem and offered his hand. "Your chase was just entertainment."

The wound in his gut burned. Blood dribbled down his throat from his broken nose. He dabbed at it, thoughts reeling. If he left with Luceran, the elves would live, until the next game, the next test, and now Luceran knew Akiem had a weakness. Elves would always suffer while Akiem lived.

Akiem closed his hand around Luceran's. "My life is yours."

Menace made the king's smile flicker and almost snuff out. He strode past Akiem and shifted in a clearing, his bulk shining white beneath the sun. Akiem shifted and took to the sky behind the king, leaving behind his first love.

CHAPTER 28

ane

METAL CUFFS, locked around his wrists, were tied to chains looped in a hook bolted to the floor. Tugging at them did little, but he tried until the cuffs rubbed his skin raw.

Opposite him, similarly chained, two elven sisters huddled together, mutely eyeing him. Clarion's bitter scent covered them. Beyond them, a tall female leaned against the corner of the chamber, her eyes distant, seeing far-off things Zane didn't want to contemplate.

He had dreamed of dragon claws closing around him and lifting him from the mud, but the claws hadn't been Akiem's, and the dream had quickly turned into a nightmare. His situation hadn't improved much on waking. Thinking on it made him want to curl into himself like the others here already had.

He tugged again on the cuffs and pulled them close to examine each link for a weakness.

"You have red hair..." one of the twins said.

Zane looked up but had no idea which one had spoken.

"He was going to kill someone with red hair."

"Guess I have that to look forward to." He wedged his boots against the hook, clamped his hands around the chain near the joint, and heaved back until every muscle in his back and arms burned. The damn loop didn't move.

Mud flaked off his boots. He looked at it, hating each flake and how it had made him panic. Jevan had saved him before. Was he here?

"Do you know Jevan?" he asked.

The twins blinked at him, but the female behind them jerked her head up.

"You know him?" he asked again.

She nodded and crawled forward, as far as her chains would allow. He waited for her to say how she knew Jev, but her eyes pleaded instead.

"He took her tongue," one of the twins said, the one with cropped black hair.

She said something else too, but Zane rocked back, needing the wall to hold him up. His head spun. The room tilted, trying to pull him down again. He breathed too hard, too fast. He should have taken the shot to kill Clarion when he'd had the fucking chance. All of this could have been avoided.

"Hey... what's your name?" the same twin asked.

He couldn't be here, and he definitely couldn't *die* here. He clutched his head. Fuck, he had to get to Akiem. The panic was back, cutting each breath off too soon. He and Akiem were going to make a difference together. That was the plan, not this prison. He couldn't die here.

"I'm Teone, and this is my sister, Helana."

"Zane," he said through his teeth, grateful for the girl's attempt to distract him.

Teone was the talkative one. The other girl, Helana, kept her head down. Her bangs covered her eyes.

"Do you know Jev?" he asked them.

Teone nodded and shuffled closer. "Yeah, he was here a little while." She jerked her chin at the closed door. "Clarion kept him in there, and then the dragon in black took him away. He's maybe... probably dead, I guess."

The black dragon was Akiem. Clarion had kept Jev in this very chamber. Maybe Akiem would come for Zane too? But no, Akiem should stay away. He'd gotten free of his past, of this place. Maybe he'd finally fly off and never come back. He should, but given Akiem's desire to get himself killed saving others, it wasn't likely.

Zane ached all over and inside too. He looked at the damp walls. No windows. He couldn't stay here. The lack of light would eat at his soul like a cancer.

"Jev's alive... I think," he said. Although the last time he'd seen Jev, he'd been standing behind Clarion, watching the lord beat on Zane. "The black dragon saved him. That dragon is not what you think."

"We're talking about the same dragon? Real tall. Golden eyes. He looked mean—like, they're all mean, but meaner than even Clarion." She shuddered. "He saved him? For real?" Zane nodded, and her big eyes widened further. "But he's dragon."

Every time someone told him Akiem was dragon, it made him love him more. His big, beautiful black prince. Alumn, he had to get out of here and back to him before he did something typically Akiem.

Akiem had saved Jev, only for Jev to turn on them.

Zane rested against the wall and stared at the door out of the prison, but his mind wandered back to how he'd seen Jevan standing behind Clarion, making no move to help. Jev had frozen. Jev never froze.

"Did Clarion talk a lot with Jevan?"

"Yeah." Teone picked at her threadbare shoes. "Sort of. Jevan didn't say much, but Clarion talked."

"What about?"

"A chase..."

Clarion had captured Jevan all those weeks ago and used him as leverage to keep Zane quiet, but that had been a ruse too, a way for Clarion to reel Jevan in without making it look as though Jev were already connected to him. Whatever Clarion had over Jevan, it was enough to make him lie to Zane for years.

"The brothers pretend to be at odds with each other to catch out any dissent at court," Teone continued, "but they're real close. Luceran and Clarion were planning something. Jevan didn't want to do it. We heard him yelling. He did it for her." Teone nodded toward the mute elf beside her.

The quiet one nodded, licked her finger, and wrote in the dust on the floor.

Zane strained against his chains to read the words.

JEVAN. BROTHER.

He looked again at the graceful elf. She had the same dark skin as Jevan, and the same proud, shapely, shrewd eyes, like little got past her.

The curl of hair in Jev's locket.

It belonged to her.

Clarion's words about finding the right motivation.

She was Jev's sister.

Which meant she'd been here since before Zane had

known Jevan, before Zane had picked a fight with Jev in the street all those years ago. Jev had kept the locket on him the entire time Zane had known him. The locket was all Jev had left of his captured sister.

Jev's insistence on returning to Bayston every year, always around the same time. His disgust for dragons. His part in a game to kill the king and restart a war. It was all because of her. No wonder Jevan did as the dragons told him. He didn't have a choice.

He should have told Zane. Maybe he'd tried, and Zane had been too wrapped up in his own life to see what was right in front of him.

"What's your name?" Zane asked.

ROSA, she wrote, smiling shyly.

"Nice to meet you, Rosa. Your brother never forgot about you. Ever. He always came back here every year. Now I know why."

She nodded, her bottom lip quivering.

He shuffled back, leaned against the wall, and draped his chained wrists over his knees. It was always the same. Dragons bullied, fucked, kept, and used elves.

He had to get them out of here. All of them.

Maybe Akiem *would* come. He always had before. But while Akiem would fight Clarion, he wouldn't fight Luceran. Akiem was different around him, like Luceran tapped into that wounded, fragile part of him and used it against him. Akiem was strong, and getting stronger, but not around Luceran.

And all for a fucking game ...

Hundreds of elves dead, a city burned, because the two diamond dragonkin were... what? Bored?

He thought of Annie and her empty warehouse, of the burning streets and ash-covered bodies.

Maybe Annie's village was safe, or maybe Luceran would click his fingers and decide it was their turn to die. Fucking dragons. They all deserved to rot in the earth.

All but one.

Zane eyed the chains tying him down. If he somehow got free, he'd then have to make it out the door. There would be guards. After that, he'd have to find his way out of the compound without anyone seeing, and he wouldn't be alone either, because he wasn't leaving anyone here to suffer under Clarion. Rosa, Teone, and Helana were all coming with him.

Whatever he did, he had to do it fast, before the windowless room sucked the strength from his veins. Elves needed light to live. The girls and Jev's sister, despite their obvious trauma, appeared alert.

"Do they take you somewhere to get light?"

Teone nodded. "The guards take us outside when the days are warm. They know we'd die without sunlight."

"Do those guards have keys to these?" He showed her the shackles.

"Yes, but we tried to take the keys once. That's when Rosa lost her tongue. They're too strong."

"Don't make him angry," Helana whispered, her voice hoarse. "He'll hurt us, not you. It's how his mind works."

She curled closer against her sister.

And that was exactly how Clarion controlled them.

Rosa tucked herself back into the corner but kept her gaze on Zane, as a warning or encouragement, he couldn't tell. Teone and Helana huddled closer still. The room reeked of blood and sex and dragon. If he did nothing, they'd all die here. Elves would continue to be used and slaughtered and nothing would change. Zane was done waiting for change. Going forward, he'd be more like Akiem and change the future himself.

"WHAT'S WRONG WITH THIS ONE?"

A boot jabbed Zane in the gut.

He dragged his eyes open and blinked wearily at the guard.

"He needs light," Teone said.

"He just got here."

Zane added a groan for effect.

"Shit," the guard grumbled and crouched. The chains rattled. "Hey, hold him, eh. Just in case."

Hands found Zane's shoulders as the chains slunk through the loop and fell to the ground. Zane flung his head back, impacting hard with the second guard's chin, and lunged forward, wrapping the free chain around the first guard's neck. He had seconds to make this count. Yanking the dragon close, he twisted the links, chinking them together. The dragon bucked and kicked, writhing and twisting. He clawed at the chain, then swung an arm behind him and snagged a handful of Zane's hair, wrenching out a fistful.

The second guard growled.

Zane glanced behind him. The twins lunged, taking his legs out as he recovered from Zane's head-butt, and then the twins were on him, scratching at his face and throat.

Citrus burned Zane's tongue.

The dragon he choked was about to shift. Zane tightened his hold, hooked a leg around him, and pulled him closer still. His thrashing slowed. The lemony bite in the air grew so potent it burned Zane's throat and stung his eyes. If the beast shifted, they'd all die, crushed under dragon.

Magic rippled up Zane's arms like heat haze on a summer's day. Zane's vision blurred. Muscles trembling, he cinched the chain tighter. There was no going back. The dragon would shift whatever happened. He had to die in the next seconds.

The guard's struggling slowed. He twitched. Zane prayed to Alumn it was over. The male finally fell still, and the pungent smell of dragon thinned.

Zane shoved the body off and twisted, grabbing for the remaining guard's kicking leg. The twins had him pinned, but he was writhing free. Zane landed a punch to the beast's throat, choking off his air, then clutched his head and smashed his skull against the floor. Something cracked, the floor or bone. Zane slammed the guard's head into the floor again, and the dragon stopped moving.

Shit.

They'd done it.

"The keys. Quickly!"

He rummaged through the dragon's pockets and found the loop of keys. They were getting out of here. He stood. All he had to do was find the right key for the right lock and—

A punch slammed into his shoulder, throwing him forward. He stumbled over a dead dragon. Another punch nailed his lower back, lighting his body of fire. Zane's knees slammed into the floor. His breaths came fast, his body ablaze with pain. Someone screamed, and he couldn't be sure it wasn't him.

"An elven bow is an effective weapon," Clarion said. "This one supposedly killed a king. I took it from our mutual friend."

Zane felt the weight of the arrows lodged in his back, one in his shoulder and the other lower, near his waist. He looked down. A bloody arrowhead protruded from his shoulder and glistened. His vision fuzzed and cracked. The shoulder wound wouldn't be fatal, yet, but the one lower, the one his brain had already numbed for his own sanity, might see him dead.

If he could just breathe for a moment and collect his thoughts. He had to stop Clarion. Nothing else mattered.

The bow clattered to the floor. Zane saw it there, Jevan's bow. Clarion probably thought his using it to kill Zane was poetic.

The twins scurried back against the wall.

Clarion's boots thumped on the floor.

Agony tore through Zane's back, and he cried out.

An arm hooked around Zane's neck, clutching him back against the hot hardness of the dragon's thighs. Clarion showed Zane the bloody arrow and tossed it to the floor. "Your dragon thinks you're alive, living a free life with the elves. He bargained his freedom on it. What a shame he doesn't know you're here."

Akiem was here? Zane opened his mouth to ask, but he tasted too much blood and choked on the words.

"The problem is... Akiem isn't so easily cowed. He plays at submissive, but it won't last, and that's where you come in, Red."

Zane had failed.

Nothing had changed. Their fates still rested in Clarion's hands.

"My job is to provide a little... insurance."

He pulled Zane around to face him, his strength monstrous. The lord grinned and pulled a dagger from his belt. "This"—he grabbed Zane's right hand—"will be the perfect gift."

The knife's hungry edge snagged beneath Zane's little finger.

Zane tore free and scrabbled back, but he only made it as far as the wall. There was no way out. Clarion stalked forward.

Behind him, one of the twins snatched the discarded arrow. Clarion hadn't seen.

Zane jerked his chin, keeping the lord's attention on him. "Akiem will stop you."

Clarion's mouth pulled into a grin. He grabbed for Zane's hand. Zane pulled away, but thick fingers locked around his neck. The dragon's smile twisted into a snarl. He tore Zane's hand out from behind him, pinned Zane's wrist to the wall, and pressed the knife against the base of Zane's little finger. "This is for Akiem. A little reminder to behave now that he's Luceran's pet again."

No...

The knife cut in.

He tried to stay silent, tried to make it so Clarion didn't win, but the cry tore free. The knife sawed, and with the strength of dragon behind it, the blade cut through muscle and bone.

Clarion staggered back and showed Zane the severed tattooed finger.

Zane clutched his throbbing hand to his chest, staring at the bloody digit, unable to believe that the finger had once belonged to him.

Helana lunged. She slashed the arrow at Clarion. He swung his arm out, backhanding her so hard she flew backward. The chains snapped tight, yanking her down. Her head struck the floor with a sickening crack. She didn't move, didn't blink… didn't breathe.

"No… no, no, no…" Teone pulled her dead sister into her lap and rocked her.

"Fucking elves." Clarion picked up the arrow, snapped it in two over his knee, and threw the pieces at Zane. "You did that!"

"Akiem will rip your wretched heart out!" Zane's voice cracked, like the rest of him, coming apart between shivers and sickness.

Clarion bared his teeth. "Akiem is Luceran's bitch."

He left. The door slammed closed.

Shudders racked Zane. He looked at the broken pieces of arrow, felt the wounds burn and throb in his back, cradled his wounded hand, and stared into Helana's empty eyes amid Teone's quiet sobs.

There was a single strand of hope left.

Clarion thought Akiem broken and weak. He was wrong.

The Black Prince was here, and that changed everything.

CHAPTER 29

kiem

BAYSTON'S FIRES HAD DWINDLED, so only a few strings of smoke trailed over the city. As dragon, Akiem perched atop the broken building Zane had taken him to and shown him what he could do with his smart mouth.

A few elves skittered among the city ruins, defying the dragons soaring above. They wouldn't be attacked, not Akiem on Luceran's invisible leash. Luceran had given his word, and curiously, Akiem believed it. Dragons were dragons. They did the things they did because they could. Luceran was no different from the jeweled thousands of miles across the sea. There was little more dangerous in this world than a bored king.

It wasn't as though Akiem hadn't suffered beneath a ruling dragon before. This was his destiny. No matter how far he flew, the same life caught up with him. Always someone else's beast, never his own.

At least Zane was safe.

His elf would see sense and move on. If he returned to Bayston for Akiem or Jevan, Luceran would kill him. Zane knew that. Despite making some questionable choices, Zane knew when to quit.

Except when it came to anyone he cared about. Did he include Akiem in that?

The king's call rang out across the city, summoning Akiem back to the compound.

He dove off the side of the building and swooped low, his gaze divided between the elves scattering below and the dragons lazily circling above. Perhaps he could keep the peace this way, with him positioned between the two, protecting one from the other. The only cost would be his freedom. Cheap, then, as what did he know of freedom?

He shifted back to man at the compound and walked the hallways, tracking Luceran down to one of the many double-height rooms the king used for gatherings. Today, he stood alone at a long table, a small box in front of him. Energy strummed around him, the type that usually signaled an imminent shift.

Akiem approached, and having abandoned any hint of pride, he knelt at the king's side and bowed his head, grateful he'd left his hair down to cover the innately vulnerable spot at the back of his neck.

"There are to be executions," Luceran said.

Akiem lifted his head, peering up the king's figure. His intricate lace-and-leather attire highlighted the purple in his eyes. "Not elves?"

"Yes."

"Our agreement—"

"—could not cover all elves," the king snapped.

Akiem rose without permission. "You knew what I referred to. Elves in this city, in your territory, at least. That was our agreement."

Luceran stared back, light to Akiem's dark. "This fascination with elves is unseemly," he snarled. "Since your return, you have given me nothing of yourself."

It had been only a day. "Allow me some clarity. I haven't allowed you to fuck me, so you will kill elves until I do?"

The king's eyes narrowed. "You are to be mine, in all ways, or the elves die. It's really quite simple."

This wasn't like Luceran. The murder of elves, perhaps, but forcing sex hadn't been his way. At least, Akiem had believed as much. But how well did Akiem know him? The brothers had been playing their game this whole time. Even Luceran had said Akiem did not know the dragon he served. Perhaps, now that the game was over, he was seeing the king's true colors. In which case, he really was like all the other jeweled. Bite, take, own, fuck. Luceran had just dragged it out, enjoying the chase more than most, but he was still dragon.

"How many elves are to be executed?" Akiem asked.

"Three."

"What is their crime?"

Luceran faced Akiem. "No crime other than being elves." His beautiful eyes thinned, lashes sharpening. "Your elf, the one that fascinates you so, he took your coin for sex? I've been known to hire elves for all manner of work. They'll do almost anything for coin..."

The switch in topic tilted Akiem's balance. His heart stuttered, the implications landing hard. He recalled Zane pocketing his coin before dropping to his knees. He didn't take payment for sex, but for Akiem he had. What else had he taken payment for? Luceran had spies everywhere —including Jevan.

Was Zane too? Nobody was that good a liar. The moments with Zane had been real. The damn kiss in the dark room—yet he had gotten inside the compound easily, and right after Akiem had handed Jevan over, Luceran had attacked, as though he had known where Akiem would be. Someone had told him. Zane.

He reached for the table, needing its solid surface.

It wasn't possible.

"Clarion would see you dead. He believes you're too dangerous to be allowed to roam freely," the king continued, but Akiem's screaming thoughts drowned out the words. "He doesn't believe you'll submit." Luceran pressed a cool hand against Akiem's chest and spread his fingers, claiming him. "He wants your head. I've refused him, of course, but he'll take the heads of the three elves in his care instead."

"Another test?" The question sizzled on Akiem's tongue.

"He wants you to lash out. Will you?"

'*Mercenary. Among other things,*' Zane had said in the elven bar.

He'd admitted to the seduction to save his friend. Had that been the only reason?

"Did you pay him to seduce me?" Akiem's voice sounded low and rough, dragging from his depths emotions he struggled to hide. *Feelings.* Real feelings for an elf whose smile warmed his cold center, whose laugh Akiem would pay to hear again. Had it all been for coin? How well did he know him? No more or less than he knew Luceran or anyone this side of the ocean. But it had seemed so real—the only real thing in Akiem's entire life.

"He is an elf, Akiem." Luceran's voice softened. "You are dragon." The king's eyes sparkled. His cool hand cupped Akiem's cheek. "Take the place I offer beside me. Submit to me, be mine in all ways, and I'll convince Clarion to stop the executions. Peace will be restored."

Peace. All Akiem had to do was submit to the king.

He'd thought there might be another life out there for him, one with an elf, *protecting elves*. He leaned into Luceran's touch and closed his eyes. Even if his time with Zane had been true, they had no future together. Akiem *was* dragon. What else was there but Luceran and a dragon life beneath him?

Akiem dipped his head, submitting. "Free the three elves first."

Luceran frowned and leaned a hip against the table. "I'll need assurances."

He flicked his gaze up. "Is my word not enough?"

The king's smile slithered as though it had a life of its own. "I hear it in your voice and see it in the way you stand: you were once revered among your kind. A ruler, even. It's that which worries my brother and that which I must control."

"What I once was does not matter. What I am here, now, is wholly yours."

Luceran stood, bringing him too close to Akiem. "Give me a promise of more." The king's simmering power tried to lure Akiem in and have him rub himself against him, but a shocking repulsion kept Akiem rooted. He'd been willing, eager even, not so long ago, before the elf had come into his life, but as the king again claimed his jaw in his grip, Akiem's heart thudded, readying for escape, not pleasure. It should be simple. Luceran was just another dragon, and Akiem had suffered under far worse, but something in him had changed. *He* had changed.

The king's cool lips brushed Akiem's, urging him to open. Zane's touches had left Akiem breathless. Luceran's left him cold.

He had to do this. To save lives. For peace. If he could control the king with a kiss, with more, the cost was hardly anything.

Akiem parted his lips and nudged the king's mouth, giving Luceran the response he wanted, even as every instinct demanded he tear away. Just a kiss.

Akiem rode his hand down the curve of Luceran's back, pulling him in close, hardness against hardness. Only Akiem wasn't hard, not where it counted.

Luceran crowded close. The table dug into the back of Akiem's thighs, the pressure reminding him that he was trapped in more ways than one.

The kiss hastened, messying tongue and lips together. Akiem pulled on the memory of Zane's kiss, the one from the dark room, the one that had started it all. *Dragon, kiss me or let me go.* The elf's eyes had sparkled in the dark, full of mischief and humor. Akiem heard his laugh now, its dirty rumble making him wish for time alone with the elf. Lies or not, Akiem ached for Zane. Finally, his cock was waking. He just had to imagine Luceran was Zane to get through this.

Luceran's hand captured Akiem's hips. The king yanked him groin-to-groin and mouthed up Akiem's jawline, nipping below his ear. Luceran's interest dug into Akiem's hip. Too hot and hard. *Unwanted.*

The king's teeth pinched Akiem's neck.

Instincts snapped. Akiem shoved him before he could stop the reflex. Luceran's violet eyes flared. He bared his teeth and lunged. Akiem swung a fist, like he had with Clarion. His knuckles struck the king's chin, whipping his head back.

A new kind of lust burned through Akiem: the killing kind. He stepped forward. Luceran recovered and swung for Akiem, but he broadcast the attack in his shoulders. Akiem ducked and sprang off his back foot. He slung his arms around Luceran's middle, tackling him to the floor. The king's skull hit hard.

Power.

Magic.

Diamond sparks danced across Akiem's skin.

The shift. Akiem had seconds to retreat. He rolled aside, flung his arms over his head, and weathered the suffocating outpouring of magic. Strength and power slammed into his back and sloshed over him, drowning him in Luceran's scent.

The king roared, the noise so loud in the suddenly small room that it shook plaster from the ceiling.

The door was too far to make a run for it, and if he ran, Luceran would pounce. Akiem clambered to his feet. Hard scale smacked him in the back, throwing him against the table. Hot breath blasted behind him. A warning. In this form, Akiem was a single bite away from death.

The shift tried to pull Akiem apart, but if he shifted, he'd fight and lose.

Luceran's massive maw shoved into Akiem's shoulders, throwing him forward, *bending* him into submission. He sprawled forward and stayed down. The king could do no more while Akiem was man and himself dragon, besides kill him.

A burbling growl rumbled around the room.

Akiem lifted his hands and slowly turned.

Luceran's shimmering diamond-white scales filled the room. The lamplight licking down his sides and over his wings made him shine. His eyes glowed violet, each orb bigger than Akiem.

The diamond king bared his teeth, reminding Akiem exactly who sat on the throne at the top of the food chain in this land. The dragon shook his head, plodded backward, and shifted back into man, blinding Akiem again. This time, when Luceran approached, there was no room on his lips for smiles. He scooped up the box on the table and shoved it at Akiem's chest.

"You need more persuasion."

Akiem breathed hard through his nose, riding out the adrenaline. He took the box and turned it over in his hand. Just a small wooden box with a simple latch. A gift? Now?

"Open it," Luceran ordered.

Akiem flicked the latch and lifted the lid. A single finger lay on bloody silk. A finger marked with the sweepingly elegant swirls of Zane's tattoos.

A growl rolled up Akiem's throat, but Luceran's hand snapped out, snake-fast, and snatched his neck, choking off the sound before it could break free. "Your wretched elf will die unless you submit to me, *prince*."

Rage set Akiem's veins ablaze. Zane was here. Clarion was likely torturing him. The deal for peace was bullshit. It always had been. Whether Zane had been paid to fuck him didn't matter. Everything was lies. Everything but the wrongness of this world. That was real, and he'd fight to see it put right.

Luceran's human snarl was no less threatening than his dragon one. "I'll have Clarion cut pieces off him and present them to you until there is nothing left."

"You lying coward," Akiem hissed. "You're the same as every jeweled."

"I didn't lie. I didn't know my brother had captured him, but I appreciate his initiative. Especially as you need a lesson in obedience." Luceran shoved Akiem to his knees. "Service me, prince, or your elf dies."

Service me, elf.

"Make me come or his cock will be the next gift I deliver."

Akiem's thoughts blurred, finding that faraway place where nothing hurt him. He threaded his fingers through the ties of the king's pants and yanked them loose. Zane's pleasurable laughter in his head turned to that of Akiem's mother's, and then to his father's every time he'd fucked Akiem into the ground. All the times he'd been used and shut in the dark, the times he'd burrowed so deep inside himself that he'd become a shadow, they should have prepared him for this. They had—until Zane had shown him kindness, shown him how things *could* be different. Lies or not, Akiem knew there was light in the world. He'd seen it, and he'd protect it for others, if not for himself. *That* was who he was: a protector of those who could not protect themselves.

Falling to his knees, he wrapped his fingers around the king's erection, barely feeling it, *refusing* to feel it. The shaft of heated maleness had lost all its appeal now that the king was forcing himself on him. He licked up, from balls to tip, tasting Luceran. The king shuddered, plunged his fingers into Akiem's hair, and held him rigid, pinning him down without choice and no escape. Closing his lips around the solid cock, Akiem sent his mind farther into that dark place.

He clamped his teeth shut, sinking sharpness into muscular flesh.

Luceran roared, grabbed him by the hair and slammed his head back. His skull hit the table or floor, he didn't know which. He smiled as pain throbbed, blood flowed, and his body went numb, unconsciousness rushing in to save him from whatever happened next.

One thought followed him down: the diamond brothers must die.

ane

THEY LED THEM, chained at the hands, in a line so very like the one that had taken twelve elflings to their deaths. No bags over their heads, although Zane almost wished there were. His back burned, his jaw ached, and his hand throbbed where his digit was missing. He was alive, though, which had to be by damn luck or Alumn's grace. Helana had died for Zane's mistake. Her sister shuffled ahead, and in front of her, Rosa led the line, pulled along by a heavyset dragonguard.

They twisted and turned through parts of the compound, rising and falling with steps and levels, until they emerged in a room Zane recognized. Dread set his teeth chattering. The chopping block in the center of the chamber bore the stains of Clarion's previous victims.

"Wait..." Jevan's panicked voice rose from the crowd of

dragonkin. He fought his way to the front, prompting a wave of snarls. "You can't do this!"

Clarion moved in fast, kicked Jev's legs out, and slammed him face down on the floor. "One more word out of you and you'll join your friend."

"Kill me," Jevan hissed. "But save my sister. Please, by Alumn. Please don't hurt her anymore!" He broke down into sobs. "She's... been hurt... enough."

Rosa frantically shook her head, and Zane's instincts simmered all over again, lessening the pain from his wounds. The crowd, Jevan's sister, the block—it was all wrong.

The guard yanked the line forward, toward the waiting block.

Luceran sat on his ugly throne, looking resplendent in leather and silk. Beside him, standing rigid, his mask back on, was the king's shadow, Akiem. Only he didn't look like his shadow anymore. He wore a deep purple waistcoat stitched with silver lace and black trousers. His hair had been pinned and tied to mirror the king's. He looked like a possession, like a doll the king dressed up and did with as he pleased.

The sight punched Zane in the gut. He tripped and fell, only to be yanked upright and shoved along. There were more guards now. So many. Too many to escape. He looked for an escape anyway. For weaknesses in those around them. There were none. The dragons looked on, hungry for blood.

A few weeks ago, he'd stood among the crowd, watching an elf lose her head. He'd believed she'd deserved it. Alumn, he'd been so wrong.

He'd stumbled from one town to the next, taking coin,

sometimes taking more, never caring about the lives around him. Until Akiem. Something about the dragon had made him see things differently. Now here he was, following in the dead elf's footsteps, and there Akiem was, standing beside the king, exactly like before.

Then it hit him. He would die here.

Akiem caught his eye, but there was nothing readable in his hard bronze glare. A terrible, all-consuming sense of dread chilled Zane to the bone. What if Akiem had been pretending this whole time, like the diamond brothers had? No, it wasn't possible. What Zane had felt between them—the kiss in the dark room and everything after—couldn't be faked. And Clarion had told Zane he was leverage to make sure Akiem behaved. Alumn, his heart ached to see him there, right back where they'd begun, wrapped in the king's diamond-grip.

Akiem leaned to the side and whispered something in the king's ear. His lips moved carefully, precisely. The king frowned and drummed his fingers on the chair's arms.

With a flick of his wrist, Luceran summoned Clarion to him. The lord abandoned Jevan and knelt in front of his brother. More murmurs strummed between them.

Akiem had said something to stop this. He saved elves now. He'd rung the city's bells for elves. He'd fought his own kind for elves. He'd see them safe. Zane was sure of it. They'd escape the block and the axe. It wasn't over yet.

"Proceed," Luceran said.

Zane's heart dropped.

The guard grabbed Rosa, unclipped her from Teone, and dragged her toward the block. She went gracefully, her head held high.

Jevan bellowed his dissent and was met with Clarion's

swift kick to his gut. He curled into himself, but his sobs went on. He'd worked for Luceran and Clarion because they had Rosa. They'd promised to release her, and now she would die. They'd all die.

Zane found Akiem's glare again. *Don't let this happen.*

Akiem was strong. He was the strongest damn dragon Zane had ever known. Nobody could survive what he had unless they knew how to fight, and by Alumn, Akiem's bronze glare told how he could fight every single dragon here. Why wasn't he?

"Not her," Luceran corrected. "The red-haired one."

Shock clinched Zane's chest, squeezing out all the air in his lungs. A guard grabbed him, unlocked his shackles from the chain, and yanked on his wrists, dragging him toward the block. His heart pounded so hard he didn't hear the dragons raise their voices or Jevan sobbing.

Akiem... Akiem could stop this.

Akiem wasn't moving. His face had the same regal blankness as the first time Zane had seen him there, beside the king.

No... it couldn't all have been a lie. The kiss.... That single damn kiss in the dark room. That had been *real. Dragon, kiss me or let me go.* Akiem wore the lies he told himself, but he'd told Zane the truth.

Zane pulled on the guard's hold, yanking him off balance. "Akiem!"

The guard's fist flew in. He crumpled around the blow, but the dragon held him up and pulled him along.

"Akiem... please stop this."

The crowd stirred. Luceran's eyes narrowed. Clarion approached with his axe slung over his shoulder, his smile as broad as his weapon's curve.

Akiem did nothing. Didn't twitch, didn't blink, didn't look away.

With every passing second, fear stabbed at Zane's wrecked heart. Could it be that Zane had been taken in by a dragon? He'd fallen in love again and fallen hard. No dragon could love an elf. The beasts weren't capable.

'You believe I'm capable of caring?' Akiem had once asked.

Zane had known they did not care or love, but Akiem had been different. Could it all have truly been lies? Another dragon game played?

The guard shoved Zane to his knees at the block.

Horror made him numb and stupid. Splinters stuck up from the block. Each jagged cut marked an elven death. Dried blood stained the wood. He blinked in disbelief. He couldn't die like this.

Hands gripped on his shoulders. Thick fingers clamped around the back of his neck and shoved him down. Splinters thrust into Zane's neck. He wheezed, his body rebelling, trying to eject him into unconsciousness.

He faced away from the king, from Akiem, so he saw only the faces of dragonkin he didn't know, their eyes hungry, and Jevan, on his feet but restrained by a dragon twice his size. Jevan's eyes apologized for everything.

He wished he'd done things differently, wished he'd shot Clarion seconds before Jevan, wished he'd spent just a little more time with Akiem. Maybe it would have made a difference. Maybe it would have made *him* different. Most of all, he wanted to feel Akiem's warm hand in his again, one last time.

Clarion moved into the corner of Zane's vision. The dragon crouched and cocked his head, peering deep into Zane's eyes. "Your pretty head will adorn a spike in the middle of the burnt city as a warning to all elves. Don't fuck with dragons."

He straightened, stepped back, and let the axe handle slip through his fingers, catching it at the right angle to swing.

Zane squeezed his eyes closed, not wanting to see, then flung them open again, *needing* to see.

Cold air kissed the nape of his neck. Clarion breathed in. Zane heard the lord lift the axe.

One second and another passed.

Alumn, forgive me.

His breath raced, body caught on the egde of fear.

The hands holding him vanished. He turned his head, expecting to see Clarion, but Akiem filled his vision instead. Akiem lunged, and the guards moved in to stop him.

Clarion's axe glinted, about to fall.

Akiem grabbed Clarion's raised arm, capturing the final strike before it fell.

"All elves are under my protection," he said, the words crisp and loud and so fucking bright in Zane's thudding head.

Zane kicked back, catching Clarion's left shin and dropping the lord to a knee. Clarion grunted, more surprised than alarmed. He swung his glare to Zane, baring his teeth.

Akiem tore the axe from Clarion's distracted grip, lifted it over his head, and swung it down. The blade sliced through Clarion's neck and rang like a bell when it hit the stone floor.

The lord's head dropped, eyes open and mouth agape. He wasn't fucking smiling now. His body slumped and fell forward with a thud, his heart still pumping dragon blood across the floor.

Silence drowned the room.

Akiem stood over Zane. The axe in his hand dribbled thin trails of blood over his boots. A tick of a smile tugged at his lips.

Zane blinked, thoughts sluggish as he tried to understand how his head was still detached from his body. By Alumn, Akiem was *everything*.

A terrible, brittle screech shattered Zane's thoughts, as if the world were breaking in two. The king jerked from his throne, shift magic crackling and sparking around his human form.

Chaos boiled the crowd into motion. Dragonkin dashed for the exits. Akiem whirled, a blur of black, and swung the axe through the middle of a guard. The axe arced again, shining like a half moon, and slammed down on Zane's chains, shattering the links apart. "Get the others out!"

Akiem moved like liquid death, cutting through any who dared to rush him. The macabre sight enthralled.

Behind Akiem's dark outline, diamond spilled into the room, bubbling out of nothing into the enormous shape of claws and scales and wings.

"Akiem!"

Akiem retreated from the diamond king. No little axe could cut down Luceran now. He turned and grabbed Zane's good hand, lifting him to his feet. He saw the wraps around Zane's wounded hand and met Zane's eyes.

The king screamed his fury and flung out diamond wings, scooping up some of the fleeing crowd and tossing them against the walls, not caring that they were Dragon. Rage had blinded him. He thrashed his brutal crown of bone into swathes of running figures. Among them, an elf lay on his side.

"Oh Alumn, no..."

Jevan.

Luceran had seen him. The diamond dragon's eyes blew wide, and fire churned behind the scales low in his throat.

Akiem pulled Zane close. "Save them," he breathed, jerking his chin toward where Rosa and Teone huddled together. He gently pushed Zane into motion. "Go." He turned away, heading for the enormous and enraged dragon.

Zane stumbled to Rosa's side. "C'mon... both of you."

Luceran's roar tore through the air, the walls, the world. Zane looked back.

Akiem was close, a smudge of black against a monster of diamond white. He circled the axe over his head and set it free. The blade whirled, struck Luceran in the jaw, flinging the king's head back, and stayed lodged there. The king thrust his head upward, smashing through the ceiling in his madness. Debris rained, but Akiem dashed in, hauled Jevan to his feet, and pulled him into a run.

They would be okay.

They had to be okay.

Zane took Rosa's hand and led her into the scattering dragonkin. The taste of dragon burned his throat and made his eyes water. Some would shift, and if that happened, this entire compound would collapse around them. They had to get out and fast.

Dragonkin funneled through the exits, carrying Zane, Rosa, and Teone along.

"This way..." Akiem and Jevan appeared ahead. A sob tried to choke Zane as Jevan sent him a sheepish smile.

Akiem flung open a door, steering them out of the chaos and into a quiet side room with one window.

Roars tunneled after them. The walls and ceiling shook. Cracks snaked across the floor.

Rosa flung the window open and peered out.

"Jump," Jevan said.

They each scrambled free and, following Akiem, ran into the remains of Bayston.

kiem

THE FOUR ELVES were in no condition to flee the city. The speechless female appeared to be the strongest among them. Zane had been tortured. The smell of old, sour blood and sickness on him made Akiem want to shift and rip into anything and everything. One of the twins from Clarion's chamber was numbed by shock, and Jevan shivered and stumbled, his adrenaline wearing off fast.

Akiem led them into the hollowed-out insides of a derelict building. Piles of burnt wood thrummed with heat. He tucked the elves into a corner and gathered anything flammable, then nursed a fire from the ashes so they'd be warm. The smoke would go unnoticed among Bayston's smoldering ruins.

With the fire stable and the elves huddled around it, he leaned next to a hole in the wall that had once been a front door. From there, he scanned the street, watching, waiting.

Occasionally, the king's roars echoed through the night. The terrible cries spoke of vengeance and torment.

Only death, or something that would make him wish for it, waited for Akiem at the compound. He glanced back at each elf, appraising their condition. They all tugged at his heart, the part he'd thought lost and empty.

Whatever the king's lies, whatever Zane did or didn't do, none of that changed the fact that elves shouldn't suffer. Protecting them was Akiem's purpose now.

He tasted Clarion's blood on his lips and smelled it on his clothes. He flexed his fingers, feeling the axe strike home again. It could so easily have been Zane's head that had fallen. Luceran hadn't reacted well to Akiem almost severing his cock between his teeth. All of the elves in Bayston had been due to be killed and butchered, starting with Zane.

It wouldn't have ended there. Another elf, another bribe. On and on it would have gone.

Akiem didn't submit.

Not anymore.

He didn't kneel, and he didn't bow, and he damn well didn't stand by and watch the innocent pay with blood for a game of peace. He tore Luceran's pins from his hair and tossed them to the ground, then loosened the too-tight buttons of the damn waistcoat. It was suffocating, all of it.

In those last moments, he'd whispered to the king that if he went ahead with the executions, he would never submit to him. Luceran had proceeded anyway, out of spite.

"Hey..." Zane approached slowly, his steps deliberate.

Akiem shifted his gaze back to the piles of rubble on the street. Rats scurried about, but no dragons. They'd come. It wouldn't be safe here for long.

"Thank you," Zane said behind him, sounding unsure.

"It's fine."

"For a while there..." Akiem glanced back and caught Zane's nervous smile. "I thought you were going to watch me die." Zane propped a shoulder against the broken wall. A smudge of dirt and blood marked his cheek and jaw. His green eyes had lost some of their luster. "You came through. You got us out. I don't think you've ever once let me do—"

"Did Luceran pay you to seduce me?" Akiem stared at the piles of rock outside.

"He told you that?" His brow tightened, lips too. "No. The whole seduction thing was a shit idea, but it was *my* idea. I wouldn't work for that worm for all the coin in the world." Zane straightened and ventured closer. His scrutiny rode over Akiem's face. "Shit, you believed him?"

"I..." Akiem winced, and closing his eyes, he pinched away a new ache. "I care. About you. He knew and twisted it, put doubts in my head."

Zane stayed silent too long. Akiem opened his eyes and found Zane's crooked smile tucked into his cheek.

"You care about me?" the elf asked. His smile twitched and grew.

He'd taken Clarion's head for Zane, and gods, he'd do it again in a heartbeat. This was about saving elves, but it was also about saving *his* Red. He turned toward him, making him look up. Akiem brushed his knuckles down Zane's bruised and gritty cheek. So fragile and so full of life. To think Clarion had almost ended Zane's life. It tore at Akiem's new-found ability to feel and almost made him wish he didn't so it wouldn't hurt so much. "Your head is too pretty to lose."

Zane arched a russet brow. "Tell me again how pretty I am."

Akiem chuckled, but the laughter died as he saw how the bruises traveled down Zane's neck. His jacket and shirt were bloody, and his bandaged hand... The dragon in him wanted to tuck Zane in close and lick him until the hurt went away. Their differences were worlds apart, that much was true, and elves were fragile, even this fiery one.

Luceran would come.

Enraged, he'd destroy everything to get to Akiem.

Everyone was at risk, especially those close to him.

"Rest..." Akiem stepped away.

Zane's good hand caught his and pulled him back. The campfire light sparked in his eyes.

"I care about you too," his elf said. A blush of heat warmed Zane's cheeks, and it was all Akiem could do not to grab him and devour him in ways dragons did not normally devour elves. "Clarion took my finger, and you took his fucking head. You think you're not worth loving? You're so wrong, Akiem."

Loving? He masked his shock by pulling Zane in and planting a gentle kiss on his forehead. "Wrong, am I, elf? I'm beginning to believe," he whispered, sliding the words down Zane's cheek, "because of you."

He drew him in tight, needing to feel Zane close, especially as he smelled a sweet sickness on the elf that would only get worse. Zane molded perfectly against Akiem and sighed as Akiem brought his arms around and held him tight. Dropping his head, he breathed in Zane's fresh scent, absorbing it into his dragonheart, where he claimed Zane as his.

Carefully, reluctantly, Akiem let him go. "We need supplies. Stay by the fire, by them..."

"Rosa is Jevan's sister," Zane quietly explained.

He nodded at Jevan and his sister, both huddled together by the fire. Akiem thought of his own broodsister, dead so long now he'd almost forgotten her face, but he remembered her love. Jevan looked up, met Akiem's gaze, and nodded.

Leaving them wasn't easy. He lingered nearby in the shadows, should any dragons slink by, but none came. Akiem scavenged food and medical boxes the elves had left behind when they'd abandoned the city. Finding anything not burned took until the sun rose. He returned, arms full of stale bread and wrapped fruit that smelled like smoke. He'd found basic medicine, but the scent of spoiled blood around their camp suggested Zane's condition had worsened in his absence.

The fire had burned down to cinders. Zane slept on his side, with Rosa and Teone watching him. Jevan approached as soon as Akiem had climbed back inside the camp.

"He's feverish," Jevan murmured.

"I have medicine." He set the bundle of goods down beside the fire and rummaged through them with Jevan, but little inside was suitable for treating the infection ravaging Zane's body.

"It's not enough." Jevan frowned and rocked back on his heels. "We need a healer. There's a deep wound in his lower back. It's hot to the touch. I can't get much out of Rosa, but I think he tried to escape and Clarion caught him. Helana was killed. It looks as though Zane was stabbed, and it went deep."

Akiem straightened. Rosa watched him rise, her face tight with concern. He approached Zane's side, and she scuttled backward.

"It's all right," Jevan said. "Akiem won't hurt you."

Zane didn't wake as Akiem knelt beside him. He'd lost his color, and his lips had blanched. The bloody marks on Zane's clothes indicated worse wounds hid beneath. "I know someone, but I'll have to shift to take him there—to take you all."

"You want us to..." Jevan swallowed. "Go with you... as dragon?"

Akiem nodded. "You'll need to hold on. I'll not be slow. The flight will not be easy."

"I don't know..."

"He'll want you there when he wakes." *If he wakes.* Akiem could not allow that thought purchase. He carefully scooped Zane into his arms and headed outside. Zane mumbled a few words, none of which made any sense, and tucked himself against Akiem's shoulder.

Flying in daylight was risky enough, but to do so with passengers would slow him, making him more obvious above the cityscape. The risk was huge, but if he didn't go, Zane would die here.

"Dragon...?"

Jevan's voice carried far in the empty street. Akiem turned and set Zane's limp body down on the road. Unconsciousness had hold of him now. Akiem stroked Zane's hair back from his face and tucked it behind his pointed ear, like he'd been afraid to do a hundred times before.

"I was wrong about you," Jevan said.

"No, you were right." Akiem backed up, gauging the distance from the building to give himself space to shift. "I was everything you said, but I've changed. Zane helped me."

"I know... and I'm sorry." Jevan stepped forward, but

Rosa's hand on his arm held him back. She nodded for Akiem to continue.

The shift happened quickly, rolling power through muscles and stretching it out through his wings. He gathered Zane's vulnerable body in his claws, careful to cradle him safely. So tiny a thing, his bright elf. So precious.

He dipped a wing and eyed the siblings. Jevan and Rosa climbed on, Teone behind them. They all settled between his wings. He prayed to the great gods that they held on, because once in the air, there would be no stopping.

AKIEM FLEW FAST and true to Annie's village. If any dragon saw him, he'd deal with the consequences later.

At the village, Annie got to work immediately, taking Zane from Akiem's claws, even as he growled a warning not to hurt him. Other villagers looked on. They watched the three elves slip down his wing and greeted them fondly, and when Akiem shifted, elves didn't flee or fling arrows. They acknowledged him, dipping their heads in respect, and waved him inside their village, as if he *belonged*.

What a strange feeling that was, and one so alien it confirmed he had never belonged anywhere before.

The elves invited him to wash up and eat, but his mind was too lost in thoughts of Zane. He waited, sitting against the wall outside Annie's house. Annie had barred him from entering. He couldn't get any closer physically, and instinct wouldn't let him leave, so he stayed there as the day faded into evening.

You think you're not worth loving.

Love. He knew it now. It kept him here, waiting outside the house, listening to every creak of the floorboards through the walls. It made his thoughts circle back to the impossible red-haired elf full of laughter and life, the bright star in Akiem's darkness. It made his body ache when they were apart, as though Zane were the missing piece he'd been searching for his whole life.

Waiting was killing him.

He paced and thought on Luceran's next move. Clarion's death would rock his world, especially as they'd been so close. Luceran would come for Akiem, but the display in the compound had shown he wasn't thinking rationally. Vicious and brutal. Desperate for vengeance. He'd make mistakes. Akiem could use that.

Luceran had to die.

As for the rest of the dragons, some would jostle for Luceran's place as the apex dragon. There had been plenty of *lords* at Luceran's court, each eager to outlive the king, but another jeweled as king would change nothing.

If Akiem were stronger, he could claim the throne. Those who had been present at the botched execution would see his attacking the lord and the king as him making such a claim, but not all. Akiem could not fight them all—alone.

In his home, half a world away, he'd seen elves rise up. He'd seen them fight for their land and their people. The elves on this side of the ocean were just as capable, but they had to *believe* they could make a change. Believing in change was the first, and most difficult, hurdle.

"You can see him now," Annie said, wiping her bloody hands on a towel.

Zane lay face down on the bed. Annie had stripped him to his waist, and cleaned and stitched two puncture wounds, one to his shoulder and another to low on his back. Both could easily have been killing blows.

Damn elves were far too fragile. He reached for Zane's peaceful face, needing to touch him and hardly understanding why, but he quickly pulled his fingers back, fearing he might wake or hurt him.

"He's drugged. He won't wake for another few hours."

"Will he..." Akiem's voice cracked. "Will he be all right?"

"He'll be fine." Annie offered a gentle smile. "Nothing I can do about the finger, though."

A growl rumbled through Akiem. He dropped into the chair beside the bed and closed his eyes. In many ways, it had been easier when he had cared about nothing, but he wouldn't change it. Caring made him feel alive and true and strong—gods, so much stronger than before.

"What happened?"

He told her everything—from meeting Zane over a month ago, to the botched seduction, the king's deception, and Clarion's head falling beneath the lord's own axe. The more he spoke, the more roughness bled into his words, the dragon in him rising to the surface.

"Luceran will come for us."

"I'm sure he will." She seemed unconcerned. "We know you didn't kill the tutor. Our elflings all told of how you tried to save her. You really are quite the dragon."

Unsure how to respond, he dipped his head.

"I spoke to Zane before you were both taken... showed him something that might help stop the king. Did he tell you?"

"No."

"I'd like to show you when you're ready. Given the king's mental state, it could prove to be the opportunity we've been looking for."

He regarded Zane's unconscious form. No power in the world was strong enough to uproot Akiem from his side.

If Luceran was coming, so be it. Akiem would die protecting Zane. That was how things were. He found it comforting.

Annie smiled in understanding. "I'll bring some food by. Let me know when he wakes."

She left, and Akiem listened to the curious quiet inside his head. Peace. It was... strange to be at peace with himself.

He looked at Zane, at the bandaged hand with its missing digit and his blood-matted hair. Zane considered himself a coward. He was wrong. It took courage to survive. Akiem wasn't giving *him* up, not for anything or anyone. He could only hope Zane felt the same way.

ane

HE'D ALMOST DIED.

Apparently, it was becoming a habit.

He groaned, fighting his bruised and battered body. He wanted to stuff his face back into the pillow and ride out whatever would happen in a drug-muddled haze, but a dragonkin sat in the chair by the bed. He looked like he'd been there for hours and would stay there until the world turned to ash around them.

A shiver trickled down Zane's spine. A good one. He kinda liked knowing that Akiem would be there when he woke. He felt unworthy too, like this enormously powerful creature had picked the wrong lover. He wouldn't blame him for turning away. He kept expecting to find Akiem gone for good, but he hadn't abandoned them. He'd kept on fighting, even when the king had tried to lie his way into Akiem's affections. He still fought for good.

That fucking bastard lizard, telling Akiem he'd hired Zane.

Zane could see why Akiem might be pissed about the whole payment for services rendered. Shit, Zane made the worst decisions. He wouldn't change it, though, because if he hadn't pursued Akiem or had him pay for those services, they never would have gotten this far.

He looked like an ancient god. His hair was a smooth black curtain down his back, his face proud and hard, mouth harder, and eyes... Alumn, those damn eyes. They turned on him, and Zane's insides skittered with anticipation.

"Hi," he croaked, sounding like he'd been broken into a thousand pieces and hastily shoved back together again. He felt that way too, and when he tried to push off his chest, his shoulder barked in complaint and his back delivered a whip-like spasm of pain. Akiem moved so damn fast Zane didn't even see him until his warm hands were holding him, helping him to roll over. Well, that felt rather nice too.

"Slow and steady," the dragon said, "or Annie will force me to leave again."

The growl underlining his words made it clear he wouldn't leave, whatever Annie said.

"Did she hit on you?" Zane asked, mostly to see him frown, which he did.

"I'm dragon," Akiem said, like that was a deterrent.

Zane chuckled and wished he hadn't. Akiem fluffed his pillows and gently laid him back. He smelled of zesty, spicy things that Zane wanted to sink his teeth into. A warm, fuzzy feeling diluted some of Zane's all-over aches.

Akiem sat back down, but the frown stayed.

He'd said he cared. He'd cared even when he'd believed

Zane had lied to him. Damn, this dragon was unique and wonderful and precious and all Zane's. He'd better not screw it up, which was easier said than done, seeing as his relationships usually crashed and burned.

"Luceran will come," Akiem said. "Annie mentioned she showed you something that might help."

The baited trap.

With Akiem as the bait.

"It won't work," Zane said. Annie could find something else to bait her trap with. She wasn't using Akiem. "Luceran is too clever to fall for it."

"What won't work?"

He told Akiem of the underground warehouse wired to blow and how it needed sufficient bait for it to work. Akiem's gaze hardened, his thoughts taking the notion and running with it.

"You're not doing it." Zane wasn't letting him go. He'd just found him.

"It has merit. Luceran is distracted. Now is the time to strike. There will not be another opportunity like it."

"It's too risky. You'd have to be down there too, and when the explosives blow... Annie doesn't give a shit if you escape. She'll blow the place with you still in there."

Akiem's cheek fluttered. He was still thinking on it, because he believed, somewhere inside that intense head of his, that he deserved to die.

"Akiem, there are other ways."

"Name them."

Zane pursed his lips. Sliding his legs off the bed, he sat on the edge. Akiem straightened, ready to catch Zane if he fell. If this prince had been raised to love instead of hate, he might have changed the world, but there was still time.

"There has never been a dragon like you. None of what

happened in your past was your fault. Don't throw yourself away because others can't see who you really are."

Seeing Akiem suffer for the sins of others broke something inside Zane. Even now, his dragon prince didn't believe how special he was. He smiled softly like he believed Zane, but doubt clouded his beautiful bronze eyes—eyes Akiem despised. How could Zane make him see that he didn't need to die to prove he had earned the right to live? Words failed him. Actions too. He did not know how to reach a dragon's soul, but by Alumn's light, he'd damn well try.

Akiem glanced behind him at the door, searching for an escape.

Zane reached out, pulling Akiem's attention back to him. He cupped his cheek and drew him closer. The tiredness showed in his eyes. He wanted to live, didn't he? Beneath all that stubborn exterior, he must believe in a future? Otherwise, why fight? And he sure knew how to fight. He'd been a creature made of pure vengeance in that execution hall.

His cheek was warm, and Zane drew him close, never letting go of his stare. He tried to drop his head, to submit, but Zane held him firm, bumping his forehead against his.

"You have a whole village out there who loves the Black Prince for all the good he's done." Zane wet his lips. "You have an elf here who loves him too." He took Akiem's hand and placed it over his heart, hoping Akiem could feel its racing beat. "It terrifies me." The dragon's eyes widened. "You terrify me, for a thousand reasons, but I'm not afraid of you."

He stroked his hand down Akiem's face. The dragon's silken lashes fluttered, and he pushed into the touch, seeking more. He'd been hurt for so long by so many that he didn't know what it was to be loved. Zane wasn't sure he was the right person to show him.

"Stay with me," Zane whispered. "Live for me. Forget everyone else. You don't owe them anything and certainly not your life."

Akiem leaned back, out of Zane's hand.

"No." Zane caught his hand, fighting off a twinge of pain in his back. "My whole life, I've kept moving on, never allowing myself to stop or care. To care is to hurt. I've seen it a thousand times. I've never cared enough to fight for something, for someone, but I care now. I'll fight for you, even if you won't fight for yourself. Even if you don't want me, I'll still fight for you, because you're the only damn thing in this world I believe in. You hear me? I believe in you. My people believe in you, Black Prince. Don't throw that away. Luceran doesn't deserve your sacrifice."

Akiem's bronze eyes shone sharply, metal slivers cutting the light. "He'll kill you all to get to me. I have to stop him."

The worst of it was, Zane *knew* that.

"Alumn," he breathed out, saying the goddess's name as though she might hear his plea and help save one dragon. Just one. The rest could burn. This one was Zane's, forever and always.

Zane pulled him closer and sealed his words behind a gentle touch of lips and tongue. Love fucking hurt more than any physical wound. Akiem kissed him back, tentatively at first. So gentle for a dragon, and so right beneath Zane's hands. He withdrew too soon, and then he was pulling away, standing, and heading for the door. Zane watched him go, knowing love wasn't enough for this prince to save his own life.

He wanted to call him back, to stop him from going to Annie, but he'd said all the words he could. He'd bared his heart. Zane had nothing left to stop him with. He watched him walk into the sunlight, heart breaking for his forsaken prince.

THE VILLAGE WAS PREPARING for an autumn celebration despite the circumstances, or perhaps because of them. Zane couldn't decide if they were all insane or absolutely brilliant for carrying on in the face of tragedy. The elves he spoke to told him they'd never let dragons take their traditions too. Fuck dragons.

As dusk crawled across the land, strings of electric lights buzzed awake through the village center. Human music played from a metal box. Definitely insane, he observed, unable to resist smiling with them. They'd gathered reserves of food from their scattered farms and bundled a feast together.

To Zane's surprise, Akiem was among them. He'd last seen him leaving the house to go look for Annie. That had been hours ago. Now he was seated among elves, taller than most but wrapped in elven clothing, helping him blend in.

A tiny elfling pulled at Akiem's jacket. He looked down at her, and she looked up at him, and Alumn, to see the pair of them... A wave of emotion hit Zane so hard he had to steady himself against a wall. She said something, her little hand still on his coat, and he smiled a softer smile meant for little elflings. Her mouth fell open in an awe-filled "oh," and then the girl's mother swooped in and scooped her up, apologizing. Akiem bowed his head and watched the mother and daughter return to their table. When she sat, the girl on her lap, Akiem turned his head and looked right at Zane as he stared like a damn fool.

Zane cleared his throat. His wounds throbbed, reminding him to take it easy, but nothing like they had before. He wouldn't be drawing any bows for a while, but he wasn't about to miss the party.

Zane slotted himself on the bench next to Akiem and nodded at the elves around them. "What did she ask?"

"Where my coat goes when I shift."

Damn good question. Zane wanted to know the answer. The staring elves at the table wanted to know too. He had a thousand questions like that one, but in between running for his life, almost being eaten, and losing a finger, he hadn't had a chance to ask Akiem much of anything. None of the small things, anyway.

Zane grabbed an apple and cut it into sections.

"Where does it go?" he asked, casually.

"The same place my human appearance goes."

Well, that wasn't an answer, but as he popped a slice of apple into his mouth and bit down, he caught Akiem smiling. Akiem knew it was a non-answer.

"Why do you shift into a human? Why no, say, an elf?" another elf asked.

"Dragonkin learned long ago to adopt the appearance of the dominant species. At that time, it happened to be humans."

"Now?" Zane asked, biting into his apple.

"Dragons."

Of course.

"Could you make yourself into an elf?" Zane enquired.

"No." Akiem's mouth fought a smile. "Our appearance is fixed from the first time we shift. It's mostly random, but always human."

Zane tried to imagine Akiem slimmer and with pointed ears. A laugh tried to bubble up. He couldn't see it. The pointed ears, maybe, but the rest of him was too large to ever be anything but dragon.

"The world you came from..." another elf asked. "There are elves there?"

"Yes. They are brave, if stubborn. Honorable. Fierce when they want to be. Ruthless too. But they don't have your open kindness. You have welcomed me here as though I have earned the right to sit among you. The elves from across the ocean would not offer the same."

"Actions are important," the elf said. "You saved us and others. Dragon or not, you've earned your place among us."

Others nodded their agreement.

Akiem dipped his chin, acknowledging the words, but to the others at the table, he remained stoic. He'd used that blank stare as a shield all his life. So much more went on behind it. Zane had seen his softer side and was seeing it now. Presented with kindness, he responded with the same.

The party went on, the music beat, and wine sloshed in cups. Zane helped himself to a few generous rounds, taking the edge off his angry wounds. The elves asked their questions, and Akiem answered them with patience and grace, melting Zane's heart. He didn't have to answer them. He didn't have to be here. He even appeared to enjoy the attention. Would the wonder of Akiem never cease?

Annie passed by the table, drawing Akiem's eye. She

dipped her chin and moved on. A great deal had passed between them in that glance. So, Akiem had found her earlier in the day, and they'd made their plans, excluding Zane.

"When does it happen?" he asked, holding his frustration at bay.

"Tomorrow," Akiem replied.

Alumn, he couldn't stand it.

Picking up his cup, he left the table without looking back. He'd planned to track Annie down and demand she tell him every detail, but she'd disappeared among the crowd. Food and dancing and laughter—Zane drifted among it all, feeling detached even as an elf asked him to dance. He declined. Maybe the wine had dampened his mood, or maybe it was the fact his damn dragon was determined to kill himself.

An arm hooked into Zane's and veered him left, toward the edge of the revelry. Akiem. Zane considered pulling away and stopping this before his heart shattered, but the thought disappeared as soon as Akiem's bronze eyes captured his gaze and lured his body forward. Akiem steered him toward a shadowy gap between two houses where the electric light didn't reach.

The crowd was close, just a few strides away.

Akiem propped Zane against the wall and braced an arm over his shoulder, hemming him in. In the shadows, his dragon simmered with power and life. He was so fucking beautiful. Zane didn't want to meet his gaze or act on the urges that demanded he *touch and taste and feel*.

He downed the rest of his wine and let the cup hang empty from his fingers at his side. People danced, swirling and singing in couples, living life while they could.

He couldn't do this with Akiem. It would just make tomorrow hurt more.

"Look at me," the Black Prince ordered.

Pleasurable tingles skittered down Zane's back, waking up parts of him that didn't give a shit about his heart. Slowly, he looked up, first seeing his coat buttons and shirt, and then landed in his dragon's gaze.

"You make me see the world differently," Akiem whispered.

His warm fingers brushed Zane's cheek, setting Zane ablaze. Heated desire strummed between them, the dragon full of want and Zane eager to submit, to feel those fingers circle and grip him elsewhere on his body, making him groan.

"Through your eyes, I see life and possibility and hope and all the things I'd become blinded to. You changed me and made me whole. I do not know how to voice these feelings you ignite inside me, but allow me to show you?"

Anger sparked at Zane's heart. How dare he speak of such things, knowing it wouldn't last because he'd chosen to forsake it all. Alumn, it hurt. His heart was breaking already. He dropped the cup and touched Akiem's hard face, feeling around the lines at the corner of his mouth, wishing he could stroke away the hurt that had made them so deep.

Akiem moved in, trapping Zane against the wall. Warmth and strength radiated through him and into Zane, stealing his breath and making it ragged. Zane curled a hand around Akiem's shirt, holding him back or holding him still, but Akiem was everywhere—in his head, on his lips, filling his vision with black-lined bronze eyes.

This kiss was like the first: gentle and seeking but fueled by a dragon's passion. Had anyone else ever felt

Akiem this way? Zane opened, luring the dragon in, letting the kiss stoke his hunger. His heart was already broken. What was another cut to his soul? He'd stroked Akiem's scales, and he'd climbed onto his dragon back and soared above a burning city.

He was falling now. Zane forgot about the party, the people, and how close they all were. There was nobody and nothing else in the world but the hot sensation of dragon molded against him, of Akiem's hungry kiss demanding more, of Akiem's hands dropping to Zane's hip and ass, claiming him.

Alumn, it wasn't fair.

Zane needed to save Akiem before fate took him, but he didn't know how. Akiem had shown him who he really was, shown him that the face in the mirror was not the face of a monster but of a powerful male with a gentle soul. Metal or jeweled, none of that mattered. Akiem was his own person.

Zane's grip on his shirt tightened and pulled. The kiss was a flame, growing hotter and brighter, consuming Zane. He needed all of Akiem on him, in him, in every way, but the dragon's touches were so terribly gentle, as though he were cherishing each one, knowing it would be their last.

When Akiem's scandalous mouth trailed down Zane's neck, he arched into the dragon and sank his hands down his back, folding him close. Too many layers. Zane needed them torn free, including the invisible layers Akiem hid inside. He needed him raw and open and beneath Zane's hands and mouth.

A growling rumble strummed through Akiem and shuddered through Zane, tightening every breath. Every part of him strained to be touched.

"Is this love?" the Black Prince whispered.

Zane's wrecked heart shattered. Akiem did not know what love was. But then, did Zane? They had each other, in a moment that could be their last. He wanted to take this dragon away, but Akiem wouldn't leave. He wanted to save Akiem in every way, but he could not save him from himself. That was love, wasn't it? He'd die for this dragon.

"Yes." Zane pulled him close, clasping his arms around him and holding on. "Yes," he whispered against Akiem's neck.

Akiem tensed and sucked in a breath, pulling back as much as Zane would allow, and then Akiem kissed him again, slowly, carefully, tasting, remembering.

"I will save you and them," Akiem said, "and this pocket of peace in a world that would see you all bullied and abused for entertainment."

Alumn, it hurt.

"Will you save yourself?" Zane whispered.

Akiem looked at him, seeing deep into Zane's soul because he'd laid it bare. The dragon's gaze unraveled him. He simply brushed Zane's mouth with a kiss that tasted like goodbye.

Tomorrow, his dragon would face Luceran, and there was nothing Zane could do to stop him, so he'd make tonight and their love last forever.

kiem

How could an elf light Akiem on fire like this? His hands found their way inside Akiem's clothes and scorched across his skin. His soft mouth was a tease of tongue and teeth, and Akiem fell into the taste of it. Both his hands swept around Akiem's waist, slid down his lower back, and sank inside his pants to cup his ass. The touch wasn't soft. His fingers groped, his arms pulled, and Akiem found he needed more of the elf clutched against him. The hard rod of his arousal brushed against Akiem's.

"Do you trust me?" Zane whispered, gently easing Akiem back against the wall.

The answer was easy, but why he'd asked had Akiem's nerves fluttering. "I do."

Zane leaned against the wall beside him, shielding Akiem from any curious glances in the crowd, and eased his hand inside Akiem's trousers, brushing his palm down the length of his erection, making him gasp. Zane's hand didn't stop there. He pushed deeper, sliding his fingers beneath Akiem's balls and lingering long enough to squeeze gently. Akiem swallowed and tilted back against the wall. Zane's intense gaze warmed his face.

Zane stroked a firm finger behind Akiem's balls, toward his rear. Akiem panted, coming undone. Pleasure crackled, and anticipation stole his breath. This was… different. Unexpected. The finger probed and stroked, but stayed in that small valley, going no deeper.

Zane was intently focused on his face, reading every signal, every gasp. He leaned in and nipped Akiem's ear, then swirled his tongue around the shell.

"Do you want more?" he whispered.

Did he? He wasn't sure what Zane was asking, but he trusted him completely. He'd said he'd never hurt him. Akiem believed him. "Yes."

Zane adjusted his position against Akiem's side and reached lower. His firm finger slid back, gently circling over Akiem's hole. Countless shivers trickled down Akiem's back, and his arousal ached. Gods, he wanted more of that. A groan pealed free, and Zane responded by stroking faster. His forearm brushed up against Akiem's balls and occasionally stroked along his cock, delivering tiny bursts of friction that sent Akiem's mind spiraling.

Zane's warm, wet tongue traced Akiem's jaw and down his neck. His sucks and nips drove Akiem toward an edge, and then his finger dipped inside, massaging a maddeningly sensitive part. Akiem blew out a breath. He didn't know what this was, but it felt divine.

Zane angled closer. Akiem was too lost in pleasure to pay any mind to what Zane was doing. A quick tug on his pants jolted his hips, and Zane plastered himself close, his hard erection nudging alongside Akiem's. Zane took both in hand, his expert fingers finding new pleasurable highs.

Akiem was Zane's, body and mind. Vulnerable in Zane's hands but strong because of it, he could hardly make sense of it and didn't care to. To think he'd been shackled and imprisoned behind the wants and desires of others all this time, and now Zane freed him. He clutched a fistful of Zane's hair and pulled him into a savage kiss, never wanting to let him go. He'd do anything for this compassionate, gentle, thoughtful elf. Sacrifice anything. His love was as fierce and dangerous as the bronze in his veins. It frightened Akiem, but it lifted him up too, made him *better* than he'd ever been. Made him new—no, it exposed the truth and made him who he'd always been inside.

Zane had helped him discover who he really was beneath a lifetime of fear and lies.

Zane was a gift, one he could never repay.

HE LEFT Zane gently snoring in their bed back at the borrowed house and met Annie in the clearing. Mist crept between the trees, silencing the world.

"You know what to do?" Annie asked. She wore her scouting leathers, blending in seamlessly with the forest's autumnal colors.

"I'll need fifteen seconds. Give me that, and I'll see it done."

The elf nodded.

Zane had been clear that Annie wouldn't think twice about sacrificing a dragon to end the king. Should it come to that, neither would Akiem. But fifteen seconds would be enough, if he dared to take them.

"May Alumn's light be with you, prince."

He turned away from her and shifted, then climbed through the mist, his wings stirring great clouds of it apart. The eastern edge of dawn brought the sun with it. Soon, there wouldn't be any mist, and nowhere left to hide as he soared toward the compound and his fate.

ane

Zane gasped awake. He reached for his dragon and found cold sheets instead. Sunlight poured in through the window, mocking him.

Tomorrow had come.

He tore from the bed as fast as his wounds allowed and dressed on his way out the door. He'd find Jevan and they'd find Akiem, and whatever happened next, they do it together.

The cleanup from the party had all but finished. Scouts were returning from their morning patrols, and hunters had returned with freshly caught rabbit and deer. Life continued. But Akiem was missing, and so was Annie.

He knew where they were, or where they might be.

Jevan and Rosa had been invited to stay with a family overnight until more permanent lodgings were arranged. Zane knocked on the door. Jevan opened it, then continued to throw on his jacket before rubbing his hands together against the cold. He grinned. "Hey, you want some breakfast…?" The question trailed off as he read Zane's expression. "What's happened?"

Jevan had been through a lot. He had his sister back. He could put down roots and settle here. Maybe it was wrong to ask for his help. "You know, never mind…"

He left but Jevan was fast on his heels. "Zane, stop…"

Zane wasn't stopping. He had to get to the warehouse, to Akiem. Jev had family now, too much to lose.

"Zane, I'm sorry. I didn't have a choice—"

"I know." He glanced over. "It's not that."

Jev's pained expression slowed Zane's pace. For years they'd fought side by side and had each other's back. Zane stopped and faced his friend. He didn't need to say a word. Regret was written in the downturn of his lips and soft eyes. He blamed himself for everything—the elves who had died and the city that had burned. He needed a second chance. "Akiem and Annie have a plan to stop the king, and we aren't invited."

"They left you out? I mean, me… I get. But you?"

"You saw it, Jev. You saw it in him weeks ago. Akiem is determined to kill himself for our cause. He knows I'll try to stop him, so he left."

"Shit."

"You said not to fall for him, but I did, and… Shit, Jev… I know I've made the worst decisions in the past. I dragged you into my fuck-ups, but this is different. Akiem is different. I can't let him do this."

Jev's steady hand landed on Zane's shoulder and pulled him close. "Then we stop him. But are you sure you want me by your side?"

"Everything you did, I get it. She's kin. You love her. I'd

have done the same." To protect someone he loved, he would do anything. He had that someone now, but for how much longer?

Jevan sighed. "I owe that black dragon more than I can ever repay. I'm with you."

Zane grabbed Jev and pulled him into an embrace.

"I'm sorry for everything," Jevan said. "For all those people who died..." He clutched Zane close.

"I know." Zane braced Jev at arm's length and held his too-bright gaze. "Let's both go make it right."

CHAPTER 35

kiem

He flew in fast and true, sweeping low over the jagged tops of Bayston's old buildings. Mist lingered below, where the sun hadn't penetrated, covering the city streets like a pale river. Ahead, dragons circled and swooped above the compound. Akiem was still miles out, but the broken walls and the collapsed sections of roof of the compound were obvious. Luceran had torn through his court, reducing it to rubble. With luck, his killing spree might have taken out some of the other lords, further weakening the king. His rage would make him foolish and blind. Akiem counted on it.

More calls split the morning quiet as dragons climbed into the blush-red sky, so many that they gathered like thunderclouds.

But no diamond.

A swirl in the mist drew Akiem's gaze downward.

A thick layer of undisturbed mist lay in the streets ahead, but behind... something large churned the vapor. Something almost invisible among its whiteness.

Luceran breached the mist, arcing skyward, jaws open and claws extended.

With a cry, Akiem rolled, narrowly avoiding the jagged walls of an old human tower. The building whooshed by. Luceran veered around the tower and flew in Akiem's wake, streamlined like an arrow. Sunlight blazed off his scales. Vengeance burned behind his violet eyes, and low in his throat, he stoked his fire.

Good.

Akiem banked hard around another tower, slicing the air apart. His insides whooshed, and his heart pumped harder. Luceran roared, unleashing a wave of flame. Akiem tilted his wings and plunged beneath the flames and into the cool mist.

Buildings sprang up ahead, racing toward Akiem. He veered and swooped, pumping his wings harder, *faster*. Luceran's roar chased him. Close. He needed to keep him on his tail, but not too close. Luceran, in his madness, would follow him through the mist, but the others, those thinking, knew the narrow streets were too dangerous to fly through.

Up, over, and around. Down, under, and through. He threaded through the old city like a needle through fabric, tucking his wings in, tilting their edges, carving through the air, and whipping his tail for balance. On and on and on. Breathless. Racing. Faster.

Diamond flashed to his right.

Luceran slammed into Akiem's side. The blow knocked

Akiem clean out of his flight. He skimmed a tower corner, but the next rushed up and slammed into him. Rock and darkness tumbled and roared over him. The pain only came once he'd blinked back into himself on the street, buried under tons of rubble.

Akiem shook his head free and pulled the rest of his bulk from beneath the rocks.

Luceran lay on the street too, unmoving.

He wasn't dead. His breathing stirred the mist near his nose.

This wasn't the plan he had devised with Annie, but what did it matter where the king died, as long as he did. Bloodlust trilled through him, voiced as a low growl. He stalked toward the fallen king. Luceran's head was turned away, the weak spot behind his crown exposed. Instinct strummed Akiem's desire to kill. It was all he could feel. His jaw ached. Saliva pooled as he thought of sinking his teeth into the king's skull and ending the abuse once and for all, abuse not just dealt to him by Luceran, but by all dragons. Killing the king meant more than a single death. It would elevate Akiem above them all.

Bite, fuck, take, own. His needs beat alongside his thudding heart.

Akiem stalked ever closer to the king, watching for the tensing of muscle that would signal a strike.

Closer now, moving silently like the mist he carved through. He raised his head, bettering the angle at which to catch the king's head in his jaws.

Luceran jerked his head around. His tail lashed and slammed into Akiem's right side. The king rolled around to face him. Akiem drove in, aiming for his vulnerable belly. The king's jaws clapped together, inches from

Akiem's snout. Akiem recoiled, summoned his fire, and blasted Luceran's face.

Luceran tore through the flame as though it were water. Teeth clamped around Akiem's neck, sinking through scale. Sparks of pain tore down his neck. His fire choked off. Akiem swung his head around and scraped his teeth down Luceran's shoulder, tasting blood and scale. He'd have gone for the wing, but he needed the king to fly, to follow... unless he killed him here.

Rage.

He'd always kept it buried deep, deep down in the darkest part of himself, because it was bronze and everything he hated, but he could feel and taste the metal in him rising. It screamed at him to take, to bite, to fuck, to own. *To destroy*.

Claws raked down Akiem's chest. He barely felt it.

He snapped at the king's wing, missing by inches.

No, no, he needed to think, to follow the plan. Rage was blinding. Rage would steal his thoughts and reason. He could not allow himself to fall into its promise and succumb to the madness of being bronze.

Akiem twisted away and whipped his tail around, slamming its spikes into Luceran's jaw. He didn't look to check the damage. The mist swirled and rolled, revealing a tower's base. He sank his claws into stone and steel and climbed the vertical façade. The old building groaned. Parts of it fell away and smashed somewhere below. Higher and higher. Luceran's flame chased him.

The mist fell away.

Sunlight warmed his wings.

He awkwardly clambered onto the roof, avoiding jutting pillars and spiked iron rods. The tower trembled beneath his feet.

Akiem peered over the side, and Luceran's snarling jaws greeted him with a snap, sending him scrambling backward. The king climbed over the side, hatred burning in his eyes.

Come for me, Akiem silently beckoned. *Chase me like you've wanted since the beginning. Chase me now... until the end.*

Akiem dropped off the building, flung out his wings, gritting his teeth against bruises and tears, and soared. Luceran followed.

The chase.

No dragon could resist and certainly not one enraged by his brother's beheading. Luceran's every breath and heartbeat sought Akiem's death. He was dragon.

Akiem flew above the mist now that they were farther from the compound, wings beating hard, lungs bellowing. Old scars burned. New wounds hissed. But he was fast. He'd always been fast.

The ruined city fell away, turning into the green crowns of forest trees.

Faster. Harder, he flew.

He could not survive a fight with Luceran, but he didn't need to.

He just needed to give the king what he wanted.

Every scale felt made of jagged glass. Every wing beat cut them deeper. He bled from places he didn't dare think about. Every inch of him demanded he land and rest, but Luceran was gaining on him. Chasing was easier than fleeing. Luceran rode in Akiem's wake, conserving his strength, and by now he'd know where Akiem was going.

There was no turning around.

There hadn't been since Luceran had seen him.

When the chase ended, the king would be dead, whatever the cost.

Fear, anger, and the thrill of it all poured strength into Akiem's veins. The destination was close. He spotted the village's trails of smoke and veered right. Luceran cut closer, his snout almost on Akiem's tail, but the turn was important; it took Luceran away from the village.

Teeth punctured Akiem's tail.

A roar clawed up his throat and burst free.

Luceran angled his wings upward and yanked Akiem *down*. The world spiraled. Akiem stretched out his wings, trying to catch enough air to keep him aloft, but Luceran's weight pulled him down and down and down. Jagged autumnal treetops rushed upward. Dread clutched his chest. He thrashed, tumbling and dragging the king with him.

Luceran's wings snapped open. His teeth tore free of Akiem's tail, but it was too late. Akiem hit the trees, heard them shatter, felt their substantial trunks splinter against his spine. Then a sudden, choking silence throbbed around him, trying to wrap him up and drag him under. The instinct to move had him rolling onto his front. Growls rumbled through his chest and up his throat. He dug his claws into the earth, gripping roots to heave himself forward.

He'd fallen just south of the village. He had to get up.

The trap was still some distance away, hidden among the trees. He'd fallen too soon.

He smelled blood.

Lots of it.

Luceran's enormous wings whipped up a storm as he landed in the clearing Akiem's crash had hollowed out in the forest. He tucked his wings in, bared his teeth, and prowled forward.

Akiem kept his head low, but the growl that emanated from him was not submission.

Rage boiled his bronze blood, and for the first time in forever, he freed the bronze inside him.

CHAPTER 36

ane

THEY'D ALMOST MADE it to the buried warehouse when two dragons fell out of the sky. One black, one white. It was impossible to watch, but he couldn't look away. They tumbled and clawed, tearing off scale and opening vicious wounds. Then the diamond king regained control, but Akiem did not.

He plummeted and vanished beyond the tree line.

The ground thundered with the impact.

Jevan set off running at the same time as Zane.

The diamond king hung in the sky, surveying the trees, his gaze landing on the village before swinging down again to where Akiem surely lay, and then Zane lost sight of him. Shortly after, great world-shuddering growls and roars began.

Trees had fallen, and some appeared to have shattered.

Wood and leaves were everywhere. Great wet splashes of blood soaked the fallen pines.

Horror held Zane rigid near the edge of the crater. The dragons fought with tooth and claw and wing and tail. They tore into each other, opening devastating wounds. Zane had never seen anything so monstrous. Akiem gave back everything Luceran landed, his bronze eyes alight.

Zane had no bow, just a small dagger he'd borrowed from a villager. Jevan had no weapon. They could not get between them, and even if they did, the dragons wouldn't see them.

Akiem got his teeth around Luceran's throat and flung him aside. Swathes of forest were swept away beneath the king. Luceran rolled onto his belly and stalked around, never taking his eyes off the towering Black Prince.

In that moment, panting out purple flame, eyes burning bronze, Akiem had never seemed more kingly. Alumn, he was a monster, but he was Zane's monster.

Luceran stilled. He lifted his head and snuffled, tasting the air.

Akiem saw Zane then, somehow, among all the broken wood and branches.

"Shit, the king knows we're here!" Zane hissed, ducking back.

Luceran whipped his head around and stared straight at Zane with slitted pupils.

Run.

If he ran, he'd die.

Akiem struck fast, his jaws coming down near the back of the king's head, but Luceran twisted. Teeth clashed. Luceran clamped down on Akiem's lower jaw and tongue and shook his head from side to side.

"I can't ..." He stepped out of the tree cover.

"Zane!" Jevan grabbed for Zane and missed.

"Get to the warehouse! Get to Annie!" Zane called back.

"Are you *insane*!"

Maybe.

"Luceran!" Zane bellowed, raising his arms. "Remember me, you fucking lily-white lizard!"

The king spat his hold on Akiem's nose and whirled on Zane.

"He took your brother's head to save my life," Zane called. "Clarion died for an elf, for me!"

Fire boiled in the dragon's throat. He came closer, lifting his head, towering over Zane.

Zane couldn't fight him. No elf could fight a dragon.

But by Alumn, he could run. He could run so far and so fast that their plan might work.

After making sure Luceran had him firmly in his sights, Zane bolted into the trees. Seconds later, the dragon thundered after him.

CHAPTER 37

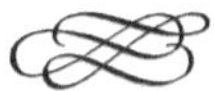

kiem

Luceran was chasing after *his* elf.

The warehouse.

Zane would get there first. He'd do what Akiem had planned to do.

Annie would see Luceran and blow the warehouse… with Zane inside.

Akiem staggered forward, one foot in front of the other. His right wing dragged. It didn't hurt. The pain was fading now.

He had to get to the warehouse.

He had to save Zane.

Bronze sizzled beneath his scales, demanding he move. The bronze in him did not suffer weakness.

The ground hardened, signaling the warehouse was beneath him. Ahead, Luceran disappeared into a gaping hole in the ground. The trap was set.

But Zane was in there too.

Akiem had told Annie fifteen seconds—the time he would have used to shift and take the stairs, slipping out seconds before the entire warehouse blew, burying Luceran inside.

Fifteen seconds or zero, if she wanted Akiem dead too.

He dragged himself and his wing, yipping as though calling Zane back to him. *Come back. For me.*

A blast of light blinded him first. Then the noise barreled into him, throwing him down into the dirt. His ears rang, thoughts rattling. Dust rained down.

A hole had opened in the ground where the warehouse had been. Only rubble remained.

Inside, buried under tons and tons of rock, lay Luceran and Zane.

Akiem clawed at the broken rocks, digging in search of the tiny body in the rubble, but the rocks were too big. He locked his teeth around them, dislodging some, but deeper down, the rocks had locked together. He couldn't break them apart.

Zane was inside.

Seconds turned into minutes into too long.

Grief tore out his weary heart, leaving him cold. He lifted his head and whined.

ane

THE WAREHOUSE WAS FUCKING VAST. As Zane ran through it, he'd never felt smaller. His thighs burned, and his lungs did too. Then Jevan appeared from the doorway at the back, a longbow in his hand.

The dragon thundered behind Zane, gaining on him.

The ground shook, and the air boiled. Faster and faster. He had to get out before Annie flicked the switch.

Jev jogged forward, nocked an arrow, and raised the bow.

"Go!" he shouted, waving Zane past. He let his arrow fly.

Luceran screamed. At the stairs, Zane looked back. Fire strafed the ceiling. Concrete collapsed throughout the warehouse. Jev's arrow had found its target and taken out Luceran's right eye.

"Jevan!"

Jevan walked *toward* the enraged dragon. He nocked a second arrow and raised his bow.

"Come on!" Zane called.

Jevan knew about the explosives. He knew Annie was poised to hit the trigger.

The second arrow flew, puncturing Luceran's throat, right where the firepit boiled. Fire spilled out, choking the king. He coughed and wheezed, vomiting up liquid flame.

Jevan turned, sent Zane a smile and raised his bow in salute. "I'm making it right—"

Fire and rock exploded, consuming the diamond dragon and Jevan. The shockwave slammed into Zane. He made it to the top step, to Annie, when a second blast rolled over them, ripping away all noise and feeling. His cheek hit the floor, and rocks pummeled over him.

At least I saved one good dragon, he thought, and the world went black.

HE CRAWLED out of the dirt, wheezing up concrete dust. Annie swooped in and tucked him against her side. They stumbled out into the blazing sunlight.

Zane coughed and breathed, hands pressed against his thighs, then straightened and squinted into the settling dust. A huge depression had eaten the ground, carving out a bowl full of concrete.

Annie sat on a rock. "We got him?" She coughed.

None of the rocks moved. A tree groaned and toppled into the crater. Then stillness settled. "We got him."

Zane shielded his eyes from the sun and searched the

perimeter. On the other side, a black dragon lay still, his torn scales covered in dust and blood.

"Akiem!" Zane called, stumbling forward.

Akiem didn't move.

Zane's racing heart stuttered with dread. He broke into a jog, opting to go over the rubble instead of around it. He couldn't run, the rocks were too uneven, so he climbed and jogged and stumbled across the warehouse's remains.

Akiem couldn't be dead, not after everything they'd been through.

As Zane clambered closer, he saw the blood, the broken scales, the bent wing. *"Alumn, you can't have him!"*

No, he couldn't stand it. It wasn't fair. This wretched fucking world needed Akiem. It needed a good dragon. The elves needed him. More than all that, Zane needed him. Without Akiem, he'd be adrift. Alone. He needed that damn black prince as his anchor.

The ground groaned and *moved*.

Zane stumbled.

More rubble moved, grinding and puffing out dust.

The ground heaved. A diamond-covered wing lifted, the scales cracked and bloody.

There was nowhere to run.

The king's head rose out of the destruction, Jevan's arrow in his eye, but his other eye gleamed with vengeance and fixed on Zane.

Luceran's jaws parted, broken teeth exposed behind a snarl. He towered over Zane, a mountain of a beast.

He was too big, too much, but oddly, Zane wasn't afraid. He'd tried. He could have done no more, and now Akiem was dead. In the next few moments, Zane would be dead too.

It was over. For good.

The king opened his mouth wider and drew his head back, about to strike.

Zane closed his eyes and dropped to his knees.

Alumn, take my hand and guide me through the darkness.

kiem

AKIEM THREW himself forward and struck. He opened his jaws, tilted his head, and sank his teeth into the weak-spot at the back of Luceran's skull. The king jolted and twitched and fell limp, dead in moments. It seemed almost too quick for Luceran, but Akiem knew death, and quick meant final. Luceran would never get back up again.

Akiem flung the body down, clamped his teeth into the diamond scales running down Luceran's throat, and ripped them off. Then Akiem dug his claws in, holding the dead king beneath him. He sucked air deep into his lungs and loosed a roar that shook the world. The king was dead. This was Akiem's land now, and these were his elves.

He'd watched, playing dead, after he'd heard Luceran breathing beneath the rocks. Zane had almost died—again. Akiem lowered his head and watched his tiny elf. He smelled like the woods and freedom and home, and

Akiem brought his head in low, snuffling around Zane, wanting to be close without frightening him. He knew how he looked, vicious and bloody, but like always, Zane wasn't afraid. He threw himself at Akiem's nose and clung on, something like sobs making him shake against Akiem's scales.

Rosa pried Zane off. They exchanged a few hushed words, and then she cried, falling into Zane's arms.

Jevan was gone.

Akiem dragged his battered bones and numbed weight off the dead king and found a flattened piece of ground to curl up in. There, he basked in the sun and licked his wounds. Only when he was clean could he shift, and he wasn't ready for that yet. Maybe tomorrow... He hadn't ever let himself think about the future. He might have one now, with Zane, with elves.

The dragons would need discipline.

Akiem eyed the king's steaming carcass.

He'd need to deal with the diamond brood eventually.

Zane strode up to Akiem's foreleg and slid his back down Akiem's scales to sit against him. He pulled up his legs, propped his wrist on his knees, and dropped his head back. Bloody, dusty, his clothes askew, and his red hair a mess, he smelled like battle and tears. Akiem sniffed him, and Zane's lips danced around a smile. He wanted to lick, to make him better.

"We need to have a talk..." Zane began, squinting up at Akiem. "You live, or I die with you—those are my terms."

Akiem huffed and resumed licking a section of his foreleg where Luceran had clawed him. Terms of what exactly?

"And no more heroics or saving my ass. I have a reputation and you're making me look bad."

Akiem smiled inside, and the hollowness he'd felt at thinking his elf had died fast became a distant memory.

"I know you're already thinking about fighting all the leftover dragons until one of them gets lucky and kills you. That ain't happening. If you're going to fight dragons, you're not doing it alone."

Elves.

They were impossible.

Akiem yawned, hoping Zane took the hint.

Zane narrowed his eyes. "If you think I'm leaving, think again. I'm staying until you shift. If you don't like it, you can eat me."

The light in his eyes suggested he referred to a different kind of meal. Akiem rested his head beside his elf and closed his eyes. He huffed out a sigh, grateful for the feel of Zane's little hand on his cheek. Maybe it would be like this now, Zane beside him, watching out for him, reminding him who he really was. He liked that thought, and as the sun baked his scales and the smell of elf overwhelmed those of blood and dragon, Akiem wondered if he'd finally found freedom.

CHAPTER 40

ane

Elves flowed back into Bayston. Zane watched them from his perch low on Akiem's back as his dragon soared above the streets.

There were other dragons in the sky, but none mobbed them, not while Akiem carried the king's carcass in his claws.

Akiem landed among the compound ruins and unceremoniously dumped the king's cold body atop the rubble. Three days had passed since his death. Decay had warped Luceran's diamond beauty, revealing his rot.

Zane climbed off Akiem's wing and walked a safe distance away to allow him to shift.

Dragons spiraled down from above.

He and Akiem had talked about how this would go.

Zane rolled his shoulders. He was armed with a

longbow and two daggers, but he didn't draw them. He sought Akiem's attention for reassurance.

Akiem nodded back, his face a mask of fierce determination.

Dragons landed all around and shifted, building in number. They eyed the king's bloated remains, recoiled at the stench, and then growled at Akiem.

Their gazes crawled over Zane. Behind them, Annie's village elves emerged from the broken buildings, their weapons stowed. She'd been crafting bows on the quiet, and with no Luceran to punish them, each elf carried a bow and a blade. Few were warriors, but Annie had promised, given time, they would be. As much as Zane was wary around her, she got shit done. She nodded at him, proving she stood with him. Her hands stayed by her sides, near her daggers.

This was about peace, not war.

"This city belongs to the elves," Akiem said, raising his voice. "Any who deny it shall suffer under me." He spoke well, considering it wasn't entirely true, but a bluff was as good as the truth if it held.

Mutterings upset the dragonkin crowd.

"If you wish to challenge me, know this: it is bronze you see in my eyes. My father was one of the first great metals, risen from the earth in our beginnings. Metal runs through my jeweled veins."

More murmurs. They knew of the bronze and their brutality. Suddenly, the shadowy black prince Luceran had found on their shores had teeth.

"Clarion died because he hurt what is mine. Luceran died because he crossed me." He paused, letting those words sink in. "This land is rich and there's plenty for all. The elves will share their skills in farming and trade, but they do not work for dragons. They are not your tools, they are not your toys, and they are not your food."

A dragon shifted and took flight, preferring to leave than live with elves. Another followed.

Akiem tilted his head. "Live here in peace, or war elsewhere. Just know I will protect every single elf in this city, and equally, I will protect you, my brood, should you need it. From this day forth, we break from the past and carve our future, one with elves and dragonkin coexisting."

Zane eyed them. They seemed remarkably calm about the whole thing. Akiem had doubted Zane when he'd urged him to come right out and say it how it was, to start as they meant to go on.

He glanced at Akiem and shrugged. *See, dragons can be reasoned with.*

Then a dragonkin fucked up and sprang for Akiem.

Zane pulled his bow free, nocked an arrow, adjusting for his missing finger, and fired into the dragonkin's heart, jolting him off his feet. He died right after hitting the ground.

Akiem raised an eyebrow. Zane's actions said what words could not: don't fuck with the elves or Akiem and they'd all get along.

The dragonkin grumbled their dissent, but with two dead dragons in front of them and a line of armed elves behind, none dared to attack. They likely would later, but Zane was staying beside his dragon. No more moving on. His heart was here, in Akiem's hands.

"Stay or go, but honor my words," Akiem finished.

The dragonkin moved off, some shifting, some walking. The lines of elves watched them warily. It would take time, but with work, they'd raise Bayston out of the ashes, working together, dragon and elf, to do it.

Zane wet his lips and asked too quietly for anyone to hear but Akiem, "How long will they fear you?"

"About a day." Akiem smiled like he relished the thought of unleashing the bronze in him again.

Zane smiled back, wondering if he had, in fact, unleashed a monster in the Black Prince, but a good one.

They stood atop the ruins of the king's court, dragon and elf side by side, watching the world shift toward good.

Maybe peace would stick, maybe it wouldn't, but with Akiem and the elves, there had never been a better time to hope for a brighter future.

Zane slipped his fingers into Akiem's, reminding him he wasn't alone. "Now, if I recall correctly, you paid for services not rendered..."

Akiem's bronze glare slid to Zane. Pleasure and anticipation trilled through him. The comment cut close to a sore subject, but Zane had always found it better to hang a lantern on these things than keep them in the dark. He winked, and his dragon smiled his private, priceless smile.

EPILOGUE

kiem

Briny dockside air salted his lips and dampened his face as he stared out to sea. A low full moon painted the inky surface gray. The ocean was calm tonight, perfect for low flying. He'd need to take to the wing soon and glide over the city. Zane said the elves liked to see him in the skies—their protector watching over them.

There would be more battles to win and dragons who disobeyed, and elves too. Annie, in particular, was one to watch. She behaved more like the elves Akiem had known back home. She was the type to inspire revolution. But they'd made progress, and it felt good. Warmth had filled that hollow, cold part of him. His mind was calm. The nightmares hadn't haunted him in weeks. It was almost too good to be true, too good for him, but he'd take it.

He rolled up a sleeve and admired the sweeping tattoos

snaking up his arm. The interwoven black ink was intricate in its design, put there by Zane's steady hand. The marks didn't hide his scars, just changed them, made them beautiful. Another gift from an elf whose love knew no bounds.

His ears picked up the *clip-clop* of horse hooves, and then the soft breeze delivered the scents of horse and elf. His elf. Akiem's nose twitched. He looked along the dock and raised an eyebrow at Zane tying his horse to a post.

Akiem allowed himself a moment to admire the fine line of Zane's waist and ass, hugged in leather and leaving little to the imagination. Zane straightened, raked his fingers through his loose red hair, and tossed Akiem a look that said he knew where Akiem's gaze had roamed and he'd been soaking up every second of it.

He approached, adding a sway to his hips. The sweet smell of horse increased, and Akiem's mouth watered. "You smell like horse."

"Do I?" Zane flashed a mischievous smile. "Not everyone has wings to patrol the city."

He knew what the scent of prey did to Akiem and had deliberately ridden in on the animal to kick-start Akiem's instincts. Zane liked to play with fire, and he burned hot when he did. They spent the nights together, some days too, discovering each other over and over. Zane was relentless in his pursuit of pleasure, teaching Akiem all the right ways to love.

He sauntered up to Akiem's side but stayed an arm's length away. Moonlight touched his face, highlighting pale skin and the dash of freckles across his nose.

"Teone is helping Rosa organize the repopulation of the city. It's going well. Rosa is... She misses Jev..." He dropped his head. His friend's death had hit him hard. His hand went into his pocket, where Akiem knew he kept the locket, recovered from the rubble.

Zane caught Akiem watching and brightened. "They've invited us to dinner. I'll warn you now, Teone wants to ask about the whole shifting thing. I told her it's magic, but she wants to know the details. She's very persistent. She also talks more than I do. I said we'd be there, but I get it if you don't want to be interrogated all evening…"

Akiem listened to Zane's melodic voice, enjoying the pride that warmed him through while wondering when it would be appropriate to pull Zane into the shadows or shift and fly him back to their *home,* where he could bury himself in Zane's wicked pleasures for the night. "She can ask her questions."

"Dragonkin are still paying for *services* farther down the docks," Zane continued, losing some of his smile. "I know how you feel about it and made sure they saw me, but it'll take more than my presence to stop it."

Akiem cleared his throat, steering his thoughts away from the idea of devouring Zane where he stood and on to more important matters. "We must select a council, not a court. Your people will nominate and vote for their council members, as will mine. Dragon and elf will draft new laws, and together, we'll police them."

Zane tilted his head, fixing Akiem in his sights, a shimmer in his eyes. "Do you think it's possible for dragons and elves to work together?"

Not long ago, he'd have said no, but he and Zane proved it was possible. "We won't know until we try."

Gods, Zane was beautiful, with lips meant for tasting and lashes that highlighted those curious elven eyes, but it was his kind and hopeful heart that Akiem loved the most. A soft heart that balanced the unyielding bronze in Akiem.

All the pain of his past, the endless torture, and the lies he'd told himself were all worth it to be standing here with this wonder of an elf beside him. Zane believed Akiem had saved him repeatedly, but he was wrong. There was no doubt in Akiem's mind that Zane had saved Akiem and continued to save him with every soft glance, every light touch, and every gentle kiss.

He loved the elf so much it hurt and frightened him. Looking out to sea, he wondered if this would last, or if fate would realize Akiem didn't deserve Zane and snatch him away.

Zane's three fingers threaded through Akiem's. He leaned close, smelling of horse and elf and freedom.

"Would you ever go back to your home?" Zane asked, staring out to sea too. There was a tightness to his words, as though he feared the reply.

"Never. My past is dead. My future is here, with you." He folded Zane into his arms and tilted Zane's chin up. Worry lingered behind his smiling eyes. He knew, the same as Akiem did, that the future would not be kind to a dragon and elf. Change did not happen overnight. Dragons would come and try to end the peace they'd created here, but together, they'd brought down a king. Together, they'd reclaimed a city. And together, they'd created true peace between dragon and elf. Change was coming, and whatever happened next, they'd face it side by side.

"You once asked me if I was looking for someone." Akiem brushed the tease of a kiss against Zane's lips and pulled back to admire the marvel on his face. This wild elf had done the impossible and captured Akiem's dragon-heart, a heart he'd thought he'd lost long ago. "I found him."

Zane smiled, threw his arms around Akiem's neck, and

pulled him into a savage kiss. Akiem's heart soared far and free. Yes, this was where he was meant to be. It had taken him a little while to find his place in life, but now that he had, he planned on living it.

The End

ABOUT THE AUTHOR

Born to wolves, Ariana Nash only ventures from the Cornish moors when the moon is fat and the night alive with myths and legends. She captures those myths in glass jars and returning home, weaves them into stories filled with forbidden desires, fantasy realms, and wicked delights.

Sign up to her newsletter here: https://www.subscribepage.com/silk-steel

The Black Prince

Ariana Nash

Dark Fantasy Author

Subscribe to Ariana's mailing list & get the exclusive story 'Sealed with a Kiss' free.

Join the Ariana Nash Facebook group for all the news, as it happens.